The Great Circle

THE GREAT CIRCLE

A NOVEL

Peter Prince

RANDOM HOUSE

NEW YORK

Copyright © 1997 by Peter Prince

All rights reserved under International and Pan-American Copyright
Conventions. Published in the United States by Random
House, Inc., New York, and simultaneously in Canada
by Random House of Canada Limited, Toronto.

Library of Congress Cataloging-in-Publication Data
Prince, Peter
The great circle/Peter Prince.
p.   cm.
ISBN 0-679-45308-3
1. Ocean travel—History—19th century—Fiction.   I. Title.
PR6066.R564G7   1997   823'.914—dc21   96-37882

Random House website address: http://www.randomhouse.com/
Printed in the United States of America on acid-free paper
2 4 6 8 9 7 5 3
First Edition

Book design by J. K. Lambert

For

Mara, Howard, Polly, Joanna, and Sue—

early readers

YOUNG MAN WAVING

42°21' N, 71°4' W

On St. Valentine's Day, 1865, the paddle steamer *Laurentia*, Captain
Donald McDonough commanding, left the Inman Line wharf in East
Boston bound for Halifax, Nova Scotia, and Liverpool. Her sailing
day was a Tuesday as usual. A three-masted wooden barque, driven by
twin paddles, each thirty feet in diameter, the PS *Laurentia* had been
built for the Cunard company in 1848 by Robert Steele & Sons of
Greenock, Scotland, and thereafter had pounded back and forth
along the North Atlantic sea-lanes for over a decade, with only a
year's gap during the war in the Crimea, when she had served as a
troop carrier.

In 1860 she was retired from the Atlantic service and sold to a company that ferried passengers between Liverpool and Bangor in Wales.
Eighteen months later, however, she was bought by Inman and returned to her previous duty. This because the outbreak of civil war in
America had created new commercial opportunities for British shipping in the Atlantic, as passenger vessels of United States registry
now either were in service to the government or else had been laid up
in dock by their owners out of fear of the nimble raiders of the Confederate navy.

Despite the wartime withdrawal of so many commercial rivals, the
Laurentia was not popular with intending passengers. Even to unsea-
manlike eyes, her lines appeared dated, she looked unsafe. Worst of

all, her speed of crossing—which had once been a marvel of the maritime world—now seemed lumbering, almost ridiculously slow, like the tread of some doomed, antediluvian monster. She still took thirteen days on the passage to Liverpool, whereas the brand-new iron-made Inmans and Cunarders, with their churning rear-mounted screws, were crossing in under ten.

So generally unappealing had she become that, at the time Arthur and Olivia Crichton booked their crossing, the joke among the company's agents on both sides of the water was that the only passengers who would consider using the PS *Laurentia* now were those who did not care how long it took them to reach their destination—or whether.

44°2′ N, 55°12′ W

When Olivia had looked in on him after breakfast and suggested meeting at one o'clock in the capstan galley, he had not thought much about it. Not even when, with a smile, she had called the place "my habitual refuge." But now, as he was climbing the first of the two flights of stairs that led up to the main deck, he recalled that on the *Persia,* which had brought them to America nearly three months back, the capstan galley, roofed against the rain and spray but open on four sides to the sea breezes, had been a kind of permanent clubroom for the smokers onboard. There had always been at least half a dozen men in there, with feet up and caps over their eyes, puffing on cigars, passing hip flasks to keep warm, if American spitting, and usually trading low stories.

The thought of Olivia, alone and unprotected, amidst such company sent Arthur hurrying up the second flight of stairs, and then threading his way speedily through the clutter of the main deck—past the officers' cabins, the baker's, the butcher's, the cow house, and the several lifeboats, which, as well as offering a doubtful refuge in the event of a disaster, served to shelter the ship's provision of fresh vegetables. He swayed a little as he went. The seasickness that had claimed him on the first afternoon out of Boston, and had kept him in his bunk all during the run up to Halifax, had only just released him this morning, when they were more than twenty-four hours' steaming out of the latter port. In all that time he had hardly eaten solid food, and had breathed nothing but the musty air of belowdecks. On the first day and a half it had been something worse than musty, for he had then been emptying himself freely, from both ends of his body, into the inadequate tin basin supplied by the Inman Line for the purpose. Whenever he rang the bell to have it emptied, his steward showed up wearing such a harassed expression that Arthur imagined the fellow was having to deal unaided with at least a score of passengers similarly embarrassed. So he had tended to wait—in the increasingly foul atmosphere—until it was absolutely necessary to summon assistance. That, he concluded now, had probably done as much to keep him sick in his bunk as all other elements combined.

At last he reached the capstan galley. And at the end of it, on a bench near the chimney that led to the furnaces below and that gave a little heat into the open galley, sat Olivia. She was wearing her plain blue dress under a gray shawl. Hiding her fair hair was a felt hat with a wide brim, tied around her chin with a blue scarf. All that he could see of her features at first *was* her chin, for her head was bowed over the book that lay open on her lap. But then she did look up, and smiled to see him, and he felt his heart turn over with love.

"There you are, old boy," she said. "I thought you must have forgotten me."

He crossed to where she sat, bent over, and kissed her cheek, feeling how cold her smooth, young skin was under his lips. Then he dropped onto the bench beside her. Nodded at the book.

"Dickens," she said.

"Great Expectations?" He knew she had bought another copy on one of their expeditions into Boston. The original, which he had given her a few months ago, had been lent to a friend—Olivia couldn't remember *which* of her friends exactly—who had never returned it.

"American Notes."

"But you read that on the way over. You said you thought it was unkind and prejudiced."

"And now I marvel at his tolerance towards the Americans. In fact, I find Mr. Dickens is generous to a fault."

"Oh, Livvy," he sighed. She was looking up at him, her head held at an angle. Her blue eyes were steady and challenging. "But do you really not like the country at all?" he asked.

She considered that. "All I can say is that for the amount of boasting and complacency that's on evidence, I can't see they really have so very much to be proud of."

"You must remember, my dear," Arthur said gravely, "that you only saw a very small part—actually only a speck—of a very large country."

(How pompous that sounded, he thought immediately. And condescending. Precisely the Voice of Experience talking to Giddy Youth. When had he started using that particular tone to his wife? Not long before she had started calling him "old boy," he guessed.)

She was looking at him now rather crossly and biting her lower lip.

"I am aware that *my* movements were extremely confined in America, Arthur."

Referring, of course, to his solitary expedition to New York. It had been a business trip, some men—a couple of cotton brokers, a general of the Federal army, a few others—who he had needed to talk to. He had not taken Olivia, though he knew very well she was longing—*dying,* as she had put it—to get away for a few days from South Hadley, Mass., and from his anxious, elderly sister and brother-in-law's dim little house. He had argued that on such a short visit it would be the height of bad manners for her as well as him to leave them. That he would be in New York for only one full day, during which every hour would be taken up by meetings. That he must concentrate during that brief time solely on business and it would be a terrible distraction if he had to be thinking of her care and entertainment as well.

Alone he had taken the cars for New York. The moment the train pulled out of the station—when it was too late to do anything about it, of course—he had regretted leaving her behind. When she was so desperate to go. On his return three days later, he had tried to make it up to her. She did not have a nature that bore grudges easily, and he thought that after a little while she had forgiven his unkindness. And perhaps she had, he reflected now, but it had clearly not been forgotten.

Still, she was smiling at him, and in such a way that he couldn't help chuckling. She slipped her hand into his, and they rested in silence for a while, side by side, looking out at the galley before them.

—

"You're alone," he said suddenly. "I come up here—and I find you all alone."

"Shouldn't I be alone?" she asked, puzzled.

"But don't you remember on the *Persia*? This place—" He looked around: the roof, the open sides, the empty benches, the duckboard underneath. "There was always somebody about, some fellows, smoking, you know, and—" Making pigs of themselves, he was on the point of adding, but didn't.

"Oh, Arthur!" Olivia was smiling. "Did you think to find me here surrounded by horrible men? Don't worry. Nobody ever comes in here in the morning. Or in the rest of the day really."

At that moment a shimmer of movement caught Arthur's eye. He looked around to see a steward making his way past the galley.

"Where is everybody on this ship?" he wondered. "I've seen hardly a soul since I got up."

"That's because there's nobody onboard." She laughed then to see his expression. "I *mean*, there's hardly anybody. There are only twenty-seven passengers in the first-class—"

"Twenty-seven! There are at least eighty first-class berths."

"Twenty-seven," she repeated. "We were thirty leaving Boston, but six got off at Halifax and only three came onboard. Mr. Hartley, the first officer, was telling me about it in the saloon last night. Nobody wants to sail on these little wooden boats now. This one may be on her last crossing, Mr. Hartley says. The last time ever she is on the ocean. Poor thing."

Arthur currently was regretting not so much this ship's fate, which he felt he could bear, as his own good nature in having spared his steward over so many hours in the matter of the slops. Twenty-seven passengers indeed. It meant there must be about one and a half stewards to each passenger.

"And a lot of the people that *are* onboard are still confined to their staterooms, as you were. So we only get about a dozen in the saloon at lunch and dinner. And they are a very odd lot."

She had slipped her arm under his. He was watching her profile, the mischievous smile crinkling her lips. She had done pretty badly in America, he thought, hadn't fitted in at all well. And he hadn't expected it. For she was true Lancashire. Her father had stumped up for a couple of years at a rather bad Home Counties boarding school, which had modified her accent considerably, but underneath, the original flavor was hardly diluted at all. And the Lancashire girls of every class, from the cotton districts anyway, had a reputation for boldness and freshness and independence of spirit quite different from the average English young lady; and, in fact, were said to be the closest human article the Old Country had to the Yankees of the New. But it had been like chalk and cheese with her and almost everybody she'd dealt with over there.

"How 'odd' "? he asked then.

Olivia sat for a moment in silence, then nodded solemnly.

"Well, there is one who is really interesting. But I shall leave him till last."

Arthur nodded, registering, without hardly knowing it, that she had used the male pronoun to refer to this most interesting of passengers.

"Very well—first, there's an old clergyman or parson or something. American. Reverend Stibbards. He told me what church he belonged to, but I've forgotten it. It didn't sound at all genuine. Anyway, it doesn't matter much because he doesn't speak to me anymore. For I have offended him."

"Olivia . . ."

"It was hardly anything at all. Judge for yourself. First night we were at dinner—we'd barely got out of Boston harbor—he leans across the table at me and says: 'Now, Mrs. Crichton, just how did you like your stay in my great country?' And I said—"

She paused considerately while her husband groaned again.

"I said, 'Not in the least, sir. Thank you for inquiring.' And since then he hasn't spoken to me."

"But can you blame him?" Actually Arthur was quite relieved that the nature of the quarrel was as relatively innocuous and impersonal as this, and above all that its active phase seemed to have ended so quickly. Olivia, when the spirit moved her, was capable of far worse.

She hated hypocrites. And fools. Nowadays, she seemed to have just one word for the both of them: Americans.

"Yes, I do blame him. Shouldn't he have had some interest in *why* I felt this way? Perhaps I could have told him something about his precious country that he'd never thought of before."

"But think always," Arthur recommended pacifically, "that the Americans—most of them—are so convinced that their country stands head and shoulders above every other that any criticism of it must seem to them not an expression of honest opinion but perverse, produced only by spite, and actually wicked."

"They could have been forgiven for believing that once," Olivia declared tartly, "but you would think they might start to have some doubts about just how wonderful they are at a time when two-thirds of the country is trying its hardest to pull away from the rest of it!"

They were in silence again. Arthur had it in mind to suggest that she seemed to have got her proportions wrong in the matter of which of the still disunited states were trying to remove themselves from the others. But it hardly seemed worth mentioning. And he had no wish to prolong a debate that seemed to make his wife angry, even though the emotion had brought a most attractive bloom of color to her cheek, a bloom that, as he watched, was now fading.

"Who else is onboard?"

Prompted, she took him on a quick tour of his prospective companions. The American gentleman—"pretty dry"—who sat at cards all day and half the night in the company of an Englishman, Mr. Burgess—"a military man, I think"—and two Nova Scotians—"the others call them 'Blue Noses,' I can't think why, their noses are actually rather red." A Miss Faversham from Kent, who was quite old— "fifty at least"—and a recently widowed Scottish lady, Mrs. Stewart, who was not, and was sharing her cabin with her two young children—"very small, very quiet...Miss Faversham by the way would actually be *from* Faversham—it is her only joke—if she didn't happen to live in the next village." There were also the Tates, husband and wife, "who would be entirely negligible except that they look rather desperate. They're very interested in you, Arthur."

"In me?"

"Mm. They found us on the passenger list, and they know just who you are. He's in cotton, but I couldn't find out exactly how. I think he may want to sell you something."

Once more Arthur groaned. Olivia gave him a quick smile. Went on to describe several other passengers, but at such a speed and so glancingly that Arthur hardly had time to register their names, let alone their attributes.

"And that completes our little society. Unless you count the captain, who indeed seems to spend as much time in the saloon with the passengers as he does about his other duties. He's a doughty old chap, lots of whiskers and so on, and—I think—a bit of a fraud. He hints at having seen action at Trafalgar, but I am sure that cannot be, Arthur. For though he is an old man, he's surely not much past sixty—at least that's what Mrs. Stewart guesses."

Arthur was smiling as he listened to her. In the ice and gloom of Massachusetts, he had missed so much this mixture of fun and teasing and sharp insights that was hers. He was so glad to see it back. He feasted his eyes on her. Lord, he thought, she is lovely. There was a wisp of golden hair escaped from under her bonnet, it lay like wheat upon her skin.

He noticed that she was tugging on his sleeve, and he was dimly aware that she had put a question to him, perhaps more than once, and he'd not answered.

"What did you say, my dear?"

"I *asked* you whether, having heard my account of the delights that await you above deck, you are planning to head straight back to your stateroom." She sniffed humorously. "I see I need not have inquired. My little bill of fare has sent you straight off to sleep."

"I was not sleeping," Arthur protested. "I was ... reflecting. And in answer to your question: why, I can't make up my mind just yet, can I? For I haven't heard a complete account of my fellow passengers. You said," he reminded her, "that you had left the most interesting one till last."

"Ah, yes ..."

She sat still. Her gaze, Arthur noted, had turned from him, she was looking toward one of the galley's open sides. She had removed her arm from under his.

"I shall take you to him."

She looked back at him then, and smiled. Got to her feet. He stared up at her. The gray shawl had been allowed to fall aside for the moment, and the breezes flowing in through the galley's open sides were pressing her dress close against her breasts and thighs. "You know where you can find this mysterious gentleman just now?" he wondered.

Olivia held out her hand, took his, drew him upward.

"I know where he is always to be found," she said.

≡

Their way led them from the capstan galley back onto the main deck. She was propelling him onward at such a speed—to view this so interesting *he*—that he could hardly catch his breath. At one moment he forgot what foot to put in front of the other, and he stumbled. She looked across at him, concerned.

"Only just out of my bunk. Haven't got my sea legs yet."

"Perhaps we should go inside, Arthur? You should sit down."

"No. I'm glad to be up."

"Can you go up some stairs?"

"Of course." I'm not yet in my dotage, he thought of saying, but contented himself with repeating, "Of course I can."

"Then pray do so, please."

And she pointed to where a set of white-painted iron steps rose from forward of the capstan galley to the poop deck. She led the way, hitching her skirt in one hand and taking the steps almost at a trot. He followed her more slowly, using the rails to hand himself along. He was out of breath by the time he joined her on the poop, just near the wheelhouse and the binnacle. But as soon as he did, and had a chance to look around him, he forgot his physical cares. For unlike the brief, obstructed glimpses he had caught from the lower deck, up here he had a free and panoramic view of all that lay around the ship. And it was not the monotonous gray stripe of water that was all he had seen from below, but an ocean boundless and splashed with color: here deep green, there green again but much lighter, like leaves in sunlight, over there an icy blue, in the distance more like purple, though darker.

The sight made him murmur out loud in appreciation. And he went directly to the rail to get a better look. He knew that, in time, constant exposure to this view would turn it into something mundane, even wearisome. So it had been on the *Persia* coming out, on those days, eighth or ninth out of Liverpool, when it seemed the ship never would come in sight of America, when everyone was watching and longing for the first shadow of land. On such days, nothing could be of less interest than the endless waste of water that was still all that could actually be seen. But not now. Not yet. Now around the ship, the ocean moved in unbroken, gleaming swells that stretched away on either side as if forever. There were no white crests anywhere, except—he pressed against the rail, looked down—except where the ocean broke against the hull. And where the great paddle beat the water into foam. Above him, the sky was a milky blue, and almost empty of cloud. It was winter cold, but to look at like a perfect spring morning in England. Just now Arthur Crichton felt there was nothing he wanted to do other than simply stand and look.

But then Olivia came up from behind and, as if recalling him to duty, touched his elbow. He quit the rail reluctantly, let himself be ushered along the poop toward where, in the distance, the single funnel—jet-black, with one white band—broke clear of the deck. All the way up to that point, the deck ran forward in a long swoop, comprising over its length the entire roofs of the capstan galley, steward's office, and first-class saloon. Along it, wooden benches had been placed at intervals and close enough to the rail so that passengers could take their ease and at the same time look their fill on the ocean all around. But there were no passengers on the poop that Arthur could see. No one except Olivia and himself to enjoy the sea and the cold, salt breeze sweeping along the deck.

"Look as though you are talking to me," Olivia muttered urgently. She had stopped, turned back toward him.

"I can do that best probably by actually talking to you."

"Don't be provoking, Arthur." Olivia frowned. She cast a quick glance over her shoulder. "Now, ever so slowly, just look towards the funnel. On the left-hand side."

He did just as she asked. Turned a little, looked—and saw the figure of a man, standing against the railing, at the farthest point of the deck. He was positioned in the shadow cast by the big funnel—which must have been, Arthur supposed, why he had not noticed him before. But now he'd located him, he had a good enough view, except there was really not much to see. A tall figure—over six feet, he looked—with his back toward them, wearing a long black or navy blue coat that appeared to be made of some waterproof material. He was bareheaded, and his hair, worn rather long, was as dark as his garment.

Arthur examined the man for a few seconds, then turned back with a shrug to Olivia. But whatever he was about to say to her stuck fast on his lips. She was looking past him at the man in the near distance with an expression on her face—but he did not want to put a name to that expression. Only he felt like an intruder staring at her, and he had a strong desire to look away. Yet he did not. Could not stop watching her.

And then he happened to blink, and the next moment all he could see in Olivia's eyes, as she watched this man, was amusement, curiosity, even a kind of pity: all perfectly ordinary, innocent emotions. He hardly knew what to think.

=

She began talking quickly then, in an undertone, as if fearing she might be overheard—which was ridiculous, of course, the man was a good thirty yards away.

"His name is Mr. John Bonney. B-O-N-N-E-Y. Isn't that a delightful name?"

"You have been introduced to him?"

"By the captain on the first night. Oh, very briefly, you know. Just names. He came aboard at Boston—I watched him. Then after we sailed, and you had to go to your stateroom, I came up here to walk about, and there he was, standing there, just at that spot. Looking back toward the town. And every time since then that I have come up here it has been the same. He is always there, just there, near the funnel. Always looking backwards. Even though there is nothing now to see, except the ocean."

"But surely he cannot be an entirely permanent fixture," Arthur argued. "He must come down from there sometimes. To eat, you know, or to—"

"Of course he comes down sometimes," Olivia said impatiently. "He's not *mad*. He is in the saloon for dinner. And sometimes at luncheon too."

But she was losing interest in what she was saying even as she spoke. Her attention was all on the man near the funnel. Arthur watched her a few moments more, then also looked toward Bonney.

"He's quite young, I believe," she said. "Perhaps not older than me. What do you think?"

"As the gentleman is standing with his back to us, I really can't judge." Arthur gazed at the long black back in the distance, then turned again to Olivia. "But tell me: does his entire interestingness consist in the fact that he stands rooted to a particular spot every day?"

She looked at him as if she couldn't see his point.

"I mean, when he does join the rest of the human race—" Arthur wondered at the scornful note that had crept unbidden into his voice. "When he is at the dinner table and so on, what account does this Mr. Bonney give of himself?"

"Why, no account at all. He is not offensive, but he won't speak if he can help it. The Reverend Stibbards has attempted to draw him out. Mr. Bonney is polite, but he don't allow it. He answers one or two questions, but then just turns the rest aside. He sits at the end of his table—I am sure he wishes he had one to himself, but that would be too impolite—and he eats his food fast, as Americans will do. And then goes straight back up here."

Arthur wondered a little how she knew that. Presumably she had followed him at least once.

"He is an American then?"

"Yes. From a western state. The Reverend Stibbards got that much out of him. He also found out—"

But whatever else John Bonney had revealed was not to be told just now, for at that moment the figure they had been watching and discussing in a manner that had by now become quite easy and dispassionate, as if it was a statue or a painting before them, suddenly came alive. As they watched, Bonney seemed to press closer against the rail, and then—but what he did then exactly they could not afterward make up their minds about. There was a throwing forward of his upper limbs, a similar forward stirring of his head and torso. Olivia *thought* she saw his legs move then too, as if he would climb up on the rail, and—heavens above!—just for a moment it looked as if he would throw himself over it and into the sea. She was about to call out, to rush forward, but Arthur was holding on to her arm. And before she had let go of her cry, she could see that the occasion for it—if it had ever existed—had passed. For the figure had settled back into immobility. And his hands, which had seemed to be flying about in all directions a moment before, were once again only gripping the top rail. And Bonney again was staring at the sea.

Husband and wife, in hushed voices, discussed what they had seen as they made their way back along the poop toward the steps.

"I think he was waving," Olivia decided.

"Waving at what? There wasn't another ship. I couldn't see even a seagull out there." Arthur paused for breath at the top of the ladder. He looked out at the great, glassy ocean. Nothing.

"Then what do you think it was?"

"I believe he was clutching at something," Arthur said promptly. "That's how it looked to me." He shook his head. "But the same objection stands, doesn't it? What had he to clutch *at*? Only the air and the sea, that's all."

He led the way down the stairs to the main deck, then turned and waited for her, holding out his hand to help her over the last few steps. The noise of the paddle wheel was loud again here, and he had to raise his voice as they turned toward the saloon.

"He certainly is a very singular passenger. I don't wonder that you call him the most interesting one onboard. I haven't met the others, but I'm pretty sure he must be that."

"Yes." She was silent for a few steps, and then, just before they turned in at the door that would lead them either to the main saloon on the left hand or, on the right, to the stairs that descended belowdecks, she added: "Unless you would think a colored man in the first class is interesting. But I don't believe I can count him. For the rest of us haven't set eyes on him. In fact, I don't think we're even supposed to know he's onboard."

—

"It's the most extraordinary thing, Mr. Crichton. The booking was made at our Montreal office. One first-class accommodation, and a premium paid for a stateroom as far as possible from the paddles. However the booking was done—perhaps by messenger, or in collusion with a white ally—there cannot have been anything untoward about it, else I should certainly have been informed at Halifax by the telegraph. Had we discovered the fellow at the point of boarding—or even just a little while after we had started out—something might have been done perhaps. But he seems to have slipped onto the ship quite undetected. It was a peculiarly gloomy afternoon at Halifax, you'll remember? My fool of a head steward showed him to his stateroom— probably the beggar was handed a lavish tip at the same time. Now he tells me that he did notice that the passenger was of a 'somewhat swarthy aspect' but thought nothing of it! And there we were, sir. Fait accompli. The matter was not brought to my attention until late the following morning. By which time I had already got myself past Sable Island and was making good progress to the Newfoundland Banks. I could hardly turn back to port at that point, could I, Mr. Crichton?"

"I'm exceedingly glad you didn't," Arthur said.

Captain McDonough tugged at his whiskers. As Olivia had hinted, the most striking thing about the man's appearance was this wild white growth. It boomed out tremendously from each cheek, and, though his chin was strangely bare, underneath it the snowy frazzle fell in cascades, to below the midpoint of his chest. For the rest, the captain's appearance was not exceptional. He was a big, bluff fellow who must have looked rather fine ten or fifteen years ago. Now there was more than a suggestion of sag about him. His belly was big under the dark blue uniform coat, and his shoulders had a somewhat abject slump. Arthur had not had time enough to discover if Olivia's further observation that the captain was a "bit of a fraud" was also accurate. But he felt he was getting close to the truth.

"I have since heard," McDonough said gloomily, "that at least one passenger thinks it was exactly my duty to have turned around, gone back to Halifax, and put the Negro ashore."

"Sounds like a piece of bluff to me. Whoever said that, I would be astounded if he—or she—had not made absolutely certain it was too late for you to do any such thing."

The captain nodded abstractedly. "It was a male passenger, of course. Actually only a few of *them* know of the situation, and thus far we have managed to keep the ladies entirely in ignorance."

Arthur thought of Olivia, smiled to himself. "I'm sure that was wise, Captain. It would not do to alarm the ladies needlessly."

The captain grunted his agreement. He was silent then. It was late afternoon, and Arthur felt rather sleepy in the cabin's close air. He was still somewhat confused as to what he was actually doing here—though indeed it was entirely at his own volition that he was. He supposed it must have been because Olivia had seemed concerned about the plight of this colored man, more or less a prisoner apparently in his stateroom, that he had thought to bring up the matter with the captain as the two of them had lingered at the table after dinner. Beneath his whiskers, McDonough had offered quite a kaleidoscope of expressions: surprise at Arthur even knowing of the matter, concern lest any other passengers overhear their conversation, depression at the size of the problem he had been dealing with all alone, ending with a very apparent rush of relief at having somebody to confide in.

"And you are exactly the man I would wish to talk this over with," the captain had asserted. "A gentleman of your stature. A *practical* man."

That was certainly flattering, Arthur thought, and flattering too, very much so, he supposed, to be asked back to the captain's cabin for a postprandial glass of brandy and water. For he knew that on any ship the captain's apartment was absolutely a place of refuge for that officer and pretty much forbidden ground for anyone else, except he be on a mission directly concerned with the running of the ship. On the *Persia*, though Captain Shannon had been courteous and affable toward all of the passengers—of the first class, at any rate—still he had never gone so far as to invite anyone to penetrate this sanctuary.

"But surely," Arthur prompted at last, "surely this situation has arisen before?"

"Never in the first class." Captain McDonough sipped at his drink. Then: "There was an instance, years ago—oh, perhaps fifteen years—

a colored fellow booked a first-class stateroom on the old *Cumbria* out of Liverpool."

"What happened?"

"He wasn't allowed to claim it when he came onboard. But he was a big swell, you know, a famous fellow, one of those abolitionists' pets, and his friends onshore kicked up a fuss. Letters in *The Times* and so on. In the Boston papers too. And Mr. Inman eventually felt obliged to write a letter for publication, apologizing to the darkie and saying such a thing would never happen again."

"Why, then, Captain, your course is clear. The man must be allowed all the privileges and freedoms of a first-class passenger. The president of your company has mandated it."

"Ye-e-es." McDonough sighed lengthily. There was a pause, during which what was visible in the captain's face behind his whiskers took on a very uneasy aspect. "Of course, to write a letter is one thing—"

"But to put its terms into execution quite another?"

"I am sure that Mr. Inman meant exactly what he wrote. But that was long ago. Eighteen fifty, thereabouts... It's these blasted Americans, of course," McDonough growled suddenly. "They just will not stand for it, you see—and then when the Collins Line came along..."

The captain seemed to be rambling. He had certainly lost Arthur. He recalled that in its heyday, back in the early fifties, the Collins Line had given the other transatlantic companies quite a scare. The Collins boats were faster and more luxurious: in fact, it was the extravagances of their cuisine and furnishings that had really put the company in financial jeopardy. And then two of its ships in quick succession had sunk without trace, giving Collins a reputation as an unsafe carrier. By the end of the decade the line was defunct, leaving to Cunard and its junior rival Inman the clear supremacy of the western ocean.

"The Collins Line, Captain?"

"Precisely. Well, they were Americans, you see. I don't think they ever even allowed a black man onboard one of their ships, unless it was as a servant. We were never *that* strict—but still, we could not allow the Collins fellows to label us as negligent in the ordinary decencies of civilized conduct."

"So that effectively ... ?"

"Effectively—" The captain stopped, mused. Then: "There *were* hardly ever any Negroes applying for passage, perhaps not a single one in twenty or thirty crossings. But any that did always bought a second-class berth. And there they were given exactly equal treatment to any other forecabin passenger ... Of course, if other second-class passengers did complain, we would try to find the darkie a separate table to eat at, and I might recommend that he limit his visits to the cabin at night. But otherwise—perfectly equal."

The captain brooded some more, as if reflecting on the company's extraordinary liberality. He tippled at his drink.

"How exactly stands the situation now?"

"The situation," said Captain McDonough, "is a big bloody mess. 'Scuse my French." He belched, poured brandy unasked into Arthur's glass, then topped up his own. "The fellow—the black fellow, you see?—we've confined him pretty much to his stateroom. He eats all his meals there—the *exact* same meals as are served in the saloon, he can have no complaints there. And I have given him permission to exercise himself on the poop in the early morning before the breakfast bell and again late at night. I have also requested—*politely* requested—that he change his accommodation into the second class. I have promised him a refund of the difference between the two fares, out of my own pocket if need be. No good. Might as well have been talking to a brick wall. Refused my every entreaty."

=

Arthur was feeling somewhat overwhelmed. He hadn't really meant to do more than ascertain the bare facts of the case, so that if things were not as bad as they seemed he would be able to reassure Olivia on the score. Actually, the facts seemed rather worse than he had imagined. Yet at least the way forward was perfectly obvious. At dinner, McDonough had hinted that he hoped for some sort of "help" from Arthur. Clearly the only kind of help that was needed was whatever would assist the captain to face up to reality.

"Who is this fellow?" Arthur asked at length.

"Who is he? *I* don't know! A black man. He seems to be a perfectly civil chap. Though he gets pretty damn cross whenever I—"

"But who *is* he? What is his occupation? Why is he crossing the ocean?"

The captain reflected. "I believe he said once that he is some sort of an entertainer. Yes. He told me he was visiting Europe to fulfill certain long-standing engagements. Singing to people, you know, in theaters—"

"Ah, then he will have friends on the other side?"

"What are you saying?"

"Whoever has made these arrangements with him—I don't know, agents, theater managers. People who will have an interest in his welfare."

"Oh, God."

"In which case they are probably in a position to make a public fuss on his behalf. And then, of course, there is the legal aspect—"

"Don't talk to me of the law, sir," the captain broke in impatiently. "That is all I need. Thank God, we have no blasted lawyers onboard this crossing. In fact . . ." His face brightened remarkably. "*That's* what I'll do. Leave things as they are till we can put it before the wretched lawyers. Nobody can blame me if I do that. And there's none of *them* closer than Liverpool."

Yes, what a fraud this old man is, Arthur thought. With his big, bold whiskers and his scared, drunken eyes. So this would be a pleasure.

"In fact, Captain, you are wrong. There is a lawyer onboard."

McDonough stared. His panic broke through the spirits, lending him a sudden insight.

"*You* are he?"

"I'm afraid so," Arthur said gravely.

On the wall a clock ticked, loud in the silence. Outside, not far away, a man shouted and was answered by jeering laughs from several throats. On McDonough's grizzled face some resemblance to a knowing smile was replacing the blankness it had worn for many moments. He shook his head then and with rising confidence said, "No, sir!"

Smiling now, mainly in relief, it appeared, he groped for his bottle.

"You will have your fun, sir, but I should tell you—it's surely not a secret—that the company tries to inform its captains of any notable passengers whom they may expect onboard. And so I know that you are not a legal gentleman, Mr. Crichton. *Cotton*, that's the thing, isn't it?"

"It is, indeed," Arthur said. "But that is because I fell away from my original vocation. It is many years ago, but oh, yes, I have eaten my dinners at the Upper Temple; I was regularly called to the bar. I even practiced for a short while on the Northern Circuit. But then, as I say, I fell away."

It was one of those times in the thirties when the cotton industry had seemed to soar like a rocket into the dirty Lancashire sky, showering sparks and sovereigns on all beneath. The rest of the country watched amazed. Great fortunes were made and lost in a month, new mills and factories opening every day. It was impossible to stand at the edge of this conflagration—as Arthur had stood—and not feel excited by its warmth. Hard not to feel that, in comparison, there was something snail-like, almost abject, about a junior barrister's progress. There were wonderful bargains to be plucked out of the spectacular crashes of that time. One morning, on Market Street in Manchester, on his way to chambers, Arthur had been stopped by a man he knew slightly and been made an offer: two mills for sale, one in Stalybridge, the other next door in Ashton-under-Lyne, the assets of a firm, bankrupted ten minutes before—would he come in for a quarter share? By the afternoon Arthur was a co-owner of the mills. He did not, of course, have the money to meet even the low asking price, but he was not required to have it—yet. Only his promise to pay before one month had elapsed. If he failed to come up with the cash in that time, he would be bankrupted himself, and his fledgling legal career would be in ruins.

Arthur still did not like to think of the risks he had undertaken that day. But in fact long before the month was up, the Ashton mill had been sold again for over twice the price at which he and his colleagues had bought it, and he was clear and free and with real money of his own to invest in the trade. Which he did, and had never stopped since. Cotton had got into his blood, and he could no more return to his old profession than he could have gone back to his dame school.

"Nevertheless, Captain, I still revere and delight in the law, and follow its development as best I can. It is always to the Law Report that I turn first when I open the newspaper. And I feel competent and would be glad to assist you in this little difficulty, from the legal point of view."

He waited courteously for Captain McDonough to respond to his offer. But the old man still appeared struck dumb by his announcement. So he went on: "It's a matter for contract law, of course. And contract has always been my special delight." Arthur smiled. "Because, I suppose, it's the only way we have of imposing good behavior on others—and on ourselves—whatever the baser instincts tempt us to do."

Silence. Nothing. The captain's glazed stare.

"You'll be glad to know, Captain, that the position here is quite easy and clear. A contract has certainly been entered into between the Inman company and this Negro. The company has given him a promise, in the form of a ticket, that it will perform certain tasks on his behalf. The Negro has provided a consideration for this promise in the form of whatever price he has paid for his passage. Thus a contract exists, and because of the element of consideration, it is certainly both legal and enforceable...Now you may argue," Arthur went on, happily pedantic, "that the Negro paid the consideration in return for your transporting him to Liverpool, and that since you *are* transporting him thither you are thereby fulfilling the contract. I doubt a court would agree. When he contracts for his berth, a passenger doesn't merely purchase the right to occupy the few square feet of his cabin during the crossing. There is the implication also that he will be allowed to enjoy onboard all the vessel's facilities and the opportunities for social intercourse that he is entitled to expect by the customary usages of the trade. I think *Hutton versus Warren* may be an important precedent here," Arthur mused. "Though I should want to check my notes on that..."

And still nothing from the captain. Only the misery in his frightened, bloodshot eyes. His fear really did seem excessive to Arthur. The Negro *had* to be allowed out of his cabin, and if there were objections from other passengers then so be it. The captain had all the law he could want on his side, and the ship would still keep steaming on to England whatever petty squabbles broke out in the saloon. To be honest—and though he acknowledged it was for no good reason— Arthur personally was not much attracted to the prospect of receiving a colored man on intimate terms as a fellow passenger. But there it was, he would have to put up with it, as would everybody else. If there were any who couldn't, then let *them* confine themselves to *their* staterooms. It was all perfectly clear.

"That summarizes the civil aspect of the matter," Arthur went on now. "One might also mention here the criminal laws pertaining to personal injury and unlawful detention. If the case reaches the courts—and if you are found guilty—there is a very strong chance of a custodial sentence." (Almost certainly an exaggeration, but something had to be said to push the fellow out of his stupor.) "You would surely not wish to pass several months, years even, in prison, Captain? At hard labor, perhaps?" (This is disgraceful, Arthur thought, I am enjoying this far too much.) "And then, let us not forget that, as well as breach of contract, the Negro may be able to bring an action for—"

"But he threatens to *kill* him, Mr. Crichton!" McDonough wailed forth in a sort of agony.

Arthur stared at the captain.

"Who is threatening to kill who?"

"Mr. Cutler is. To kill the Negro."

"And who on earth is Mr. Cutler?"

"Have you not met him? Also in the first class? One of those damned Americans. He knows the Negro is onboard. And he threatens to shoot him down like a dog if he ever sees him outside his stateroom."

———

On the Cunard vessel *Persia,* as the Crichtons had discovered back in December, the usual order of teatime and dinner was reversed. Dinner was served between four and five o'clock of an evening; the covers were cleared afterward; and then a light tea made an appearance at seven. The custom at dinner was for a passenger to choose the place where he wished to sit at the beginning of the voyage and then keep to the same seat all the rest of the way. They had found this to be a limiting and quite irksome system. For a dozen fairly lengthy dinners in a row, one was stuck with the same faces, as well as much the same conversation, prejudices, fatuities, and peculiar eating habits. To attempt to exchange for another table was, it seemed, not to be thought of. It was unlikely that a place would open up elsewhere, and if it did, the insult to those left behind would be considered serious. And in any case:

"It could be a matter of out of the frying pan into the fire," Arthur had remarked, third day out on the *Persia*.

"Better the devil you know?"

"At least we're not sitting opposite that man with the huge carbuncle on his forehead."

"Or next to the woman with the mad laugh."

However, teatime on the *Persia* had been a much more casual, fluid affair. After the bell rang at seven o'clock, people began to drift into the saloon in ones and twos. They sat wherever they fancied among the red plush banquettes, or along the tables that lined the sides of the room, to be served their beverages and little cakes fresh from the ship's bakery. Many remained where they had first sat down, but it was quite in order for one to get up after a while to visit with acquaintances in other parts of the room. Little groups formed and broke up and formed again. The blue-uniformed stewards moved among the crowd with their pots of tea and coffee. On a couple of nights on the *Persia*, once the cups and saucers had been cleared away, there had been some kind of entertainment offered. One evening an American passenger had given a lecture on "spirit rapping," a new method of communicating with the dead. Another evening an Irish passenger had sung, unaccompanied, several of the beautiful ballads of his native land.

But on all the other nights on the *Persia*, when tea was over the passengers were left to make their own amusement. The cards that had been put away to allow the tables to be set reappeared. Whist, brag, and loo were the usual games. Another group would be keeping the backgammon board rattling, and still others, who did not play, would be sitting or standing at various points around the room, continuing the conversations that had begun over tea.

There *were* pockets of relative peace in the *Persia*'s saloon during those hours. There was a table where a pair of Germans, commercial travelers from Cologne, used to sit facing each other over a chessboard night after night, on any of those nights hardly uttering a half dozen words between them. And some people preferred just to take a book from the shelves that lined the wall on either side of the door at one end of the saloon and sit solitary under a chandelier. But what Arthur Crichton remembered best was the animation of the *Persia*'s saloon, the moving, shifting throng, and especially the unceasing hum of voices. So that the first thing he thought when he pushed open the saloon door one hour after quitting Captain McDonough's apartment was how eerily quiet and still it all seemed.

Yet, as he waited for a moment in the doorway, he could see that, in fact, matters in the Inman world were arranged in much the same way as in Cunard's: there were the same cardplayers, gossipers, tea takers, and the solitary readers were there too. The difference in noise level was entirely a function of numbers. Well over a hundred passengers used to crowd into the *Persia*'s first-class saloon at teatime, and sometimes the throng was so dense that in parts of the room conditions reached that comical curse of the modern age, when the ladies' crinolines got so tightly wedged together that any movement—by man, woman, child, or steward—seemed impossible. Here there was not a quarter of that number present. And though the saloon was smaller than the *Persia*'s, the little band of passengers presently in it seemed lost in the midst of vast open spaces, like a few solitary grazing animals adrift on the plains of America or Africa. Arthur had met most of them at dinner, but it was only now, looking at them when they were allowed to move freely around the saloon, that he really comprehended how very few they amounted to.

But then as he moved from the door and toward the populated end of the room, the feeling of being cast away in an almost infinite space started to fade. Faces were turned to him as he approached, there were smiles of greeting. A steward came forward to take his order. Having given it, Arthur stood waiting. At the nearby card table a well-dressed man, distinguished by a set of imposing mustaches, who he guessed to be Mr. Burgess—Olivia's "military man"—looked up at him speculatively, then nodded and looked down again at his hand. Also nearby, on one of the banquettes, sat a woman of about thirty-five, with a fine full head of hair, as dark almost as the black dress and shawl she was wearing. There was a decided air of melancholy about her. She had been introduced to him at dinner as Mrs. Stewart, and so he knew her to be the poor lady Olivia had described to him, so recently widowed. On her lap now was an open volume of what appeared at a glance to be scriptural commentaries. Looking up from her book, her eyes—which were a lovely deep violet, Arthur noticed—met his. Arthur bowed. Mrs. Stewart inclined her head very slightly. Then she returned to her volume.

Arthur looked around then for the steward who had gone for his tea things. The man was nowhere to be seen. He located Olivia, though, at last. She was standing in a corner of the room almost hidden behind the bulky form of the ship's first officer, Mr. Hartley. With them was a tall, middle-aged lady, very thin—Miss Faversham, Arthur remembered. He made his way over to the group and, with an apologetic smile at the other two, abstracted his wife from their midst.

"That was cruel, Arthur," she protested as he took her over to sit at an empty banquette. "I believe I was starting to make headway with Mr. Hartley. But do you think that the existence of a Mrs. Hartley in Liverpool and five little Hartleys will prove a barrier to our future happiness?"

Arthur smiled into her eyes. "There is also the objection that you are already supplied with a husband."

"So I am," she said, rather wistfully to his ears. But then she laughed. "Although I don't think Mr. Hartley was particularly eager to offer me his *hand*."

As ever Olivia was capable of stunning indelicacy when she chose. He shouldn't be surprised by it anymore. And he could not deny that he found those moments quite stirring. The angel's face and the wicked words, well...Arthur found he was becoming stirred right now, and would be visibly so, he feared, if he was not careful. He hunched over in his seat and hushed her as she seemed to want to pursue her humor. "Olivia, I've something to tell you," he started. But then had to fall silent himself, for the steward had found him at last and, as if to make up for his dilatoriness, made a great fuss of setting up the plates and offering the cakes and pouring the tea, so that it was minutes before they could get rid of him.

"Is anything wrong?" Olivia asked as soon as the fellow was gone.

"Not wrong, exactly. But it's very odd. Something the captain has told me..."

What he had to tell her was still surprising even to himself, though he'd had an hour to digest it. He had spent the time first walking about on the main deck, then sitting in his stateroom, mostly brooding over the request McDonough had made to him near the conclusion of their interview. It was not a request that had at all appealed to him.

"I can't be expected to play the spy among my fellow passengers!"

"Not the spy, Mr. Crichton. Not that at all. The *diplomat*. That's the word." The captain's red-flecked eyes were imploring him. "All I ask is that you ascertain the state of mind of the saloon. See how it feels about having the Negro introduced there... But, of course, if you can give it a certain push in the right direction, I would be most grateful to you. The company would be most grateful."

Hang the company, Arthur had nearly said. The meeting had ended a few minutes later without him giving a definite response to the captain's proposition. He had certainly felt very irritated that it had been made, and a subsequent twenty minutes' pacing on deck had not driven that feeling away. By the time he reached his stateroom, he had pretty well decided to have nothing to do with this affair. Increasingly, outside the world of business, Arthur Crichton did not like much to put himself forward with new people. For instance, when he traveled with his wife or saw people socially, he preferred to leave it to Olivia to break the ice and reserved for himself the right to watch the progress of a new acquaintance for a while before deciding whether he would have a share in it. And now to be expected to go around accosting a set of people he had hardly yet been introduced to, talking to them on a matter that for several—the Americans especially—might contain the potential for strong emotions, even violence...

No, such a mission was quite out of the question, Arthur had decided for the tenth time as he rested, deep in the armchair in his room. Even though, he supposed, the object was a worthy one. He looked around his stateroom. It was one of the more expensive cabins among the first class—as was this Negro's, he understood—but even so it was terribly small. It measured—what? perhaps eight feet by six—and the ceiling was so low that Arthur, standing at five feet nine, always instinctively stooped when he came in through the door. There was room only—he had made the experiment—for three short paces in any direction from the center of the carpet. For furniture, there were two sleeping berths, one above the other. There was a sofa, small, covered in oilcloth and, like the bunks, screwed to the floor against the threat of shifting if the boat should meet foul weather. There was a washstand with a jug on it, and the painted tin commode hanging at the side from a hook. There was a looking glass on the wall above the washstand. There was a porthole, thickly glassed. And there was nothing else.

Arthur had grown pretty tired of looking at this meager arrangement during his sickness. At least the thought that his captivity would be ended before too many more hours had passed had helped him endure the final stages. To have had nothing to look forward to but day after day of such confinement, nearly a fortnight of it, until their slow approach to Europe at last brought the prospect of relief—

It would have been unendurable.

"And so you are going to do it? You're going to talk to the people here."

"I think I have to." Arthur grunted. "What else *can* I do? Those cabins are so damn narrow, Livvy. Like a coffin. But the captain's behavior is outrageous. You were right: he's an utter fraud. And a coward. My God, if he has a passenger onboard making threats like that, isn't it his duty to arrest him straightaway? Have this Cutler fellow taken down to his own stateroom, put a guard on the door?"

While he was saying this rather loudly, Olivia's gaze had drifted away toward the card table in the center of the room. Arthur turned to look in the same direction.

"In the olive green jacket," she said.

Mr. Cutler proved to be quite a small man, aged about forty, clean shaven, hair parted in the center, with angular, rather blank features. He was frowning now over the hand he'd just been dealt by Burgess, but still he did not look a very threatening prospect.

"Has he even *got* a gun, Arthur?"

"D'you think our gallant captain had bothered to find out?" Arthur shook his head. "He seems to have taken it on trust that the man is armed simply on account of his being an American. For he went off on a great ramble then into his past, not quite as far back as Trafalgar, but into the twenties, when he was a midshipman on a sailing packet and the American passengers were notorious for their armament: pistols and blunderbusses and huge knives and cutlasses. Duels fought on the quarterdeck every morning after breakfast."

"But has Mr. Cutler a gun? It's important that you should know."

"At this moment one of the stewards is searching Cutler's stateroom to find that out. My suggestion, of course."

Olivia put out her hand, touched his arm. "It is good of you to do this, Arthur," she said seriously. "It is brave."

"I don't see how I can dodge it, really." He covered her hand with his own, smiled at her. He felt ridiculously pleased at her praise. "The situation . . . well, it's not good enough, is it? This poor chap—"

"Still, I think it is very much to be preferred that the man should stay in his room for the entire voyage than you should put yourself in danger for a single moment."

A proposition with which he sincerely agreed. But: "There won't *be* any danger. Not a chance." He pressed her hand again, sat for a moment wondering how he could best reassure her. "Olivia, you were the first to tell me of the existence of this Negro. Yet according to the captain the ladies are not supposed to know about him. So how did you hear?"

"From Mrs. Tate. She told me." And again Olivia's gaze moved past his shoulder. Arthur glanced around to catch—standing a little way off—a middle-aged couple staring at *him*. Particularly with the male half of the couple, there was something extremely hungry about this stare, which puzzled Arthur, until he remembered with a pang Olivia's guess that Tate was hoping to sell him something. So as to give not even a chink of opportunity, Arthur nodded at the couple and hastily turned his back on them again.

"D'you think the other women know too?"

"Of course they do. Mrs. Tate had it from Mrs. Stewart, and so I am sure it has gone from lady to lady."

"Very well. Then let us, you and I, divide up the passengers between us." He smiled into her eyes. "Now, d'you think if I feared there was any danger at all in the work that I would ask you to share it?"

A long moment. And then she shook her head.

"And you'll enjoy it, Livvy. You *like* talking to people." She was watching him gravely. "It's just a matter of asking them how they will feel if the Negro is allowed into the saloon, eating at the table with them and so on. No reason for you to get into arguments. It is only information that is wanted."

=

Leaving the saloon, Olivia turned away from the stairs that led down to the staterooms and toward the door that gave access to the main deck. As she came near, it swung open and a blast of wild, cold air was flung in at her. The ship's third officer stepped in from the deck. He was about to shut the door behind him when he saw Olivia. He stared at her. The open door still let in the sea wind, making the lantern that hung from the passageway's ceiling sway back and forth.

"You're going on deck, Mrs. Crichton?"

She nodded.

"Pretty cold out there. I'll get a stewardess to fetch your cloak."

"It's all right," she said. "I'm only going out for a moment—a breath of air."

Just then a great volley of wind through the doorway took her own breath away. But she felt so hot now from her excitement, it was as if she never would be cold again. This thought must have lent her aspect conviction, for after a moment the officer nodded, touched his cap brim, and stood back to let her pass.

She stepped out on deck into a momentary lull in the wind. She moved quickly along the side of the saloon. The windows were fogged up mostly, but here and there she could see enough to spot some of her fellow passengers: the cardplayers, that awful parson, Mrs. Stewart, Miss Faversham...And there was her husband too. He seemed locked in some complicated exchange with the Swiss passenger Monsieur Charvet. That gentleman was wearing a look of polite confusion. Arthur himself had his back to the window, but, knowing his mission—and his dreadful French—she could guess at his current expression. Sheer embarrassment, mixed with a gloomy determination to see things through to the end. How he would dislike his present task! Thanks to her years at the Misses Robbins' in Twickenham, her French was much better than his. She would have to get back as soon as possible and take Monsieur Charvet off his hands.

But that was a falsehood really, Olivia thought, as she hurried on. She would not be returning as soon as possible but as soon as... as soon as she had done what she had come out here to do. And that was? Really, she did not know exactly, and rather than think about it for a second—a second that might have recalled her to good sense and duty, and sent her straight back to the saloon—she hurried on faster. She came to the iron steps, same steps as she had climbed with Arthur this afternoon, and, burning ever hotter in her excitement, scurried up them.

She was on the poop deck now, under a thousand stars, bracing herself against the sweeping wind. Nearby was the faint glow where the officer of the watch stood near the compass. There were other lights visible along the deck, hung up on the masts and on the paddle boxes. She moved on, having in sight the distant lamp fixed to the now indistinct outline of the funnel. Again a great surge of wind swept by and almost, it seemed, right through her. Now at last she did feel the cold, and she drew her shawl close about her body. She could hear the sea muttering to itself far below her and then, as if at the peak of an argument, suddenly roaring out loud. This she heard even above the monotonous clanking of the paddle wheels. She heard then too, from behind her, piercing through the darker tones of engine and sea, a human cry, a yell from the front part of the vessel, beyond and below the poop, from that quarter she had learned to call the fo'c'sle, where the common sailors lived. The yell—of delight or misery, she couldn't tell—was followed instantly by another voice, much deeper, growling forth an oath. And then there was silence—or rather, there was again only the noise of paddles and sea. And even to this now she was paying scarcely any attention. She was walking on, just seeing enough by the light of the half-moon to avoid the benches and other furniture that cluttered the deck. She found her way to the rail on the starboard side and then was able to move much more steadily toward her goal.

He was there. She had been sure she would find him, in that exact spot, but still the confirmation of it—dark outline of coat, thickness of muffler around the collar, the glow of a cigar—made her uncertain for a moment, brought her to a halt. It was something, she thought, what she was doing, something pretty forward—*fresh* as the detestable Americans would put it. But then she caught herself and was truly surprised and shocked to find herself so hesitant. Like some timid, fluttering Miss, not of her own day but the type of shrinking violet that she imagined must have been characteristic in her parents'—or, well, Arthur's—youth, all delicacy and vapors. Olivia prided herself on being modern. And even more on being a Lancashire lass, famed as they were throughout England for their boldness. Above all she was proud of bearing a name of real consequence in the greatest commercial city in the Empire, and—and so she would speak to any man on earth if she wanted to. Particularly when she came to him on such an important, serious mission. She was Mrs. Olivia Crichton of Stormont House, Chorlton, near Manchester, Lancs, and at this moment, in effect, she was a woman of business.

"Mr. Bonney," she said as she came close, wishing the next moment that her voice had not sounded so near to a squeak. But his big, coat-shrouded shoulders did not turn. He had not heard her. Nor did he seem to hear the second time she spoke. At last, growing a little irritated, she reached out and tapped him on his upper arm. At that he swung around, his fist clenched. And in the moonlight she was able to see on his face such an expression as to cause her to take a quick backward step. "Mr. Bonney," she gasped. "It is only me!"

＝

He stared at her. And as he did the expression—whatever it was: anguish, fear, anger—slipped from his eyes, giving way to one of puzzlement, almost disbelief.

"Mrs. . . . Crichton?" he inquired haltingly at last.

She felt quite absurdly pleased that he should know her name. Their introduction at dinner the first evening out of Boston had been so rudimentary and brief—and he had done nothing then but mutter and look away—that she had doubted he'd even noticed she had a name. And since that occasion they'd had no speech together at all. But he had remembered.

As if in confirmation: "Mrs. Crichton?" he said again, still sounding almost doubtful that she did now indeed stand before him. And his hand went to his head as if to lift off a hat. But then came to a stop as he remembered he was bareheaded. At the same moment, watching his little blunder with some amusement, she realized that she too was hatless, bonnetless. For she had come out in such a rush, unthinking, and now the wind was blowing up ever stronger, seemed to be seeking all the time to drive her hair into a wild, shameful mess. And was making her really very cold, she noticed again. In a moment her teeth would be chattering. It would never do. She must go on with her business.

"Mr. Bonney," she said in a quick, high voice, "my husband has asked that I ascertain your views on a certain subject."

"Your *husband* has sent you to me?" Bonney asked after a moment, wondering. His voice, she noted, while inevitably marred by a distinct American cast, was at least quite free from the harsh quacking noises the people in New England made. In fact, if one forgot where in the world it came from, the accent had sounded melodious, almost pleasing to her ear, even as he had raised his voice to speak above the wind. He was looking down now at the cigar still burning between his gloved fingers. With an abrupt motion, he flung it over the rail.

"He did not precisely ask me to talk to you," Olivia admitted. "Rather my commission was of a general nature…" And then rapidly, for she felt herself likely to be overcome at any moment by an onset of the shivers, she told him what she had been asked to discover. He watched her at first with a kind of curiosity, but very soon his expression returned to that flat, uncaring look he had worn on almost every other occasion she had seen him.

At length she came to a halt. They were silent for a moment, then he stirred, and in a voice as empty of feeling as his look, said, "What are you asking me, ma'am? If I care whether or not this colored man is allowed full use of the saloon and the decks?"

"Yes," she almost whispered, brought suddenly low by his cold, empty manner. "That is it."

"It's a matter of indifference to me."

Again they were silent. How penetrating now the wind felt. She wondered how he could stand it for such long periods, even dressed as warmly as he was. As for herself, in her evening gown and shawl, it would be well to go inside before she caught cold by this disappointing adventure. But she could not go, it seemed she was rooted to the spot, though she knew he wanted her to be off, desired only to turn back to his interminable contemplation. Of nothing, darkness.

"There is something else," she murmured. "I . . . I believe my husband thinks there may be trouble. This man—Mr. Cutler—may have a gun. He has certainly threatened to use—"

Before she could finish she was overcome at last by the cold, and had to clench her teeth to stop them making her ridiculous. Seeming a little surprised by the abrupt ending of her speech, he peered closely at her. She felt a sharp pricking on the skin of her face then and would have cried out except that she was trying so hard to keep her jaws locked. At first she thought it was the wind cutting her ever deeper, but then a sudden reek of coal smoke made her see it was only that a shower of cinders from the funnel had descended upon them. Bonney now was dusting several sparks from his coat. She smelled burning rubber. He stopped what he was doing, looked back at her again.

"I think, Mrs. Crichton, that you must be cold."

"Y-yes. I am."

"You should go below . . . If you wish it, I suppose I could escort you."

But how coldly and reluctantly he had said that! It was so clear he had spoken only out of politeness. And it came to her now (what she had known all along, but had hidden from herself) that as she had hurried toward this meeting she'd been hoping that their conversation at last would wind to a point where she might, without awkwardness, suggest that he come back with her to the saloon, where he might warm himself a little in the society of his fellow passengers. This vigil he was keeping, hour after weary hour, this staring backwards—at

what? at America? or at a woman? or at a fortune thrown away?—
while rendering him so interesting and even, she conceded, romantic
in her eyes, must be such a burden to have to sustain. An hour or two's
genial company, something to eat and drink—they served an excellent supper at about ten o'clock—might do so much to thaw out that
chilly, careworn look of his, might even put a smile on features that, if
not set in such an unhappy mask, could certainly have been described
as ... *quite* attractive.

But now. "I suppose I could escort you" indeed.

"Thank you, s-sir," she stuttered, in the most scornful voice she
could command. "I would not think of k-keeping you f-from your *ob-
servations.*"

And she turned and, gripping the rail, hurried away from him. And
did not look around again until she was well past the halfway mark
along the deck. It was as she'd expected. His back was to her, once more
a cigar glowed in the dark: He had resumed his vigil, and it was as if
she had never interrupted him. It *is* a woman, she thought as she hurried on, he is looking back toward the One he has left behind. Perhaps
his wife. Or else it is a woman he has ruined and now has deserted.

As she went down the stairs to the main deck, two men coming up
them pushed rudely past her. She could not see them clearly in the
dark, but she was certain they were not fellow passengers, rather men
of the crew, sailors. They certainly smelled like workingmen. At the
top of the stairs one said to the other something of such inconceivable
vulgarity that she simply refused to recognize what had been said
until she was safely through the swing doors and standing outside the
saloon again.

=

By ten-thirty, only a half hour after the supper service, the saloon was
nearly deserted. Most passengers had left for their staterooms. A couple of the men had gone to smoke a last cigar on deck. The card game
had broken up early, to the loud disgust of Mr. Burgess. He now sat
alone at the table, frowning, a glass of warm whiskey punch at his side,
dealing himself a hand of solitaire. Also still in the saloon was the
Reverend Stibbards, who for the past twenty minutes had been giving

an account of his church—the Third Inspirational of Boston—and of the particulars in which its doctrine and practices differed from those of the other reformed churches of that city. Listening to this discourse with flattering attention were two ladies, Miss Faversham and Mrs. Stewart. Also in attendance, and serving thereby the company's policy of indefatigable attention to the passengers, however few, and at all times of the day and night, was the first officer, Hartley. Lurking in a doorway that led out to the pantry, a steward waited for final orders. Every now and then he yawned behind his hand.

At last, near a quarter to eleven, Burgess grunted, threw down his hand, and pushed back his chair. The noise of chair legs scraping on the parquet floor startled the Reverend Stibbards out of his monologue. He watched as the cardplayer nodded a curt good night, then headed for the saloon's main door. He turned back to the others then and smiled apologetically.

"We are the last survivors. I fear I have been talking for far too long, and you will be anxious for me to finish?"

"Not in the least," said Miss Faversham fervently. "It is most interesting."

"Most interesting," Mrs. Stewart repeated. "As indeed I find is any subject of a truly religious nature."

At this Miss Faversham gave the other lady a rather hard look. However, Mrs. Stewart did not seem to notice it. At that moment her lovely violet eyes happened to be glancing toward Mr. Hartley. That gentleman said nothing at all, either in support of or against the notion of the Reverend Stibbards continuing, but his silence appeared to signify consent and so, buoyed up by these encouragements, the clergyman resumed his discourse and in fact for a while was able to speak with even more enthusiasm than before.

But eventually even he grew drowsy, and his reminiscences turned intermittent. In the last of these gaps, Mrs. Stewart seized her chance to inquire the time of Mr. Hartley, and on being told—after the officer had hauled out and displayed a handsome fob watch—that it was twenty minutes after eleven, she gasped in surprise.

"And I had particularly meant to retire early tonight," she sighed as she gathered together the small pieces of sewing with which she'd been occupying her hands during the Reverend Stibbards's discourse and placed them in her reticule.

"At sea, ma'am, it don't signify what time one retires." The first officer smiled. "You are in a floating hotel, you may come and go as you please."

"And so I should," Mrs. Stewart responded, with a faint note of reproof in her voice, "were I not the mother of two children who have needs to be met—and met usually at a very early hour of the morning."

"Give them into the hands of the stewardess," Miss Faversham shrugged. "It is what she is there for."

"Ah, but a *mother's* particular care, Miss Faversham…" Mrs. Stewart sighed. And she looked at the spinster lady opposite as if she could add more but chose not to. Miss Faversham was left looking rather bleak. Mrs. Stewart rose in triumph and prettily bade her farewells to the company.

"I shall see you tomorrow," she concluded. And then shuddered half-humorously. "If, indeed, I should be so fortunate as to survive the journey to my stateroom tonight."

All knew what she meant. As she had explained at dinner on her first evening aboard, Mrs. Stewart's presence on the *Laurentia* was only because of the Christian generosity of her neighbors in Nova Scotia, who, following the unfortunate death of her husband—influenza—had collected sufficient funds to buy a first-class berth in which to send his bereaved family back home. Yet besides generosity, they had used the opportunity to show a proper attention to thrift and a dislike of needless display by paying for the very cheapest possible of the staterooms. The other first-class berths, which were situated beneath the saloon, required no exposure to the open deck in going to and from meals, et cetera. But Mrs. Stewart's stateroom was sited well forward, almost to the point where the second-class cabins began. This meant that every time she wished to pass between her room and the saloon she was forced to go outside, and in rough seas the *Laurentia* shipped quite a lot of water onto the main deck. There had been a fair blow the night before last, and Mrs. Stewart had had a tale of woe to tell at breakfast. Her clothes had been soaked and she had almost fallen twice.

It was thought by several of the passengers rather mean of Captain McDonough not to offer to remove the widow and her two children from these inconvenient lodgings when there were so many other empty first-class berths available. But Mrs. Stewart herself declared that she was perfectly satisfied with her lot—"whatever the Creator chooses to send me"—and would not think of applying to the captain for a change.

Nevertheless, hearing now the wail of the winds outside and glancing at the black night that lay beyond the windows, where she would have to go, Mrs. Stewart began to look a little apprehensive. And seeing it, Mr. Hartley—who had already got to his feet when she had risen—stepped forward and bowed.

"Mrs. Stewart, you'll permit me to accompany you to your stateroom?"

And as the wind *was* blowing so, and as Mr. Hartley, by virtue of both his uniform and his extremely respectful manner, showed that he was only offering his assistance in the capacity of a servant of the company, not even Miss Faversham could see anything improper in this arrangement, though she looked fairly hard for it. She watched as the couple headed for the door, and as the officer opened it and stepped back to allow Mrs. Stewart through. And then, with something of an anticipatory gleam in her eye, she turned back to the Reverend Stibbards.

He was fast asleep! His chin had sunk onto his white shirtfront, and he was breathing so loud and regular that she could be sure that only a thorough shaking would ever rouse him. While the thought of shaking the Reverend Stibbards hard was at that moment tempting, she had to recognize that their relationship was as yet hardly such as to entitle her to do so. She waited beside him with mounting impatience for a minute or two (by now he was positively snoring), and then, feeling the awkwardness and even indelicacy of her position—keeping company so with a sleeping male—stood up. She cast a look, a silent command, at the steward waiting near the pantry door, and then she gathered her shawl about her and headed for the exit.

The steward, when he'd finished clearing away the few remaining wineglasses, stood for a moment over the unconscious clergyman and then, feeling none of Miss Faversham's compunctions, reached down, grasped the Reverend Stibbards's shoulder, and gave it a violent tug.

═

Mrs. Stewart and the first officer, meanwhile, had negotiated their passage in the open and were now back indoors. The deck had been pretty slippery, and the ship had lurched heavily each time it came down the far side of an especially large sea swell. Mrs. Stewart had been forced to lean rather hard at those times on the supporting arm of Mr. Hartley. So hard indeed, and by necessity pressing herself so close to his portly body, that the officer discovered that he was becoming quite aroused. She began to apologize for this inadvertent physical intimacy. She sounded sincere; yet at the same time Hartley had a curious notion that she was well aware of what effect her closeness had produced in him—and that she was not altogether displeased by it.

"Worse things happen at sea, ma'am," he winked.

They were both silent then. It was not yet midnight, and the corridor lamp was still burning. It hung fortuitously near to the stateroom door, and Hartley was able to observe the widow's pleasing features quite clearly. At the same time, Mrs. Stewart appeared to be inclining her head away from the officer's perhaps too-penetrating gaze.

"I must go inside," she murmured at last. "The children…"

"Ah, the children. They seem very quiet children," Mr. Hartley said.

"They are angels. They are—"

"I have children," Hartley interrupted in a solemn tone. "I have five children."

"Yes, I think you have mentioned—"

"I miss them very much, Mrs. Stewart. It is hard to be a sailor, and so often away from one's family."

"My poor Donald also was a devoted papa. I have heard him say—"

"It would give me extraordinary pleasure to be allowed to view your children now, Mrs. Stewart. There is something about a child sleeping that, for a father—" But he could not go on.

A request such as this, accompanied by a look of almost painful supplication, would have melted the coldest heart. Mrs. Stewart paused to consider it for a moment only, and then quietly turned the handle and pushed the door open. Hartley followed her in. As she closed the door, he looked around the room and nodded his appreciation. In truth, on land the apartment would have been regarded as modest in the extreme, but Mrs. Stewart had tricked it out with certain small items of adornment that gave to its rather utilitarian foundation an attractively feminine flavor.

Across the room, separating perhaps a third of it from the rest, was a large curtain made of some flimsy but opaque muslin material. It hung at about head level. Mrs. Stewart, seeing Hartley looking at the curtain, nodded toward it. Thus invited, he stepped stealthily across and looked over. He beheld a charming sight: two young children in a narrow bed, fast asleep in each other's arms, their golden hair mingling on the shared pillow.

Hartley stared at this affecting vision for a while and then nodded.

"They sleep pretty sound, ma'am," he said.

"They do," she murmured. "They are good sleepers."

He stepped back then from the curtain, and she too turned away. She crossed to the little table and set her reticule upon it. Then she straightened up, looked across the narrow space to where the first officer stood on the other side of the room.

"I thank you for showing me your little ones," he said.

"As you are a father, I could hardly refuse."

"Yes, a father, ma'am. A married man ... It is hard for a married man being away at sea so much. He has needs."

"I am sure you miss your dear wife very much," Mrs. Stewart murmured. Again her eyes flickered away modestly from his steady gaze.

"Needs, ma'am, of a personal nature—" His voice had sunk to a sort of mellow growl. "Needs which only a woman can understand ... or satisfy—"

"Speaking thus," said Mrs. Stewart very smoothly, "you remind me so much of my poor husband. He was of all men the most attentive, the most *ardent* I might almost say, and I shall never admit that it was his fault that he has left us almost penniless. Nor that I should be thrown upon the generosity of a hard world in order to find the wherewithal to feed and shelter my two dear—"

At that moment there came a small, helpless-sounding cry from beyond the curtain.

"Drat!" said the widow.

"It's all right, ma'am," Hartley put in hastily. "The nipper's only calling out in a dream."

They waited in silence for a moment, and then, hearing nothing more from behind the curtain, both began at once to speak, though much more quietly than before.

"A man's needs, Mrs. Stewart, they just get *bottled up* on these crossings. For though it be but thirteen days Boston to Liverpool, you have to add to that another two weeks going over, and then a few days' layover in Boston—ma'am, that's a clear month away from the comforts of home, which is not endurable—"

"They told us life would be cheap in Canada, but you know, Mr. Hartley, I really think it was more expensive than in Scotland, for certainly we were unable to save—"

"Of course I might have taken advantage of the...the *facilities* in America, but, Mrs. Stewart, I could not go to those women. Only with an English—or Scottish—lady could I for a moment consider—"

And thus—he talking about his needs, and she about money—they arrived at an understanding at last. By this time, she had seated herself on the cabin's single chair. Before her, in quite a gallant fashion, the officer had lowered his heavy frame onto his haunches. He held out his hands.

"Your little feet are still wet, ma'am," he said gently. "We must have your shoes off...and then, I think, your stockings..." A minute or so passed away. "And now your drawers, ma'am...Ah no." The first officer sighed then, in tones of great gratification. "I see there's nothing at all like that we have to bother about..."

=

At just the time the first officer was making this discovery, the Crichtons were meeting in Olivia's stateroom to discuss the evening's events and check on each other's progress.

"The Charvets are all right," Arthur noted. "At least, as far as I could understand him he is—and he answers for Madame too. Or did you get around to her?"

Olivia shook her head. She was sitting in the armchair; Arthur was lounging on the lower bunk.

"The big surprise," he said, "was the Reverend Stibbards. And I went to him almost first as I wanted to have one certain scalp on my belt before I tackled the harder cases. But not a bit of it."

"But surely—?"

"Exactly what I thought. A minister of the Bible. From *Massachusetts*—"

"Aren't they all on the side of abolition?"

"Oh, he *is*. A furious abolitionist, he. Kept telling me so. It's just that it seems never to have occurred to him that freeing the Negroes might lead to such horrors as the Reverend Stibbards actually having to meet any of 'em in a social sort of way. That is, somewhere other than on a platform at a public meeting."

"Blow him."

"Agreed. But you know I think the Reverend is a bit of a reed and in the event will probably bend in whichever way the majority goes. Isn't that how those fellows hang on to their pulpits in New England? In general"—Arthur frowned as he rolled onto his elbow to look at his wife—"it's the Americans that are the most likely to make a fuss. They keep going on about the insult to the ladies. *Do* the ladies feel insulted?"

"Miss Faversham don't much. Mrs. Stewart says she has learned by her sad loss that all matters are in the hands of the Creator, and if He chooses to send a Negro into the first-class saloon then still she will bow to His wisdom."

"Good Lord." Arthur stared at her. "Poor Olivia. Have you had to listen to an awful lot of guff tonight?"

"Not so much."

It was as if he had expected more from her, for he let a few seconds pass before he spoke again. "Who else?" he said then, now back to contemplating the upper bunk. "Well, the Nova Scotians weren't so good. Especially the one called"—Arthur wrinkled his nose—"*Harris.*

Nasty, blustering fellow. Too many damn niggers in Halifax, according to Mr. Harris, and he did expect to be free of 'em out on the ocean. On the other hand, *Burgess,* who I managed to draw away from the cards for about half a minute, said it was all a damn nonsense, if the fellow had paid for a ticket he had a right to be treated same as any one else—"

"Good for Mr. Burgess."

"Yes, but unexpected, isn't it? I don't know why it should be so . . . And isn't he a little chap? I'd only seen him sitting down up till then. What is he, do you think? Five feet? Less?" Arthur didn't expect an answer to that. He yawned, stretched his arms above his head, winced as his knuckles came into unexpected contact with the upper bunk. "Oh, and I spoke to a chap called Farrow, do you know him?" She shook her head. "I think it was his first time in the saloon, been seasick like me up to now. Has a place in our consulate at Boston. Pretty low one, I should judge. Said he had no objection to the Negro but wished to make it clear this was a personal reaction, not an official one. I thought he was joking at first. He wasn't. Ass."

Arthur ran through the rest of those he'd spoken to. "That red-faced fellow from Ontario? Harper? Doesn't care one way or t'other. I would say the majority are pretty indifferent. One or two—Burgess, for instance—might actually speak up in favor of the man being admitted. Four or five are definitely against it, but even they, I think, would submit in the end."

"Did you speak to Mr. Cutler?"

Arthur shook his head. "I thought it best to find out the mood of the company first." He was silent for a while. Then: "Oh, well. I dodged talking to him, that's the truth, I funked it. I don't *think* so much because of what he might do to me—but who wants a blazing row in the middle of the saloon, everybody staring at one? Oh, the devil take that coward of a captain." Arthur half-laughed, half-groaned.

They were quiet again for a few moments. Then Arthur snapped his fingers in irritation.

"I forgot to talk to that man Bonney."

"You may place him among the indifferent, Arthur."

Her tone was flat, without emotion. He stared at her.

"You *spoke* to him?"

"You asked me to approach the passengers—"

"Only the *lady* passengers. I didn't imagine—"

"But you directed me particularly to speak to Mr. Tate."

"Yes, but—I had special reasons there, I didn't want to talk to the fellow—"

He stopped. She sat unmoving, upright in the armchair. In profile her face seemed cold, remote.

"Bonney wasn't in the saloon tonight," Arthur began again slowly.

"No. I went up to the poop." For a moment he thought she might try to justify herself, but in the end she shrugged, saying, "Oh, well— I'm sorry, Arthur. Not very becoming, I know. I just thought it might be interesting to talk to him."

He watched her carefully. "Was it interesting?" he asked at last.

She flashed a look of gratitude at him, then again turned away.

"Not much. As I said, he is entirely indifferent."

They left it at that. For another five minutes they spoke about the Negro, and the problems he posed, and then, with something of re-lief, drifted on to other, much more pleasing topics, in which the steady approach of England and home, now with luck only a week or eight days away, was preeminent. At last Arthur got to his feet and pressed a good-night kiss to her cheek. He was heading for the door when she said, "Would you like me to undress before you, Arthur?"

He turned back. She was standing now, she had one hand on the middle button of her dress.

"Won't you be cold?"

She shook her head. Then, as he watched, she unbuttoned her dress and stepped out of it. She removed her chemise, and then her stockings, then her underdrawers, laying each garment neatly over the armchair back. At the end she stood before him, artless, relaxed, naked. She was like that for a few moments, then she began to slowly turn herself before him. Her breasts, and below them the subtle impression of her ribs, swell of belly, then the soft fleece beneath, the small buttocks, the long white thighs, passing under his vision in the candlelight. Every now and then she would stop and hold a pose.

"Do you like me like this, Arthur?"

"Yes, my dear."

Turning again in the dusky glow. Stopping. "And like this, Arthur?" Then, without waiting to hear him, as if she were listening now only to voices within her, turning once more, lowering herself, then rising again, lifting her arms above her head, arching her back.

"Thank you, my dear," he said at last.

She nodded and, certainly feeling the cold by now, went quickly to the closet and took out her nightgown.

"Am I a nice bit o' first-class cunt, Arthur?" she asked, just before she put her head into the gown.

He was still gaping at her when her face reemerged.

"Livvy!" he said. And "*Olivia.*"

"I thought you liked me to talk naughtily, Arthur."

"I do...I just...I never thought to hear you say—"

"Some men called me that tonight."

"*Which* men?"

"Oh, ordinary men. Sailors."

"We will go straight to the captain. He must throw them in irons. Could you recognize them?"

"It was dark. I couldn't possibly."

"Still, we should go to the captain. He ought to be informed if there are a few individuals who are disgracing his crew."

"No, Arthur. Let it be. Perhaps it would not look well. The captain will think I should not even know it was a bad word."

She came to kiss him again at the door.

"But you didn't answer me."

"Yes, my dear. First class, that you are."

"Thank you, dear old boy," she smiled.

He opened the door then—to disclose one of the stewards standing just outside in the corridor, with his fist upraised, about to knock on the oak. Both parties were taken aback at the unexpected encounter. The steward, recovering, bowed.

"Madam—Sir—Captain's compliments and wishes to inform you that an hexhaustive search of a certain gentleman's stateroom 'as failed to discover any sort of firearm whatsoever."

Arthur and Olivia exchanged glances. He smiled with relief. He was not ashamed to feel such gratitude at having the heavy burden taken from him. He felt—even at his age—that he could stand his ground in most types of dispute, would be prepared to use his fists in this case perhaps, if it came to it. But guns introduced another dimension entirely to a quarrel, and one completely unfamiliar to him. He had never had anything to do with the wretched things, not even in a sporting way.

The steward was knuckling his forehead, preparing to take himself off.

"But is it certain there is no such item in the gentleman's cabin?"

"Done the search meself," the steward answered promptly. "Ain't nothin' there at all."

Now Arthur let him go, watching the man head off down the dim corridor. He turned back then, smiled at his wife.

"And so Cutler is only a blowhard after all."

"I hope so," she said gravely.

"You hope so? You just heard that fellow. No gun in the stateroom—"

"But what if he should be carrying one concealed on his person, Arthur?"

Arthur walked down the corridor to his stateroom door, two along from hers. When he looked back, she had already disappeared into her room. He stood for a moment more, inspecting the empty corridor, so feebly lit by a single lamp at the far end. Down there was Cutler's stateroom, he thought. And beyond that, in the choicest part of the vessel, farthest away from the engines and the paddles, was the Negro's. For a moment, standing there, Arthur imagined that he could hear from those recesses the sound of a human voice, deep and tuneful. Again for just a moment, he imagined that it was the Negro's voice he was hearing, and that—in the immemorial habit of the race—the poor fellow was seeking to pass the long hours of his captivity by filling his prison with song.

But by the time Arthur had turned into his own room—the man was coming down the corridor now, extinguishing the lights; he would have to undress in the dark—he'd concluded that it was just a piece of fancy on his part, that what he had really heard was only the keening of the sea wind filtered down through the decks from above.

LOVING LIVVY

45°4' N, 51°45' W

In the night Arthur dreamed of his first wife. He knew this was so—even though he did not recall a single detail of his dream—because he experienced on waking a familiar blend of affection, and frustration, and relief. He always felt ashamed of the last, of taking comfort, even in an unconscious state, in the fact that Laura was dead. Certainly while she lived he had not wanted her to die, and had honestly mourned her. It was only several weeks afterward that it came to him that the novel feeling of lightness he had been experiencing, as of a burden kindly taken from his shoulders, was connected with her death.

It had been a horrible thought then. It was horrible now. For several minutes he lay staring miserably at the base of the upper bunk. But gradually he became aware of another, a physical sensation within, which was drawing him steadily away from the confusions of the night. It was something . . . it was not an unfamiliar feeling, and yet for a few moments he could not place it. Tentatively he explored himself, letting his mind probe this way and that. Yes, there it was. A faint pulling, a craving, just there below the breast, it was—

It was hunger. Hunger! Delightful. He was out of bed as soon as he realized this and splashing warm water on his face (as usual the steward had entered his room while he was still asleep and refilled his jug). Hunger! First time he'd felt it on waking on this voyage, first time he hadn't risen out of an exhausting, agitated doze to find himself still in the grip of the great sickness. *Le mal de mer.* He was whistling as he dressed—forcing down as he did all remaining memory of his guilty dreaming—and in the same determined, carefree spirit quit his room and hurried along the corridor. He took the steps up to the deck two at a time.

While he was still in the corridor he had paused for a moment to knock on Olivia's door, but there had been no answer. Early as it was, apparently she had got up even earlier. He was anxious to find her, and, as a first step, he looked in at the saloon. A glance from the door-way showed that she wasn't there, but then the sight of the breakfast things set out on the far table made him linger a moment and then lured him in. He felt so well now, so marvelously *hungry,* that even though the atmosphere in the saloon was still somewhat rank from the night before, the long array of cold tongue, ham, chops, salmon, cod, eggs, tart, hot rolls, et cetera appeared to him quite irresistible. He went to the table and filled a plate, and took a cup of coffee from the hands of the presiding steward. Dropping into a chair at random, he set to work.

Glancing up from his food at one point, he saw that the cardplay-ers had taken their usual table and were already on the first hand of the day. The Englishman Burgess looked particularly cheerful and expansive this morning. He called out to a passing steward for brandy and water and asked the other men if they'd care to join him. They all declined, pointing to the early hour, saying they'd stick to coffee and tea—a gesture at moderation that Burgess greeted with good-natured scoffing.

Arthur moved on to contemplate the American, Cutler. The fellow sat there, his small, neat head bowed over his cards. In this posture his expression was somewhat hidden from his companions. Yet Arthur could see it clearly from where he sat. He thought he had never seen such contempt before on any man's face and wondered at whom it might be directed. Burgess was talking loudly again now, complaining at the slowness of yesterday's play, proposing higher stakes. The two Nova Scotians were objecting to the idea. The American kept silent, his head still bowed.

The sight of Cutler, recalling to his mind the still unfinished business he'd allowed himself to be persuaded into, took what remained of Arthur's appetite away. He pushed aside his plate, looked around for the steward to refill his coffee cup. Across the room was Mrs. Stewart. She had her two children with her and was making sure that they made a good breakfast. It was an affecting sight, Arthur supposed, the attentive mother, the two pretty infants. He wished he could linger on it, yet his gaze kept being pulled back to Cutler. With a sigh of irritation, he threw down his napkin and heaved himself to his feet. He bowed a good morning across the room to Mrs. Stewart; she inclined her head toward him in return.

≡

Arthur was delayed for a while after leaving the saloon. A full quarter-hour had passed before he stepped out onto the main deck and began making his way forward to the capstan galley, where he expected to find Olivia. The day was gray and gusty, though at present the sea looked as if it was keeping pretty low. There were again sails on all three masts and, as Arthur looked up, he could see a couple of sailors working in the yards, appearing to his unnautical eye as if they were unraveling some parts of the rigging that had become entangled in the night.

On the deck itself there was a fair deal of traffic. Supplies of fresh vegetables for lunch were being plucked in quantities from under the lifeboats and ferried across to the little kitchen gallery. At the same time he found, dodging among the hurrying chefs and stewards, the Tates, man and wife, who were attempting to play shovelboard. On the *Persia,* Arthur recalled, the game had often been accompanied with much noisy mirth as the roll of the ship sent players and skittles sliding in all directions. The Tates seemed to be playing it in a grim silence. In fact, they were quite a grim couple altogether, Arthur decided. Grim. Intense. A sort of barely restrained anxiety about everything they did.

Disaster, Arthur decided, as he touched his cap to Mrs. Tate. He was looking at disaster certainly. Some kind of financial catastrophe. He had seen the look the Tates carried around with them on other faces over the past few years as the war in America had produced hard times in the English cotton districts, and those who had been imprudent or unlucky reaped their reward. Whether it was always a just reward he could not say. Yet he had heard enough men on the Liverpool and Manchester 'Changes, in the boom days before the war, ascribing all their good fortune to their own cleverness to be skeptical when the same men now blamed their hardships on political events. Other men had prospered in spite of the so-called cotton famine. There was always money to be made in a crisis. He had made money, for instance.

"Care to play, Mr. Crichton?" the male Tate spoke up. "*We* do every morning after breakfast. It assists the digestion, you see."

As her husband was speaking, Mrs. Tate—a bony, sallow woman, about forty, Arthur guessed—was sending out a sort of muffled echo of her mate's speech, though only the more emphasized words, as in *play, breakfast, digestion,* could be heard, the rest being lost in the sea breeze. It was an eerie accompaniment; together, the voices coiled into a strange, beseeching duet. Arthur looked uneasily from one Tate to the other.

"If you don't mind awfully, fresh air and a stroll about the deck will see to my digestion quite adequately, I'm sure."

He touched his cap again to Mrs. Tate, and with a smile of apology went on his way. Mr. Tate called out to his retreating back: "We must have a talk some time, Mr. Crichton. Perhaps at tea?"

Arthur's step did not falter. "That would be grand," he called over his shoulder, and kept on walking. In silence the Tates watched him go; and then, without a glance at one another, bowed their shoulders and turned back, as if duty bound, to their play.

=

Approaching the capstan galley, Arthur saw a man leaving it from its farthest end. He came to a stop and watched as the man too paused. He had his head down, seemed to be deep in thought. Then, after a few moments, he gave an odd little motion of his shoulders, as if shaking himself out of his previous state of mind. He headed off now, away from Arthur, on a course that would take him soon to where the first-class promenade turned right to double back along the starboard side. He did not seem, at any point, to have noticed Arthur, who now, as the man receded along the deck, started again toward the galley.

Olivia was sitting in the same place as yesterday. She had on her long coat, warm russet in color, and a bright red muffler tied at the throat. She wore no hat or bonnet, and placed as she was, with her profile turned toward him, she appeared, he thought, pretty as a picture, although looking uncommonly thoughtful.

"You look as if you've been posing for one of our celebrated younger painters," he teased her as he sat. "Languorous and lovely— a sigh made flesh!"

She turned and touched his arm and smiled at his fun. But he thought, watching her, that the smile was somewhat mechanical and hardly reached her eyes, which were troubled and preoccupied. He looked away from her then, and they sat in silence for a while. He wished suddenly that he was a smoker. This was the place for it, after all, and he imagined that something as mellow and everyday and good-fellowish as the smoke from a fine cigar would be an improvement on the present atmosphere, which, without wishing to rebuke Olivia, seemed to be mostly composed of female unease and melancholy.

"Was that Mr. Bonney I saw leaving here a moment ago?"

"Yes," she said promptly. "He was here."

"Ah ... He has deserted his post, has he?"

Pause. Then, with unmistakable irritation: "What are you talking about, Arthur?"

"I thought he was always to be found on the poop. Staring out to sea."

"He came to apologize to me."

For a confused moment, Arthur imagined that it had been Bonney who had said that vile thing yesterday to Olivia and had appeared before her this morning to tell her he was sorry for it. But then he realized it could not be. She had specified it had been one of the crew who had done that.

"He was a little abrupt when I spoke with him last evening. It had been troubling him. He came to say he was sorry ... He need not have. Poor man."

"I see." Poor man?

He held her hand, and tried to look perfectly contented and un-worried as he gazed out upon the capstan galley's uninspiring vista. Above all, he told himself, I don't want to play the part of the posses-sive husband. It is one thing to be unfortunate; one does not have to be a clown as well. He remembered there was something he had meant to tell Olivia. He could not recall what it was at first. Some trivial ad-venture of his own...

Yes.

"Would you be interested to hear that I've had another interview with the captain?"

"Of course I would," she said, though hardly looking it.

So he told her how he had met McDonough when he quit the sa-loon after breakfast. He'd given him his report. "Awful man." He frowned. "I thought he'd have cheered up when he heard that there were no guns in Cutler's stateroom. Turns out, though, he's had the same idea as you."

"That Mr. Cutler may be carrying one around with him?"

Arthur nodded.

"But this is dreadful. It can't go on, Arthur, can it?"

"No, it can't. The captain agrees that the Negro must be allowed to leave his cabin, by this evening at the latest. No matter what the con-sequences."

"What consequences? What did he mean?"

"Cutler will have to be restrained. He can't be allowed to wave guns around in the saloon and fire them off. We may not be much of a crowd, but a few flying bullets would do some damage even among us. So the captain will be detailing a couple of the crew to seize the gen-tleman before dinner and carry him off to his cabin. There to stay until he's promised to be a good boy. He will be replaced in the saloon by the Negro—if the fellow is fool enough to want to join our com-pany in such circumstances."

"Oh, bother them both," Olivia said in disgust. "I wish them both overboard—Mr. Cutler and the black man too. Nuisances."

"I would nominate the captain to join them," Arthur sighed. "For he is the greatest nuisance of all."

"At least he cannot expect you to involve yourself anymore."

"On the contrary. He has asked me to double my efforts. I am even to speak to Cutler himself, and urge him to withdraw his dreadful threat. Our captain still has hopes that it can all be settled, if not amicably, then at least without the embarrassment of having a first-class passenger imprisoned and fuming in his cabin. Not a *white* passenger at any rate ... It is his last voyage as an Inman captain, you see, and he wants to leave a good taste in the company's mouth, just in case they ever have a job that only an experienced and reliable old sea dog could fill. So I said I'd do what I could."

He was smiling as he said this, but won no answering smile from her. She looked away from him as he finished. "I think you are wrong, Arthur," she said. "I think you should have nothing more to do with it."

He felt obscurely hurt to hear that. "But yesterday you seemed mightily concerned for this Negro's misfortune."

"Oh, *yesterday,*" she said, as if referring to an era impossibly distant. And seemed about to say more, but then stopped again.

=

When he looked back on the near two weeks spent on the *Persia,* Arthur had a memory of what seemed like great plains and prairies of time, to go with the sense of near-infinite space and sea that lay all around them. Every day had seemed to contain at least twice the normal allotment of hours; the week and a half of crossing had appeared to occupy a month at least. And it became a great labor to find things with which to fill up all this time. Meals were looked forward to with desperate ardor on the *Persia,* always from a point long before their serving. They were prolonged in the eating as far as humanly possible, even the American passengers delaying their customary headlong charge at the vittles. And when the meal had to be declared over, it was discussed and analyzed at immense length. All in the interest of wasting time. But even these regular great bites out of the day did not keep the remaining hours from hanging very heavy. Desultory wanderings about the deck, reading old novels from the ship's dog-eared store, hanging over the rails staring at the stupefying uniformity of the sea, wondering how long till the next bell for the next meal—how the time had crawled by.

And how different on this boat, Arthur thought grimly as, on leaving his wife, he made his way back along the main deck (he chose the starboard side this time to avoid the Tates). Since the seasickness had released him to the upper decks, it seemed he had done nothing but hurry from one engagement to another. Except for a brief glance from the poop deck yesterday, he'd not had the time to even look at the ocean, let alone get bored with it. And it struck him very hard now that all this motion had a quite random and pointless quality to it. It was not at all what he wished to be doing. Nor what he wished to be thinking about. Just now, he realized, he should have stayed in the capstan galley, had it out with Olivia about this Bonney fellow. It did not require him to be too unpleasant either, he realized. He could suggest that together they could confront the young man, he could introduce himself, reintroduce Olivia as his wife—in fact, put the acquaintance on a reasonably suitable and regular basis. They could have gone now to find him, got it over with. Instead of which, his immediate prospects included maltreated Negroes, rampant Yankees, a frightened old fool of a captain, bullets flying in the saloon. None of it (unless one of the latter struck Olivia—or himself, he supposed) essentially mattering a damn to him.

He looked through the window of the saloon door. At the far end of the room, the stewards were clearing the last of the breakfast things. He could see three passengers still at their meals: the parson Stibbards and the Swiss couple, the Charvets. Also present, of course, were the cardplayers, and it was on them that Arthur's gaze reluctantly settled. They seemed deep in their game. Burgess was dealing. He said something as he threw a last card before Harris, something humorous apparently, for he grinned at the others. But they appeared too occupied with their hands to acknowledge him.

Arthur had no relish at all for interrupting their play. He stared at the small, hard-featured person of Mr. Cutler, very neat today in a well-cut suit of dark cloth, a blue cravat at the neck of his white linen. What if the man should not wait to confront the Negro and should suddenly draw out a concealed pistol—or one of those ferocious knives he had heard Americans employed in settling their quarrels—and start using it upon the nearest human being who happened to be annoying him? Who very shortly would certainly be Arthur himself. He swallowed. He believed he was not a coward exactly. But he knew for a fact he wasn't armed. He studied his quarry through the glass. Like Olivia, he suddenly, devoutly wished the man at the bottom of the sea. And let the black man—the cause of all this trouble—follow him as soon as he liked.

A murmur at his ear. "'Scuse me, sir."

He turned to find a steward waiting to pass into the saloon. "Yes," Arthur said, but made no move to get out of the man's way. "Will you wait for a moment?" he asked then, and fumbled at the inside pocket of his jacket. While the man stood patiently by, Arthur brought out a card case and a stub of pencil. He selected a card, held it against the doorjamb, wrote a brief note, then handed it to the steward, asking him to give it to Mr. Cutler. Then he stood back and let the man go through into the saloon. He watched him through the glass door until he had approached within a few feet of the gaming table, then turned away and headed for the stairs leading below.

A few minutes later, in his stateroom, the same steward brought him an answer. Compliments from the gentleman. Would Mr. Crichton care to meet him on the poop deck directly?

=

"I know just the place, sir," Cutler said, in the drawling voice that Arthur had hitherto only heard calling for cards in the saloon. "Just convenient for our little talk."

He led the way across the poop to a bench located a few yards behind the compass stand, which being so sited was fairly protected from the headwinds. It faced toward the stern, and, as he sat down, Arthur looked all the way along the deck to the side of the funnel. Yes, inevitably, the long, black form of Bonney was standing there, leaning upon the rail, staring out at the ship's wake. Presumably he'd come up here straight from the capstan galley.

"What do you make of that fellow?" Cutler asked casually as he settled himself, crossed his legs.

Arthur looked again toward Bonney. He hesitated.

"Crackpot, ain't he?" Cutler nodded. "Touched, I'd say. And I'm sorry for it, seein' as he comes from the same part of the world as myself."

Arthur nodded, then said, a bit heavily, "From America? Yes, of course—"

"From the West, sir. From the valley of the great Ohio River."

Cutler bit off the end of the cigar he'd just plucked from his waist-coat pocket, then took from his frock coat a box of lucifers. One of these he struck on the bench, then held it to his cigar tip till it glowed. He blew out a cloud of smoke with great satisfaction. Arthur started to protect himself against it by putting up his hand over his mouth, but then, not wishing to offend his companion before it was absolutely necessary, let it drop away.

"Now then, Mr. Cutler—" he began.

"Major Cutler, if you please. I have been favored with an honorary commission by the governor of my state."

"Well, then . . . *Major* Cutler—" Arthur stopped again. Already he felt himself floundering. What on earth was he doing up here? With this appalling major? "I am sorry to have interrupted your play," he resumed at last, carefully.

"Not at all," Major Cutler singsonged nasally. "Been expectin' you'd get around to me. And in fact, been lookin' forward to it. I have long wished to meet a representative of the British aristocracy."

"I am far from being that," Arthur said earnestly. "And further from any wish to be that."

"I have to say," Major Cutler added, "you do not at all look like my idea of an aristocrat."

"No doubt that is because I am not one."

"I thought you were all tall, well-set-up, out-of-the-ordinary-looking fellows. Whereas you—"

"But I tell you I am *not*—"

"Then how come my friend Burgess has been sayin' you are a cotton lord, rich as Croesus?"

"That is not at all the same. And, in any case—"

"And that other British fellow, Tate, he says it's gen'rally known you had at least five thousand bales of Middling Orleans at store in Liverpool last July when cotton hit sixty-five cents a pound. Sold it, didn't you? Good thing you did. Sherman took Atlanta, and the market goes all to hell. What's Orleans now? Twenty cents a pound? Good luck to you, sir. Tate figures you must have made yourself near a cool quarter million—"

"I thank Messrs. Burgess and Tate for their interest in my affairs," Arthur said angrily, "but still I assure you—"

"But maybe," said Cutler, winking and smoking and generally giving the impression of a very acute customer, "maybe you didn't sell just *all* of that cotton. Who knows what's going to happen this year? Could be a few more jumps in the market before this war is through." He looked around, then dropped his voice. "Here's what I heard from a couple of fellows who know a thing or two. Early spring, Gen'ral Lee's goin' to move out of his Petersburg lines. He'll catch Grant nappin'—and incidentally that won't be too hard, that fellow's been caught nappin' plenty of times. Lee'll head south. Meet up with Joe Johnston in the Carolinas. One big rebel army under Lee. They'll turn on Sherman—and remember Sherman's never faced a first-rate gen'ral before. Lee'll beat him before Grant can come up . . . Oh, the rebels'll still lose in the end, but hell, Mr. Crichton, this war could go on till Christmas. Till next fall, for sure. If you got any cotton still in store, then damn! hold on to it a mite longer, that's my advice; it ain't over yet."

═

Arthur closed his eyes for a moment. It was no good. When he opened them, the major was still there, nodding and chuckling in an intimate and thoroughly offensive manner.

"Major Cutler," he began again grimly, "you said you had expected that I would be approaching you sometime soon. Which must mean that you have talked with some of the other passengers."

Cutler nodded.

"And so you will know what I wish to talk to you about?"

"About the nigger, hey?" Cutler shook his head. "Not much of a subject for conversation between gen'men. *I'd* say."

"I don't," said Arthur carefully after a pause to consider his tactics, "exactly want to talk to you about this Negro—"

"Good!" The major smiled. "For if you did, we should surely quarrel."

"I want to talk," Arthur pressed on, "about certain unwarrantable threats you have been making in the presence of Captain McDonough."

Silence. Cutler's blue eyes, which had shown quite a humorous glint a moment ago, were now chips of ice.

"Aside from the…unfortunate target of your anger—you must consider the danger to every other soul onboard. Particularly your fellow passengers. Particularly the ladies."

Cutler frowned. "Sir, you cannot think that I would even dream of endangerin' the ladies."

"Then you did not mean it," Arthur cried out in relief, "when you said you meant to shoot the Negro?"

"Oh, I will shoot him. But I will be tidy about it. Only the nigger will fall."

After a moment, Arthur dragged his gaze away from his companion's now-cheerful gaze. For relief, he looked down the long deck. His gaze rested at last on the motionless form of Bonney. Another mad, unpredictable Yankee. Arthur felt almost giddy, he was floundering. He turned back to the major. "I do not believe you," he muttered. "You would not carry out this monstrous threat—"

"Monstrous is it?" Cutler frowned. "Have a care, sir, in what you—"

"Good God, man! You propose to shoot down another human being in cold—"

"Said nothin' about human bein's. Talkin' about a nigger here."

Arthur found that for the moment he could not go on. Cutler watched him, and then nodded in quiet satisfaction. "Yes, a nigger, sir. Attemptin' to force his way into an intimate social relationship with white folk. With white *ladies,* sir—"

"But have you thought of the consequences to yourself? If you murder this man, the captain will certainly have you placed under arrest. You will be handed over to the police as soon as we arrive at Liverpool. Eventually you will find yourself in a court of law. And from there, I can almost guarantee, you will be taken to the place of your own execution—"

"No jury," Cutler interrupted cheerfully, "would convict a gen'man for enforcin' the Laws of God and Nature upon the body of a goddamn African. Certainly not in England. Your homeland, sir"—the major offered a sort of sitting bow—"and—I cheerfully acknowledge it—the actual Mother of our American Laws and Liberty."

Arthur stared at the incomprehensible American next to him. He felt like laughing in his face; he felt, too, as close to weeping as he'd been since he was a child. Tears of rage they would mainly be, and frustration. It was by far the worst, but not at all the only occasion he'd been rendered almost dumb with surprise by some piece of unfathomable American conduct in the past few weeks. Indeed, he thought he'd understood the country rather better before he got there than he did now, coming away from it.

Major Cutler, seeing his perplexity, nodded in satisfaction. "I guess," he said, with an air of restrained triumph, "an aristocrat such as yourself would not have fallen in with many examples of the free, enlightened, and democratic citizenry of the great West of my country?"

"None at all, to my knowledge. But—" Arthur had decided at last that there was no profit to be had in mincing words, nor in persuasion. "But I have met a few violent blowhards in my time."

"Blowhards?" Cutler frowned.

"Blowhards. Bluffers. You're a cardplayer, aren't you, Major Cutler?" Arthur's spirits were rising fast as he felt free at last to confront this wretched man head-on. "Doesn't that make you by definition a bluffer?...I think you lack the means to carry out your threats, sir. I don't believe you're in possession of a firearm at all."

Cutler stared at him. "Is that what the problem is?" he said at last, wondering. He reached inside his coat. "Why of course I have a firearm." He drew it out. It sat, small, snub barreled, in the major's hand. He looked down at the evil thing with a kind of affectionate disparagement. "It ain't much to look at, is it? But I guess it'll stop the nigger cold. Unless"—he chuckled throatily—"unless I do a damn fool thing like shoot him in the head!"

And having given his companion a good look at the revolver, the major slipped it back inside his frock coat.

═══

For Arthur, the rest of that morning could hardly have failed to be depressing. Major Cutler had taken himself off the poop deck very soon after his little joke about shooting the Negro passenger in the head. There followed a painful interview with Captain McDonough in the latter's cabin, painful mainly for the captain's cowardly initial response to the news that Cutler not only was still issuing bloodthirsty threats but now had been confirmed as having the means to carry them out.

"Of course, you and your men will have to use the greatest care when you go to place him under restraint," Arthur had urged as he came to the end of his account. After that, for several moments, he eyed his silent companion curiously. The man was still sitting looking stunned, as if, like a poor bullock in the shambles, he had been hit once but terribly hard on the forehead. It dawned on Arthur that, although the captain had earlier mentioned his suspicion that Cutler might be armed, he had really put his entire faith in the steward's report yesterday that the man's stateroom was free from weapons. He was mentally quite unprepared for this new development.

Arthur thought of what he could say to help put a bit of backbone into the frightened old man. He began, "You must—"

"I *must*?" cried out the captain as if he'd been stung. His eyes swiveled around to meet Arthur's. "What must I do, Mr. Crichton? Meet this armed criminal, is that it? With my bare hands?"

"Surely," said Arthur, speaking as calmly as he could, hoping thereby to calm the agitated atmosphere in the cabin, "surely you must have some kind of weapon onboard? You must have"—what did sailors habitually employ, he wondered, when they wished to slaughter a fellow creature?—"a blunderbuss?" he hazarded. "A cutlass?"

"I have a gun," the captain snapped, "which I have used occasionally to shoot at seabirds. It is years since I last indulged in the sport. And I never brought down a single bird when I *was* indulging. I am a very bad shot, sir. And you are proposing now that I should exchange fire with Mr. Cutler—"

"Major Cutler," Arthur corrected him.

"Good God! He is a military man?"

"I don't think he is a military man in the way that you and I would understand the term," Arthur said encouragingly. "He told me it is an honorary commission, and I believe over there they distribute such titles like rice at a wedding."

McDonough wore an expression of tremulous scorn, as if he was not to be deceived by such fairy tales. Arthur considered the matter as calmly as he could. The old man was gripping the sides of his chair, evidently to stop himself from shaking.

"Captain McDonough," Arthur said at last, "if you do not find yourself adequate to this task, the remedy is clear. Order one of your officers to do it."

"My officers!" the captain sneered. "Have you *seen* my officers? Have you *met* them? They are the dregs of the company's service. Why else do you think they are assigned to a dying old tub like this?"

"But— The first officer seems a fine-looking chap."

"A poltroon, sir! A knave. I had to spend ten guineas of my own money to get him out of jail in Boston. He had put himself into a very dirty mess…And the second officer? A mere boy. Feebleminded. Family connection got him his berth here. The third officer—you've seen him. He's as old as me, perpetually drunk, and his incapacity is amply testified to by the fact that he has not received one tittle of advancement since he hauled himself out of the fo'c'sle near forty years ago. It is not," the captain concluded unhappily, "that they would not obey my orders, but it would be murder to put any of them up against this American hooligan. A *military man,* you say?" And he rolled his eyes in fear.

"The crew then?" Arthur came in quickly. He was beginning to feel quite desperate. The number of those qualified to stand against the murderous major was shrinking so fast. He dreaded to find that at the last would be found only himself—who was not, of course, qualified at all. "*Surely* among the crew there is some stout young fellow. The boatswain, for instance, or—"

"I do not know my crew," the captain said flatly. He was sitting forward now in his chair, staring at the Turkish carpet under his feet. "I don't know them. Don't know who's aboard. Don't know how many."

Watching him, Arthur felt a thrill of real fear steal up the back of his neck. "How do you mean?"

"I mean that I had the devil's own job to get out of that bloody Boston this time. Lost near fifty men. The army crimps took a score of 'em out of one tavern alone. I did what I could. Brought our consul into it. No good. The damn drunken fools had signed papers, taken money. Been spirited out of town, probably on their way to Virginia while I was still looking for 'em." McDonough looked up angrily at Arthur. "And wastrels though those fellows were, they were the best I had. They were *sailors*... As to what manner of men have taken their place in the fo'c'sle—the Lord alone knows. We had to take any that offered themselves. Drunkards, deserters, boys who had never gone to sea before, fugitives from justice. Murderers even, perhaps—and worse... I dare not hand any of them a gun. They would as likely turn it on myself—or on the passengers—as on this ruffian Cutler."

"Are you saying," Arthur asked slowly at last, "that your ship is presently outside your control?"

"My ship," said the captain, with some sort of return to dignity, "is proceeding steadily upon the Great Circle route to Liverpool. Meals are served in liberal quantities at regular intervals, and the decks and sleeping quarters are kept clean and orderly. As long as that state of affairs continues, I do not think that any passenger, Mr. Crichton, has just cause for complaint."

═══

All these matters Arthur communicated to his wife as they settled at their table for luncheon, just after the noon bell. Olivia shook her head when she heard of the captain's timidity. "It is a wonder," she remarked, "that he did not ask you to go up against that dangerous man."

Both then glanced to where the dangerous man was seated. The cardplayers were occupying their places till the last possible moment. Two stewards were waiting to cover their table for the lunch service. As the Crichtons watched, the last card fell. Mr. Burgess laughed loudly and gathered to himself the rather large pile of wooden counters from the center of the table.

"They are worth a dollar each counter," Olivia whispered. "Mr. Burgess has won a great deal this morning, and yesterday too."

Arthur shrugged. It did not affect the present emergency one way or the other that Major Cutler had been losing money—except, he thought suddenly, that his annoyance at that might render the man more violent and intractable when the time came for somebody to challenge him.

"In fact," he said, "I think McDonough had some idea of asking me to step into the breach; take his wretched old gun and face the brute myself."

"You are not going to do anything of the sort?"

"I am not. Before he could exactly put the question, I told the captain there were some privileges of being an Inman passenger that I must avail myself of. And one of them was not being required to face an armed assassin."

"Of course," Olivia said, "you were quite right, Arthur... And so, will nothing at all be done?"

Arthur waited as the steward filled their glasses with ice water, then, when the fellow had left them, said, "An attempt will be made tonight to disarm Cutler. The captain knows it must be done or he risks everything. If he involves the company in a lawsuit on such a matter, they will undoubtedly deny him future employment—or even his pension."

"But isn't there a still worse risk in the other course?"

"Not so much for him personally, I'd say. Even now our gallant captain is conferring with his officers, and one of them will be chosen to lead the forlorn hope. I wish the choice may not fall on the second officer—he is so much younger than the others."

He smiled when he said this, expecting to see an answering smile on her lips. The ship's second officer—a boy called Thompson—was not only young, he appeared to be the essence of heedless, virtually mindless youth. He seemed to have no duties onboard except to wander the decks offering a sweet and silly grin to all and sundry. Often he was to be seen at a distance on the second class's diminutive promenade playing uncomplicated little games with the children. The idea of this amiable, foolish youth taking on a cold killer like Major Cutler—well, it was not to be thought of without a shudder or a smile.

But Olivia did neither. There was no reaction, almost as if she hadn't heard him. And in fact, from now on her manner was rather that of a person who was hard of hearing: she reacted slowly to the things he said, and sometimes frowned at him as if she could not quite work out the sense of his words. Too, her eyes strayed often from his, seemed to be looking past him, searching for someone else. It did not please Arthur to find he needed no time at all to work out who that someone was. In the end, she was disappointed. Bonney did not make an appearance in the saloon while they were there.

But for all her inattention and low spirits, it was Olivia who, at the end of their meal, as they were pushing back their chairs, made the most intelligent suggestion he'd heard all day.

"Why don't you go and see the Negro, Arthur?" she asked, and he could not think why it had not occurred to him before.

"Of course! I can talk to him. I can persuade him, perhaps—"

"If he knew that other men would be risking their lives on his behalf, surely he would not persist in his attempt to join us?"

Arthur was so delighted at her idea that he wanted to visit the man straightaway. Olivia complained of a headache, said she would go out on deck for the fresh air. And so they parted in the narrow corridor outside the saloon door.

=

When he was still yards from his goal, Arthur's walking pace had slowed almost to a halt. What had reduced him to this unwilling crawl he could not tell at first. The mission he was on was delicate, certainly, but it stole over him gradually that what was truly bothering him was that he had never before, beyond a few unimportant brief exchanges with servants, held a conversation with a person of color. Free or enslaved. He knew he was not illiberal in his views, believed that the African race, a few individuals at least, was capable of high attainment in certain restricted fields. Believed too that the generally abject and ignorant standard presented by the mass of the race was a result of circumstance, of the heathen backwardness of their native continent, and of the curse of slavery, past or continuing, there and elsewhere. And though his own acquaintance with the Negro was so limited, he had spoken with men who had known coloreds they could describe as cultured, cultivated beings—"as good as any gentleman in England," he had actually heard that phrase used, and by a man he respected.

And yet, and yet: the fact remained, as he contemplated the forthcoming interview, Arthur felt as uncertain, truly as "all at sea," as if he might be about to hold a conversation with a being from the far side of the moon.

And almost worst of all—it hit him the moment after he had knocked on the door—he did not even know what to call the fellow. He had come here in such a rush he had neglected to discover a name. Hadn't thought of just glancing down the passenger list before he'd raced off. Oh, it was a blunder, no question. He listened to light footsteps approaching the door from the other side. Fool, he condemned himself. Bloody fool. Idiot.

The door opened.

"How d'you do?" Arthur cried out enthusiastically—more so than he had planned, and at a much higher pitch. The room he was looking into was brightly lit, which threw into greater contrast the figure of the man who stood before him. A Negro man, not very tall, in a sober suit of dark cloth, with a dark muffler wound around his neck. Lit as he was from behind, Arthur could not make out his features. Only the whites of his eyes gave contrast to the surrounding obscurity. Those eyes, Arthur noticed with a stir of discomfort, were fixed on himself and, he thought, showed about as much caution and unease as he himself was feeling.

At last the voice came—deep, rather resonant, certainly hostile.

"How do I do? I do not do particularly well, sir, as it happens."

A pause, mainly occupied by Arthur with thinking how remarkably like an educated American the fellow sounded. Then the Negro bowed slightly, said, "Thank you, sir, for inquiring."

"Ah...I should so much like to talk with you," Arthur put in quickly. The door had actually been about to be closed on his face, he realized. As if he was some front door vendor, or an importuning Bible missionary. Extraordinary. "If you could spare me...fifteen minutes, say?"

The Negro studied Arthur for a moment or two. Then he held the door wide open again, stood back from it.

"I have an infinity of time to spare, Mr. Crichton. You are welcome to choose as large a portion of it as you require."

Instinctively ducking his head, Arthur passed through the doorway. The Negro closed the door quietly behind him. Looking around, Arthur saw—with a very faint throb of resentment—that the colored man's stateroom appeared much more spacious than his own. Though the difference, when he reflected on it, was a matter of a few feet only, this chamber, lit as it was by half a dozen wax candles set all about, gave an impression almost of airiness when contrasted with the gloomy confinement of his own room. The furnishings were much more luxurious too. A fine Chinese rug, a handsome mahogany table, a really comfortable-looking sofa, velvet covered, and an armchair, similarly adorned. The portholes—two of them compared with his own one—had lace curtains, whereas his were bare. There was even a grate wherein burned a cheerful coal fire—a luxury that was certainly not to be found in Arthur's cabin. He had not even known such a thing as an open fire was to be found onboard outside the saloons, the galleys, and the captain's cabin.

He looked around then to see that the Negro was watching him. He hardly knew how to begin his argument. (Or plea for mercy, as it increasingly seemed to Arthur.) Seeing his embarrassment, the other gestured courteously to the sofa. Arthur sank into it. Very soft, very comfortable, much more comfortable than the one in *his* cabin.

The Negro settled into the armchair. Gazed at his guest.

"You know my name," Arthur said at last.

"I saw you entering your cabin last night." The Negro nodded. "I was just about setting off on the nocturnal ramble I am permitted. On my return I checked the passenger list against the number of your cabin."

"Ah . . . the thing is, I don't know your name, I'm afraid."

"It is Stuart. Charles Stuart."

"Stewart? We have another Stewart aboard. A widow lady. Of Scottish origin, I believe."

"I do not think we can be related," the Negro said gravely. "On the passenger list Mrs. Stewart's name and mine are spelled differently. Mine inclines towards the royal usage."

Arthur glanced keenly at the man, wondering if he was being mocked. There was something ever so slightly ironical, even insolent, about the Negro's demeanor, and in the extreme formality of his speech.

"I see."

Now Arthur, with some little difficulty, eased himself forward from the sofa's luxurious embrace.

"Mr. Stuart," he began, "may I say in the first place that I am very sorry that you should be subjected to your present confinement. I think," he added, when Stuart made no response, "that I speak for the great majority of our fellow passengers. Your situation"—he gestured at the distinguished fittings of the Negro's stateroom—"is quite disgraceful."

"It is illegal," Stuart said in a deep, firm voice. "I have paid for a first-class ticket. I have entered into a contract with the company—"

"Exactly. I can assure you of that, Mr. Stuart. I know something about the law, you see—"

"Don't need your assurances, Mr. Crichton. I've been fixing my own contracts for years. I never yet let a man pull a fast one on me. And some of those theater managers are cute birds, I can tell you."

"Well, then... There you have it. Legally, the situation is clear as day. And I know that Captain McDonough feels this aspect of the business particularly."

"Then why has he not released me?"

Unexpectedly, Arthur felt a pricking at the corners of his eyes. Good God, he would be weeping next. Yet the tone of the man's voice had been so anguished then. He waited for the moment to pass. And then gently: "You know why he doesn't. He fears bloodshed."

"At the hands of that damn cracker?" Stuart snorted. "*I* do not fear him." He seemed to brood angrily for a while, staring at his fine floor rug. Then looked up again. "It can't go on, Mr. Crichton. I won't be transported from shore to shore, all the way, confined as I am. I won't accept it."

"And the captain intends now to effect your release. Have you not been informed?"

"I've received a note. The attempt will be made after dinner tonight." The Negro looked again at Arthur. "And so I cannot see what we have to talk about, Mr. Crichton. It will be done."

—————

They were at the point Arthur had dreaded reaching. He must come out with what now presented itself to him as a thoroughly craven appeal. Or else hold his tongue and get himself out of here, leaving all unsaid, and all dangers yet to be faced. Hesitating, he looked around the room. The walls too were decorated much more interestingly than his own. Really, he thought, the pampering of this fellow approached the absurd.

Suddenly he noticed that what he was looking at were not the usual company-supplied land- and seascapes, and sentimental sketches of elderly British peasants, but framed playbills—printed items, mostly in black and red, and decorated with woodcuts: dramatic masks, a plump lady singer, a Negro buck grinning and kicking up his heels. They were from various theaters, a number of cities: Pittsburgh, Cincinnati, Indianapolis. One from an establishment called the Marble Hall in Evansville, Indiana. Examining these bills, Arthur discovered a constant theme. Always in the list of attractions, usually in the bottom third, but sometimes rising halfway and even above, was the name Mr. Charles Stuart. Always adjoining it, or immediately below, was some such description or puff as "The Colored Tenor" or "The Sweet-Voiced Singer from the Schuylkill" or "Direct from Europe" or "Lately Appearing in New York." In one of these notices there was a woodcut of the sweet-voiced singer himself. Arthur looked around from it to check if the artist had caught his man.

Stuart was staring at him impatiently.

"Yes, Mr. Crichton?"

"Ah, yes. Yes…" All the burden of his mission returned to Arthur. He sighed. Thought of what he must say. "You do know that this man Cutler will have to be subdued before you can appear among us? Someone will have to take hold of him, restrain him—"

"That shouldn't be hard," the Negro chuckled.

"He has a gun, Mr. Stuart. A pistol."

"I doubt it."

"I've seen it."

Silence. Stuart looked away. He crossed his long legs, his small feet were encased in polished slippers of a burgundy hue.

"You're saying somebody is liable to get hurt?" he said at last.

"Somebody is."

"If I should claim my rights?"

"Yes."

"So you're asking me not to?"

Arthur could only nod. He felt spiritually very small all at once, small and shabby. Stuart again looked down at his feet.

"Would you stand for continued imprisonment, Mr. Crichton? When you might go free?"

"I don't know. Perhaps not," Arthur said at last. He hesitated, almost appalled at the words that came into his mind to say. "I suppose," he faltered, "that I hoped . . . that a man such as yourself—with the experience of your race—that you might be able to bear it with greater fortitude—"

"That I could stand being clapped up for no reason and for as long as it pleases some white man because I am of *color*? Is that what you thought, Mr. Crichton? Leave the nigger in captivity—he won't mind; he's used to it!"

"I certainly held no such illiberal—"

"Mr. Crichton, I was born in Philadelphia, Pennsylvania. Free. My mother and my father before me were free. I have had no such experience of life that would enable me to bear an unjust imprisonment with any greater fortitude than yourself. Or any other *gentleman* onboard . . . I will assert my rights, sir. Tell your people not to interfere if they don't wish to. I will go into that saloon alone if I must. No help. I don't need it."

Now in Crichton admiration for the Negro struggled for primacy with self-contempt. He saw how truly cowardly had been his request, had been his whole mission. And he saw too how excellent this noble fellow was. He felt exhilarated, swept up by the other's courage. He leaned forward and stuck out his hand.

"Bravo, sir!" he cried. "You must defend your rights. And I will stand by you."

The colored man looked down at Arthur's outstretched hand, seemed to inspect it rather cautiously, and then, with the very faintest of shrugs, accepted it into his own. The touch of his skin, Arthur noticed, was very cold. Somewhat to his mortification, his own hand was dropped very quickly, almost as if its touch was offensive to the other. Who now again resumed his contemplation of the area of rich carpet that lay beneath his slippered feet.

"I told you," he murmured, "don't want any man's help."

"You may not find it sufficient to approach this Cutler fellow armed only with courage."

Stuart glanced at him in surprise. Then: "T'hell with that," he chuckled.

He eased himself out of his chair. Arthur was struck suddenly by how lean and well muscled the fellow was. It showed even under the restrained cut and hue of his garments. He moved easily, powerfully across the room to a mahogany wardrobe. He slid open a top drawer, reached in his hand, and then drew out of it an immensely long and shining steel blade. Arthur stared at the ghastly thing. His lips had gone suddenly dry. He licked them.

"Good God. Is that a *sword*?"

"It's a bowie knife," Stuart said easily. As he seated himself again, he tossed it from one hand to the other. "And I know how to use it. Damn Cutler better not miss with his first shot. Else I will stick this toothpick right into his goddamned white belly."

To that Arthur had nothing to add, nor could he see any very good reason for prolonging the interview. He opened the door for himself, the Negro choosing not to leave his seat. After he'd done this, though, Arthur stopped, and without looking around said, "Mr. Stuart, this door is not locked. You could leave your cabin at any time."

"Yes."

"Then why do you not?"

"Gave my word I wouldn't. Besides"—Arthur looked around, Stuart smiled at him faintly—"I'd as soon not be chased all over the ship by a bunch of white men and caught and brought back to my prison . . . like some poor scared nigger found hiding in the swamp."

＝

Arthur spent most of the hours remaining before dinner in contemplation of the rash promise he'd made to "stand by" the Negro. He did not see how he could entirely repudiate this agreement and still keep his self-respect. So it became a matter of weighing up the extent to which "standing by" another person actually committed one. He would have liked to talk the matter over with his wife, but she was nowhere to be found—not in her cabin, or on the decks, or in the cap-stan galley.

Verbally was the limit, he decided at last. When the time came, he would speak up, he would make himself heard on the Negro's absolute right to be accepted into the stateroom.

And then what? he thought, as he lowered himself into his seat at the dinner service. He looked around at the various tables, wondering which of them he would be diving under the moment the speech-making had finished, the bullets and knives started flying, and America finally blew asunder the peace and coziness of this little English world.

Olivia arrived then at the table, five minutes late, with some story about having spent the past hour with Madame Charvet in her stateroom, talking about England, which the Swiss couple had never visited. They had planned on arriving at Liverpool to take the railway straight to London. But she thought she might have persuaded them to linger for a few days in the North, to see the sights—the 'Change at Liverpool, Market Street in Manchester, Blackstone Edge... She chattered on brightly, and Arthur had no chance to discuss with her what was most concerning *him* before, just as the first course was being set out, he learned that whatever sacrifice of dignity—or life—he might have to make would not be required from him in the immediate future. A note was handed him by a steward in which the captain—not present at the meal—stated that owing to an indisposition on the part of First Officer Hartley, who had been chosen to lead the storming party against Major Cutler, the attempt to introduce the Negro would not now take place until the morrow.

=

The evening wore on. The dinner things were cleared away. Teatime came and went. Such as it was, the crowd in the saloon seemed to melt away earlier even than the night before. Only the cardplayers appeared unmovable. Arthur and Olivia Crichton went downstairs together at about ten-fifteen. They paused outside her stateroom, and he asked her if she wanted him to step in and chat for a while as on the previous evening, but she said she would rather he didn't, she felt very sleepy. Just at that moment the ship gave a sudden great lurch, throwing him against a doorjamb, and Olivia against him. They disentangled themselves, smiling at each other, and then he kissed her cheek and they parted.

The ship's sudden movement, which had almost pitched the Crichtons onto the corridor floor, also nearly tipped over two people who were at the time walking together on the main deck. Having nothing solid nearby to hang on to, they hung on to each other, and in that way managed just to remain upright. The sea subsided again, the ship became comparatively still, but the couple did not disengage from each other instantly, and in fact not until a voice that, though reproving, could not be said to be entirely unfriendly, spoke out: "I think, Mr. Babcock, we are no longer in danger of falling over."

With some reluctance, the man let the woman go.

"Didn't expect it," the Nova Scotian muttered. "That wave."

"Indeed not," Mrs. Stewart agreed. She gave a laugh as silvery and tripping as the moonlight that glanced upon the deck. "I thought for a moment that a whale—some great Leviathan—had passed under our ship and raised us on its back."

The Blue Nose stared at her in incredulity as they resumed their journey. "Not likely!" he said at last, and let out a loud, jeering laugh. The moon had drifted behind a cloud just before, and so he did not see the rather irritated frown that gathered on the widow's brow. It was somewhat by chance that Babcock had won the right to assist Mrs. Stewart in negotiating her nightly passage between the saloon and her distant stateroom. For Mr. Hartley, who might be said to have official supervision over her, being indisposed was not present in the saloon that night, and the Reverend Stibbards, who earlier in the evening had volunteered to be her escort, was seized about ten o'clock with a wretched headache and had to go below. Miss Faversham went with him as far as her own stateroom, for, she declared, she had a bottle of eau de cologne in her trunk that was most efficacious in soothing headaches. The Reverend Stibbards's feeble objections were tut-tutted aside. They left the saloon together, and neither returned.

That left Babcock, who in a little while came over to say that he felt like turning in pretty early and whenever Mrs. Stewart had a mind to leave it'd be all right with him, he guessed, if she wanted him to escort her. This not very gracious offer, Mrs. Stewart—who, of course, had spent some time among the Nova Scotian people and knew their ways—calmly accepted. Babcock went back to explain matters to the card table, which was not pleased by his defection. Nevertheless, ten minutes later gambler and widow left the saloon together and went out into the moonlight and salt breeze of the main deck.

Now they passed down the stairs to the cabin deck. Left at the foot of the stairs led to the second class, right to the few first-class state-rooms that were located so far forward, only one of which, Mrs. Stewart's, was occupied. They came to her door. She used her key to unlock it. Then looked up at her Blue Nose escort and, smiling, dipped into a slightly satirical curtsy.

"Thank you, kind sir. I believe I am quite safe now—"

"Like to come in."

"I beg your pardon?"

"Understand from Hartley the tariff's five sovereigns. Or twenty-five dollars American." Babcock sighed. "Well, I'll say that's pretty steep—still, I'll go for it." Under the dim corridor lamp, he leered into her face. "Long as you can guarantee me a helluva good time."

She stood quite still for a moment, then opened her door, went inside, and closed it in his face.

Repeated knockings at last induced her to open it again.

"Look, Jesus, I'm—"

"Will you be quiet? You will wake my poor children."

"Uh-huh? I've heard they're pretty good sleepers, those two. Laudanum, ain't it?"

"Go *away*, sir, or I shall be forced to ring for my stewardess."

"I want to say I'm sorry—"

"Very well. You are sorry."

"I got it all wrong, I guess. That fellow Hartley—"

"Must be a brute of the first order!"

"Well, I guess he must be," Babcock said humbly.

She was biting her lip angrily. Under her shawl, which on her reappearance proved to be slightly disarrayed, her breasts were rising and falling rapidly in her agitation. He could hardly keep his hands off them.

"He sure is a brute, that Hartley—"

"Out of the foolish kindness of my heart"—she was gasping for breath, she was so outraged—"I allowed him into my room. And it was only because he so piteously lamented the loss of certain comforts of the marital state that I permitted him to achieve a degree of intimacy which..." She shook her head, she could not go on.

"Well, that's just the fix I'm in," Babcock said eagerly. "Those marital comforts? I miss 'em too... even though I ain't exactly married." He watched her, hope brimming in his eyes. "So can I come inside?"

And not waiting for her answer, he pushed on the door—only to find that in her hands it stayed absolutely rigid. He looked down at her with some respect. She must have quite some muscle on her, he thought, to hold the door like that against his shove. That led to thoughts of strong, firm arms gripping him, powerful thighs wrapped close around his middle...

"Entirely unconnected with those kindnesses I was prepared to offer Mr. Hartley, he, understanding my worldly situation and sympathetic to the plight of my two fatherless children, elected to make a small contribution to their future welfare—"

"That's what I heard!" cried the Blue Nose. "I want to make the same contribution."

"To you it is seven sovereigns, Mr. Babcock," she said demurely. "As you are not exactly married."

He stared at her in horror. She was standing against the quarter-opened door, her eyes downcast. She was certainly a fine-looking woman, and those images, the strong arms and thighs, were so clear before his eyes... But seven *pounds*. When a clean whore at Halifax never cost more than five dollars. For Chrissake.

But at that moment her eyes slid upward, and she looked at him in a way that made the hair on his neck stand up.

"Just tell me," he begged in a whisper, "d'you have a fine, full bush? For I do like that on a woman."

She put out her hand and laid it on his arm. "Everything will be just as you wish," she promised. Her hand slid down his arm and clasped his own hand. Then she opened the door a little more, and drew him inside.

===

Precisely as the widow was fulfilling her pledge, Arthur Crichton was finding out that the captain's had not been worth the paper it had been written on. For as he undressed for bed, he received another note from McDonough, this one pushed under his stateroom door. "As tomorrow is Sunday," he read, "and the risk of violence and bloodshed on the Holy Day being one I cannot contemplate, the business we have spoken of will not now be effected until the following day, Monday."

"Holy Day, my arse!" Arthur grunted as he crumpled up the note and threw it scornfully into a corner. "Poor wretched Stuart. This is quite intolerable."

Yet after all he slept very well that night, and woke in the morning in excellent spirits.

46°37' N, 45°50' W

The condition hardly survived Arthur's first glance toward the port-hole. Even through its near-opaque glass it was apparent that it was a filthy day outside. After he had washed and dressed, and gone up-stairs—there was no response to his knocking on Olivia's door—he went onto the main deck to see if, perhaps, the view from the porthole had overestimated the foulness of the weather. It had not, rather the opposite. It was such a dark, dreary morning. Clouds of dingy vapor seemed to wrap the ship like a shroud. Some of it resulted from the funnel smoke settling on deck in the heavy, almost windless air. For the rest—was it fog? Arthur wondered. Had they been closer to land he would have had no doubt of it. He was uncertain whether the con-dition persisted this far out on the ocean—but what else could it be?

At that moment they broke clear of the thickest clouds. Around them banks of mist gathered and parted. Above, through the smoke, was a flat gray ceiling, through which a persistent small rain was falling, making the deck slippery underfoot. Even though there was little wind, the sea rose and fell all around in oily, gray swells, the peaks higher and troughs lower than he had seen before. The ship lurched across them, unsteady as a drunken man. He had to hold on to the rail tight to keep his balance.

He went inside to the saloon. There were hardly any other passen-gers there. The stewards stood about in listless attitudes. Arthur took a tray, helped himself to eggs and cod and fresh-baked rolls. He saw the Swiss, Charvet, sitting at a table alone, and thought of joining him. He could ask him whether it was really the case that Olivia had spent the hour before supper last night in his cabin, talking to his wife about England.

Of course he knew he couldn't possibly do it. Anyway, he couldn't speak French worth a damn, and the Swiss had hardly any English. Useless. He nodded to Charvet, went to find his own table.

It was the black fellow, he knew. Foul weather and a cheerless saloon could not alone make him so depressed. He felt the tension of this unresolved affair knotting his stomach. And a kind of tedium too, dull, weary, as if the problem had been going on for weeks, instead of—when had he first heard of Stuart's plight? Day before yesterday? That afternoon.

When he was midway through breakfast, the chief steward sounded a small hand gong and told the handful of passengers present that there would be a service of worship at eleven o'clock sharp, here in the saloon. The news seemed to plunge the sparse company into a greater depression than before. People hardly spoke now, and when they did their voices drifted across the room in spectral whispers. Before he had nearly finished his meal, Arthur had had enough. He threw down his napkin. At that moment, a shadow fell across the table. He looked up to find the gaunt, beseeching presence of Mr. Tate looming over him. He was holding a tray of food.

"Would you mind if I sat at this table, Mr. Crichton? It will not inconvenience you?"

"Not in the least," said Arthur, rising, and already admiring the deftness of his escape. "For I am leaving it, as you see. Good day to you, sir!"

He was away, heading for the doors before Tate was able to get off another word.

=

The small infusion of pleasure from this victory did not last long. The rain was now falling hard, which disinclined Arthur to go outside. He thought for a moment of paying the Negro another visit. But he found that his anger at the mishandling of the man's release had spread to include poor Stuart himself. Arthur did not want to see him in this mood. He would be bound to accuse the Negro in some way of being the author of his own woes. And that would be thoroughly dishonest. The only other option was to go below to his stateroom. Of course, in the corridor downstairs, he tapped again on Olivia's door. Again no reply. She could be sleeping—but he knew she wasn't. Olivia always got up early; morning was her best time. Perhaps he should raise the alarm. She might have gone exploring and locked herself in somewhere by mistake. She might have fallen overboard. But he knew none of that was true either; he had not the least fear of it. He went on to his own door, turned the key slowly in the lock, trying to prolong every action, to use up the morning until the faint relief of attending divine worship in the saloon came around. It was half past nine, an hour and a half to get through.

What to do, what to do? And then, as if in answer, there came drifting toward him unwanted thoughts, thoughts of the past that he never harbored willingly now, never wanted to harbor...

No. Not that. Definitely not that. From his bunk, he leaned forward and picked up a book that lay on the sofa. It bore the yellow wrapper that showed it had come from the ship's little library. Olivia had taken it out on the first night and had kept it for him after reading it. Volume One of *Lady Audley's Secret.* By M. E. Braddon. He had never heard of this author before, though Olivia assured him that Miss Braddon was all the rage, considered to be the equal of the Brontës, or even of Miss Austen. Considered so, he'd decided after reading a couple of chapters, by not very exacting judges. Still the lady was competent, at least, and had held his attention for an hour or so the first time he'd opened the book.

But this time Miss Braddon's spell lasted only five minutes at most. He found himself staring not at the pages but beyond them, at the sofa opposite. And not seeing the sofa either.

It was no good. He could not resist what he'd taken up *Lady Audley's Secret* to avoid. He got up and returned the novel to the sofa, then crossed the few feet of carpeting to where his cabin baggage was stored. He opened his trunk and took out of it a bulky leather-bound volume, which he carried back to the sofa. He seated himself, then began turning the leaves of this volume, many of which were loose, held to the attached pages with brass clips. It was a kind of commonplace book, in which Arthur liked to jot down items that had taken his interest, usually from the newspapers: statistics, odd stories, a phrase or two from a political speech that had caught his eye. And legal judgments that had interested him, for he had not been deceiving Captain McDonough when he'd said he still had a curiosity about such things. Also he occasionally wrote in it memorandums to himself, in which he looked at matters that were preoccupying him and tried to examine his feelings about them as he wrote them down.

He found the pages he was looking for. He had written them three years ago, a few days after Laura's death.

Laura Laura Laura Laura Crichton Laura

Laura Brightwell she was—daughter of Salford mill foreman—educated by the Quakers till she was ten—sent to work at the looms—got out of that somehow—brave clever girl—set to work in the mill's office—keeping the correspondence straight, filing so on

(She told me once—the room she sat in after she got her deliverance would shake all day from the churnings of the great machines sited just a few feet away, behind a flimsy partition. Perhaps it served as a warning of what lay in wait for her if she should fail at her new task. But she DID NOT FAIL DID NOT

The first note broke off here. He thought probably a day or two had passed before he nerved himself to try again. He was struck by how strangely this new effort read, so detailed and yet so detached. And the handwriting—the last time it had flowed unchecked across the page; now it appeared controlled and amazingly neat, as if a policeman had patrolled his every line that day:

When the agitation against the taxes on bread began late in the 'thirties, and the Anti-Corn Law League was formally constituted in Manchester, there was great need to bring order into the chaos that inevitably accompanied the opening weeks of such a vast effort to change the whole bent of public opinion. Publicity, membership lists, appeals for funds, booking lectures and lecturers throughout the country: the office was overwhelmed. Laura's employers were friendly with some of the League's leading lights. It was a slack time in the cotton trade, and so natural that they would offer to lend her services for a few weeks. So she came to the League's headquarters in Newall's Buildings, at the junction of Market and Cross streets. By the time the League was in a position to hire full-time staff, it was known how good at the work she was, and she was offered and accepted a permanent job in charge of the postal arrangements.

I met her at Newall's Buildings late during the second year after I had moved to Manchester. I was still then practicing at the bar, though pretty unsuccessfully. Nursing secret political ambitions, I was in the habit of dropping in at Newall's on most days, my lack of occupation giving me a great deal of free time, and I volunteered to help with whatever work needed to be done. Thus, as an addresser and stuffer of envelopes I fell under the direct supervision of Miss Laura Brightwell. I found this an intriguing, indeed a quite amazing experience. The fact of a woman being employed at serious work in an office was much less common then even than now. And to have that woman actually in charge and having the direction of several male subordinates—well, it could only have happened at the League, which had a generally liberal and encouraging attitude towards the capacities of women. At least Richard Cobden had, and even at this early date Cobden generally got his way in League business.

Though even here, liberalism had its limits, of course. Laura was paid, I later found out, about half the wage that the male clerks were getting, but from what I could see from my position as a regular volunteer she was worth two of those gentlemen put together—and they were not bad workers either, for all of us, waged or not, were in that office because we wanted to be, because we so detested the unfair taxes that a selfish agricultural oligarchy had placed on the bread of the workingman, and so looked forward to the boundless blessings that were certain to accompany their removal.

Reading what I have written, I fear I give the impression that our whole intercourse in those days revolved about political questions.

I do believe that the sharing of generous hopes for our fellow man, and our keen arguments as to how those hopes could be realized, gave an intensity to our relations almost from the beginning, something not possible, I think, with the usual measured development of affection between man and woman. But I would cancel that statement even as I write it. I am talking only about the two of us. What I mean to say is that my own diffidence and shyness as a young man, and that which I came to know as Laura's innate skepticism, would have probably kept us from admitting our liking for each other for a much longer time than in fact it took.

We could not of course make a parade of our feelings in the office. The last thing Laura wanted was to be accused of frivolity or flirtatiousness at her place of work. But often she let me walk her home at night, across the river to Salford. And occasionally, when work was slack, we would walk about the town together. On rainy days, I remember we used to stroll in the covered passageway of the Manchester Arcade, between the shops. Sometimes she let me buy her little trinkets, or ribbons, pincushions—though she was always rather on edge in the Arcade, for it was next to Newall's Buildings and, as she'd say, no telling who might happen to see us.

The second note ended here, high on the page. The rest of the sheet was blank, white all the way down, white as a sepulchre. Arthur could not be sure, but he believed it was just after this that he had given way utterly to his grief. Dismayed by this, friends had contacted his brother, who had come up from Birmingham and had stayed with him through the worst of that time. He couldn't now remember whether Samuel had been with him still when he had gone back at last to his notes:

I mostly amused her at first, I think. It helped my cause greatly when I revealed to her early on that, as the son of a master tailor, my own background was reasonably modest, so that we were not too far apart in the matter of class. And though I was certainly a professional gentleman now, I also was, as she could see, the least inclined to claim any particular deference on account of my rank. In fact, she could not get over my dilatory and indifferent attitude towards my job. I tried to explain that while the Law, abstractly speaking, had a certain fascination for me, the business of being a barrister, of having to get up on one's hind legs to argue the toss against other fellows in a court of law, in front of numbers of other people, had none at all. I don't think she listened to my explanations. "Lazybones," she'd call me, though she had the evidence of my assiduous work in the League office to give the lie to that. And she'd say, "You must settle to your work, Arthur, or you'll never amount to anything much"—though later, when indeed I did find some work I could settle to, and proved I was no sloth after all, she didn't like it so much.

What else about me appealed to her? I don't know. I think I was reasonably pleasing to look at then. Hair and teeth all present, and my midriff not so unfortunately swollen as it has become. But again—I don't know . . . Who can say how one seems to another person? Twenty-five years ago.

For myself . . . Laura Brightwell. Laura Brightwell. I liked her laughter—even though it was mostly directed at myself. And her dry Lancashire wit. And her clever mind. Her competence. And her bright little eyes and her full mouth, smiling usually then whenever I saw it. She had a trim, dainty figure, and I'd walk beside her feeling tall and masculine—yet knowing that with a couple of trenchant words she could cut me down. I'm not sure if this would attract other men: for myself the feeling of being both protective and vulnerable at the same time was rather pleasing. Exciting, I suppose. Of all the young ladies that I knew—not so very many really—the girls I danced with (badly) at my married colleagues' houses or at the public subscription balls which were popular then—Laura was the only one who sought to deal with me without the usual employment of feminine wiles and posturing. I thought frankness was the core of our attachment, and so that we could not go wrong, for neither of us was being deceived in the other. Looking back, I think this was the greatest mistake I made. Neither of us, it was to turn out, had been frank with each other at all. Yet truly I think we were not aware we were guilty of this then.

Anyway, this period, before our marriage, was the happiest we were ever to be.

We married in '42. By then I had already abandoned my profession and had taken my first steps in business. Our first child—the boy—was born the following year. He did not live out his first day on earth. Our second child was a little girl. She lived long enough to be given a name. Maria

And so this note too dribbled away into nothing. Three years ago he had not had the heart to add any more, and before this morning he hadn't looked again at what he had written then. Hadn't the courage to, he supposed.

What can't be cured must be endured. Laura was fond of saying that. The young Laura said it—when she grew older she seemed not so certain that there was even this much comfort to be had in the world. Yet what had she to be despairing about? Or angry? Arthur wondered, angry himself now. Wealth, position, a fine house: such afflictions!

There was a knock on the door. He looked up, almost flinching, expecting to see it fly open and Laura standing there, furious and implacable and tireless.

The door was opened, but only a little way.

"Did you say to come in, Arthur?"

"Yes, my dear," he called out, laying his manuscript book aside gladly, feeling himself in a moment passing from darkness into . . . half light at least. "Please do."

—

He had an impression of some dishevelment as Olivia advanced into the room, though she was quite properly dressed. The cardigan thing she wore over her dress was not buttoned exactly right, so that one side hung lower than the other, and her hair was escaping wispily from under her cap. He noticed too, as he got to his feet, that she wore a look of great determination: clenched fists, set jaw. He smiled at her, trying not to appear the least bit uneasy, or curious.

He pointed at the yellow-bound book on the sofa.

"Been investigating your Miss Braddon. Thought she was rather dull at first, but, you know, there are some good things in it."

"Arthur, please listen to me."

"Of course I will, my dear. Won't you sit?"

She settled on the sofa, her back very straight, head held upright, alert.

"I'm so glad to see you, Livvy. I couldn't think where you might have—"

"I've been with John."

He lowered himself onto the bunk.

"Who is John?... Is he one of Mrs. Stewart's children?"

"Oh, I mean Mr. Bonney, of course," she said impatiently. "I've been talking to him all morning, and he has agreed—"

"John? You call him John?"

"Oh, please, Arthur, listen. It is a matter of life and—"

"*Where* have you been talking to him, Olivia?"

"What does that matter? In the capstan galley. There!"

Not a speck of rain on her that he could see. Of course the galley, though open on the sides, had a sheltering roof. But when she left it there would have been quite a bit of deck to negotiate before she could have got back under cover.

"It wasn't the first time," she said, her words setting off another alarm rocket in his mind. "Yesterday, don't you remember? You saw him leaving the galley after speaking to me?"

"I remember."

"He told me about it then, most of it. I would have told you—I wanted to, Arthur—but he begged me not to speak of it to anyone. Not even to you."

The novelettish mists of M. E. Braddon seemed to be swirling very thickly around the room. He was about to say something like "Do you hold secrets from me, Olivia, from your husband?" But his lips actually would not form the words, and before he could change them to something less Braddonish, Olivia said, in a low, thrilling voice, "Oh, Arthur, he is in desperate trouble."

"Most people have troubles, Olivia. And do you know..." He was trying for the note of neutral cheerfulness. "I begin to think the less interest we take in the misfortunes of those who aren't family or good friends, the better off everybody is in the end. This Negro business, for instance—"

"That is quite different. Of course, the Negro has no claim on us at all—"

"Actually, my dear, I think a detached observer might say that of all the persons on this ship, it is *only* the Negro that has any claim on our concern. Not that it's a good enough claim to risk getting shot at for, of course."

"What on earth are you talking about, Arthur? The black man means nothing to us."

"Doesn't he? Think about it. How have I made my living all these years? Cotton. Buying it. Selling it. Long ago I even used to mill the stuff. Always cotton. And who picks the cotton?"

"Not Mr. Stuart, I am sure."

"Black men. Black men and women held in slavery. Held prisoner as Stuart is."

Olivia's pretty little mouth tightened in exasperation. And he couldn't deny he felt some sympathy for her. His argument had sounded pretty flaccid even as he had spoken it. He did not really believe it—or rather, whether or not he believed, he hardly cared about it. He was just talking. Mainly, he knew, to stop himself thinking.

"Please try to concentrate, Arthur. I say Mr. Bonney is in trouble."

"Well, then, my dear, I am sorry for it. There."

"And I've persuaded him to speak to you."

"Why would Mr. Bonney wish to talk to me?"

"Because I have told him that you are wise." The preoccupied, concentrated cast of her countenance broke up, she smiled at him teasingly. "Awfully wise, dear old boy." (He watched this tactical shift with interest. Of course, it worked. He felt himself, as ever, relaxing and softening under her flattery.) "And when I said that you had once been a lawyer, he was very keen."

"Bonney's difficulty is a legal one?"

For the first time she seemed to grow uncertain. "I don't know exactly... It appears to be how it presents itself to him. He talks a lot about wanting justice." Then she reached out, and took the hand he gladly raised to meet hers, and she smiled at him cozeningly. At least it was a familiar Olivia he was seeing now, not that intense, direct, unfeminine (Laura-like?) creature who had been staring at him a few moments ago. "Oh, won't you meet him, Arthur? I am sure you will make everything right."

"Very well. When I see him next I'll have a—"

"He's outside."

"I beg your pardon?"

"He is in the corridor. I told him to wait."

At last he sighed, and took out his watch. Still forty minutes to go.

"All right, then, I'll speak to him now. Meanwhile, I would like you to get ready for Sunday service in the saloon. Perhaps you should ring for the stewardess to help you."

"I think I will not attend service."

"Yes, Olivia. I wish you to be there."

She watched him curiously. "But why? We never go to church at home."

"At Easter," he reminded her. "And Christmas."

"Hardly ever, then."

"I want you to be there," he repeated. "At my side."

He gazed at her levelly. She nodded then, rose to her feet. He stood up too, watched her as she went to the door. She looked back, and smiled at him.

"Thank you, Arthur. It is kind of you to see Mr. Bonney."

"Not at all."

"You are always kind to me."

She sounded, he thought, quite sad, regretful, as if she were looking back tenderly at something she had rather liked once and had since mislaid.

"If I am, my dearest, it's because you make me want to be."

She smiled again, then, with her hand on the door handle: "I have told John there will be no difficulty at all in his settling in England. That you know lots of important people and one of them is bound to give him employment."

═══

In a minute or so John Bonney was sitting upon the sofa that Olivia had vacated. After ushering him in, she had cast a look of mingled thanks and encouragement at her husband, and another glance, which Arthur did not try to interpret, at the young man, and then had closed the door quietly behind her.

"It is very good of you to see me, sir," Bonney said immediately.

"Is it? Yes, I suppose it is, particularly as we have not yet been introduced." Too acerbic, Arthur decided immediately. The young man was staring at him almost in consternation. He did his best to smile at him. "But my wife has never been one to stand on ceremony, and I suppose through her we have in some ways effected a meeting."

"She is very kind."

I am good, she is kind, Arthur thought. He sat down again on the bunk. "I'm afraid this is not the most commodious of meeting places. I would suggest a turn on deck, but—" He nodded toward the porthole. It looked, through the film of rain or spray that lay on the glass, as dark almost as night.

"It's bad up there," the young man nodded.

Young man. Lord, how young he is, Arthur thought, staring across the table at Bonney. Most impolitely, he supposed, but he was so taken by the other's appearance. Seen only at a distance on deck in his great raincoat, or else hunched over his food during his brief visits to the saloon, John Bonney had given an impression of a rather formidable maturity. His dark looks lending him, at a glance, a somewhat saturnine menace even. But close up like this—he was a boy. Twenty-two, perhaps? Twenty-one? Olivia's very age? His skin looked almost smoother than hers, his color as fresh, his long black hair as soft...He is a child, thought Arthur, and, unfortunately for me, a beautiful one.

"My wife tells me I may be able to help you in some way, Mr. Bonney?"

Bonney looked embarrassed, then nodded.

"She tells me the fact that I was once a lawyer was of particular interest to you?"

"Not that exactly," Bonney said. "What interested me was when she told me that you are an authority on the law governing contracts."

"Ah, she remembered that?" Arthur said. "You know, I am never quite certain what Mrs. Crichton takes in, and what she doesn't."

At that Bonney looked quite uncomprehending. Or perhaps it was, Arthur guessed, that, like a child, he was so full of his own immediate concerns that he could take nothing else in at all.

"Perhaps," he urged mildly, "you should tell me what your difficulty is. I can't guarantee that I will be of much help. It's many years since I practiced at the bar. But whatever assistance I can give is yours, of course."

The young man's large, dark eyes glanced at him gratefully, and then seemed to take aim at the porthole. He took a breath, then another. He began to speak, changed his mind, and then at last: "Mr. Crichton—I am not what I seem!"

Arthur waited courteously for a few moments, but Bonney appeared to have reached the end of what he could say unassisted. He had closed his eyes now, and was shaking his head slowly from side to side. He did seem to be under the sway of some considerable emotion. Arthur remembered the phenomenon from his professional days. People came to you for help, and then sat dumb as gateposts, expecting you to extract from them what their difficulty was, item by painful item. Though, of course, there were the other types too, who you could not get to stop prating of their wrongs, like complaining waterfalls.

"I am not certain, Mr. Bonney," he began, trying to keep his tone cheerful and encouraging, "that I have any great sense of what you *seem*. Only that you spend a great deal of time on the poop gazing at the sea...I personally find," he resumed, Bonney not having spoken in the meantime, "that after a few days the ocean strikes me as rather a bore, and—"

"I am a soldier, Mr. Crichton. That is what I am. Not—" He made a gesture that included his ordinary though well-cut suit, his white linen, his dark green cravat. Not a civilian, Arthur guessed all at once he meant.

"A soldier?"

"Army of the Potomac. Second Corps. Gibraltar Brigade. Fourteenth Regiment of Indiana Volunteers. Company J. I hold the rank of sergeant."

The words, the names rolled from the young man's lips like muffled drumbeats. The light around Bonney seemed to grow darker. His white shirt gleamed. His eyes were lustrous, wretchedly sad. Arthur suddenly thought of a criminal he had met once. He had accompanied a senior barrister to the jail in Salford to interview a man held on a charge of murder in the first degree. The man was from a wealthy family, could afford the finest representation. But there was nothing at all to be done. The crime had so clearly been committed by the prisoner—and was in its details so hideous—that he could not be saved from the rope, no matter how brilliant the defense. Arthur had had the strongest feeling of this as they talked to the still-living wretch. Something abominable had been done; the guilt was inexpungible, could not be changed, ameliorated, nothing.

He had just a flavor of that feeling now, hearing Bonney. Something final, irrevocable had been done; it could not be helped.

"I think you must be some long way from your encampment, Mr. Bonney," he said at last, not really knowing what to say. "Or should I call you Sergeant Bonney?"

The other looked at him reproachfully. "Do you make fun of me, sir?"

Arthur shook his head. "Not at all." He thought for a moment. "Surely, Mr. Bonney, what you need is someone who is expert in military law. And as I have no knowledge of that field whatsoever—"

The young man laughed scornfully. "God knows I don't want to have to do with military *anything*, Mr. Crichton. Least of all military justice, so called."

"I admire your coolness, sir. For I think the usual military punishment for the offense you appear to have committed is severe indeed."

"What offense have I committed?"

"Are you not telling me that you're a deserter?"

"Oh, plenty will call it that, I daresay."

"You are on a ship. A thousand miles and more from the American coast, and still heading away from it. Unless you have been sent upon some extraordinary mission by your military superiors—well, what else would you call it?"

"I'd call it—getting myself out of a damn bad deal," Bonney said.

=

"Lord, whom wind and seas obey," Arthur sang with the rest of the congregation,

> *Guide us through the watery way;*
> *In the hollow of thy hand,*
> *Hide and bring us safe to hand.*

The choral efforts of the dozen or so passengers in the saloon were unaccompanied by any musical instrument. The ship's piano had broken up in rough seas on the previous crossing (Captain McDonough had explained this to the congregation before the service began), and the ship's carpenter had not yet got around to fixing it. Entirely because (as McDonough was to tell Arthur privately some time later) he was dead.

Keep the souls whom now we leave,
Bid them to each other cleave;
Bid them walk on life's rough sea,
Bid them come by faith to thee.

The carpenter had been one of the few regular members of the ship's company that the captain had managed to purchase out of the hands of the army or the police in Boston. Back onboard, he had celebrated his escape with reckless, fatal enthusiasm, with the result that he had been buried quietly at sea near the entrance to Chebucto Bay, two hours before the *Laurentia* docked at Halifax. None of the passengers had even noticed, McDonough would say proudly.

Save, till all these tempests end,
All who on thy love depend;
Waft our happy spirits o'er;
Land us on the heavenly shore.

As the congregation was seating itself, the Reverend Stibbards stepped forward and, having waited for the noise of scraping chair legs to subside, raised a glossy, waterproof-bound copy of the Bible to within an inch or two of his spectacles and began to intone in a stern, though oddly gloating voice: "Forty years on I grieved with this generation, and said: It is a people that do err in their hearts, for they have not known my ways…" And Arthur's thoughts, as always when he heard the lesson read in church, began to drift. He glanced at Olivia sitting beside him, and she, seeing him looking, gave him a private smile. She had certainly done him proud this morning, he thought, facing front again. No trace of that disheveled party he had first met this morning. She looked quite elegant, composed, very pretty, really it was wasted on the handful of passengers that had bothered to leave their cabins and make an appearance in the saloon.

Of course, he thought, suppressing a yawn, the weather was so ugly, and rumored to be about to turn even worse. One couldn't blame them really, it was a time for staying put, battening down the hatches... He caught sight of Burgess on the far side of the group, lounging negligently in his chair. Surprising that, him being here. And also one of the Nova Scotians—Babcock or Harris, he could never remember which was which. Of course it was possible that they were even lazier than their cardplaying fellows, and had just not bothered to leave the saloon at all. Though both looked as if they had spruced themselves up a bit for the service. The Tates were sitting next to... to *Harris*. Yes. Harris it was. The female Tate looked close to tears, the male just looked exhausted. Arthur removed his gaze hurriedly, before it could be noticed by either of them. He moved on to the person sitting on Mrs. Tate's far side.

Bonney. Yes. Bad business that.

Well, the facts were clear enough. (If the fellow wasn't lying, which was certainly a possibility. Clients so often lied.) When the war broke out, Bonney was just completing his freshman year at the University of Indiana. He had not enlisted to fight in the first year of the war, nor in the second. His father was strongly against him doing it until he had finished his education. By the third year, however, though he was still in college, he had insisted on volunteering. A conscription law had been passed by the Congress, and he did not want the shame of entering the ranks only because he was legally bound to. Neither did he wish to purchase an exemption by paying another, poorer man to go off and fight in his place. All this was somehow bound up with the political career that he hoped to pursue when the war was over. ("Since I was quite small I've had hopes of going into politics someday, Mr. Crichton. And I know folks are not going to vote for a man who was made to fight. Nor one who bought his way out of his duty.")

This coveted career was also the reason why he tried very hard to find a regiment that would allow him to enter it as an officer. ("Folks look up to a man who's been an officer, Mr. Crichton. Lot more than they do to some poor bummer.") Though he appeared to have no other qualifications for such a rank than a few afternoons of drill with the university cadet force, the climate of the times encouraged his hopes. Many new regiments were being formed to replace those decimated in the previous years' fighting, old regiments were seeking replacements for their threadbare ranks. One afternoon Bonney met an officer, a Captain Ames, sent home from a veteran Indiana regiment of the Army of the Potomac on a recruiting mission. From him, at last, Bonney received an offer close enough to his demands to persuade him to sign up: he would enter the regiment with the rank of corporal, and in return he had a promise that he would be nominated to fill the first vacancy for a lieutenant that occurred.

Bonney went off with hundreds of others to the training camps in Indianapolis; the captain who had recruited him set off back to his regiment. By the time Bonney caught up with his new comrades, several weeks and the battle of Gettysburg had intervened. The regiment had been heavily engaged in that memorable conflict, taking nearly forty percent casualties, including fifteen officers killed. One of whom was Captain Ames.

═

Arthur looked again at Bonney now. He wasn't quite certain whether it was a good thing, or the opposite, to find out that the man who appeared to have attracted Olivia's interest was such a bad lot after all. His behavior really was pretty distasteful. Though according to him he had waited a perfectly respectable amount of time before, as it were, claiming his prize. Three days at least he had delayed, until the moment, in fact, when he had realized that the several vacancies for lieutenants that had occurred in the regiment because of Gettysburg were being rapidly filled, and none of them so far had been offered to him. As per his agreement.

It must have been quite a sight, thought Arthur, this young cub standing forth in the midst of men still freshly shocked from battle, still mourning dead comrades, still perhaps, some of them, nursing wounds of their own, to claim his entitlement to a post of authority over them. He who had done nothing saying this to those who had risked all. Because of a bargain he claimed to have struck with an officer now dead. Unwitnessed by any man now living.

("You had nothing on paper?"

"No. It was just—Captain Ames made his offer. Saying it, you know. And I accepted it the same way. Was that wrong?"

"Always better to have it in writing. But an agreement doesn't have to be so to make it a contract. A handshake will suffice. Did you shake hands when you struck the bargain?"

"I . . . I don't remember. At some time, we may have shook hands, I guess.")

Of course what was most detestable about Bonney's performance was that he was not claiming the right to fill an officer's place because he wished to be foremost in the fight for the cause he now served, but only because he hoped by filling it to feather his nest in some way when the fighting was over. Arthur glanced again at the young man. What kind of a society was it where a fellow could say that he had wanted to be a politician "since he was quite small"? Outrageous.

In any case, Bonney's "deal" had got him nowhere in the end. He had persisted in arguing for it for weeks, had taken his case to each of the regiment's senior officers in turn. All of whom had showed what sounded to Arthur like exemplary patience in hearing out the importunate young man, and then in gently explaining that what he asked for was impossible to grant. Still, Bonney had persisted—and it had taken in the end actual threats of violence from his immediate comrades, the privates and corporals that surrounded him daily, to convince him to desist at last from his nagging demands.

"You must make him see reason," Olivia had begged when she came back into his room five minutes after Bonney had quit it. (She and the young man must have been talking out in the corridor. Or had he actually gone to her stateroom?) "I have told him that he did absolutely the right thing to leave that horrible country. And there will be no difficulty at all if he wishes to settle in England."

"But he has not asked me about any such matters, Olivia. It's a point of law—or justice, I suppose—about something that has happened to him—"

"He's bound to find suitable employment in Lancashire," Olivia carried on, as if he hadn't spoken. "He has been to the university, you know."

"So I gathered. But not finished his course of studies, I understand."

She had looked at him rather hard, as if detecting a skeptical note in what he had said. Luckily, the bell for service had rung just then, and for the moment there was no time left to discuss the affairs of Mr. Bonney.

=

"Glory be to the Father," the Reverend Stibbards was praying now. "And to the Son, and to the Holy Ghost. As it was in the beginning, is now, and ever shall be: world without end. Amen."

"Amen."

"I shall now read the second lesson," the captain announced confidently. "The Gospel according to St. Luke, chapter seven..."

Mrs. Stewart, standing on Arthur's other side, gave a loud, almost rapturous sigh at the news. It won her a suspicious stare from Miss Faversham. The captain opened his personal Bible, and cleared his throat. Bits of cracked leather sprayed from the old book's binding.

"Now when he came nigh to the gate of the city, behold, there was a dead man carried out, the only son of his mother, and she was a widow: and much people of the city came with her.

"And when the Lord saw her, he had compassion on her, and said unto her, Weep not.

"And he came and touched the bier: and they that bear him stood still. And he said, Young man, I say unto thee, Arise."

A sad though not unpleasing emotion was stealing through Arthur. The captain certainly read well, and Scotch was the very best accent, of course, for reading scriptural things. And these stories always had the effect of casting him back into his childhood. His father used to read them aloud of an evening by the fire. As a reader he hadn't been in the McDonough class, but he'd had a fair voice, and there was something of the orator, even the actor, in him that he got very few other chances to reveal. Of course the attitude toward these tales at that long-ago fireside had been entirely uncritical (his parents were devout Methodists of the New Connection). It was revealed truth, and that was it. It did not even need talking about. He had had to wait for Laura Brightwell to laugh him out of his remaining attachment to the old stories. Miraculous ones, like the one the captain was now telling, in particular roused her angry derision. "Conjuring tricks" she used to call them.

"And he that was dead sat up, and began to speak. And He delivered him to his mother."

He wished she was here. Wished suddenly, fervently that she was here. Standing at his side. Instead of Olivia? Yes. Perhaps. Yes, in spite of everything, he wished it was Laura who was next to him now. The bride of his youth. His youth.

When the little girl died, when Laura knew at last that she could never be a mother, she had wanted to throw herself back into her old work at the League. But it was too late. Three weeks after she returned to Newall's Buildings, it was over—the League had won. The Corn Laws were abolished in Parliament. And like the League's, Laura's usefulness was at an end.

He'd urged her to find new employment for her good mind and efficient habits. "You wish me to go back to the mill, Arthur? Or to seek employment in a haberdasher's shop, perhaps?" But by this time they had moved into the house at Ardwick, the first they'd ever owned. Obviously she could not both reign as mistress of that establishment— they employed a large domestic staff now—and set out to a place of work each morning. Was there then no good cause, no charity she could support and put her energies into? None that appealed to Laura.

His business career progressed; they got older, richer. The house in Ardwick gave way to a bigger one in Moss Side, and then a veritable mansion at Chorlton. Laura's inertia continued. If you were a man, Arthur mused sometimes. But I am not a man, Arthur, so there's an end on it. It was at the heart of her unhappiness, he thought. If she was a man, there were any amount of useful and practical occupations she could have taken up. As it was...Even as it was, Arthur argued, there were opportunities. There were women in Manchester, and Liverpool too, deeply engaged in work of intellectual and social value. I am not a bluestocking, Arthur, I don't wish to become one. Not a question of becoming a...

He came at last to see that there was only one thing she wanted, and that she could not have. It was her old position in the old building with the old League. It was as if she was some supremely fine-turned tool, of absolute worth in the function it was made for but utterly incapable of being adapted to any other. The only thing to do with it when its occupation was gone was throw it away. Which Laura had more or less done with herself for the rest of her life. And turned all her energy and rage against herself—and upon Arthur.

Once on a day of despair she had described herself as "a scrounger upon a money-grubber." Two birds with one stone, he'd congratulated her. Well done, my dear.

He had always nursed the hope that one day, like a ship finding its way at last out of a tempest, he and Laura would reach some peaceful place. Where all passions were exhausted, all disappointments had lost their sting. And they could be together, without much feeling, but in tranquillity. "Like two boulders sitting side by side?" she had scoffed when he had been unwise enough to mention this hope of his to her once. But the condition had not sounded so unpleasant to him, in comparison with what they had. He persisted in looking forward to it.

But she was dead at forty-four, a cancer in her breast. The illness had taken only five weeks to finish her. And nobody had touched her bier, nobody had raised her up. She had just died, and that was the end of her.

=

The congregation sang one more hymn—Arthur knew it well: Charles Wesley's "Lo! He comes, with clouds descending"—and remained standing while the Reverend Stibbards delivered the final invocation. Afterward the little knot of worshipers stayed largely in place, only the Charvets choosing to leave the saloon. There was an atmosphere in the room now, generated by the simple, singular service, of something homely, something fondly though not precisely remembered, which people were reluctant to leave. There was also the fact of the wretched weather on view through the windows, which offered no other alternative to the saloon than going below, solitary, to one's own cold and stuffy little cabin.

But it developed as the passengers stood talking that even more serious concerns had become attached to the weather. For several had been told by the ship's third officer (a gruesome old scalawag called Bennett) that to his ancient mariner's eye all the signs that he could read in the sky and on the ocean pointed to just one thing: hurricane.

The word skittered from one little group to another, creating its own miniature eddies of alarm and despondency wherever it landed. According to the diplomat Farrow, who had become friendly with the Charvets, the reason the devoted old couple had just left the saloon was that they wished to spend the last hours before the onset of the storm, and consequent breakup of the vessel, with no other company than each other. Somebody inevitably then brought up the *Pacific,* the steamer that had disappeared on a run between New York and Liverpool a few years ago, no trace of passengers or crew ever having been found. Somebody else mentioned the *Arctic,* which had also been lost about that time. There were survivors of that disaster, almost all of them belonging to the crew, for they had commandeered every lifeboat except one.

"Oh, the crew always see to their own safety first," someone said, and the group turned to cast bitter glances at the inoffensive stewards who were waiting for the company to disperse so they could begin laying covers for luncheon.

"But those boats were both of the Collins Line," the gentleman from Ontario, Mr. Harper, reminded them. "And remember Inman's motto: We've never lost a steamer nor a mail, nor even a passenger, except by his own fault."

"There's always a first time for everything," Farrow said.

"And what does 'except by his own fault' mean?" demanded Harris, querulously. "We're to be blamed for it if we get killed on this old tub, is that it?"

The atmosphere was calm and homely no longer but growing almost panicky, and at last even the captain could not remain unaware of it. When he understood what the problem was, he took charge of the situation immediately. To get the attention of the passengers, he tapped with his penknife on one of the cruet holders that hung suspended from the ceiling over the dining tables. As they turned toward him, several were already looking ashamed of the agitation they'd been feeling and spreading. They were ready to be reassured now, and the captain did it perfectly.

"Ladies and gentlemen, it has come to my notice there are rumors abroad that a hurricane is about to strike us. Please allow me to explain to you some facts about weather on the Atlantic—an ocean I have known since I was a boy aboard the old *Pelican,* chasing and boarding Yankee frigates from the Irish coast to Chesapeake Bay."

There were various wry grins and chuckles at that from the North Americans present, with the exception of the female member of a couple from Rhode Island, the Barlows, who, in a contradictory spirit, had chosen this day of unsettling weather to make their first appearance in the saloon.

"What is he talking about, Frederick? Is he a Rebel?"

"Hush, dear. I think it must be the 1812 War."

"The what?"

Having established his credentials as a sea dog, McDonough went on to give a calm and easy account of present conditions. There was no question of such a thing as a hurricane hovering anywhere in the neighborhood. The season for Atlantic hurricanes had long passed away, and whoever was spreading such rumors—"It was Bennett," called out several passengers meanly—well then, Mr. Bennett was merely indulging in a bit of old sailor's humor. Very reprehensible— he would be reprimanded—but in its way a tradition of the sea. "Putting the wind up the landlubbers," the captain chuckled. "We've all done it."

Almost all his hearers by now were willing to accept his assurances. And he won them over completely by what he said next. It was a bold stroke: "I must tell you, however, that there has indeed been a serious threat to us on this crossing." (Moans of alarm from the ladies and the Reverend Stibbards.) "That bit of warm weather at the beginning of the month, before we sailed from Boston? It affected the sea as much as the land. I was given reports in Halifax of icebergs seen considerably further south than usual for the time of year." (Shudder of fear from almost everyone this time, for all knew that the great ice mountains were the most dangerous foes to shipping on the ocean, worse than any tempest. It was said to have been an iceberg that had finished the *Pacific.*) "Consequently, I chose a Great Circle route more southerly than usual, to put us as far out of danger as I could. Yet have any of you noticed that we've been sailing on this rather uncommon course?" (General shaking of heads, smiles of relief.) "Naturally not, because it is my job, ladies and gentlemen, always to be looking ahead on your behalf, and to take appropriate actions having at all times your comfort and safety foremost in my thoughts. For instance, I do think present conditions indicate—not a *hurricane*, of course—but that we may be in for a spell, forty-eight hours of it perhaps, of choppy seas and moderate winds. I have given my orders, the sails have been shortened, and we should ride through this little blow with the greatest of ease."

Arthur was much impressed by the captain's performance. It made him feel that he might have misjudged the old man. Perhaps he had not exactly been a coward in the matter of the murderous major, just out of his depth. For a time McDonough was surrounded by a crowd of passengers, all eager to shake his hand or tell him how grateful they were. When this crowd had peeled away, Arthur went up and put out his own hand.

"Congratulations, Captain. You have wonderfully set our minds at rest."

McDonough was flustered, chuckling, really bemused by the reaction to his speech. Arthur guessed it had been some long time, if ever, since he had been the recipient of such universal praise.

"It was nothing, Mr. Crichton. Matter of sizing up the situation, and then taking it by the scruff of the neck."

"Well, I was most impressed."

"Were you, sir?" The captain was peering at him now in a hopeful, slightly furtive manner. "You were impressed by my conduct?"

"I said I was."

"Would you be prepared to make your opinion public?"

"In what way?"

"A letter perhaps. A few lines only. Addressed to the company's headquarters. I can't tell you how obliged I would be. Such a statement, coming from a passenger of your stature, would do much to counterbalance the false judgments and erroneous assertions of lesser individuals."

"Have there been any such?"

"One or two," the captain admitted. "Not every crossing of the *Laurentia* has been as smooth and uncomplicated as this one."

"I see," said Arthur thoughtfully. "Well, Captain, I shall try to remember that letter—"

"You're very kind."

"—for I certainly did admire your behavior just then."

"It was nothing; not for one with a lifetime's experience of—"

"It made me think of another difficulty onboard that could be, as you say, taken by the scruff of the neck, and resolved with equal firmness."

"What is it, Mr. Crichton? Just say the word. It shall be done."

"It is the Negro, Captain."

All the captain's delight and bonhomie died in his eyes as Arthur watched. It was almost a shame to have to do this to the old man.

"Ah, the Negro... well, I have explained that, Mr. Crichton. To-morrow, without fail—"

"Today would be better than tomorrow," Arthur said gently. "Far better. We have had our service, sung our hymns, there can be no question now of desecrating the Holy Day. Indeed, Captain, I can think of no more Christian deed that we could perform today than to release a fellow creature from an unjust imprisonment."

McDonough looked as if he could very easily think of half a dozen more Christian deeds than *that*. But before he could speak, Arthur broke in again.

"It is the kind of decent and resolute action that I should so much like to include in my letter to Inman, to back up my excellent opinion of you, Captain."

The captain stared up at him with a mixture of hope and fear that was almost pathetic, and Arthur was moved sufficiently by it—and also because he had genuinely been inspired by the way the old man had taken charge and settled the passengers' fears—that the next thing he said came from him almost without conscious thought.

"I have told the Negro he can count on my help. I mean to give it in as full a measure as I can. When the time comes, I shall be at your side, Captain. You may count on me."

Captain McDonough stared at him a few moments more, then, convulsively, he gripped Arthur's hand.

"We will do it, Mr. Crichton. By God, together *we will do it*!"

═

The captain's reassurances also seemed to have broken the spell that had kept the congregation riveted to the saloon, for when Arthur turned from the old man, he found the room to be almost deserted. Only his wife and John Bonney stood near the far doors, evidently waiting for him. As he walked toward them, he was unable to stifle the thought that they made a fine-looking couple. Olivia's face was flushed, eager. He couldn't remember when he'd last seen her looking so engaged and excited.

He put on a placid smile as he reached them. "I trust we all feel elevated by the captain's service? But who would have thought the old chap had such a gift for speaking the Scriptures? That tremendous growling Scotch—"

"Arthur, are you ready now?"

"Ready for what, my dear?"

"To give me your verdict, sir," the young man said.

Bonney's gaze was very serious, his jaw jutted and his mouth was tightly clenched. He looked like a schoolboy who expects a flogging but is determined not to cry. Arthur couldn't help but soften a little toward him. He agreed to talk to Bonney right away. When Olivia said she wanted to join the discussion, Bonney shook his head. "I would rather you didn't, Livvy," he said.

Livvy? Arthur was too shocked to object, to speak at all. *Livvy.* His own pet name. Not even her father and mother called her that.

Disappointed, Olivia took herself off. Still outraged, Arthur surveyed the young man. Who looked back at him in all innocence, evidently having no idea that he'd given offense.

Arthur took a deep breath. Started speaking, with difficulty: "Before we begin, Mr. Bonney—"

Bonney was staring at him curiously, and Arthur guessed suddenly that the words were coming out of his mouth like bullets. As if spoken by a murderer in a stage melodrama. He stopped, then started again, in a more measured fashion: "You see, I was planning to pay a call just now on a certain passenger. I have some good news to give him. Perhaps you wouldn't mind accompanying me?"

"Of course." And as they went through the doors: "Which passenger?"

"Mr. Stuart."

"I don't think I've met a Mr. Stuart," Bonney mused as they went down the first flight of stairs.

Shouldn't wonder if you hadn't met nine-tenths of your fellow passengers, Arthur thought of saying, for they are not generally to be encountered where you might see them, out on the waves, beyond the farthest point of the poop deck.

"Mr. Stuart is the black man. I want to tell him that he will be released tonight."

"Ah." Bonney came to a stop. They were at the foot of the stairs, and it was very gloomy down there. Arthur strained to see his expression.

"I have never paid a social call on a Negro before," Bonney said slowly. "Where I come from—you see, we're just across the river from a slave state and . . . my aunt, Miss Eunice Dix, in Frankfort, Kentucky, she owns a few slaves, and we always visited her every summer for a few weeks, and . . . well, like I say, to my knowledge I have never—"

Arthur's exasperation boiled over. "Well, there you are, Mr. Bonney. If your standards are too high to allow you to accompany me, then we must part—"

"I was about to say: I certainly do welcome this opportunity." There was hardly a trace of rebuke in Bonney's voice. "For I know that after the war there will have to be changes in the intercourse between the races, and it's best to get started on it early."

Arthur recognized that an apology was due from him, but then he thought how Bonney had so carelessly said "Livvy" and decided the tally was about even. He turned and walked on toward the farthest end of the corridor, the other following. He came to Stuart's door, knocked on it. No reply. Knocked on it again. No reply. Knocked a third time.

"Perhaps he is out?" Bonney hazarded.

Arthur glanced at him. Was the man a fool? He was raising his fist to knock again when they heard from beyond the door a shuffling footstep. Then the handle turned, the door opened a crack, Stuart looked out.

"Yes?"

"It is I, Mr. Stuart . . . Arthur Crichton?"

"Yes?"

"Yes." Already Arthur was fumbling for the words. He couldn't understand why the fellow wasn't opening his door wide, inviting them in. "This is Mr. Bonney. A countryman of yours."

Stuart's gaze drifted beyond Arthur, gave Bonney a brief inspection, returned to Arthur.

"I am rather busy just now, Mr. Crichton. Was there anything—?"

"I wondered if you had heard from the captain?"

"Not since yesterday. He told me that, for religious reasons, I am to be confined to my room another full day."

"Ah. I have just spoken to him. It has been decided to effect your release this evening after all."

Surely at this, he thought, the fellow would open his door to them. But he didn't. The gap remained at a few inches only. Stuart appeared to be thinking.

"That is good news," he said at last.

"Yes. I imagine you will be getting confirmation soon from McDonough. But I wanted you to know as soon as possible."

"I appreciate that, sir." The Negro sounded now genuinely grateful. "It is certainly courteous of you."

Arthur thought he had never held so long a conversation in which he had seen so slight a fraction of the person he was talking to.

"Well . . . think nothing of it."

"And now," Stuart went on, "as I *am* rather busy . . ."

"We won't detain you a moment longer," Arthur said rather stiffly, and watched as the other nodded, and then closed the door.

"What could he have to be busy about in there?" Bonney wondered as they walked back along the corridor.

"Who knows?" Arthur shrugged. He was actually quite hurt by their treatment at Stuart's hands. Particularly as he had not long since volunteered to risk his life on the fellow's behalf. In a manner of speaking.

=

On the other side of the door, Stuart stood waiting, listening to the receding footsteps. When they were gone, he turned and looked back into the cabin, at the woman who lay on her side upon his bunk.

"That Crichton fellow," he said, in response to an interrogative raise of her eyebrows. He came away from the door, went to the fire, held out his hands to warm them. "What do you reckon on him?"

"I've heard he's rich," said Mrs. Stewart. She was hugging a blanket to her. Underneath it, she was wearing only her shift.

"How rich?"

"Very."

A pause as Stuart thought this over. Mrs. Stewart was watching the Negro curiously. For a moment it seemed as if she would say something more, but then she shut her mouth. Stuart looked away from the fire then, studied her thoughtfully.

"He looks kind of sappy to me," he said. "Kind of a weakling."

"You do well to be careful there," she said. (They talked together easily, casually, as if they had known each other for years. In fact, it was the first time they had met. She had come down to his cabin after the service in response to a note that he had slid under her door during his permitted wanderings late last night.) "Many Englishmen have that look," she went on, "yet it may not be a true indication of what lies behind it."

A moment, then Stuart nodded.

"Thanks, I'll remember that."

They watched each other, both smiling faintly.

"Now where were we?" he murmured. "Before I got interrupted . . ."

For answer, she threw aside the blanket, sat up, leaned toward him. Her breasts, through the open top of her shift, hung heavy before his eyes. He came and sat beside her. Began unbuttoning his shirt. She stopped him, took over the task herself. He watched her as she worked, put out his hand, touched the creamy white of her cheek.

=

By then, on the top deck, near where Bonney had kept his long vigil, Arthur and the young man were deep in their discussion. The rain had ended. The sea was very flat. There was something odd about the sky—Arthur had remarked on it as they sat down—it was colored, at the limits of its circumference in every direction, by a hazy reddish tinge. It was eerie, Bonney agreed. Still, it offered no barrier to their sitting out-of-doors.

Arthur had not known quite how to begin. But he remembered a tactic that his master at the bar had urged on his pupils: "From the first you must absolve yourself of final responsibility. You are not wizards who can tell a man exactly what will be; if you pretend that you can, when you get things wrong, as you will, your authority—with your client, with your colleagues—will crumble away like dust."

He took a last look at the red blush on the horizon; it seemed to be spreading even farther toward the center. "Mr. Bonney," he began then, turning back to the young man, "you know that I am not a judge who can decide a case at issue; I was once a barrister, and all I could do in that office was to advise a client whether or not I thought he might have a case in law. You mustn't therefore take anything I say as final; it is only a suggestion."

Bonney nodded. His eyes were sunk deep in their sockets; they gleamed at Arthur with longing and apprehension.

"Very well. So, I have tried to decide whether or not you did make a contract, valid in law, when you came to your agreement with Captain Ames. By the way, please remember that I am really only familiar with the statutes and cases that are to be found in English law. American precedents are outside my competence."

"English law will be fine by me."

"It is the basis of your system." Arthur nodded. He smiled. "As the gallant Major Cutler will be happy to assure you. And courts in both countries," he hurried on, as Bonney stared at him in perplexity, "are used to referring to each other's decisions. Well, then, Mr. Bonney, as far as I can understand it, you did make a contract with Ames."

An exultant sigh escaped from the other.

"In return for his promise that you would have the first vacancy for lieutenant, you offered a consideration in agreeing to choose his regiment to enlist in and shunning all others. Thus a contract was established. But was it a legal contract? Could such an item as a military commission rightfully be offered in return for consideration? Well, you tell me that in your country it can, and it is an established principle of English law that a contract may be deemed to incorporate any relevant custom of the market, trade, or locality in which it is made. *Hutton versus Warren* is the precedent you want. What it means is that if, say, in a particular locality it is the custom that the word *dozen* is taken to refer to the number fourteen rather than to twelve, then if a man contracts there to buy a dozen bushels of wheat, he is entitled to require delivery of the full fourteen."

"Is there anywhere on earth where a dozen means fourteen?" Bonney asked, mystified.

"I don't believe so. But you see the principle, Mr. Bonney?"

Bonney nodded. He looked up. A grin was beginning to show at last on his lips, lighting up his troubled features.

"Then I was right. I was right to do what I did. For I had a contract, and I was cheated on it."

"Not necessarily. For we move on to consider the difficult question of whether the extinction of one of the principal parties to the contract does or does not render said contract null and void."

"Ames's death?"

"Precisely. Do you know *Hall versus Wright*? No, why should you? Interesting case. About five, six years ago. Breach of promise: the young lady sued the gentleman for failing to keep his end of the contract to marry her. His argument was that he was a very sick man and marriage, and especially the performance of his marital duties, would most probably tip him over the edge." ("Roger himself through the Pearly Gates," as a lawyer friend had put it to Arthur in a coffeehouse near the Manchester 'Change. "Lucky bastard.") "I can't remember the exact deposition of the case, but the principle was established that if a contract can be performed only by the promisor in person, it is subject to the implied condition that he shall be alive to perform it. I've been wondering if this is a precedent that is useful to us. I can't quite make up my mind."

Another sigh from Bonney, this one, Arthur guessed, more of exasperation. He had better make it short. It was clear the young man did not share his own enjoyment of these nice calculations and hypotheses. Of course, he had rather more depending on the result.

"There are other interesting precedents. *Taylor versus Caldwell*, for instance…But the fundamental question is, I think, was Captain Ames acting purely on his own responsibility—in which case his death extinguished all claims you might have—or was he fulfilling the function of an agent to the true principal of the agreement? And if he was an agent, who was the principal? And can he be bound to fulfill the contract?"

He saw that Bonney was in a fog.

"In other words, could you bring an action for nonperformance against...well, your regiment—or your army—or even your government—as being the true principals in the contract?"

"Could I, Mr. Crichton?" Bonney's eyes were imploring him.

=

The devil you could, Arthur thought. The young man was really talking about a suit directed at the heart of his nation's government. Arthur did not exactly know what were the powers of the executive in American courts to dodge and duck and evade litigation, but he expected they were formidable. Certainly in the English courts the ability of the Crown to throw up a smoke screen of exceptions and immunities was almost limitless. Crown agents could wear down an individual, his stamina and his purse, with ease. The private litigant thought in terms of months, years if he was feeling gloomy. The Crown took a longer view. It was content to watch a case amble its way through the best part of a decade. Arthur knew there were suits in which the Crown was the defendant that were not expected to be settled in the present century, and were bound to ruin all the parties involved—except the Crown. And the lawyers.

As a professional barrister, he would never have recommended a suit against government unless the certainty of success was almost absolute. Which was hardly the case here. On the other hand, he was not a barrister, and there would be no actual legal consequences to whatever he might recommend. And, as irritated as he still felt with Bonney's oafish behavior—"Livvy," for God's sake—he supposed it would be a mean thing to unnecessarily add to his trouble. Tempting though.

"Well, Mr. Bonney." He chose the words carefully. "It would certainly be interesting to see the issue tried before a judge."

"I have a case?" breathed Bonney.

"Well, I suppose you may."

The young man got up, stepped toward the rail. Stood there as he had done so often and for so long before, staring out at sea. Arthur watched him for a while. Then looked up at the sky. The redness he had seen before seemed not to have spread much farther than since he'd last looked. Only a few trails of it could be glimpsed from where

he sat. There seemed to be no wind at all. He looked up at the sails to
see if they were stirring. There appeared to be as full a complement
of them as usual. If the captain really had given orders to shorten sail,
it looked as if nobody had bothered to carry them out. Arthur
breathed in deeply. It was curious. They were out so far on the ocean,
where the air must be purer and freer than anywhere else on earth.
Yet the atmosphere seemed close, hard to breathe. Airless. He felt uncomfortable now in the heavy overcoat he had put on to come outside. He thought of taking it off.

He heard a sound. Looked up toward Bonney. He was bowed over
the rail. Another sound. Lord, he is crying, Arthur thought, rather
horrified. Again the noise. As if it were wrenched from the young
man's body. It sounded not so much like a sob this time though. But
before Arthur could exactly locate it, Bonney gave him the answer by
massively vomiting over the rail.

"Ah, God" came a hollow groan. And then another enormous up-
rushing. Arthur was on his feet. And then, having got up, was uncertain how to proceed. From his recent memories of his own similar
predicament, he knew that the last thing he would have wanted was an
observer to his miseries. On the other hand, just to walk away from
Bonney in this crisis did not seem right. Bonney groaned again, then
spat thickly. He straightened up, so that he was still clutching the rail
but no longer hanging over it.

Arthur took a handkerchief from his pocket. He guessed Bonney
would not have one on him; he knew from experience with Olivia that
it was the sort of humble but necessary article that young people
often neglected to carry. He came up behind Bonney. Wordlessly offered him the handkerchief. Bonney grabbed it, wiped it across his
mouth. Attempted to give it back. Arthur declined it.

"Poor fellow," he said. He helped the young man back to the seat.
"But it's late in the voyage to get the seasickness. I wonder if it wasn't
something you've eaten. I have always regarded those pickles that appear at every meal with suspicion. They have a peculiarly bright
shade of green that I've never encountered before. But can one become ill from eating pickles?"

He was talking away mainly to allow Bonney to compose himself.
But a quick glance into the young man's eyes showed that he was

pretty well along that course. Though still sunk deep in their sockets, they seemed clear and calm. It was a remarkable transformation.

"How do you feel?" he asked curiously.

"Very well." Then, as if he had been checking himself carefully, "I feel relieved."

They sat in silence. Arthur was thinking: I have given my advice. I have seen him through his little crisis. I can now get up and walk away and that's an end to it. And whenever I see him from now on till we reach England, a nod and a How d'you do? will be quite sufficient. And I shall ask Olivia to observe the same restraint. The Crichtons have done quite enough for this particular young man.

He said, "You know, Mr. Bonney, I remember a somewhat similar case from when I was in practice. A client came to me with a story. It mattered a great deal to him, that was obvious. Something or other, I can't remember what, some injustice that had been done to him. It had been churning around and around in his mind for months. He told me what it was. We talked about it, I gave my advice. And then, it was rather like what just happened to you. Not vomiting though. The man's nose began to bleed. Most copiously. He said it had never happened to him before. Lord, how he bled. Quite a lot over my carpet unfortunately. It was the getting out of his story. Seemed to release him. Then, when he had recovered, he told me what was really troubling him. Which was something quite different from what he'd been talking about before. The other story, you see, the first story, that was just to hide his true concerns. Without him really knowing that he was doing it."

The young man did not look at him. He seemed to be thinking, and then he spoke, so quietly that Arthur could hardly hear him: "You think that I have another story?"

Arthur sighed. "I think," he began carefully, "that a man doesn't stand by a rail, as you have done, hour after hour, and day after day, staring back at what he has left behind with such longing—because of a contract."

Bonney's head was bent over, his chin lowered to his chest. He stared down at the deck. Shook his head once. Then was still again.

"You have guessed what I am," he said. "A deserter..."

"All I have guessed is that you are certainly a good and brave soldier."

Bonney looked up. "Why would you say that?"

"Well…" Arthur thought about it. "After such a start in the army as you described to me, to attain the rank of sergeant must mean you have performed your duties gallantly since then."

"I attained that rank mainly because the other candidates were dead or wounded out of the service."

"But you have been in battle?"

"Oh, yes… The Wilderness. Spotsylvania. The North Anna. Cold Harbor. Petersburg…."

=

The last engagement Bonney fought in had occurred a few days before Christmas. It had been a muddled, toing-and-froing affair, fought south of the city of Petersburg, as the Federals attempted to move closer to one of the few roads still open to General Lee that connected his lines with the areas of Southern Virginia and North Carolina from whence he drew his supplies. Bonney's regiment was in the van of the Federal movement and had made good ground against a weak defense, until a large Confederate reinforcement drove them back almost as fast as they'd advanced. So briskly were they forced out of their leading positions that it wasn't possible to retrieve all those on their side who had fallen. Among these was a friend of Bonney's. In fact, there would have been just time to retrieve his body and carry it back, except it was strewn all over the frosty ground. Bonney's friend had stopped with three other soldiers to fire parting shots at the pursuers. A shell had landed in their midst, and when the smoke cleared it was no longer possible to say which bit of humanity on display had belonged to which particular human being.

("Mr. Bonney, please, a little less graphic if you don't mind—unless you want me to take your old place at the rail and offer *my* contribution to the ocean."

"I'm sorry. But we were all so struck by what had happened. Many times we'd seen a shell take off a fellow's arm or leg or head even, but that particular effect—none of us had seen *that* before. It was remarkably interesting. And yet I had loved poor Harry Langford like a brother.")

The regiment returned to its camp with the rest of the corps. The calm that had existed before the expedition against the Rebels returned, which meant the days were punctuated only by occasional far-off artillery fire or the rare crack of a sharpshooter's rifle. Bonney felt very low. The excitement and tension of battle no longer protected him. He felt flat, sad; in particular he mourned Langford, who had been his closest friend in the regiment. He went about his duties without enthusiasm. At night he lay on his bunk in the wooden shack that had been home all winter long, listening to the wind and rain beat upon the roof. He stopped speaking except when, militarily, he absolutely had to. His gloom began to infect other members of his company, most of them new men, conscripts. Because they were still unsure of themselves, the attitude of their sergeant, who could hardly bring himself to talk to them, undermined them considerably. Also they generally liked Bonney, and were concerned for him. A couple of them spoke to the lieutenant, who had a talk with Bonney and, as a result, recommended to his superiors that the sergeant be given leave. And, in view of Bonney's good record since that early bother about his rank, and of the fact that he hadn't received a furlough since he'd joined the regiment, leave was granted—a full thirty days to allow him to get to Indiana and back, and have a good rest at home in between.

("But I didn't go home. I meant to, even wired my father I was coming. But when I got to Washington, I changed my mind. Sent another wire home to say my leave was canceled. And I got the railroad warrant changed to Boston."

"Boston?"

"Harry Langford was from Massachusetts originally. He went out West after he'd finished college, to make his fortune. But his people still lived back East. He'd talked of them often, and I knew he'd written them about me. I thought to go see them. Tell them what a friend he had been to me. And how he'd died."

"Smashed to smithereens by a cannonball?"

"No. Not that. I would have lied. But I wanted to tell them I was sorry I couldn't get hold of his body to send him back home.")

But when Bonney arrived in Boston, he did not immediately arrange to go on to the little town twenty miles distant where Langford's family lived. He had a considerable sum in back pay on him, also some money his father had sent him at Christmas that he'd not had the chance to spend. He took a room in a small hotel where they did not seem to mind his uniform and set out to walk about the city. He was stopped three times within half a mile by army provosts wanting to see his papers. He resolved to get out of the uniform and found an outfitters where he bought off the rack a suit of civilian clothes, and shirts, cravat, boots, a hat. In another shop he bought a carpetbag, into which he bundled his uniform. He deposited the bag back in his room, and then set out again to see the city.

All that day he walked about, untroubled by army busybodies, looking at the houses and the shops and the office buildings and the monuments with which Boston is so well supplied. And at the people, above all at the people. He thought he had never seen such carefree folk. Walking about their city with such confidence. Not ducking and running and hiding, not anticipating that the next second a shell would fall out of their clear Boston sky and smash them all to kingdom come. And the ladies. Bonney had forgotten about the ladies. He couldn't keep himself from staring at them as they walked by, and he got many annoyed frowns and tosses of the head in return. Though one or two returned his stares frankly and loitered near him, waiting for him to approach. But they were disappointed. For now he only wanted to look and pass on.

For two full days he walked about the city, and then past the city limits into the countryside and the small surrounding towns. He had left the bitter winter behind in Virginia, here it had grown suddenly warm. The sky was a gentle blue. He could imagine spring not far away. It seemed to him he had woken as if from a terrifying dream. All that had happened to him in the past eighteen months, up to and including Harry Langford's death, was revealed to him as abnormal, mad, grotesque. *This* was normality, this calm sky and these peaceful folk walking about beneath it, pursuing their everyday occupations. What he had been living in—it was making him more and more angry to think of that.

He had pictures in his mind that horrified him. That he had not thought of since the events they described had happened. He remembered men, friends of his, screaming as they burned to death in the Wilderness. He remembered at another battle the butt of the rifle he was holding descending on a man's head and the bone and brains spattering all over himself. He remembered after Cold Harbor when some men of another regiment caught an enemy picket and, in some sort of twisted retaliation for the massacre the army had just endured, hung the Rebel by his feet from a tree. They used him for target practice for a while, then cut him down still living and bayoneted him over and over again; finally they dragged him to a corduroy road, placed him between the stumps, and watched until the wagons that rolled along the road had turned the body to a pulp. Bonney had taken no part in this, but he had witnessed it. And he had not objected.

=

In the early morning of his third day, he was walking out beyond the city limits in the direction of Cambridge. He found himself by the river, which the warm spell had rendered mostly free from ice. Some college boys had brought a couple of rowing boats and were racing with them. The boats had to keep dodging remaining chunks of river ice as they raced, and between the dodging and the racing the effect was fairly ludicrous. The rowers could hardly maintain their stroke for laughing. Along the bank other boys were trotting to keep up with the boats and shouting mock encouragements at their friends. Bonney lingered for a while, watching the fun. It occurred to him that behind the charade of what he had been back in Virginia—sergeant in a mighty army, veteran of major battles—was a far more real self: a college boy, with his senior year still to come. It could as well be him out there on the river or running along the bank; he could be just as happy and heedless as they.

As he thought this, the pleasure with which he had begun watching the college boys darkened. He turned away from the riverbank. He started back toward the city. Why me? he was thinking. Why did it have to be me? Those boys back there were his age, and as healthy as he, and as fit to carry a rifle. Yet they were playing on the river, and he was trying to nerve himself to face a dead man's family—the mother, father, young sisters of a friend whose body had exploded like a cascade before his eyes. He would do this. And then in a little while he would go back to the place where such things had happened. And would happen over and over. Until, certainly, it happened one day to himself. When it would be his body lying on the grass, brains leaking, face smashed, or else in his belly the gut wound from which no one recovered. Grave dug by evening. His corpse laid in it. Earth falling on his face. Inevitable.

He did not for a moment blame the boys he had seen on the river for keeping themselves prudently away from such mischances. He admired them for it, he wanted to be like them—safe, and with no horrors feeding on his mind. But he was not.

Why me? Why me? All morning he walked, now back in the city, now taking a ferry to some destination and then walking again, all the while churning over the same question. If there had to be a war, it was clear that someone had to fight it. But it was just as clear, as he looked into the faces of those he passed by, that so many who could have taken up the burden had decided that those someones need not be their own precious selves. And he could have chosen to be just like them. Even if he had been drafted, three hundred dollars would have bought him an exemption. No great sum at all—he had almost three hundred dollars on him now. But what was the use? It was too late to spend it on something so necessary as preserving his life. He had not even waited to be drafted. No, he had hurled himself willingly into the charnel house, he had *volunteered* to be killed.

He stood there, directly in front of a building, churning and churning. People had to step around him, they looked at him curiously. His lips were moving, and several stopped, thinking he was addressing them. But no words came from his mouth, and the people shrugged and moved on. After a while Bonney shook his head, and his anguished self-questioning died back a little. He looked up. Found that the building he was standing before housed a passenger shipping company. Inman. A British line. Quite a famous one, he had heard of it even back in Indiana. Now he noticed a tang of salt on the air he breathed. He guessed he had come out to the east side of town and was somewhere near the wharves. There was a notice chalked on the blackboard that hung beside Inman's door. He stepped up to read it.

THIS AFTERNOON THE PADDLE STEAMER *LAURENTIA*
WILL SAIL FOR HALIFAX AND LIVERPOOL AT 4 O'CLOCK.
BERTHS AVAILABLE IN FIRST AND SECOND CLASSES.
A FAST CROSSING AND EVERY COMFORT WHILE ONBOARD.

━━

"And so—here you are."

"Dammit, I didn't mean to—" Bonney shook his head, as if still baffled by what had happened. "It seemed—just a great joke. A sort of... *wonder.* The idea that, by putting one foot in front of the other, I could walk up a gangway, step onboard a ship, and it would sail away from the land, and I would be on it, and everything—the army, Virginia—it would all just... *vanish.*"

He put a hand to his head, was speechless. Arthur watched him, then looked away. He was glad now he hadn't taken off his coat. Though the atmosphere was still close and airless, sitting in one place for so long had chilled him. He felt sleepy as well as cold, wanted to yawn, but refrained so as not to hurt the young man's feelings. He listened to the clanking of the paddle wheels for a while, then even above them heard his stomach growl angrily. Thoughts of the luncheon spread out in the saloon below returned to him; he wondered if they would have any of the roasted jacket potatoes that he liked. Nothing better to take a chill away.

"A fast crossing and every comfort while onboard." Damn cheek that "fast crossing." Actionable? Probably not.

"You thought it was a joke?" he prompted at last when the young man still showed no signs of returning to his story of his own accord. Bonney looked up at him sharply, as if surprised to find him there. Then collected himself, nodded.

"Yes. A joke. And yet I did everything that was necessary to make it real. I bought my passage. I just had time to get a cab back to the hotel to collect my baggage. Another cab to the wharf. I was sure someone would stop me, it couldn't be this easy. I think I wanted someone to stop me—I'm not sure. There was a troop carrier a couple of berths away from Inman's. Hundreds of men going onboard, officers and noncommissioned walking all around as I got out of the cab. They looked at me with hardly any curiosity at all. I was just another civilian. Going about my business. And so I walked up the gangway."

"And have regretted it ever since?"

Bonney was silent.

"Which is why you spent so much time at that rail, looking back at the mistake you made?"

"I have stopped doing that."

"Regretting it?"

"What is the use?" Bonney said stubbornly. "I must look to the future now."

"Indeed."

"England," said Bonney with little enthusiasm. "I shall need to get work, I suppose."

"Mm. My wife said that might be the case. Well, it shouldn't be difficult, an educated man such as yourself. Perhaps I will be able to help there. Of course, my contacts are almost exclusively in the cotton trade, and I don't know if that line of business will suit you."

But Bonney wasn't listening. He had hunched himself forward in his seat, his elbows resting on his knees, his hands clasped together. He was staring at the deck. Arthur thought of what he might say next, and then, suddenly, decided that he would say nothing. He had an instinct that they were dropping to another, deeper level in the young man's odyssey.

"I can never go home," Bonney muttered at last. "After what I have done."

"You know," Arthur said quietly, "time is kind. It covers up everything. In a few years, you'll find, people forget. Even the law forgets."

"My father won't. Until the day he dies, he won't forget."

"But didn't he want to keep you out of the army?"

"He did. But since I chose to go in, since I swore an oath to serve..." Bonney shook his head. "He will never forget." He was silent for a while, then: "What I was doing when I was standing at that rail was trying to make up my mind to throw myself overboard."

Arthur remembered suddenly his first sighting of the young man. How he had seemed for a moment to be trying to do just that—climb up on the rail and launch himself at the sea. Olivia had wanted to run and save him. He'd had to hold her back.

"I did not have the courage even to do that."

"Now, sir," Arthur said sharply, "there is no need for that. Your courage is not in question. It has been called upon too many times, that is all."

Bonney gave him a grateful glance, which for a moment succeeded in lightening the gloomy cast of his features. But it was a moment only, and soon he was again staring unhappily at the deck. And Arthur knew he had not really been cheered at all by anything he had heard. The fact of his desertion lay upon him so heavily that he could not contemplate any future. The past was crushing him so. Arthur guessed it was like murdering someone in a dream. Only the act of waking and of finding that it had never really happened brought relief.

And this was the strategy Arthur had been contemplating almost before Bonney was through with his story. If the reality was so terrible, best to turn it into a dream.

"You know, Bonney," he began, "Inman operates boats that sail both ways upon this ocean." The young man looked up, stared at him, puzzled. "West as well as east. And not just Inman. Cunard, of course. The Allan Line. Must be others." Still Bonney looked confused. It was as Arthur had suspected. The thought had never crossed his mind. He had taken this great, fatal step, and could not see that there was any way to deal with it except by plowing on and on in the same desperate furrow.

"When did your thirty days' leave begin?"

"February ninth."

"Very well. You must be back with your regiment by around—is this a leap year?—around March tenth? Eleventh? We should dock at Liverpool on the morning of the twenty-sixth of February. Boats of one company or another are leaving for Boston and New York every day of the week. And few of them are as slow as this old villain. Ten days to Boston is quite common now. Eleven to New York. Say you got a passage on a good, fast ship that was leaving on the twenty-sixth. Or the twenty-seventh, say. With luck you would be back in New York on...the eighth? Ninth? Would that give you time to be with your regiment by the tenth? Or even, were you to be a day or two late, would that matter so much?"

The young man's expression was at first uncomprehending, then interested. Then his face was like a sunburst. He beamed at Arthur, he shone, he was far too excited to speak.

"What do you say, Mr. Bonney? Shall we shrink this matter to its true proportions? An ocean voyage to recruit your health after arduous campaigning. Better! Two ocean voyages. You will return to your comrades fit as a fiddle. Won't they envy you? And *nobody will know a thing.*"

=

Most of the dishes had been cleared away by the time Arthur was able to get to the saloon. But there was no problem about having a plate of roast beef and jacket potatoes quickly put together, and a glass of beer to wash it down. Gratefully he accepted them from the hands of the steward, and then turned around to choose a table. He was not sorry to see that one of them was still occupied: the diplomat Farrow and Harper the Canadian were sharing a bottle of wine. Nor that, seeing him looking their way, they waved to him to join them. The interview with Bonney had stimulated him. For once, he felt like company. He had thought simply to eat whatever he could as fast as possible, and then go to look for Olivia. But really a sit-down and a chat with a couple of fellows who he didn't know very well but who seemed reasonably congenial appeared a much more inviting prospect just for the present.

Farrow, once he'd got through the diplomat's obligatory bag of tricks—the little knowing smiles, the constant hinting at possession of vast stores of secret and earth-shattering information, the self-important silences—proved to be an interesting conversationalist. He made it a point early on to tell the others that his career in the service had been obstructed by lack of political and family connection, saying this, Arthur could only suppose, to forestall the rise of any questions in his hearer's mind as to why at his age—he was about forty-five or fifty—he had got no further than a vice consulship in the Boston office. Horrible it must be, Arthur thought, to have to begin every dialogue with a stranger on an apology. But before long he had forgotten that, becoming interested in what the man was saying. Farrow thought that Britain had lost a magnificent opportunity in failing to take advantage of the civil war in America to cut the United States down to size by siding with its opponent. Arthur had known such sentiments expressed before, of course, in both private conversations and in the newspapers, though there the desire to see the American Union dismembered was commonly disguised with appeals to morality, Christianity, and the need to stop the "useless effusion of blood." But he had never listened to them from an "official" source before, nor heard them expressed with such force and anxiety. Farrow appeared quite distraught at the consequences he expected from this lost chance.

"It will never come again," he kept saying.

He had traveled extensively through America, both before the war and since, and was hugely impressed—oppressed rather—by the size of the country in actuality, even more by the vastness of its potential. He believed that even in those quarters where such things ought to be known—his superiors in the service, their political masters—there was no real conception of what Great Britain would be dealing with a few decades hence.

"A nation of fifty million, then soon perhaps a hundred million. A continent of staggering resources united under a single political control—it will be irresistible. Forty, fifty years from now, there will be nothing for us to do but submit and obey. Our only diplomatic option will be to ingratiate ourselves with the Americans at every turn."

"Well, now, stop just there," Harper broke in impatiently. "For a start it ain't a whole continent, just a half of it, if you don't mind. And we in Ontario have beaten those damn fellows to the south every time they've tried to grab a piece of us." (Farrow and Arthur exchanged quick, condescending smiles at the Canadian's rude fervor.) "And you'll see. If they should threaten Old England one day, the Empire'll rally round, don't you fear."

"And after all, Mr. Farrow," Arthur said, "why should the Americans threaten us, however great they become?"

"Because they hate us" came the quick reply. "Oh, yes, I am convinced of that."

"I have never been so kindly treated by strangers as in the past few months," Arthur protested.

"Oh, individually, man to man, they are most friendly. And I believe genuinely so. But collectively—trust me, sir, they hate us. They want to see us finished. They want to supplant us. They mean to do it."

It was just the kind of argument Arthur most enjoyed: serious, informed, long ranging, and without an end in sight, for onboard ship nobody had anywhere to go or anything really to do except wait for the next huge feast to appear. They could sit here all day if they wanted, thrashing out any and every question. He had enjoyed several prolonged debates aboard the *Persia:* on the French threat, on the Bishop Colenso affair, on the advantage to Great Britain of becoming a republic. He had despaired of finding any such on this ship, with its curiously unsettled society, in which all questions asked seemed to pose some very direct threat: Shall the Negro be allowed upstairs? Is there to be a hurricane? Are the crew to be trusted? It was important for the success of these disputes that there should be no serious personal investment in their outcome. A debate on what international relations would be like in fifty years' time, when all present would be dead, matched the criterion perfectly.

Some of his present enjoyment too, he knew, was because of the feeling of satisfaction he had taken away from his interview with John Bonney. Reviewing his performance, he did not see really how it could be faulted. The skills he had developed so long ago when he had practiced his profession had not yet quite deserted him. He smiled to himself as he half-listened to some more imperialist bombast from Harper. He had behaved toward his client with careful moderation, not encouraging his hopes too high, but not reinforcing the worst of his fears. In the end he had shown him that he might take a path that would lead him away from extreme solutions—suicide, lifelong exile—and yet would restore to him all he believed he had lost.

Whether Bonney would in the end take that path was something which he suspected was still not settled. Of course, when he had left him, the young man had been certain that this was what he wanted to do, and his first intention, he'd resolutely announced, was to hunt up the purser—*was* there a purser on this boat? Arthur wondered suddenly; he didn't believe he'd met him—and obtain from him a list of Inman's and, if possible, other companies' westward sailings. However, there was time enough left on this present voyage, Arthur guessed, for Bonney to recognize the fact that while returning to America might restore his honor to him, it would also place him squarely back in the predicament he had fled from. Whether in the end the fear of dishonor would outweigh the fear of death—well, Arthur looked forward to finding out the result of that debate.

Meanwhile, in the present one, Farrow was saying something that Arthur just could not accept. He shook his head impatiently, waited for his moment to jump in and put forth his own argument. He could see that Harper too was waiting his chance. He would have to get in very quickly. Farrow was evidently winding down. Arthur leaned forward, opened his mouth to speak.

"Oh, Arthur—how could you do anything so *vile?*"

═

It was astonishing. One moment he was sitting around a table with a couple of congenial fellows setting the world to rights. The next there was a blur of movement, and he found himself staring directly into the bitterly disapproving eyes of his young wife. And of the congenial fellows there was no sign at all.

"How *could* you, Arthur?" she repeated, shaking her head slowly from side to side. "Oh, how could you be so cruel?"

A steward arrived at the table at that moment and, with his eyes, inquired if Arthur had finished with his meal. Arthur nodded and waited in silence for the plate to be taken away. He expected Olivia at least to do the same. But she did not.

"I did not imagine that you were capable of such—"

"Be *quiet.*"

Reluctantly, she closed her mouth. At last the man left them. She started to speak again, but now, rising, he said, "Please sit down, Olivia. And tell me what you are talking about. And don't speak so loud."

"Speak!" she cried disdainfully. "Loud!"

"Don't be ridiculous. What is the matter with you?"

She sat. She stared at him, distraught. "I have come from John. I know what you have done. He is so grateful to you, poor boy. But I know, Arthur. I know."

"What do you know, Olivia?" he humored her.

"He is returning to America, he is going back to the war—"

"I know he says that now. But I shouldn't wonder—"

"—where he will be killed."

"There's no special reason to think that will happen. Of course he will have to take his chances with thousands of other young—"

"You sent him back because you hate him. Because you hate all the young men who are my friends."

The clink of cutlery behind Arthur reminded him that they were not alone. He got up and went to his wife's side. Put his hand on her arm, drew her up.

"We will talk about this outside."

"I want to talk about it *here*. Now!... You are *hurting* me, Arthur!"

Glancing back once at the steward, who was polishing spoons with unusual concentration, Arthur moved her, still protesting loudly, across the saloon and beyond the swinging doors. In the little corridor outside, they turned on each other. "Have you gone mad?" "Not mad enough not to know what you are doing—" "I am doing nothing. I have done nothing." "John told me—"

"Stop *calling* him that."

Out of breath, they glared at each other through the gloom.

"Stop calling him that," he said again. "It is disrespectful to me."

"Disrespectful!"

"Yes. It is."

She shook her head once more.

"It's you that is guilty. How dare you accuse me?"

"What am I guilty of, Olivia?"

"Did you not tell—*Mr. Bonney*—that he should go back to America?"

"I pointed out to him that if he did not wish to accept the consequences of his desertion, then he might reverse the process. Yes, by sailing home."

"But I wanted him to stay in England." Her anger seemed suddenly gone. A long, dismal sigh escaped her. "I wanted him to be our friend,

Arthur. And we would help him. We would see that he was established in some good place of business. And he would come and visit us on the weekends…"

Her voice trailed away. In the corridor's shadows, she looked so grief-stricken. He wanted to comfort her, but he didn't know whether she was ready for that. Before he could make up his mind, she turned away from him, and went out through the door that led onto the deck.

After a moment he followed her out. She had gone no farther than the railing that lined the vessel's side opposite the door. He approached her slowly. It was raining again, but very lightly. He wondered if he should mention it, warn her about it. She caught cold easily.

"My dear," he said at last. "We can't just organize other people's lives to suit our wishes—"

"Oh, but you have," she said spitefully. "You have organized his life, thoroughly. Haven't you, Arthur? You are sending him back to his death. Because you are jealous. Like that horrible man in the Bible, whoever he was."

Silence, and then he couldn't help saying, "It was King David. He sent Uriah the Hittite—"

"I don't *care*," she shouted.

They were silent again for several moments.

"Why would I be jealous?" he muttered then.

"You are always jealous. Of any young man. That's why you took me away from Manchester before Christmas. You didn't want to see me at the parties and dances. You remembered last year—"

"Are you referring to the time you drank too much punch at the Ashworths' ball and made an exhibition of yourself?"

She gasped at that, and he felt a twinge of shame. Still, he steadied himself to stare back at her. She set her head proudly.

"I'm referring," she said, "to all the times when I was happy. When I was enjoying myself with my friends—"

"Curious how so many of your friends seem to be unattached men of no great age."

"There," she cried out triumphantly. "You *are* jealous. You admit it!"

It had been a blunder to say that, he knew it. He turned from her, angry with himself. She followed him, staring up into his eyes, making him look at her.

"Jealous. And that's why you took me away and put me in a horrible little town in America. With your tedious old sister—"

"Olivia, stop this—"

"And when there was a chance of letting me escape it for just a few days, when you went to New York, you would not take me. You wouldn't *take* me, Arthur. You left me in that horrible town. With a horrible ladies' seminary full of big, ugly American girls. And old people shuffling about everywhere. But no young men. I didn't see one in all the time—"

"Perhaps because they were away serving with the army. Did that ever occur to you?"

"I don't care what they were doing. They weren't—"

"Or did it occur to you that perhaps they were already dead?"

"*Dead.* Like you want poor Mr. Bonney to be—"

"And finally, does it by any chance occur to you that it's the least bit disgraceful for a married woman to be bawling out hungrily for young men like you are doing?"

She stopped at that. Seemed uncertain for the moment. "I don't mean that exactly." Stopped again. Shrugged. Then, defiantly: "I like young men, that's all."

"Then why didn't you marry one?"

She dropped her gaze. "You know why, Arthur. You were ... importunate."

"Oh, I was? Really?"

"And I ... I was flattered—"

"I gave you every chance, Olivia. Again and again I asked you to reflect, to consider whether you really wished to connect yourself with a man of ... of my age. And every time you said you did."

"I was under such compulsion," she sighed.

"Not from me," he said bitterly. "And it was unknown to me that you were in that plight. I wish I had known. Perhaps I could have found some other way to help. But I didn't know. Not until your father came to me and presented his bill. How long after the wedding was that? Two days? Did he wait that long?"

"Arthur," she said. She had begun to look frightened. "Don't say this. It's not like—"

"Not like me? I thought it wasn't like you to be cursing my sister and yelling out your appetite for young men. But I found out differently...You've said what you wanted, Olivia. Loud as you wanted. Very well. My turn now. You married me—and I saved your father's mills. Perhaps I would have been grateful to know that he was on the edge of bankruptcy before I accompanied his daughter to the altar. It might have given me a clearer sight of the contract I was making. And if I had, I'm not at all sure that I would have gone ahead with it. It's not sound business to do business with a fraud."

═

Whether she said anything after that—or even whether he did—he could not afterward remember. They parted. He spent much of the rest of the day roaming about on the upper deck, most of the time staring at the planks under his feet, once in a while looking up to gaze out across the ocean. The red haze he had seen earlier in the day had gone. Dark clouds rolled across a gray sky, the rain came on harder, then stopped, then came on again though less so than before.

They had never spoken such words to each other. Had hardly ever even quarreled before. The great blight of their life together—her physical repugnance for him—if anything made them less rather than more inclined to fight, for both in their own ways felt apologetic toward the other. Yet, Arthur acknowledged, the strain of living with this blight must have created a deep well of anger within him, and he guessed it would be the same for her. It had just never shown itself before. Only the sudden passion she had conceived for this *deserter* had flung it out from her.

In fact, he saw Bonney at one point during the afternoon. He was in a party comprised of himself, the Reverend Stibbards, Miss Faversham, and the Canadian Harper. They wandered about the poop for a little while before the increasing rain drove them below again. As they were walking, Bonney noticed Arthur and waved to him. He did not return the greeting. Even at a distance, he noticed how relaxed and cheerful the young man looked. He was smoking a big cigar. He was chatting animatedly with the others.

When the bell rang for dinner at four o'clock, Arthur went below to change out of his wet things. Leaving his cabin again, he hesitated, then crossed to Olivia's door. A moment standing before it, then he knocked. Silence. He knocked again. Came a muffled voice at last: "Who is there?"

"Livvy. It's me. Are you coming to dinner?"

Silence.

"Olivia?"

"Please go away."

So he did. He ate his meal quickly, and did not talk to anyone during it. The noisiest part of the room was the group around John Bonney. Having come out of his shell at last, the young American was making a great impression on his fellow passengers. For them, after several days of growing progressively weary of one another's company, it was like having a stranger suddenly come aboard. Everybody wanted to talk to him. In a gap in the general commotion, Arthur heard Mrs. Stewart laughing at something Bonney had just said. It struck him how flirtatious that laugh was, quite unexpectedly so from such a pious source. Evidently—Arthur ground away at the thought—the young man's power over women approached the prodigious.

He left the table without waiting for dessert and went below again. After five minutes in his cabin he was bored to death, yet he couldn't face the society of the saloon. He considered going back out on deck, but he'd had enough of rain and wind. He picked up the novel Olivia had given him, Miss Braddon's masterwork, and tried to read it, but the candle's dim light defeated him. At last he moved himself to his bunk and just lay there, staring at the base of the upper berth. Eventually, still in his clothes, he slept.

He was to wake much later, long after the lights had been put out on the passenger decks. It was pitch black. Something was burning in his mind, it was what had woken him. Something he had done. No. Something not done. Christ, what was it?

It was to come to him after five minutes of furious probing. *The Negro.* Tonight—or rather it was already last night—the Negro was going to be introduced to the saloon. In defiance of convention, and of Major Cutler's pistol. And he, Arthur, had volunteered to take a leading role in the attempt.

He had slept through it. He had deserted his post in the face of the enemy. In war, soldiers were shot for the crime. He would lie awake until dawn, berating himself for his feebleness. Then he would fall asleep again for several hours more.

47°55' N, 40°11' W

He was in stylish undress this morning. Crisp white linen shirt unbuttoned at the top, a silk scarf wrapped around his throat, brocaded dressing gown worn over these. He looked Arthur up and down—in contempt, Arthur could only suppose.

"I'm glad to find you in, Mr. Stuart." He shook his head, hoped he looked as apologetic as he felt. "I am so sorry about last night. The truth is I fell asleep and did not wake till the early hours. But it must look as if I funked my duty, and you have every right to believe that is so."

The Negro put his head on one side, apparently the better to study him. He had not offered Arthur either his fine armchair or his excellent sofa. Arthur didn't blame him; he had no right to expect hospitality. He stared down at the luxurious carpet. He tried to think of more words to express his regrets—but then what he had already said seemed to him to encompass all he had meant. He had failed. He had not been there at the moment of action. It had been inadvertent, but he would not insist on that being recognized. He would bear the shame. He deserved to.

"At any rate, I hope the action passed off without incident." He looked up at Stuart and offered a wan smile. "At least, you do not appear to have been seriously wounded. And I am glad for that," he added sincerely.

"What are you talking about?"

"Last night," Arthur said, surprised. "When you were introduced to the saloon. I was—"

"Never happened. Cap'n put it off again."

Arthur stared blankly at the man.

"He put it off? Again?"

"Uh-uh."

"Because I wasn't there?"

"No, sir. It was the bosun this time. He was s'posed to lead the party. Fell through a hatch. Broke his leg. No time to find a substitute."

Stuart's tone was bitter, and clearly disbelieving. He watched Arthur, who was still coming to terms with the news.

"Weren't you informed? The steward who told me said he was on his way to tell you."

"When was this?"

"Oh, 'bout six o'clock. I was just getting ready. To go up to the saloon, you know. Mingle with the folks."

"If the steward knocked, it didn't wake me." Arthur remembered the last time the news of one of the captain's retreats had come to him. "Perhaps he put a note under my door. But I didn't look this morning."

"Well, that's how it is. Twenty-four hours' delay. I am to remain in confinement down here till this evening . . . and I am glad to see that it amuses you."

"I'm sorry, Stuart, It's just that I'm so glad that I haven't, after all, missed the action . . . But it's disgraceful—" He had no difficulty now controlling his smiles, as the import of poor Stuart's continuing plight at last struck him. "Disgraceful," he said again. "But it *will* happen tonight. If I am the only man to accompany you, the attempt will be made."

The Negro shrugged. Lowered himself into the armchair, waved Arthur to the sofa. "I don't know," he sighed. "I'm not certain I care much anymore. Lord, I've come so far in this damn prison"—he waved a negligent hand at the splendid furnishings all around him—"might as well go the whole way. Have a better case against the company, I guess. Sue 'em to perdition. That's what I wrote back to the cap'n, anyway."

"Good." Arthur leaned forward, spoke earnestly. "Anything you can say to stiffen McDonough's resolve is good. But on the point of law: while I believe you certainly have a right to be recompensed for every day you have to spend in your stateroom involuntarily, I think it cannot be so for any time during which you are offered a means of escape but choose not to avail yourself of it."

The authority of this pronouncement was somewhat compromised by the rumbling report from Arthur's stomach that immediately followed it. The Negro opened his eyes wide at it, in almost feminine dismay. It made Arthur a little impatient. A natural occurrence after all.

"Beg pardon. Sea air makes me so confoundedly hungry. And then I missed my breakfast from sleeping so late . . ."

Stuart nodded. Glanced then toward the sideboard. Arthur followed his gaze. Over there was a contraption, a sort of chafing dish, under which several candles burned.

"You might find something in that," Stuart said. "I didn't eat much this morning."

Arthur was quickly on his feet, and crossed to the sideboard. He removed the covers one by one. Bacon. Sausage. Deviled kidneys. Crimped cod.

"Coffee in the pot," Stuart called. "I believe you'll find cutlery, plates, all that in the sideboard."

Arthur spooned out a generous helping from each of the chafing dish's compartments. Poured himself a cup of coffee, which still was hot enough to be steaming. Exultantly, he brought his plunder to the table. Sat down, attacked it.

"Do they feed you this well every morning?" he asked after a while, finding a gap in which to speak between the sausage—prime, just how he liked it—and the cod.

"Feed me? As in a zoo?"

Arthur put down his knife and fork.

"I say, no need for that."

"Is there not?" Stuart shrugged. "I am well fed. Cared for. There appears to be an interest in preserving my well-being. Yet I am a captive."

"You make me feel ashamed, Stuart."

"I'm sorry for that. Don't exactly mean to. Not your fault, I know ... Crichton."

Arthur bowed his head, and finished his meal. He had never thought in his life to be addressed by a person of color familiarly, by his surname alone. But when it happened, really it mattered hardly at all. No more than a twinge of dismay, and that was soon gone.

He looked over at the other man, sprawled so elegantly in the arm-chair.

"Tonight—" he began.

"Tonight somebody else will break a bone. And it will be called off again."

"No. No, sir. I have said. If I alone am left to accompany you, I will—"

"*Will* you, Crichton? When the moment comes? When you look at Major Cutler, and he has a pistol pointing at your breast—what will you do then?"

He was studying Arthur with a degree of interest. Arthur shook his head at last. "I will do my duty, I hope." Silence. Stuart's gaze did not waver. Arthur shook his head again. "I don't know," he sighed. "I can't tell."

He stared down at his empty, greasy plate. Then looked up, past Stuart's handsome profile. Looked again at the cabin's walls, the decorations, the many mounted playbills that the Negro had put up there to replace the pictures provided by the company. It must have helped Stuart, Arthur thought—still gloomy at the poor showing he was making—to have these reminders of his profession about him. Testimony that somewhere, if not on this ship, he had a place and a reputation and the dignity of a profession. Davis Hall, Galena. Gaiety Theatre, Memphis. A night of "Ethiopian Soirees" at the Bryan Hall in Chicago.

"Will you be appearing in Liverpool? Or Manchester?"

"What say?"

Arthur nodded toward the wall. "Wondered if you'll be giving a concert in Lancashire."

His question seemed to unsettle the Negro somewhat.

"Well, I just don't know about that. Couldn't say at all…It's my agent. He'd know. And he's already over there. Went on an earlier boat. He'll be seeing to things before I get there."

Arthur nodded. "I hope you will appear. I should so much like to attend. My wife too, I am sure," he added uncertainly. In his delight at finding that he had not failed Stuart, he had momentarily forgotten about the argument with Olivia yesterday. Now the memory of it threatened to overwhelm him. The terrible things they had said to each other, the ugliness of their complaints.

For relief, he looked again at the cabin's walls. Sanford's Hall, Cleveland. Wood's Theatre, Cincinnati. Columbus Armory. "The Colored Balladeer." "The Melodious Minstrel." "The Voice of Africa"…And then the details of these notices were lost to him. Lost too his depressing memories of the conflict with his wife. He was staring at the walls without seeing anything that was on them. A minute or two went by in silence. Stuart yawned and stretched in his armchair, perhaps impatient now for his guest to be gone. Arthur didn't notice. At last he turned his gaze away from the wall.

"Do y'know, Stuart…I think I may have had a very good idea."

━━

A half hour later Arthur was in the saloon. Having quite quickly got Stuart's assent to his proposition, he had gone to find the captain. He had located him in his cabin, the first place he'd looked. Once McDonough understood that Arthur had not come to browbeat him over last night's failure, he settled down to listen.

"Could work," he said thoughtfully when Arthur had finished. He pondered the question some more, then beneath his whiskers a smile grew. "It *will* work. Well done, Mr. Crichton." At once the old sea dog was a man of action, direction, in command. "I shall reassemble my force tonight, but distribute them more discreetly than I had intended." He ran down the list of his "force." "Hartley. Myself, of course. You are still ready to take a part, Mr. Crichton? Excellent…The bosun—"

"I thought his leg was broken."

"Ah…No. It turns out his injury is much less serious than first reported." The captain giggled uneasily. "D'you know, I have an idea the fellow was only funking it last night!"

Arthur's mood as he entered the saloon shortly thereafter was finely balanced between his curiosity and excitement about what would happen with the Negro tonight and the constant wash of sadness about Olivia. On leaving the captain, he had gone down again to the passenger deck, and had knocked on her door. There had been no answer. He could have gone in search of her. But something held him back, and, considering why he was so reluctant as he made his way slowly back upstairs, he knew it was because the quarrel was not over, deep down he was still angry with her. And so he did not see why it should be him that went in pursuit of her, as if in supplication, as if to apologize. He supposed he would go halfway to meet her—and even that appeared to him generous. It had been her behavior over Bonney that had brought on the conflict. And so it should be her role to seek ways of making the peace. He would not insist on unconditional surrender. But there would have to be concessions, large concessions on her part, before he would consider making friends again.

That was clear. And yet, he felt this sadness pouring in upon him. He would much rather not feel it—and he thought he knew how he could arrange this. He sat at a table, and in a few moments a steward appeared at his shoulder.

"Please, I would like a drink."

"Sir?"

What would fit the bill? Wine? No, taken in quantity wine made him melancholy. Which was not at all what he needed. Rum? To fit the nautical setting? But he disliked the taste. And beer made him gassy, which on the present performance of his insides was something to be avoided. It would have to be whiskey then. Or else: "There's a drink they serve in America. In the hotels, you know?"

The steward put on a look of keen intelligence. If the gentleman could be more specific?

"Well, I don't know—it's sweetish, you see, and it's rather good on a cold day, and—*sherry*, that's it. Got sherry in it. It's—"

"It's a sherry cobbler" came a voice from beyond the steward. "Excellent idea. Two great natural wonders of America—Niagara Falls and sherry cobblers. D'you know how to make 'em, steward? Two, then, if you please. You don't mind," asked Burgess, dropping into the chair opposite Arthur's, "if I join you?"

The drinks arrived after a short interval. Were pronounced "Excellent" by Burgess and "Just as good as in New York" by Arthur.

"Best to order two more while our friend is here," Burgess advised. "Just to be on the safe side. In fact"—to the steward—"Best to keep 'em coming until we tell you to stop. That is more or less how we organize matters when we're playing cards," he told Arthur, turning back to him. "It seems to serve."

"Where are your companions just now? It is strange to be in the saloon and no game in progress."

"Ah, we're giving the cards a rest. We rather broke the rhythm of things when two of us stayed away on account of the forthcoming hurricane." Burgess chuckled. Then turned more serious. "Though at times yesterday, I began to think the captain might have got it wrong. Did you catch sight of that strange reddish color that spread across the sky? Never seen anything like it before, and I've crossed this bit of water a dozen times. Lord, I thought we were in for it. But there, you see, nothing happened, and it's all gone today. Bit of fog coming in, though, I noticed just now. But fog's harmless enough. Long as it doesn't cause us to hit anything."

Arthur was interested to hear that Burgess had crossed the Atlantic so many times.

"Been to most parts of the civilized world more than once, but America most often. I'm a traveler, old man. Commercial traveler. Salesman. Peddler, if you like."

"What do you like?"

"I've rather taken a fancy to the American term. Drummer, that's what they call chaps like me. Drummer, that's what I am."

"Yes? On whose behalf?"

"Represent several clients. This trip was for a German company. Stuttgart. They make lenses. High quality lenses."

"There is a large demand for lenses in the United States?"

"Has been for the past few years," Burgess nodded. "You see, my lot specialize in telescopic lenses for rifles."

"Ah."

"Yes. Quite a call for the item. From both sides, y'know."

Burgess downed his sherry cobbler. His third? Fourth? Arthur couldn't decide. Whatever—he looked down at the drink in his own hand—he had been matching him glass for glass. He must be careful. He had intended to drink pretty deep, but the speed with which it was going down was alarming.

"You're familiar with the circumstances surrounding the death of General Sedgwick at Spotsylvania?" Burgess asked, looking around for the steward.

Oh, why the hell do I have to be careful? thought Arthur suddenly. Today I shan't. Today shall be an exception.

"I'm afraid not."

"Sedgwick was rallying his men to face the fire of the enemy, who were several hundred yards away. 'Why,' says the general, 'they couldn't hit an elephant at this distance.' Next moment, he falls dead, drilled through the forehead by a Confederate sharpshooter. Using one of our products," he added proudly.

"Really?"

"Well…" Burgess hesitated. Then, as his eyes lit up at the sight of the steward reappearing with two more glasses, "It could well have been. Our line is very popular in Lee's army. I could show you letters… And customers do like to hear the Sedgwick story. Yes"—he raised his glass in toast to Arthur, or perhaps, Arthur thought, rather to a defunct general months in his grave—"the old boy has sold a lot of telescopic sights since the unfortunate occurrence."

They started on the newly arrived sherry cobblers. Arthur was relieved to see that Burgess was going at it a little more slowly than previously. The next batch arrived before they had finished the present ones. Burgess indicated where he wanted the steward to leave them. Arthur expected to hear him tell the man to delay bringing another round until he was called to. But he didn't, and Arthur was too slow to say it himself before the steward had gone.

Poor General Sedgwick. Shot through the head. Dreadful shame. And Burgess had contributed.

He tried to pick up the threads of the conversation before they'd got onto Burgess's business affairs.

"But you… you do intend to play cards tonight?"

Burgess nodded, reached for his next glass.

"You will have to delay the start of the game, then. Mr. Stuart will be giving a concert."

"Stuart? The nigger?"

"Himself. He is a professional singer, you know. And has kindly consented to entertain us tonight."

"Well..." Burgess sounded a bit mystified. "That will be jo-jolly. I suppose."

"Of course it is a ruse to facilitate his introduction to the saloon." Arthur was impressed by the way his tongue had slipped so smoothly over the word *facilitate*. No difficulty at all. Whereas Burgess was already tripping over quite easy words. "My... our hope is that once he has become a presence among us, it will be hard for anyone to insist that he be excluded thereafter... Of course, by 'anyone' I mean Major Cutler."

He watched Burgess, anxious to hear his reaction. The other sipped thoughtfully at his glass. At last looked up, nodded.

"Might work... Good idea to bring him in as a singer. Minstrel show will it be? Bloody good idea... Yours, I take it?"

Arthur bowed modestly.

"Yes." Burgess frowned then. As if automatically, his hand stretched out for the new glass that had just arrived at the table. He drank. "But you know, Crichton, I'm damned if I see why we have to go through all this song and dance. Bally Cutler's just a little fellow after all—"

"But armed."

"Even so. Why doesn't the captain tell off half a dozen of the big chaps in his crew to seize the fellow and hold him somewhere till he sees sense and swears he won't be a bad boy anymore?"

Arthur started to explain the true state of affairs in regard to the ship's crew, and the captain's fears about the extent of his control over them. Burgess broke in before he had done more than outline the predicament.

"Mutinous are they? The swine. Should be clapped in irons." Burgess was silent for a time. Then he shook his head. "I don't like this ship. Something wrong with it, thought so from the first day. And it's so bally slow... I thought I'd save a bit of money by going on it. They gave me a d-damn good price for a stateroom at the New York office. But you know, I wish now I'd waited and gone on one of the others."

He peered across the table. "But you—Crichton? Why are you here? You don't have to be careful about money, surely?"

Arthur shook his head. Tried to remember. What *was* he doing here?

"My wife," he said suddenly. "We were booked on the *Scotia*. Sailed in five days' time. But Laura wanted to leave America straightaway. And this was the first boat out. She would not stay another day."

"I see. Who is L-Laura by the way?"

"I mean Livvy, of course," said Arthur heavily at last. "Olivia. My wife."

=

"Want to say," Burgess slurred, as he leaned forward on the table in a confiding sort of way, "greatest respect, of course. With the *greatest* respect. My God, sir, your lady, w-wife is such a p-pretty girl."

Arthur, who had just discovered a full tumbler beside his hand, was not able immediately to respond.

"Greatest respect, mind—lovely, lovely. Wouldn't do for me, though. Beautiful girl like that. Have a curious problem. I can't—how shall I say?—never can *function* with a really beautiful girl. Only the plain ones. Don't know why it is. Show me a pretty girl, can't get it up. Curse of my life... But you have no problem there, eh, Crichton? My hat off to you."

"Sir! Now—now, damnit!"

Arthur had realized at last that he should put a stop to his companion's ramblings, which certainly were becoming offensive... And must be stopped. Certainly...

"No offense. No offense," Burgess burbled on. "Yes, I have such difficulty... F'r instance, I haven't even been able to avail myself of Mrs. Stewart's services. Just because she's such a handsome w-woman. Great pity that. I haven't been accommodated since I was in Washington City, three weeks ago. Frightfully ugly woman, that one was. Marvelous. Anyway, I'm damned randy now. Cough up La Stewart's price like a shot, I would, though it *is* confoundedly steep."

Arthur could hardly believe what his ears had told him. "*What* did you say?"

"Sorry, old chap? Said what?"

"What you said about Mrs. Stewart. You implied—" Words failed Arthur.

Burgess gazed at him curiously. Then he started to smile.

"Don't you *know*, Crichton?"

Arthur shook his head. He had a new sherry cobbler in his hand. He had not noticed its arrival. Perhaps it was an old one he had forgotten to drink. A puzzle certainly. Yet it did not stop him swallowing half of it with a gulp. "I refuse," he said, licking his lips to catch the overflow of delightful liquid, "*refuse* to believe—"

"Oh, come now. Her tail's for sale. Definitely . . . Babcock's had her. Harris. The first officer . . . Everybody's had her. 'Cept me, worse luck."

"You must be mad."

Burgess chuckled. Arthur stared at him. He thought of Mrs. Stewart. Could see her almost, head bowed over an improving. Or smiling down fondly upon her little. It was like a . . . whatsit . . . what the hell was it? . . . Michelangelo did it . . . absolutely. And yesterday, how her voice had soared above all others as the congregation had sung the.

But on the other hand . . . No, *impossible*.

"I remind you, Burgess, she is a widow. A widow with, you know, children."

"No reason to doubt the widow part. Not sure about the children. Ever heard one of 'em call her Mama? I haven't. They could be beards."

"Beards?"

"Disguises. Decoys. Throw the Inman people off the scent. They're very fierce on these seafaring tarts, you know. Once they spot one, they circulate her name among all the other companies, and the poor g-girl can't get a berth from then on, not for love nor m-money."

Burgess's casual erudition unsettled Arthur. And yet he could have sworn . . . A seafaring tart? The woman must be a consummate actress.

He brooded some more on the extraordinary prospect Burgess had opened up to him. A bubble of air rose from his stomach, he tried to stifle the incipient belch. Was unable to. It was pretty loud. Burgess grinned cheerfully at him across the table. Arthur felt disgusted suddenly. With himself. With his companion. Certainly with the conversation. He shook his head, frowning.

"Whatever you think Mrs. Stewart is or is not, I'm sure we shouldn't be sitting here, like blackguards, discussing her case in a public—"

"Not a bit of it, old boy. Sure she wouldn't mind. How she gets her business, y'know. Word of mouth. Best form of advertising. Well, look at poor old General Sedgwick."

Burgess was looking around now for the steward. Arthur gazed at him. Then he got up suddenly. Burgess turned back.

"What's up, old chap? You're not leaving? I was about to suggest we switch to champagne cocktails. I'd advise it strongly. Refreshes the stomach, you know? Get rid of that wind."

"Excellent idea," Arthur mumbled. He was having difficulty speaking, for he was also currently using his tongue to hold back about a gallon of sherry cobblers that threatened to leap out from between his teeth like a fountain. "But I must just go and find my wife."

And he turned from the table and, disregarding Burgess's further appeals, lurched across the room to the swing doors.

═

On deck the fog that Burgess had mentioned earlier had settled clammily upon the ship. Arthur did not notice it, though he did think, as he stumbled toward the rail, that it had grown uncommonly dark and gloomy. And still not yet lunchtime. As far as he knew. He held on to the rail for a while, expecting shortly to vomit over it into the sea below. Like somebody else. Who was it? Couldn't remember. Anyway, it didn't happen. The open air seemed to settle him enough; the fit of nausea largely passed away. He had a powerful desire to urinate though, and this seemed as likely a place to do it as any. He had finished relieving himself before the truth struck him: he was standing in the open, in a public place, with his trousers open and his member in his hand. He stuffed it away immediately, buttoned himself up. Looked around furtively. Dear God. Thank God. No one else to be seen. Or to see.

He remembered that he had wanted to speak to Olivia. It would be natural therefore for him to go below to her stateroom, the likeliest place to find her. But instinct kept him on deck. He went forward along it, not steadily but with purpose. Shapes loomed up at him out of the murk. The cowshed, the lifeboats, the colored lights on the paddle box, glistening damply. To hand himself along, he grasped bits of wet railing and the edges of decktop constructions he couldn't identify. He had to be passing the officers' little quarters. A smell of fresh bread then told him he was near the bakery.

He came at last to the capstan galley. For some reason, he did not just walk into it but loitered near the entrance. The fog swirled in front of him. He peered through it. Two figures on the far bench. He'd been right. One of them was Olivia. He said her name. Rather he thought he said it, and he moved his lips. But no sound came out. Anyway the two people—the other, of course, was Bonney—did not notice him. Olivia was leaning toward the young man. As Arthur watched, she turned his head to hers and pressed a kiss on his lips. But that wasn't the full horror. He seemed to see—though in patches, and never once the whole picture—but he *seemed* to see that her hand moved upon John Bonney's thigh, moved along it, and then, as he watched, pressed hard between his legs.

=

Mrs. Stewart was turning away from closing her stateroom door. She heard the sound of footsteps on the stairs. She expected to see a steward, there were no other passengers with rooms on her corridor. What she did see, a few moments later, made her gasp in surprise.

"Mr. Crichton," she said at last—he had come to a stop a few feet away—"are you quite well?"

He was sweating. He looked ghastly. His cravat was awry. And, she couldn't help noticing, his trouser buttons were done up in all the wrong holes.

"Mrs. Stewart," he said then, staring at her with great intensity, "it may be that I am the victim of foolish gossip." He stopped, concentrated, then with painful accuracy, "Or rather, it is you who may be the victim. If it is so, I apologize in advance. But—pray tell me—are your children with you presently?"

"They are not, sir. The stewardess has charge of them ... For at least an hour," she added, the vaguest suspicion dawning on her of what—remarkably—this visit might portend.

"Then, madam," he said with a formal tone that quite took her aback, though in a way that rather pleased her, "I must ask you: may I purchase your services—for an hour at least?"

She looked him over. He was drunk, of course. But that did not bother her. Most often the gentlemen were drunk, particularly the married ones. As long as they gave off no threat of violence. This one—well, she could sense some rage boiling around in him, perhaps a lot of rage. But she did not think it would be directed at herself. It might be interesting to find out who had caused it. Most probably that doll-like little wife of his. It hadn't escaped Mrs. Stewart's notice that for days the little doll had been mooning over that handsome American boy. And now this one had finally noticed.

She made up her mind, gave a neat little curtsy, and put her hand on the stateroom door.

"I am at your disposal, sir," she said.

She opened the door a little way. From the cabin beyond came to Arthur a pungent aroma mixed of perfume, powder, children, sweat, urine, drink, shit. His stomach tightened. He stared at the half-open door, then at Mrs. Stewart, who was now smiling at him. With the slightest inclination of her head, she invited him to walk in.

=

Later, back in his own cabin, he thought, it would have been sufficiently disgraceful if I had chosen that moment to desert her. If I had turned and headed away from her up the corridor, fumbling out an apology as I went. Bad enough that—but the reality had been so much worse. He had gone into the room, had heard the door closed behind him, listened to it being bolted. She had begun to undress. Had taken off her gown, unlaced her chemise. Her breasts had tumbled into view. By this time, sitting on her sofa, he had only managed to untie one shoe. Her breasts seemed to transfix him. They were very large. The flesh was white and heavily veined. The nipples were dark and prominent. She smiled down at him confidently. Waited considerately for him to catch up with her.

He had removed his shoes and trousers, and was just lowering his underdrawers, when it struck him that this was the second time in less than an hour that he had exposed his private member in a place that was far from private. And this time his prick was not even confining itself to a decent state of reticence. He stared down at himself. The thing was thickening and strengthening, first making a tent of his shirtfront, then protruding sturdily between the divide, all veiny root and purple head. He heard Mrs. Stewart give a little murmur of appreciation and found himself wondering fatuously if she had genuinely liked the look of him, or if her reaction was simply a part of her professional technique.

The next moment, under her surprised eyes, he was pulling on again his drawers and trousers. He replaced his shoes, but got to his feet without bothering to retie them.

"After all, ma'am"—he gasped, through teeth that were almost clenched together—"I find that it won't be necessary." And he turned and hobbled to the door, unbolted it, and left the cabin without once looking around at her.

Oh, contemptible. Contemptible.

He was so ashamed. The poor woman. To expose her like that. To expose *himself* before her like that. How could he face her again? Even in a crowd in the saloon? He would have to stay down here the rest of the voyage. Swapping roles with the Negro... But he couldn't. Of course, he couldn't. Perhaps in her shame she would confine herself to her own cabin. Amidst that stink of perfume and piss and—

And that too was so contemptible. Whose cabin didn't stink, close quartered as they all were? (Not the Negro's, he suddenly remembered. The fellow's ventilation must be of a quality to match all the other facilities he enjoyed.) But Mrs. Stewart was not the pampered ward of a guilty company; rather she was bravely facing on her own charge the dangers and confinement of the crossing in almost the worst of surroundings—saving only the second-class berths, of course—and sharing that so-limited space with two children, who had no doubt added more than their share of ordure and vapors to the communal privy. What right then had he, after sneaking a look at her in her nakedness, to show his disdain so obviously, and flee from the scene, like a fop of olden days escaping the stink of the mob with a bouquet of flowers pressed to his nostrils?

But it was not only that. He couldn't pretend.

Olivia. The name came from him like a moan. And again: Olivia. So very reckless. But he did love her; unhappily for him, he loved her. That was what had sent him away from Mrs. Stewart, not the smell of her room. Also what had sent him to her in the first place. Pay Livvy back for taking his affection, and squandering her own on such as John Bonney.

No. He looked up, stared sightlessly across at the porthole. No, pay her back for the many months that she had denied him, shrunk from him, refused him. How often had he grumbled to himself, If she doesn't want me, I know where to find those who will—at a price?

Never really meant it. Anyway, never did anything about it. Only did this time—because of Bonney. And the drink. And didn't do much this time either. Popped the question, pilfered a look, then ran away. Georgie Porgie...Contemptible.

The thing was, in his heart he didn't blame Olivia. Why should spring lie down with winter? Or with autumn even? He did not think he was so...so very bad looking. Indeed, he thought, and had been told—certainly by Olivia, and he believed she meant it—that he still made a decent appearance. Portly perhaps, but not yet grossly so, still some hair left on his scalp, beard only tinged with gray, most of his teeth. But all the same, why *should* spring lie down with anything later than summer? Just because she had promised to? But then she had been flattered. And it had been exciting for her. The grave, *well-appearing* gentleman, arriving at her door. To take her out for drives in a handsome phaeton, to walk with her arm in arm on Market Street. Looking in at the windows. And anything that caught her fancy... anything at all almost...for he was so rich. And there was her father, whose need of a rich son-in-law was about to become so pressing.

And, too, she had loved him. She loved him now. He knew she did. He had no real doubt of it. Or at least that she was very fond of him. Set aside the romantic note, they enjoyed each other greatly, laughed much together, talked incessantly, were vitally interested in each other's outlook on life. They were *friends,* but to a high measure of what that word can mean. Loving friends. It was just that...flesh to flesh, the well-appearing gentleman fades away somewhat and she finds herself in the arms of—he supplied the words to himself: heavy

stomached, balding, bollock hanging, skinny legs, drooping buttocks...Though a lady should not notice these things. But she does.
She does. From the start she is unexpectedly quiescent in bed. Which,
of course, he puts down to her maidenhood. But it doesn't change.
Then he finds she shrinks away from him when he comes to her. And
this happens often. And then all the time. And he, hurt, starts to shrink
away too. He doesn't come to her anymore. But they don't speak of it.
And it doesn't get mended. For months and months now.

She is twenty-one—and in three months he will be fifty. It is that
simple. It is a catastrophe.

=

It was getting late. The darkness moving to cover his porthole window
was more than just fog. He must have missed lunch. But he didn't feel
hungry—or drunk anymore, he noted, in a detached fashion. It didn't
surprise him. He was so unused to drink that it affected him more
quickly than was normal in other men; on the other hand, he always
seemed to recover faster from it too.

He wondered about the truth of what he'd been thinking. Not that
she shrank from him, he couldn't be unaware of that. Nor that she
loved him in her way. But he wondered whether, even if he was young
again, as young and comely as John Bonney, Olivia would have been
content to give all her focus to one man. Soberly, he knew that what
she loved most was the attention of many. It was why she took such
delight in parties, parties which he heartily disliked. Just before, and
in the first months of their marriage—while she was still accepting
him into her bed—he had attended numerous such functions with
her. The guests were mostly her old crowd, from the days of her girl-
hood—which he had taken her away from. Young men and girls in
their early twenties, or late teens. They treated him with deferential
respect. And, having done so, moved on to another part of the room
and surrounded Olivia, and, while he made elderly conversation with
various other chaperones, he had to listen to her distant squeals of
laughter and delight. Sometimes things got quite out of hand. There
was that party last Christmas at the Ashworths', the business with the
mistletoe, Olivia in the arms of one boisterous young fellow after an-

other—there seemed to be a troop of them, kissing her with fantastic ardor, which she had most passionately returned. Dodging and peering between all the arms, collars, hair ribbons, and bare shoulders, as the young people milled around her, he even thought he saw one boy actually fondling her breast as he kissed her. It could not have been so. Yet it had seemed so.

Olivia's words in his ear: "And that's why you took me away and put me in a horrible little town in America. With your tedious old sister—" After all, it seemed to be true. He had taken her three thousand miles across an ocean because he was afraid of a repetition of that Christmas party. Where would he have to take her next year? Where would he feel safe? China? Van Diemen's Land? Tierra del Fuego?

He thought he had seen her fondle that boy's private parts in the capstan galley. But that could not be true. *Could not be.* It was the darkness. He hadn't seen clearly. Fog. In the fog, nothing is clear.

There was a knock, uncertain, almost timid, upon his door. At first he resented its breaking in on his thoughts. But then he started to smile. Livvy, he thought. Come to make it up. All his anger seemed to fly away. He would make up with her gladly. Explanations could be left till later.

Another knock. How shyly she approached him.

"Come in," he called out.

The door opened. The voice that then spoke appeared unattached to any particular person. Its actual owner was still skulking somewhere in the darkness of the corridor.

"If this isn't a convenient time, Mr. Crichton, I'll take myself off right away."

The speaker then appeared out of the gloom.

"I hope, sir, that I'm not bothering you..."

He looked like a dog cringing forward on its hindquarters, expecting to be driven off at any moment. Arthur had no intention of disappointing him.

"But you are, Mr. Tate. You are bothering me greatly."

"I beg your pardon?"

"And well you may beg my pardon. You have been bothering me since I first laid eyes on you. Always about to spring on me—it is confoundedly uncomfortable. And I've no desire to talk to you, sir. Please go away."

When the first shock was over, Tate composed his features. Without the sneaking, ingratiating look he had always shown before to Arthur, he revealed himself to be quite a proper-looking man. There was dignity in his high forehead, and in the plain line of his lips, intelligence in his eyes. He nodded, more with regret than apology, and without another word closed the door. It suddenly occurred to Arthur that the fellow had appeared so wretchedly before simply because he had hated what he was screwing himself up to do. It was pride, not sycophancy, that had been distorting him.

He got up off the sofa and went to open the door. Tate, his head bowed, walking slowly, had reached the end of the corridor.

"Mr. Tate," Arthur called out. Tate stopped, turned, regarded him steadily. For the first time, Arthur noticed that he was carrying a briefcase under his arm. "Mr. Tate, I apologize. I have much on my mind. Please—you wished to speak to me?"

"But you have said you've much on your mind, Mr. Crichton."

"I would rather not have it there, frankly. And if you have anything to say that might replace it, I'd be grateful."

"Not at the risk of troubling you, sir."

"Well, you may do so. I can't tell. Only one way to find out, I suppose."

He stood back from the door. Tate seemed to consider the invitation. Then he walked back along the corridor.

=

After Tate had left him, about an hour later, Arthur took up the briefcase he had left behind and carried it to his bunk. There he opened it, and removed the papers that were inside. These he began sorting into two piles. The pages of figures—initial costs, running costs, estimates of this and that—in one pile; and the pages of densely written prose—in which Tate had described his dream, and given a model description of how it would all work in one hypothetical instance—in the other. He then took the pages of figures to the table and began to go through them. He would read the prose pages eventually—he would read everything Tate had left him—but he already had the broad outlines of Tate's scheme in mind, and now he wanted to take a long, cool bath in the numbers.

"I have been in New York," Tate had begun. "Massachusetts too. And then I went South—"

"You were in the Confederacy?"

"I don't know what they are calling it now. I don't think the poor folk themselves know what to call it. I was in Georgia, and the Carolinas—"

"Bad there, is it?"

"Georgia is pretty bad. I entered South Carolina about the time General Sherman was leaving it at the other end. The destruction there is pitiful... Anyroad, wherever I went I tried to find the prominent men of the locality. It wasn't easy, many are still with the Southern armies. And those I did meet, it was hard sometimes to get them to concentrate on what I wanted to talk about, they are so much in a condition of shock at the disaster that has befallen their country. But there were some I talked to who could bring themselves to think of what must come after this war. They recognize that the old South, the plantation South, is doomed. The future—they know it—must rest with industry. There are pockets of manufacture all through the South; they could not have armed their soldiers for four years without them, even granting their importation of guns and powder from ourselves. But there must be more than little local centers in the future. Great industries must be started, or moved there, if the country—the region—is to have any chance of regaining its old prosperity."

"Cotton mills," said Arthur quietly.

Tate gasped. "You have thought of it yourself?"

"In a cloudy sort of way... No. Not even that. In the back of my mind. A long way back. Please go on, Mr. Tate."

At first he had listened to Tate so closely, almost urgently, because it was the best way of blocking out thoughts of Olivia and the sadness that had come between them. Yet as the man had talked on, he had grown genuinely interested in what he was hearing. Tate was a revelation. By occupation a mill manager (he'd explained), he had lost his job more than a year ago when the mill closed down, as hard times came to Lancashire. Since then he had been "on my own hook," as he'd called it.

"Living on savings, Mr. Crichton. Doing some thinking. Aided by my wife, I must say, who has a good, clear head for business... Anyroad, I have been thinking. And lately, as I say, I have been traveling—"

"And now you must do a bit of selling?"

"I must, I must find capital now. Can't go forward without it."

"Which is where I come in?"

Tate had shaken his head. "I am so unwilling to trouble you, sir. I had no intention of even thinking of my affairs again until I had got back to Manchester. It was to be a rest, this crossing, for both myself and Mrs. Tate. But then we saw your name on the passenger list and... But I am really so unwilling—"

"Oh, come now, Tate," Arthur had laughed. "You make such a wretched salesman."

"I know it." Tate was smiling now too. "I hate it. I would much rather be managing, any day."

At some point, as he worked through the columns of figures, Arthur felt hungry, and he rang for the steward. When the man appeared, he gave him half a sovereign and, without looking up from the pages, asked for coffee and sandwiches.

"What kind of sandwiches, sir?"

"I don't know. Any kind."

The man must have brought the sandwiches to him, for he found himself some time later trying to turn a sheet of paper with fingers that had a bit of buttered bread clinging to them. He was mortified to find he had put grease marks on one of Tate's perfectly clean and neat pages. But then he lost himself again in the figures, and forgot about all that. He finished them by candlelight. Then reached for the prose pages. The careful, bold sentences marched on beneath his eyes. He thought of nothing else as he read. He was so happy to be holding a piece of serious business in his hands again. He'd had nothing like it to occupy his talents since his meetings in New York, six weeks before. And how he had enjoyed those. And what good business he had set under way with those men. He could hardly tear himself away from them, had gone so reluctantly down to the railroad station to take the train back.

Back to Olivia. Who could have been with him all the time. Who should have been. Wouldn't any other man have been proud to march into the lobby of a great New York hotel with such a woman on his arm? Would any other have been so small, so cowardly, as to hide her away in a dark house in dark Massachusetts?

Yet it was because he could not trust her. If only he could have trusted her. If only she would not shrink from him . . .

("I like young men," she'd cried out, like a martyr for her faith. "Then why didn't you marry one?" he'd snapped.)

Enough. Enough. The figures. He could trust the figures. He clung to them like a life belt. He remembered Tate's words, remembered how— once he had flung off his diffidence—he had spoken so earnestly, with such conviction.

"Cotton, then. And why not? The advantages would be immense. In the first place, you have the source of raw material bang-up close to the site of manufacture. No more costly freight charges to bring the crop to New England or Liverpool."

"But surely that's counterbalanced by the fact that the cloth, when it's made in your Southern mills, will still have to be shipped North to be finished and exported?"

"Not when you consider the cost of labor there." Tate had tapped his briefcase. "I have all the figures . . ."

How thoroughly Tate had compiled his numbers, Arthur thought as he scanned them again. And how carefully had he written them down. Good man. Arthur felt strong admiration for the manager, even though he knew that almost all these figures were more or less fiction. At best, informed conjecture. They usually were when they concerned a scheme not yet beyond the planning stage, when they had had no chance at all to come into contact with uncomfortable facts.

Yet, though he knew the figures were highly suspect, still in a way he did trust them. Something could always be discerned in the neatly inked rows, some movement under the surface that gave a clue as to the deep direction of things. Though each individual number was not to be taken seriously, put together, he knew, in the right light, they told the truth. If only he could find that proper light to see them by. The light of God, he sometimes thought of it as, and had no sense of being blasphemous when he did. Only a sniff of atheistic disapproval from Laura at his elbow.

So involved was he in this endeavor that he did not hear the first knock on his door, nor the second. The third was much louder, and made him look up from Tate's pages. He was puzzled to hear it. It had definitely been a masculine sort of knock—he did not think this time it was Olivia come to apologize. Yet he was sure he had not rung again for the steward. Wishing he didn't have to—for at just that moment he thought he had spotted a bias in the figures that, unhappily for Tate, seemed to make uncertain an important part of his scheme—Arthur called out, "Yes?"

The door opened. It was the steward. Arthur gazed at him impatiently, still holding the page he'd been reading.

"Beg pardon, sir. Captain's compliments. Says to say: 'We're ready for you now.' "

"What on earth are you talking about, steward?"

"The black gent, sir. He's ready to go up ... Captain says"—the steward looked up at the ceiling as he strove hard to remember—"says 'e does hope that your absence from dinner this evening did not indicate that you are unfortunately suffering from some malady, and cannot therefore be one of the party who will be accompanying the black fellow to the saloon, as per what you promised." The steward took a breath, then, still gazing at the ceiling: "In which case, the captain suggests the attempt is postponed until tomorrow evening, this time, at the latest."

≡

Wishing that he was several hundred miles from where he actually was, Arthur got slowly to his feet. He had entered the saloon about ten minutes ago, just as the last course was being served. He had taken his usual seat next to Olivia. He had hardly seen her though, she was a blur of white dress and white arms and face. She had not looked at him, of that he was certain. It was what he had expected. Of the other participants in the drama that had swollen so quickly and fetidly into life around him, he took no notice. Indeed, Arthur could not say even whether Bonney was present or not. And as for Mrs. Stewart... He sat staring at his plate, shaking his head at the steward's queries as to whether he wanted serving, and crumbling a bread roll between his fingers.

Now he struck a fork against his empty wineglass. The subdued murmur of conversation fell away into total silence. A sea of faces all staring at him, waiting for him to utter: the exact vision that came to him in nightmares. Olivia too was gazing up at him, he was suddenly aware.

"As most of you, I think, already know," he began, "we have a most interesting prospect before us this evening." (Then why did it sound, even to his ears, that he was announcing a forthcoming execution?) "One of our fellow passengers, Mr. Stuart, is a celebrated professional singer in his own country. Which is the United States," Arthur added hurriedly. "He has performed"—for a moment all the playbills on Stuart's cabin walls seemed to whirl in front of him, but so fast that he could make out none of the details printed on them—"has performed in many important cities in America and is now on his way to fulfill engagements in Great Britain and in Europe. We are most fortunate that Mr. Stuart has consented to favor us with a demonstration of his art—as we voyage between the scenes of his previous triumphs and those of his future ones."

This last flourish Arthur had been working on since he'd sat down at the table. He had expected that it would bring him—and the cause of Charles Stuart—rather more than the faint spattering of applause that in fact greeted it. He had never felt more ridiculous, like a barker at a fairground. He wanted to collapse again into his seat. Actually, he wanted to go to his stateroom and creep into his bunk and forget the whole damn thing: black men, murderous Yankees, cowardly captains, his wife, his rival, poor wicked Mrs. Stewart—the lot.

"There is something else... As you are also all no doubt aware, Mr. Stuart is of the colored race. In other words, though a free man himself, he is a representative of that people which, in his homeland, is only now, in the rush of contemporary events, rising up from its historic state of bondage—"

"Here, here!" somebody called out. Was it Burgess? Tate? The Reverend Stibbards?

"I think it would be wrong—and illiberal—and *contemptible*—for any person here to manifest towards Mr. Stuart, who has been so kind as to agree to sing to us, the least hint of distaste or prejudice towards him." He had turned and was staring directly now at Cutler. "Such a manifestation would be heartily resented—and not only by Mr. Stuart."

There could be no mistaking to whom Arthur was speaking. Cutler returned his stare boldly for a moment, then, with an almost imperceptible shrug, looked away. Arthur finished quietly: "If any do feel within themselves a disposition to show such distaste or prejudice, I think it would be best for all if he quit the saloon directly, and leave the rest of us to our enjoyment of this fine artist."

Now every eye rested on Cutler. Who made no move, but only sat staring ahead. The silence was becoming oppressive. There was a flurry of movement, which caught Arthur's attention, and without thinking he looked in that direction. Found himself staring directly into the eyes of Mrs. Stewart, who had begun to fan herself. Appalled, he felt himself on the verge of blurting out an abject apology for his earlier conduct. He tore his gaze away. Around him the motion of fans was constant, as other ladies took up Mrs. Stewart's example. It seemed to Arthur too that the room had suddenly got very hot. He didn't know exactly what to do now—bring the fellow in, he supposed—but he felt rooted to the spot. God, it was warm. And the silence—deafening.

Suddenly little Burgess, who was leaning against a column some way down the room, spoke up: "What if we just plain don't admire the chap's voice, Crichton?"

There was relieved laughter around the room. It broke the tension. Arthur smiled.

"Then you must not applaud the 'chap,' Burgess."

More laughter, and people were turning to each other now, talking, relaxing. Arthur nodded his thanks to Burgess over their heads. He had meant to say something about the advisability of the ladies retiring now to a place of safety, but he realized it would hardly be in keeping with the agreeable picture of the forthcoming entertainment that he had been trying to paint. Nevertheless, he could not stop himself, as the swell of conversation rose around him, from muttering out of the corner of his mouth: "Olivia, perhaps it would be best if you left now." It was no surprise to him to see her shake her head. He did not see what else he could do. It might be his duty to protect her—but he couldn't forcibly drag her from the scene. And in truth, after such commotions as they had been through, he hardly knew where his duty lay anymore. All seemed in flux.

=

He got himself out from behind the table and made his way down the saloon. In the corridor outside, Stuart was waiting in the company of a curiously cheerful-looking bosun and a shrinking first officer. Hartley was holding the captain's fowling piece far away from his body, and as gingerly as if it were a dangerous snake. The weapon had an almost comically lengthy barrel.

Arthur was struck again by how gorgeous the Negro's appearance was tonight. He had on an impeccably tailored suit of fine cloth dyed the deepest, darkest purple. Underneath that, his silk shirt was a rich cream, and around his neck his cravat was burgundy. His boots shone in the flare of the oil lamp; they appeared made of the best and softest leather, not a crack on their gleaming surfaces.

At the moment, he was uttering various small yips and whoops—which concerned Arthur, until he realized it was only some kind of voice preparation before the performance. Seeing Arthur watching him, he smiled fairly warmly. Arthur—feeling quite impressed by the other's relaxed good humor—nodded, then indicated Hartley: "He is under orders not to fire."

"Never?" asked Stuart.

"Never," repeated Hartley thankfully.

"That piece really is too dangerous." Arthur nodded at the gun. "And mostly to its user."

Stuart again inspected the trembling Hartley. "Then I think I shall stay close to this gentleman." He glanced rather flirtatiously at the bosun. "Whatever weapon he is carrying under his jacket, he looks as if he means to use it if he must."

"It's a club, sir."

"I kind of thought it was."

Hartley stirred fretfully, spoke out of the corner of his mouth. "Can't we get this damn thing over with?"

"Are we not to wait for the captain?" Arthur asked.

There was a silence.

"He has failed us again?"

"The captain is unavoidably detained," the first officer spoke up spiritedly. "He is closely engaged in the navigation of the vessel..." Then he seemed to run out of steam. Bowed his head, muttered: "It is just us four. The captain has sent to tell us: good luck!"

"How kind of him," Arthur sneered. "Well, I wish you would do this for me, Mr. Hartley: when this wretched business is over, please inform the captain from me that I find his conduct unworthy of his office, and—" He struggled to find more ways of condemning the cowardly absentee. Could not. "Just tell him that, will you?"

Hartley stared straight ahead, making no acknowledgment of any kind. Arthur glared at him a few moments more, then shrugged and, after a last doubtful glance around him, pushed open the door to the saloon.

Once inside, Hartley and the bosun quickly dropped away left and right and took up positions in the uninhabited forward part of the saloon, putting themselves out of the sight of most of the passengers but not—by design—of Cutler. Arthur and Stuart continued to advance through the room. They came to a stop at last in the space before the passengers' tables. All eyes were on the Negro. Several of the ladies looked rather frightened, though not, Arthur noted, as much as did the Reverend Stibbards. He caught a stir then at one edge of his vision. Burgess had moved away from his pillar. Was now standing within convenient distance to make a grab at Cutler. Another stir on the other side of the room. Bonney had also positioned himself within striking range of the major. Who, with a calm smile on his thin lips, had leaned back in his chair, placing his hand conveniently on his chest. It would take hardly a moment for him to reach in under his jacket and get hold of the pistol that Arthur knew was concealed in there.

"Ladies and gentlemen—" It was coming out as a plea rather than an introduction. He strengthened his voice. "Ladies and gentlemen, Mr. Stuart will now give us a short recital of songs old and new...I give you—Mr. Charles Stuart."

Silence. Not a single clap. People appeared frozen in their seats. Arthur retired to stand at Olivia's side. The Negro looked his audience over, gazing from face to face. A slow and almost arrogant smile spread on his lips.

"Say, Charlie," Harris called out. "How 'bout singing 'Camptown Races' for me? That's a good un. Or 'Nigger on de Woodpile'?"

Stuart inspected the plump Nova Scotian. His expression showed the remote fascination of a scientist examining a specimen under a microscope. The broad grin fell away gradually from Harris's lips. "Say—!" he said again, angrily this time, and he looked around as if for support. But no one was looking at him, and he subsided into an aggrieved silence. The Negro continued with his study—or appraisal, it felt more like to Arthur—of his audience. At last he nodded.

"I should like to thank Mr. Crichton—"

At that moment Cutler's hand dived into his jacket. On either side Burgess and Bonney took purposeful steps forward. Arthur, unthinking, gripped Olivia's shoulder...But a second later Cutler's hand reappeared, bearing in it a large white handkerchief. Upon which he proceeded to blow his nose. Those watching the Negro had noted that he hadn't ducked, or even flinched at Cutler's movement. And some admiration for the fellow's pluck began to spread among the passengers, perceptibly warming the atmosphere toward the singer. He himself seemed unaware of any change and, after pausing to allow Cutler to finish emptying his nostrils, carried on as smoothly as before.

"I do, however, have to disappoint Mr. Crichton's—and your—expectations. I cannot give a recital tonight."

A murmur of surprise. Major Cutler began to grin. The Negro held up his hand.

"The reason is that my repertoire has been created around a close collaboration with my piano accompanist. That gentleman—Mr. Alan Fortescue, native of Columbus, Ohio—has been unavoidably detained on family business, and will not be joining me in Europe until a week after I shall land. I do not feel it proper to expose the art that we have created—in harmony, I may say—in his absence. Besides"—the entertainer smiled indulgently—"I see there is no piano in this saloon, so even if he was with me we could not perform."

After a moment, a rising murmur of complaint grew from the passengers. The good feelings Stuart had earned by his courage were dissipating fast. Though a number of passengers had been fearful, and a few had almost dreaded the proposed concert, now that it was about to be taken away from them, all united in a disappointment, which was quickly turning to anger. Cutler sat back in his chair and laughed once scornfully. And Harris, rising from his previous humiliation as if he had been reinflated, cried out, "Why, what a sell!"

But then, just as the protest threatened to become unmanageable, the Negro held up one slim, authoritative hand.

"However—" And the din died away. "However, it did occur to me that there was just *one* song that I have been accustomed to sing without accompaniment. That, indeed, we—Mr. Fortescue and I—have found, after experiment, to be actually *enhanced* by being sung unaccompanied... And with your kind permission, ladies and gentlemen, it is this song that I would be glad to sing for you tonight."

Again Stuart's searching gaze raked his audience. The members of which, having found one restored when they thought all were lost, now generally wore expressions of agreement and content. The Negro's eye fell on Harris, and he smiled aloofly.

"It is not, I regret to say, a plantation chant—nor a minstrel jig."

Harris looked away, muttered to himself, something about the "goddamn airs the fellow takes"—but Stuart had already moved on to include the other passengers in his gaze.

"It is called 'Your Mission.' Perhaps some of you will know it. It is a favorite of our president—"

"Our president." Cutler snorted very audibly.

"I beg your pardon." Stuart nodded. And then, misunderstanding brilliantly: "I refer to the gentleman who currently guides the destinies of we Americans. Of the Northern persuasion, at any rate."

At this, several passengers who had not till now shown themselves remarkably forward in defending the Negro's rights turned and smiled boldly at Cutler's presumed discomfiture—though to be sure, the latter was not showing too many signs of that. Stuart meanwhile was carrying on in his smooth, elegant way: "This air was sung before Mr. Lincoln at the White House not long since by my distinguished colleague Mr. Philip Phillips…Ladies and gentlemen, 'Your Mission.' "

He waited, head bowed, until the last cough and the last scraping of chair had died away. Then, raising his head, staring at some point above the tallest of the standing passengers, placing one hand upon the rich imperial cloth on his breast, he opened his mouth and sang:

> *If you cannot on the ocean*
> *Sail among the swiftest fleet,*
> *Rocking on the highest billows*
> *Laughing at the storms you meet,*
> *You can stand among the sailors*
> *Anchored yet within the bay;*
> *You can lend a hand to help them*
> *As they launch their boats away.*

The level was deep; the tone mournful, tender. It was not as strong a voice as might have been expected, considering it was customarily employed to reach the farthest corners of the great theaters and concert halls of the New World. No doubt, Arthur decided, the singer was adapting its force to the space it was presently required to fill, and certainly the solemn, melodious notes dominated the area where the passengers sat. Arthur accepted them gladly, put up no resistance, let the fellow's music just flow around him. He was so glad, so relieved that this difficult business had been seen through without violence, and with no backing down on the side of righteousness. A show of unified determination had done it. And a bit of gumption. Looking past Charles Stuart's ebony head, he noticed the bosun, his purpose fulfilled and himself presumably no music lover, slipping out of the cabin. Hartley was probably still there behind his pillar, Arthur thought. Poor fellow, rooted to the spot, still gripping that terrible old weapon. Yet he had done his job tonight; unlike his wretched captain, the first officer had been there, present for duty.

He looked then to his left. The genial features of Burgess nodded back at him. Good fellow!—hopeless gambler though he might be. And may he win every dollar he could—Arthur smiled to himself—from those two Blue Noses and from that damnable Yankee. Then he glanced to his right—at Bonney, another inexplicable Yankee. Whom he ought to hate for stealing the affections of his wife. Whom he would soon have to—what? Warn off? Go to law against? Challenge? Yet he had shown himself willing to take a stand on the right side tonight. That could not be denied, and at the moment Arthur—soothed by the sweetness of the Negro's voice—did not want to deny it.

> *If you have not gold or silver*
> *Ever ready to command,*
> *If you cannot towards the needy*
> *Reach an ever open hand,*
> *You can visit the afflicted;*
> *O'er the erring you can weep;*
> *You can be a true disciple*
> *Sitting at the Savior's feet.*

Now here and there, among the ladies, a handkerchief appeared, a dab at the eyes, a sigh. And several of the men were having to swallow and clear their throats: the Swiss, Charvet, blew his nose noisily. Yet these were not somber faces, Arthur noted: in many now shone a light almost of exaltation. Which may, he thought, as in his own case, be stemming from relief at the apparent safe outcome of a dangerous situation. Yet it must also be owing something to a quality in the singer's voice. For underneath the majestic solemnities of his delivery lay an element more humble, yet quite as in keeping with his message: it was the note of common humanity, something homely, yearning, a democratic note, the cry of the ordinary man and woman. And didn't the words support this particular note, and seem to penetrate particularly the hearts of *these* hearers? For they were all ordinary, none of them could pretend to be of the very first rank in anything at all. (It was practically a condition of having taken passage on this old, slow, dying boat that none should be that.) And none of them—unless young Bonney be the exception—were heroes. Yet, the lyric said, even beneath that lofty level, there was work to be done; and though of a rather mean kind—"You can visit the afflicted"—yet it still might lead to a glorious end: "sitting at the Savior's feet." And noplace came higher than that.

And though Laura was there instantly to ask him whether he really believed in such fairy stories, such falsehoods, Arthur decided that, for tonight, he was not required to deal with questions so far beyond his capacity to answer. He would just listen to the song.

> *If you cannot in the conflict*
> *Prove yourself a soldier true;*
> *If where smoke and fire are thickest,*
> *There's no work for you to do;*
> *When the battle-field is silent,*
> *You can go, with careful tread;*
> *You can bear away the wounded,*
> *You can cover up the Dead.*

The mournful notes died away, a long, appreciative silence followed. And then, just as the applause was about to break out—hands were raised everywhere, ready to clap with grateful enthusiasm— John Bonney suddenly pushed away from the pillar he had been leaning on. His face was contorted. He said some things—not loud, but with a chilling note of fury in his voice. Arthur thought he heard the word *lies* several times repeated. Miss Faversham, who had been sitting nearest to the young American, indignantly reported to her friends later that the man had called out "Fools!" in a most derisive fashion. Whatever it was—he said it. And then strode directly past the Negro, and all the way out of the saloon, leaving behind a group of people so astonished by his behavior that they forgot entirely to applaud the recent sublime entertainment provided by Mr. Charles Stuart.

Hours later Arthur Crichton was strolling upon the poop deck, accompanied by Burgess, whose idea it had been to go outside, for he wished to smoke a last cigar before retiring. Arthur was agreeable. This evening's eventually successful outcome had left him feeling exhilarated, and so somewhat restless. He would be glad to walk it off under the stars.

As they strolled, they reviewed the evening's events. Really, they decided, there had been only one sour note.

"I was surprised. The chap seemed to have come out of his shell at last. Given up all that hanging about over there"—Burgess turned and pointed toward the distant funnel, the lights on it shining against the night—"like some bloody actor in a play. Appeared to be a thoroughly congenial fellow. Then he had to behave like that. Why on earth?"

"I think the song affected him."

"Affected us all," Burgess grumbled. "Wonderful bit of singing. I was ready to blub, I can tell you. No need to go shouting abuse, though, like that young chap."

"He has been in battle, you see."

"What's that got to do with it?"

"The words Stuart was singing?...'You can bear away the wounded/You can cover up the Dead'...I think Bonney has had some unfortunate experiences on the field of battle. With the wounded, as it were, and the dead. Of a kind to make him find such words sentimental and, I suppose, almost insulting."

At that suggestion, Burgess's anger subsided quickly. He drew on his cigar. "Poor fellow, I didn't know that...Still, he did give offense, you know, Crichton. I think a lot of the people are expecting an apology. *I* am expecting one. Someone ought to talk to the boy."

"I believe," Arthur said evenly, "that I saw my wife leave the saloon not long after. It's possible she may have gone to speak to him."

"Ah..." Burgess glanced quickly up at his companion, then looked away. When next he spoke, his tone was mild and kind. "Well, you know, Crichton, that's probably a good thing. He's more likely to listen to someone—well...someone his own age, you know."

"Yes, I daresay."

In silence they walked. They reached the end of the deck and turned and began walking back toward the funnel. Arthur was thinking that what made this evening's success so satisfying was the contrast it offered to all the other problems he was confronting. Olivia. His nagging memories and regrets about Laura. Mrs. Stewart even. Female problems. Problems about females. Drifting webs of frustration and complaint, insoluble if only because one could hardly even get one's hands to close on the damn things. How different from tonight's events. A thoroughly masculine show that. Presented: a singular, limited problem. Needed to solve it: decision, initiative, and, though he said it himself, a sort of heroism. There was a brief struggle (not physical, thank God). At the end of it: the villain overthrown, the right side triumphant, the whole problem disposed of. Arise, Sir Arthur, knight of the Saloon Table!

"Thing was, Crichton—poor Stuart . . . After he had sung so well— and then nobody clapped at all. Poor chap was just left standing there. Bonney dashing out through the doors, and everybody else struck dumb."

"But do you know," Arthur mused, "I shouldn't wonder if it didn't make things easier for him in the end. Sympathy, you know. I mean, after he'd sung so well—and not got his rightful applause—nobody felt like pushing him straight back out of the saloon."

"Not even Cutler." Burgess agreed. "At least he kept mum, didn't he?"

It was Burgess who had come forward first after the sensation created by Bonney's departure.

"Mr. Stuart," he'd said, "that was a fine performance—very fine."

Stuart had bowed. The swelling murmur of agreement that arose from the passengers must have done something to soothe his indignation at the lack of applause. Burgess had turned away from him then and had stared around him, focusing at last particularly on Cutler.

"About now, Mr. Stuart," he'd said, "a number of us find it helpful to take something to settle the digestion. The brandy punch is not too disagreeable." Then turning back to the Negro: "I hope I may persuade you to stay and take a glass with me, sir?"

Stuart had accepted Burgess's invitation gracefully. The brandy punch appeared. A larger number than usual felt obliged to take a glass in order that they might toast tonight's great success. For half an hour or so Stuart was the center of an appreciative crowd. But in time, quite naturally, the interest in him began to fall away. A number of passengers drifted off, out onto the deck or down to their cabins. The singer himself proved not to be a fluent conversationalist, answering most questions and compliments very briefly, sometimes with only a nod. Eventually, even Burgess repaired with relief to the card table, where the night's game was already under way. And even Arthur Crichton was driven into silence at last by the Negro's monosyllabic answers and took himself off to a banquette where he fell into conversation with the Barlows from Rhode Island.

So Stuart had been left alone at last, nursing the remains of his second glass of punch, looking increasingly disconsolate. And it had looked very much as if in a few minutes he would be getting up and quitting a saloon that had somehow—without anybody particularly intending it—turned inhospitable to him. It would have been a dispiriting end to an evening that had begun so well. It would be, Arthur had thought, as he listened with half an ear to Mrs. Barlow, as if Cutler had won at last after all. Not gaudily by the bullet but by patience, certain that in the end it would be demonstrated by the natural course of events that the Negro could not be assimilated to their company, that there was no perch at all for him here, no place of refuge, except confined below in his own cabin.

Oddly, it had been Cutler himself who had, unwittingly, opened the door to Stuart's full admission to their company. Burgess explained it now to Arthur. "We were playing a hand of loo," he chuckled. "Stupid game, I can never really keep my mind on the cards when I'm playing it. I was watching Stuart half the time. The fellow was looking rather down by then—remember how he was looking? Anyway, I said to the others: 'Bit of a shame, ain't it? Poor fellow looks rather lost, don't he?' The other chaps—well, Babcock and Harris—agreed, damn shame. But that rogue Cutler just sneered in his way, you know: 'Black son of a bitch, I told you it would never work' et cetera. Then he says to me: 'You feel so damn bad about the nigger, Burgess, you ought to go and ask him to step over and play a hand with us. Why don't you do that?' And he laughed like a fool. But I was already thinking: what a bloody good idea!"

Cutler, of course, had reacted with incredulity to the idea that the Negro be seriously invited to take a seat at their table. ("He can come over here and I'll rub the wool on his head for luck—but sit down and play with us? Never!") However, the two Blue Noses had become quickly interested.

"Hang it, I've played with darkies at Halifax a few times," Babcock had reported. "I was as happy to take their money from them as off any white man."

"And you know," Harris had urged Cutler earnestly, "it'd be a hell of a lot more fun with five. It's hard to keep the interest up with just four playin'."

Cutler had shaken his head in disbelief, and when he spoke sounded like someone trying to hold together the last shreds of sanity in the face of total madness.

"How d'you know he's even got enough cash on him to buy into this game? Niggers ain't too flush with the readies gen'rally in my experience."

"Hell, he's a showman, ain't he? An entertainer," Babcock had argued. "I bet he's got heaps of money."

At last Cutler had shrugged. "Christ, he's sung for us. He's drunk with us... What the hell, it's too late by far to object to *anything* now—"

"Exactly!" Burgess had said, and the Blue Noses had cheered.

"Go ahead," Cutler had said carelessly. "Ask the nigger over. Jesus Christ! The world turned upside down—I'll say!"

Burgess had got to his feet. But he had held his ground for a moment, looking down at Cutler.

"If he does agree to join us, Major Cutler, you must not refer to him by that appellation, for he will be our guest."

"What did I say? I just said 'nigger.'"

"Well, that's all right among ourselves, we all say that kind of thing, and no harm done. But that nigger over there is a cultivated fellow, you see, and may object. So we will call him 'Mr. Stuart' when he's with us. Agreed?"

It was a mark of how much Cutler's earlier failure to defend his position had reduced his prestige at the table that the Nova Scotians had not even bothered to look his way for permission before they'd nodded their agreement. And at last Cutler had shrugged his too.

The Negro, on Burgess's application, had proved most ready to take a hand. At a very distant hint about the necessity of there being a sufficiency of money in order to play, Stuart had pulled from his trouser pocket a neat wad of greenbacks and had riffled through the notes. At a very rapid estimate, Burgess had guessed that what was in his hand amounted to about eight hundred Federal dollars. The Negro had asked if that would be enough: if not, he could repair to his cabin and bring back whatever sum was required.

"I told him he had enough right there. Lord!" Burgess chuckled. "The most any of us had won on a hand up till now had been about twenty dollars."

Stuart had a condition to make, however. He would only play a particular game, for it was the only one he knew. Said he'd had a hard enough time learning that game, and he would by no means put himself to the task of learning another, not with money at stake. So unless the gentlemen would agree to play at his game, he must decline their kind invitation.

"What particular game? And did you know of it?"

"I knew it. It's a Yankee game, it's come on pretty strong over there the past few years, 'specially in the South and the West, I believe. Bears a resemblance to brag. Stuart used some coonish name for it"— he thought for a moment—" 'Pig stud,' that's what he called it. But generally it's known as poker. Heard of it?"

Arthur shook his head.

"Needs no particular skill, but the play can get fast and furious. It's hardly known in England, but there are a couple of houses in London where they play it, and I've sat in on a few hands...And we'd been stuck on just loo and whist for days. I thought it would make a change, do us all good. Sharpen us up."

"Strange though," Arthur mused, "that Stuart should so insist on one particular game."

"Yes." Burgess hesitated. Then: "I might as well admit that for a while I suspected that he was so keen because he happened to be a dab hand at that game. And when he sat down, he took over the dealing, and the way he shuffled the cards, so neat and practiced, I said to myself: 'Watch out, Harry, my boy!' And I resolved to keep my stakes bloody low for the time being. But—" He stopped, grinned. Then, cheerfully: "My word, he's quite a duffer. We've been playing just an hour now, and he's seventy dollars down already."

"Which seventy dollars is now reposing in your wallet?"

"Most of it," Burgess smiled. "Cutler had some luck too."

"So," Arthur said, in an admonishing tone that he tried to make sound humorous, "we have released this poor man from his captivity only so that he may fall into the clutches of an experienced card-player. For shame, Burgess."

Burgess glanced up in some surprise. "Oh, Lord," he said, "I'll go easy on him. If his losses get above two hundred, I'll not play with him anymore. I've promised myself that. I'm not a damned 'sharp, you know, Crichton."

———

Arthur was sorry to realize he had offended his companion. It was the last thing he wanted to do. He knew how much the evening's success had been due to Burgess's several genial interventions. Besides, he liked the little gambler. The drummer. He tried to explain that he'd been joking, and Burgess nodded and told him not to fuss about it. They talked quite easily for a few more minutes before Burgess went below, yet Arthur was left feeling that he had not altogether been forgiven for his blunder.

He stood for a while longer looking down over the rail, running through his mind the list of those onboard who he appeared to have wounded, insulted, or otherwise distressed in the past few days. Major Cutler, of course, but that hardly mattered: he had shown himself to be a man of straw tonight. The captain, perhaps—definitely if Hartley had delivered that message he'd given him just before they entered the saloon. Mrs. Stewart, certainly—oh God, he could not bear to think of *that* episode. And now Burgess. It was, he decided, a lengthy list to have to contemplate on a night of unqualified triumph.

It struck him then that he had forgotten to include Olivia in the inventory. She who had most right to be included. He had not even begun to address that problem. All her wrongs still lay unrequited; his wrongs too if it came to that. The foul words, the horrible deeds. He must think of what he should say to her when next they met.

If he could ever find her.

Far below, the water was invisible to him in the darkness except where, by shifting his position a little, he could see the foam spun upward by the port-side paddle. On the *Persia,* an officer had told him that it took approximately a quarter of a million revolutions of the wheels to take the ship from one side of the Atlantic to the other. As the *Laurentia* was of smaller proportions, it was likely, he supposed, that even more rotations were required. Sixty tons of coal were consumed in the furnaces every twenty-four hours. All day and night the dead cinders were raised from the engine room in buckets on ropes and thrown overboard to sink to the bottom of the sea, forming down there—it was supposed—a thin trail, thousands of miles long, to mark each steamer's passage. It was the stokers' joke, the officer had said, that what they were really being employed to do was to lay the foundations for a future transatlantic railway upon the ocean bed.

And then suddenly, for just a moment, Arthur saw it. And seeing it, forgot everything else: Major Cutler, the captain, Mrs. Stewart, Burgess. Dismissed from mind. Even John Bonney. Even his wife…But it was not a passage across or beneath the ocean floor that he saw. Rather a bridge, a bridge of silver, soaring above the deep. And a railway train, a silver line of cars speeding across it. All aboard at New York for Liverpool and London. Three thousand miles to go. Thirty miles an hour. One hundred hours in total. Four days to cross an ocean. What a piece of business to build *that.*

He stood for a few moments more, gripping the rail. Then he sighed and let go of it, turned away and began to walk carefully under the moonlight toward the stairs that led below. It would come one day, of course, that bridge—or a tunnel more likely, like the one that would certainly be built beneath the English Channel before the century was out. He still hoped for the former, though. Much better to soar with the clouds than creep along in darkness. But whichever, it would not be in his time. For him, there was only the vision. It was something, but it was not enough, and he ached suddenly to be granted just one peep into the future. At a hundred years from now. Nineteen sixty-five. Everything would be clear by then.

=

Belowdecks, as he turned the corner into his corridor, he at first did not recognize, in the feeble light of the lantern, what appeared to be a bundle of laundry lying outside his door. He was thinking that it was a curious way to deliver laundered garments but decided that it was quite in keeping with the erratic and unorthodox standard of service on this particular ship. But then, as he came close, he heard a woman's voice moan wearily, saw a hand come out of the bundle to push aside the covering shawl, and the face of his wife appeared at his feet.

"Livvy!"

He knelt beside her, put his arms around her, and helped her into a sitting position against the wall. She was mumbling, half asleep. Then she called out clearly, "Arthur? Is it you?"

"Yes, dear. Hush. What—why are you—what are you doing here?"

"Had to see you. You weren't in your room. Mustn't miss you. Wanted to say I'm sorry."

"Come, dear. Sssh. How long have you been here? You'll catch your death—" He felt her forehead, it was cold, moist.

"Had to see you, Arthur. I've been so bad."

He raised her to her feet. She clung to him. He used his key on the cabin door. Pushed it open, and then helped her in. He led her to his bed, and sat her upon it. Went back to the door and closed it. Then crossed to his trunk, from which he extracted a small bottle of brandy. He took it over to the washstand, where there were a couple of glasses. Poured a measure in one of them and brought it to her. She had fallen back against his pillows. He raised her head, put the glass to her lips. She opened her eyes and studied his face.

"We mustn't quarrel, Arthur. I hate so to quarrel with you."

"I know, dear. I hate it too. It was my fault. Now, drink this."

She did so, coughed only a little, lay back against the pillow. Her breathing, he noticed, was becoming labored and harsh. He felt her forehead again. It did not seem much warmer than before. But she was sweating copiously.

"Not your fault," she breathed. "You have done nothing wrong. I have—I must confess to you, Arthur. I am so ashamed."

He got up, went to the washstand, and poured out a little cold water into the basin. He took his towel and plunged it into the water, then wrung it out partly. He went back to her side, pressed the cold towel against her forehead. She murmured her pleasure at its touch. When he had finished, she seemed to have fallen asleep. With her head now turned as it was upon the pillow, he could see only her profile. There was a spot of red on the cheek that was visible.

He saw her wince. He leaned over her.

"What?"

She put her hand to her throat.

"Hurts," she whispered.

"I shouldn't wonder. You couldn't have chosen a colder place than that corridor in the whole ship. How long were you sitting out there?"

She shook her head. Seemed not to be interested. She closed her eyes again.

"Tired," she said. "I must go to my cabin."

"Don't be silly. You'll stay here."

She was silent then. He feared she would fall asleep before he could get the bed linen up to cover her. He got to his feet and began doing it, trying not to disturb her as he brought the sheets and blankets over her shoulders. She muttered something that he did not catch.

"Go to sleep, dear."

"But I haven't confessed," she sighed.

"Time enough in the morning." She said nothing. "Or we could just not bother."

"Yes, I must confess."

"Livvy, if you're troubled because of some . . . indiscretion with Mr. Bonney, then let's not—"

"Ah, not only with him," she whispered. She was silent. Then, the faintest murmur: "Poor Arthur."

He guessed that at last she slept. He sat down and studied her. Her forehead had lost its gleam of sweat, appeared dry. The angry flares on her cheeks were still there, however. He was looking at them when the light in the room was extinguished. In darkness he went over to the sofa and made up a bed composed mostly of his greatcoat and Olivia's shawl. The sofa was so short that his legs draped over the far end. He lay unsleeping for more than an hour, listening to his wife's labored breathing, and kept waking all through the night.

48°57′ N, 33°57′ W

By early morning, she was much worse. He rang repeatedly for the steward. When the fellow finally came, he looked sleepy and sulky, but at the sight of Olivia became quickly alert.

"I'll fetch the stewardess, sir."

"It's disgraceful," Arthur said bitterly, before the man could leave the room, "that a ship this size can sail without a doctor onboard."

"But we do have a doctor," the steward said, surprised. "Dr. Davies. I'll fetch him too."

The doctor, when he arrived, turned out to be a small, red-headed, full-bearded man Arthur had noticed more than once about the saloon, usually at mealtimes, without ever quite catching his name or occupation. Later on, he was to learn that, like the *Laurentia* and its captain, this was Davies's last crossing, and he'd been doing his best to ensure that it was a peaceful one by lying low in his cabin most of the time, reading his way through the complete works of Edward Bulwer-Lytton, a treat he'd long promised himself. He came to Arthur's cabin with no less reluctance than had the steward, but equally the sight of Olivia concentrated his mind quickly. He sat on the bed, held her hand, touched her forehead, murmured questions at her, and listened to her low, gasping responses.

Arthur, standing over by the porthole, could hear neither questions nor replies. He watched as the doctor opened his bag and took out a brass stethoscope, then turned away as Olivia's nightdress was opened. When next he looked, she was under the covers again, her head turned toward the wall, her eyes closed. The doctor was standing by the bed, looking down at her. At that moment, he looked around at Arthur and gave a wan, preoccupied smile.

"Yes?"

"I think there's no doubt of it—the symptoms all point to pneumonia."

"Is it dangerous?"

"It's certainly most uncomfortable. Great deal of coughing—sore throat, very bad that can be. Fever."

"What will happen?" Arthur was watching her. Her face was in shadow, he could hardly see it now. "Do you know what will happen?"

"Yes, I think we can be pretty confident about that: the fever will last six or seven days, then reach a crisis, after which she'll be on the mend. She'll be weak for a good while longer, but once the crisis is passed she'll suffer very little."

"In six or seven days' time?"

"Can't be entirely sure of that. It may come on earlier, for we don't know how long ago the disease first took hold. When did you first notice that she was ill?"

"Last night. Just last night."

"You noticed nothing unusual about her in the days prior to that?"

Arthur thought. "She has been—perhaps, she has been a little high-strung lately. Could that have been from the disease?"

"Might be. Hard to say. In any case, the crisis will take place no later than seven days' time."

"And then she will recover?"

The doctor nodded, though not with as much assurance as Arthur had hoped to see.

"What can we do for her?"

"Not very much, I'm afraid. Make sure she is as comfortable as possible. Keep her warm—does she possess a flannel nightdress? That would be ideal. I can give her a demulcent to soothe the throat. And tincture of opium to help her sleep. For the lungs' sake, it's important that she not lie flat in bed. She should be propped up against pillows, as many pillows as we can get under her." He stopped then, looked from the patient to Arthur. "But this is your cabin, in fact, is it not?"

"What of it?"

"If you like we can shift her to her own room, put her into her own bed—"

"Of course not. I can move my things into her cabin. Of course we won't shift her."

"Very well." The doctor looked across at the stewardess—a tall, rather gaunt Scottish woman, of uncertain age, called Mrs. Logan—who waited by the door, and she nodded and left the room. "Here, Mr. Crichton, perhaps you will help me raise her up."

Arthur came to the bed and put his arm around Olivia and lifted her as the doctor piled up the pillows. The stewardess came back with more pillows in her arms, and these were added to the pile. Gently Arthur laid his wife back against them. She had made no sound during this operation, nor opened her eyes. He stood over her.

"I shall stay here with her," he told Davies.

"Yes. Of course. But try to encourage her not to talk."

COLORADO

50°5′ N, 29°50′ W—50°20′ N, 20°59′ W

Over the days of her illness, Arthur spent less time in his wife's presence than he'd expected or wanted. Where he was concerned, Olivia proved an irritable, intolerant patient. She did not at all like him to be near her when, as she felt, the sickness must have made her unattractive. In vain he argued that this was her delusion. What could such concerns matter at such a time? You see, she'd retort, you don't deny it, I have become revolting to you. Of course, all such intimate sickroom details as bathing, expectorating, use of the commode, et cetera, were banned from Arthur's observation as furiously as if he were a heathen being driven from the gates of Mecca.

Yet in the intervals when the sickness relaxed its grip on her, when she didn't feel sticky with sweat and her throat wasn't red hot and the cough had died away, she liked him to be there. She would sit, propped up against the pillow, and let him feed her the whey and toast water and thin broth that was all Dr. Davies permitted her to consume. She thought—and made Arthur bring her a glass to confirm it—that she looked very dramatic and touching at such moments. And she had a repertoire of trailing hand movements and downward glances and poignant sighs that added greatly to the effect. Sometimes she overdid them, and then first Arthur, and then she would start to laugh. But most often her laughter would end in a single cough, then there'd be a prolonged painful fit of them, the spots on her cheeks would flare up, and she'd turn from him, waving at him in a gesture that meant he should get out of the room quick and send Mrs. Logan in to her.

Though she would fall into a doze at any time, she slept mostly at either end of the day, and those were the times he remembered most clearly afterward. The light coming up against the porthole window, or dying away from it. That window was always closed, Dr. Davies being no believer in fresh air, indeed very much the opposite. He wanted the room kept as draft free and as warm as possible. To aid in the latter effort, Captain McDonough had dug up from his sea chest a little wood-burning campaign stove, Peninsular War vintage at the latest. It reeked and smoked horribly, but undeniably it kept Olivia's sickroom pretty hot.

Arthur was usually sitting in shirtsleeves as he watched the dawn rise outside or—at the other season of Olivia's rest—the sunset. Now she was unconscious and could conceal herself or act for him no more. He would listen to the harsh, toilsome breathing, hear her murmur and groan in her sleep. Often she sounded frightened, and he would lean over and say what he could to calm her. Sometimes his interventions worked, and, still sleeping, she would settle back against the pillows and be still. Other times he could do nothing, the moaning and the calling out would go on until whatever it was that was scaring her would startle her finally out of her sleep. As he listened to her unconscious struggles, it came to him how gallant was all her wakeful coquetting and performing and ordering him about. It kept him from fearing for her for much longer than he might have.

Banned so frequently from her cabin, and having as little ability to sleep in this period as she did, he spent much time roaming the ship, or else sitting and talking with whoever was available. A remarkable number of such people came his way, and in time it occurred to him that there must be some sort of informal agreement in operation among the saloon passengers to keep him occupied, and so not brooding on his troubles, by sitting with him whenever he was alone. For it was a fact that he could hardly settle anywhere in the ship, at almost any time of the day, and long into the night, without somebody appearing beside him with an apparently ardent desire to talk with him for as long as he liked. The officers too were in on the scheme—except for the captain, who he hardly saw in this time. But he was treated to several lengthy, disordered, and faintly offensive reminiscences from the third officer, and the second officer also appeared before him and showed him a number of simple tricks with cards and bits of string, none of which entirely came off. After those two, Arthur greatly preferred the approach of the first officer, Hartley, who sat with him for several long sessions, in more or less complete silence. On only one occasion did he significantly break it, when, in response to an idle question from Arthur about the progress of their voyage, he launched into an enthusiastic explication of the principles and advantages of Great Circle sailing.

"You know, Mr. Crichton, a lot of people don't believe that the shortest line between two points at sea may not be the straightest one—"

"They are right not to believe it. The straightest line *must* be the shortest."

"Aha!" Hartley's pale eyes lit up with anticipatory delight. "Now there, Mr. Crichton, I think I may be able to confound you. For instance..."

Within a minute or two he had lost Arthur completely, and had to be stopped in full flow.

"Forgive me—in all technical matters, I am a complete dunce. It is not that I will not learn, I cannot."

"You, sir?" Hartley said skeptically. "A great man of business such as yourself?"

"Believe me. I owned mills once, and the foremen used to try to explain the processes to me. I could never follow them. And it didn't seem to matter much. I found there was a good profit to be made from the manufacture, even though I did not know in the least how it was carried on."

Saying that left Arthur feeling rather flat. Though he had spoken no more than the truth—as a "cotton man" he had never felt himself handicapped by his lack of mechanical knowledge, least of all, of course, in the years he had spent on 'Change. Yet he felt very sorry suddenly that even in those distant days in the mills, when for a little while he had had a closer relation to the manufacture on which his fortune had been based, he'd shown so little curiosity about it. It seemed like a gratuitous insult he had hurled at—someone. He couldn't think who. The poor folk who labored at his frames? Or the honest, industrious men who had built the mills and installed the machinery? At all those whose heavy toil had served to make him so rich—and kept them always close to poverty?

Yet it was late in the day to be caring about *them,* he thought dourly now. Much too late to be indulging his conscience so. *They* wouldn't thank him for it.

Sensing the passenger's sudden despondency, without in the least knowing the reason for it, Hartley made haste to put an end to the apparent subject of their conversation.

"I have a book in my cabin. It explains very well the principles of the Great Circle. Perhaps I can lend it to you?"

Arthur agreed distractedly. Yes, perhaps he could. And with that the first officer fell back into his usual companionable silence. The sad, guilty feelings stayed with Arthur awhile and then seemed to drift away at last in the long stillness between them. Glancing up gratefully at Hartley, Arthur recalled that the captain had once described him as a "poltroon" and had suggested he'd been involved in some disgraceful and even criminal activities in Boston immediately prior to the *Laurentia's* current sailing. Looking at the blandly guileless countenance before him, it was hard to credit this. Besides, the man had stood reasonably firm during the battle for Charles Stuart's liberation, and for that Arthur honored, and preferred not to think ill of him.

=

So nearly universal was the attention showed to him during this time by his fellow passengers that Arthur couldn't help but be aware of those who did not approach him. It was no surprise, of course, that their number included Major Cutler, nor at least one of the Nova Scotians—Harris—but he was rather sorry that Charles Stuart avoided him. Bonney too stayed away, as did Mrs. Stewart, and again in neither case was he much surprised. In Mrs. Stewart's he was greatly relieved at it. If there was anything at all to be grateful for about poor Olivia's condition, it was that it gave him the best excuse in the world for not attempting to explain himself to Mrs. Stewart, or excuse himself, or otherwise deal with the ludicrous misadventure that had taken place in her cabin. Already the scene was taking on an air of complete unreality in his mind. It had not happened. Or else it had happened so long ago, in such another era, it had become irrelevant, of no weight, like a dream.

Was it a dream too, a fancy of his, that as the days went by the whole ship became attuned to the course of Olivia's illness? A hush seemed to spread through the vessel; even from the fo'c'sle one hardly heard anymore the usual catcalling and raucous laughter of the sailors. In the saloon he was aware now, during the times he passed through it, that the passengers were habitually talking among themselves almost in whispers. But it was not, he thought, a gloomy or mournful silence that was being perpetrated. Rather the *Laurentia* had taken on the soothing aspect of a hospital, a convalescent ward.

One form of activity onboard did not change at all, however: the card game in the saloon still proceeded all day and every day and long into every night. Arthur was glad that it was so. At intervals he liked to drop into a nearby seat and watch the progress of play. Other passengers, seeing him thus apparently preoccupied, would feel permitted for once to leave him alone—which, he guessed, came as a relief to them as much as to himself. It mattered not at all that he understood almost nothing of what he was seeing. The cards were dealt and studied by the players and then either held or thrown away and all in obedience to rules that were a near-mystery to him. He heard the low, lulling murmur of voices that accompanied their rise and fall—"Ante up, sir," "Jack to the queen, two to the trey," "Possible flush," "Raise you," "See you," "Check"—he saw the wooden counters, which looked so inconsequential but which he knew represented real, hard cash, being shifted across the table—and none of it meant a thing. In fact, he came to believe that his pleasure in watching the game was actually enhanced by his ignorance—the play took on so much the aspect of a ritual: remote, formal, inexplicable except to the initiated. It was a mystery indeed, and serene and calming to the soul.

So restful were the feelings the game engendered in him that he did not notice the moment when it shed two of its members. It was only that when he *did* notice it, he also realized that the game had been down to three players for some time—for several hours at any rate, during which time he had made at least one visit to watch it—without him consciously acknowledging the loss. It was the two Nova Scotians who had left, though whether because they were driven from the table by bad luck or had just walked away from it, he did not know. For a time he watched the progress of play with more alertness than before, wondering if—now that Burgess was the sole barrier between the mortal enemies Cutler and Stuart—the harmony of the proceedings would begin to crumble. But the game appeared to go on much as before. Apparently it was one that could entertain three players as easily as five—though he did hear Major Cutler once wondering aloud whether it would be worth recruiting the Canadian fellow Harper. Burgess said nothing, Stuart shrugged, called "Ante up." The game proceeded.

=

Of all those passengers who came to share Arthur's vigil, the most unexpectedly congenial turned out to be Miss Faversham. Their first encounter had taken place in the saloon. He had come up there in the gap between the clearing of the breakfast covers and the laying out of the luncheon. Olivia had just told him that the sight of him sitting beside her, "glaring at me like that," would surely send her into a decline if he remained much longer. Catching sight now of his unshaven, yellowy, and bleary-eyed visage in a mirror on the wall above one of the saloon's banquettes, he understood her revulsion entirely. He decided that he would go back belowdecks and see what he could do to improve matters. But then another idea overwhelmed him, as he looked down at the banquette's soft, plush seating. How welcoming it looked; how, he thought, he could sleep on it, for twenty-four hours at least.

At that moment, though he had no awareness of her coming into the saloon, Miss Faversham appeared beside him, and then, after a brief and—as Arthur read it—sanctimonious little smile, settled herself on the banquette he had been coveting, occupying with her lean frame just that portion of velvet he had been so looking forward to stretching himself out upon. The whole maneuver, in its absolute disregard for his rights in the matter, reminded him forcibly of the behavior of women in the trains and other public conveyances in America. A female there, seeing a man occupying a place where she desired to sit, would merely present herself beside him. And the man was expected to leap up instantly, turning the seat over to her without a murmur. This was the case even when there were other unoccupied places all around. And any man who objected to, let alone resisted, this imperious behavior was thought by all other passengers to be a cad, a thug, a brute. At least, Arthur supposed he would be thought so. He had never actually seen any man in America brave enough to resist this assertion of female power. Including himself, and the memory still rankled. It was not at all the giving up of the seat but the absolute absence of any asking or thanking or even acknowledging on the women's part that had exasperated him so much.

So now too with Miss Faversham, he thought darkly. Not only plain, not only a canting religious bore, but evidently corrupted by American female manners. Having taken over one side of the banquette, she tapped the other with a bony hand to indicate he should sit down beside her. He was on the brink of making a curt apology and stalking away from her, out of the saloon—but a suddenly noticed resemblance between the lady and a certain schoolteacher who had used to frighten him badly when he was about eight years old confused him about what he had meant to do. He sat down beside her, resolving though that no matter how strong the resemblance to past tyrants, she would get no more than a quarter-hour from him.

At first the conversation hovered at about the level of interest he had feared. Questions about Olivia's progress, of course. Then a violent attack on the venison pie that had been served up at dinner yesterday afternoon. Then a description of the village of Litchfield in Connecticut, where she had spent the last five months as the guest of friends. Followed by a description of the village of Faversham in Kent, which was next to the village of Teynham, where she happened to live. Of course, had it been the other way round, she would actually have been Miss Faversham of et cetera. But it was not to be. Have you ever been to Faversham, Mr. Crichton? Or to Teynham?

He had not, he had not. He was answering her, and certainly listening to her, with considerably less than half his mind, and so the oddity of what she next said took some time to penetrate to him. He had to ask her to repeat it.

"I said—what is your opinion of the Reverend Stibbards?"

Arthur at last began to explain that he would rather not commit himself on the question, on the general grounds of being unqualified to make such a judgment, for he hardly knew the man, and no doubt had never been fortunate enough to see him at his best. Miss Faversham shook her head firmly.

"Candidly now, Mr. Crichton—what is your opinion?"

"Well, then—I'm sorry to say, Miss Faversham, it is a rather low one."

She nodded in satisfaction.

"I *thought* so. But I could not be sure, for I do not know gentlemen very well. Yes, he is a poor specimen, isn't he? Feeble. Tedious."

Arthur felt obscurely moved to defend the absent reverend, but before he could do so—he was still trying to think of anything to say in the man's favor—Miss Faversham was speaking again.

"He has asked if he might visit me at home during his tour of England. I shall say no." She shook her head again. "Don't want him around. Not on any account. I must seem to you, Mr. Crichton," she added with scarcely a pause, "a rather ridiculous figure."

"Madam—Miss Faversham—I don't know why you would say—"

"Hungry old maid? In search of a husband? Making a spectacle of herself?" She grinned at him suddenly, a phenomenon almost as surprising as what she had been saying. Then her features became sober once more, she nodded. "Not far off the truth, I'm afraid. My parents have now both died, you see. I looked after them"—she closed her eyes for a moment—"for so long . . . And now I am alone. And in need of a companion. I expect I will have to settle for a female companion, and it would probably be better for me if I did. Yet I cannot help thinking it would be more—more *stimulating* to share my life with a gentleman. A kind man of Christian principle is what

I want. The problem is, Mr. Crichton, at my age, and with my features, the choice is necessarily limited. Tiresome old men are what
appear to be available to me. But *not* the Reverend Stibbards. There
is a limit after all."

When he had collected his dazed thoughts, Arthur began on a
rather feebly gallant objection to what she had said, on the lines of he
was sure the situation could not be as desperate for her as that. She listened to him, watching him thoughtfully all the while, then she raised
her hand, cutting him off.

"Would you mind telling me, Mr. Crichton, how old you are?"

"Not at all. I will be fifty in July."

"Fifty—and married to a person who is, I think, not even half your
age. Oh, I don't condemn you for it, perhaps I would do the same had
I the chance. But where does it leave us ladies of—of a more mature
aspect?... As it happens, I am younger than you by several years. Yet
if you were to find yourself suddenly free, I do not think you would
even consider me. Would you?" There was a pause, then she said with
a quite altered voice, "I'm very sorry, Mr. Crichton. In the circumstances, that was a most heartless thing for me to say."

He shook his head to show he understood she had meant no allu-
sion to his wife's illness.

"I'm still thinking over your question, Miss Faversham. I'm not sure
but that you may be, perhaps, too quick to—"

"Come now, Mr. Crichton, when we were talking just now, you
were so bored by me you could hardly keep yourself awake. Isn't that
so? But if I was twenty-one and lovely, I think you might have discovered some compensation for my dullness."

Pause, then stiffly:

"I'm very sorry, ma'am, if I was rudely inattentive—"

"You certainly were. I could scarcely keep myself from boxing your
ears!"

"Well, you know," he retorted, "our conversation was not exactly of
the liveliest."

"It seldom is, sir, when only one person is taking part."

They glared at each other. Then she put her head back and laughed
as freely as a girl. He shook his head in rueful admiration.

"You are right. You are quite right, Miss Faversham, and I was a clod. I promise to do better in future."

"Very well. But not just now. For I see you are plainly very tired and want to be left alone. I should have known it at the beginning, but then I have so little experience talking with gentlemen, and I tend to rush at it, without thinking. If I did think about it, I should do nothing at all. No, sit," she commanded, as he followed her to his feet. "In fact, stretch out and sleep, as I'm sure you've been wanting to do all along. We will have other conversations, and, as you say, we will do better."

=

They had other conversations, and they did do much better, and it was to her that, early one morning, he told more of the secrets of his marriage than he had ever revealed to another person.

"I blame myself mostly. I was the older. By a great deal." He tried to smile. "As once you pointed out. Certainly I had so much more experience—yet I was greedy, thought of little but my own gratification."

"She was young, but not a child. And she consented to the match."

"As I say, I am *mostly* to blame. Not entirely, I see that. But it is not I that will pay the greatest price for the mistake. For I have lived, and she has not. She has known so little. I think she is just beginning to realize all that she may have to forgo. When she understands everything, she will be terribly bitter, I fear."

It was the fourth day of Olivia's illness. All through the previous afternoon she had been querulous and uneasy. She had talked more than at any time since her confinement began, mostly complaints and repeated requests for glasses of ice water to ease her burning throat. As it grew dark outside, she lapsed into incoherence. The sweats broke out all over her body. The doctor was summoned and confirmed that the crisis had been reached. He ordered more blankets to be placed upon the patient and wrapped tighter around her. And that the fire in the stove be built up. The atmosphere in the cabin grew incredibly stuffy and hot. Arthur protested at one point, he could not think such extreme conditions could aid the sufferer, particularly when her body was producing such amounts of heat on its own. The doctor resisted his arguments grimly. He knew what was best to do. He had watched this disease run through its course scores of times—could Arthur say the same?

He could not, and soon enough he ended his arguments. But at length he could no longer bear to stay inside the furnace that the room had become. He went out, climbed up to the main deck, and stood breathing in great gulps of fresh, cool air. Then he walked along to the capstan galley, where Olivia used to sit, and settled in a corner of it, wrapping his coat around him. In a while he fell asleep.

When he awoke, the dawn was coming up. He knew he should get up right away and go below to see how Olivia was. But he felt unable to move. He looked around the little galley. It came to him that it was here, in the fog, that he had seen Olivia and John Bonney. Seen them kiss, seen her—perhaps—touch him intimately.

No, no perhaps. Of course, she had touched him. What had she said the night she became ill? He remembered he had asked her if she was troubled because of some indiscretion with the young American.

"Ah, not only with him," she'd said, opening up an abyss before him.

"Coffee, Mr. Crichton? It's freshly made, if no longer very warm."

He looked up into the thoughtful gaze of Miss Faversham. She was holding out a china mug to him.

"What are you doing here?" he asked, struggling into an upright position.

"I'm here because I'm a bad sleeper. I get up every morning at dawn and walk the decks. Usually at that hour I only meet the men who scrub them. Today I saw you. You appeared to be on the verge of waking, so I went and found a steward and asked him to make some coffee. Which I now present to you. Won't you drink it?"

He took the mug, and she settled down beside him. Asked after his wife. All his unhappiness and fears over Olivia's suffering of yesterday flooded from him, followed at last—with shameless abandon, as he was to look back on it—by almost everything else that troubled him about his wife. She listened, trying, he saw, with all her might to comprehend his disaster. He knew it was almost cruel of him to force all this upon her, but he could not stop himself.

"But is it," she said now, "that you think she does not love you at all?"

"Indeed, I know she does. And the longer we know each other, I believe the love she has for me grows stronger. As does mine for her."

"Then what can be the—?"

"But don't you see?"

She shook her head. "Please explain. I am so stupid in these matters."

"Well, then—it is just that the love she has for me does not include every way in which a man might hope that a woman would love him."

Incomprehension in the spinster's eyes gave way at last to the dawning of understanding. There was a moment when her eyes flickered with unease, almost fear. Then, as he watched, she mastered herself.

"You say—you are saying she is not affectionate towards you. Not...ardent?"

"I believe you have understood me, Miss Faversham."

"But why is she not?"

"Ah, you would have to ask her that, I suppose." Then, as she continued to stare at him, perplexed, he added: "I think my appearance tells against me with her—and my age—and—"

"But you are in the prime of life!"

"Thank you, ma'am," he said. "But you know, I suspect that sort of judgment rather depends on—well, the position of the judge."

"You mean that you will naturally look well to an ugly old hag such as myself? You are very ungallant, Mr. Crichton."

He chuckled at her shrewdness. Put his lips again to the coffee mug.

"Is it," she started. Then had to stop while she chose her words. "This lack of ardor—is it such a handicap—when you say that you do love each other in other ways?"

"I think it is an awfully great thing for a young person to have to forsake—perhaps forever. I know that young ladies are meant not to have the same desires as young men, and it may be so. I only know that in my own youth the—the marital love I shared with my first wife was a great joy to me. And to her, I know that to be true. At least in the early days."

"Then you were married before," she said.

"Yes. Of course. Olivia and I have been married less than three years. Did you think I had been a bachelor all my days till then?"

"I did not think . . . it didn't occur—"

"Laura," he said, finding for once some relief in saying it. "Her name was Laura. We were married for twenty years. Until she died."

"You were happy then, in that marriage?"

"No, ma'am," he said. "Except at first. We . . . we fell to quarreling after a few years, and never thereafter ceased."

"Quarreling? About what?"

"I could not exactly tell you, Miss Faversham. She was not happy that I left the bar to go into business for myself. That I remember as the first cause of dissension between us. But it was only the first cause. After that, what we quarreled about—" He shook his head in despair, and almost in awe, as at a phenomenal life-form, endlessly complicated and reproducing. "It was a habit, a terrible drug, that neither of us could stop indulging in. But why and what and who was to blame, I can hardly say. I never understood it. I never understood *her*. . . ." He bent his head; his voice became harsh, began to shake: "And then she died, and I knew I never would understand. And now if Livvy too dies—"

"*Stop it*," Miss Faversham commanded, and he did. They looked at each other. With the greatest of frankness. More so in that moment, he would remember afterward, than he had ever looked at another human being. She put forth her hand, touched his, and he felt the fear receding a little. He nodded then to show he was composed again, and she took her hand away.

"After Laura died," she said at last, "how long before—?"

"I married Olivia? Seven months. You will say that I was hasty. Imprudent. Perhaps I was. Yet I was so lonely—and I thought, at least this time there will be no arguments. For I had soon found that Olivia has little taste for quarreling. And there *haven't* been any arguments," he added forcefully, as if Miss Faversham had challenged him upon the point. "We are very amicable, on the whole. We have been amicable," he remembered then, "until we came aboard this blasted boat." He was silent for a while, thinking it over. Then shook his head. "But still you will say I was imprudent—"

"I shall say no such thing. As I know nothing about the circumstances. But this I will say," the spinster added, "you have said that you
enjoyed... enjoyed marital bliss once with your first wife. And yet it
did not save you or her from unhappiness. Perhaps the absence of
such bliss may not therefore be an absolute prohibition upon your
happiness now. I am saying," she went on bravely as he seemed to take
little notice of her words, "that life *can* be lived without such rewards."
She tried to smile as he turned to face her, to make light of her next
words, but they came out at length with equal earnestness: "You know
that I am an authority on the subject, and I say it can be borne."

"But would you recommend it, ma'am?" He looked away from her.
"I would do almost anything to spare her from the necessity. The
trouble is, there's nothing I can do. For we are locked in the deepest,
snuggest contract there is... I've considered divorce, many times. But
that won't do."

"Of course not," said Miss Faversham, shocked. "Not even to be
thought of. It would be utterly unchristian."

"Oh, believe me, I have thought of it. And I'm sorry to say it's not
for that reason I reject it. I would let her divorce me, of course I
would. But what would her existence be then, even if she was found to
be the innocent party?" He was speaking very quietly now, as if only
to himself. She had to lean in closer to hear him. "Can you imagine
Livvy's life then? She'd have to go back to her wretched father's house.
She would embarrass them terribly. She'd be kept out of the way. If
she went anywhere, there'd be whispering and snickering behind her
back. So she would go nowhere. Livvy! Who needs her friends, needs
company, needs to be loved and amused. The only sensible thing
would be for her to leave, to go away, some big town, London would
be just about big enough. Or Paris, perhaps. But Livvy couldn't live
away from Lancashire, she wouldn't be happy. A room in lodgings in
Bayswater, or off the Strand? Surrounded by people who don't know
her, or love her? No means of entering any society but the disrep-
utable—?"

He stopped, and shook his head. Was silent for a full minute, then
added in a sighing voice: "Yet we should part. For her sake. But I don't
know how it is to be accomplished. Except by death. I have even

thought ... but I am not that honorable a man. Yet it should not be she who dies, for she has scarcely lived, poor girl."

"Nobody will die," Miss Faversham said sharply. "And you are not to think upon such things. It is dreadful, and ... and there must be another way."

He saw the dismay in her eyes, heard it in her voice. He had tested her too far, and whatever else was welling up in his thoughts he would have to keep from her. For he did know of "another way," and thought it most likely the way he and Olivia would have to tread. He dreaded the prospect. So far he did not believe she had become entirely vicious. He supposed her indiscretions to this point amounted to no more than kisses, fondling, intimate caresses received and—though this he had not yet guessed till he'd seen it with his own eyes—given.

The young men with the mustaches and the lively eyes. The opportunities. Dances and parties, they led a gay social round—at least she did, and he tagged along. And then, he was much away at the office, and of course his wife had the right in his absence to receive visitors ... Well, bad enough all this, but bearable, he supposed. Or ignorable at least. But in a year or two or three, perhaps when Olivia saw in her glass the first traces of age upon her smooth and lovely skin, she would find just that small increase of motive that would propel her to the next, the final stage. She would take a lover. Some young man. Like Bonney. Though probably not Bonney. Somebody met at a dance or a dinner, son of a neighbor, or of a colleague of Arthur's. And he—he would just have to put up with it. And he did not think he could.

"It would all be so much easier if we were French," he tried to joke.

"Beg pardon?"

Not suitable in the present company. Not at all. What was he doing revealing himself to this poor spinster? And yet for a moment he felt an urge to tell her exactly to what point his and Olivia's marital life had dwindled. Her occasional exhibitions of her naked form. Her speaking filthy words. And that they excited him—and, he had long been confident, excited her too.

It was the devil's prompting, he knew. Miss Faversham's gaze was kind and uncertain. He smiled to reassure her.

"So sorry, Miss Faversham. I was wool-gathering. Yes," he pushed on, "I'm sure you are right. We will find another way. There must be one."

"Of course there must." She was smiling back at him, so relieved, he saw, that he seemed at last to have come out of the dark wood. "Or else many a pithy saying would have no truth in it at all."

"Such as that every cloud has a silver lining?"

"Or that it's a long, long lane that has no turning." She watched him then, her smile fading. She put out her hand, again held his. "Truly, Mr. Crichton, I know that your difficulty is very great. And that I am no use at all in solving it. But if you could—I don't mean to preach at you—but if you *could* think of taking it to Him who sees all our sorrows and ask for His help, I am sure you would never regret it." She looked up, and when next she spoke could not disguise the note of relief in her voice. "There! It is the steward beckoning to you. I am sure he wants you to accompany him back to your dear wife. And you'll see, Mr. Crichton, everything will be all right."

He rose to his feet. Olivia is gone, he thought, and this man is come to summon me to her deathbed. She is dead, and he has come to send me straight to Hell.

But after all the man only desired to pass on a communication from the doctor: that there had been no change in Mrs. Crichton's condition, but that she was holding her own. There was no need for Mr. Crichton to attend her, indeed it was strongly implied that his presence would be much more of a hindrance than a help.

"But is she still suffering?" Arthur wanted to know. The steward only gazed back at him with polite, unhelpful eyes.

=

The hours of that awful day crept by, so slowly that each one seemed to cover a full day in itself. Twice more Arthur got word from the sickroom that she was no better, but no worse either. The second time he was so undone by worry that he asked the man who had been sent to him whether Olivia had been asking for him. Of course the fellow had nothing to say on the subject. The only message he had that concerned Arthur directly was a repetition of the advice to stay away.

Arthur disobeyed it so far as to go down to the corridor and wait outside what had become his own door, looking all the while toward Olivia's. After about twenty minutes, Mrs. Logan emerged from the latter room, carrying a chamber pot under a wrap. As she passed by, she gave Arthur a look that he interpreted as one of strong reproof. As if she blamed him for his wife's plight.

Helplessly, he accepted her censure, he assumed the guilt. After she'd gone, however, he realized that in looking at him so, the stewardess probably had been doing no more than trying to show sympathy for his fears. Or perhaps her look was meant to convey nothing at all. Why should it? She was merely doing the duty she was paid to do. A tedious, messy duty—and in the midst of it poor Livvy lay close to . . .

He could not end the thought.

He loitered miserably for five minutes more, then dragged himself away up the corridor, seeking some other spot to wait out this vigil. First he went to the saloon. It was unusually full. There was something different about the room, he noticed, as he stood just inside. What could it be? Then he saw that the poker game was gone. Absent. Missing. And none of the players was in the chamber. And it was, he saw, as if a great tree had fallen in the forest—the light playing freely now on the forest floor had allowed other forms of life to spring up. In particular, a circle of the ladies had gathered at the spot where the card game used to be. A half dozen were sewing and darning; one—it was Mrs. Stewart—was reading aloud from a book. She had just begun.

"It lay down in a hollow," she read in her melodious voice, "with fine old timber and luxuriant pastures; and you came upon it through an avenue of limes, bordered on either side by meadows, over the high hedges of which the cattle looked inquisitively at you as you passed, wondering, perhaps, what you wanted; for there was no thoroughfare, and unless you were going to the Court you had no business there at all . . ."

"*Lady Audley's Secret*," Arthur murmured, remembering now that, having failed to make further headway on his last two attempts on the novel, he had returned it to the library.

As if his mutter could have been heard across the room, and so had interrupted her reading, Mrs. Stewart looked up from the book and stared directly at him. Arthur wilted under her gaze, looked away. The reading continued. He watched another part of the room, where Mrs. Stewart's two children were engaged in some game with another child he had not seen before, dressed very plainly, perhaps invited up from the second class for the day. The children's laughter blended pleasantly in with the mother's steady recitation. It was all too pleasant, too homely for him on this horrible day. Miss Faversham looked up from where she sat in a banquette at nearly the far end of the saloon, reading a magazine. She saw him, waved to him to join her. He shook his head apologetically, backed out of the room.

Livvy. *Livvy.*

He went quickly along the deck. Skirted the capstan galley, walked on. Remembered the last time he had been this far forward, when he had hurried along here to escape the Tates. He'd misjudged that man. Lesson worth remembering. Never estimate a fellow only by his . . . by his . . .

He could not keep his thoughts straight, couldn't keep his mind off—

Livvy.

On that day Olivia was already ill. Should he have seen it? Of course he should, and surely if he had seen it, and persuaded her to rest at that early point in the disease's course, it would never have reached the dangerous proportions that it now had. If he had noticed . . . but how could he have? He'd been too busy running around liberating stray Negroes, bursting with self-importance. So flattered by the responsibility put on him. The only man onboard who could bring this off. What had produced this—this *murderous* inattention to his own wife's failing strength? Guilt at the black man's suffering? Perhaps. Admiration for his own wondrous liberality? Certainly. Oh, a great Christian gentleman he was. Wilberforce and the slaves, no less. Shaftesbury and the factory operatives. Richard Cobden and cheap bread for the masses—

Before he could finish sneering at himself, a gang of men came around the corner carrying buckets and mops and pumice stones. The third officer was accompanying them. He touched his cap.

"Sorry to disturb you, sir. The men must scrub the deck."

"Not at all." Arthur began to move away. Something held him, though, in spite of the general distraction of his thoughts. He watched the men for a while as they set to work, then drew the third officer a little aside.

"Those men are chained," he pointed out.

"Yes, sir. They are malefactors. They have been removed from the fo'c'sle, and when they are not at work are now being held in a vacant cabin in the second class until the captain can consider their cases."

"Then," said Arthur, feeling a slight lift of spirits almost in spite of himself, "this must mean that the officers have reasserted their dominance over the crew?"

"Not entirely, sir. It was the crew themselves who delivered these fellows up to justice. Their crimes, apparently, have been so vile down there that even their shipmates wish to have nothing more to do with them... Though we can't be sure about that yet," the third officer nodded. "It may all just be a dispute about wives, and these men are the losers in it."

"Wives? There are *women* down there?"

"No, sir. But there are some young boys, I believe, who go under the name of wives, and there is fierce competition for their favors, I'm sorry to say. I have known crossings"—the third officer's mouth had become somewhat loose lipped and slavering—"when murder was done in this cause. And I can certainly tell you a few strange stories— if you find that sort of thing interesting, Mr. Crichton?"

Unwilling to contemplate any more circles of Hell on this day— and particularly not in the company of the third officer—Arthur declined the offer and, refusing to look any more at the men, hurried away toward the starboard deck.

=

He kept his head down. There was nowhere to go, but he felt it would be all right, he could hold the demons at bay, if he could just keep walking. But he was going too fast. Running out of room on this pestiferously circumscribed boat. He had already reached one of the white-painted sets of iron steps that rose from the main deck to the poop. He stood there wondering whether to mount it. And then it occurred to him, as he looked up, that there was a place onboard the *Laurentia* that was in a way already reserved, consecrated even, to be a refuge for men driven by guilt and lashed by angry fate.

Such as himself. He hurried up the steps. Reached the poop. Ignored the tremendous view. Strode along the deck. Toward the place, against the rail, close to the funnel. Where Bonney used to stand and repent that he had lost his honor and America.

He was standing there now.

He was standing there! Looking out to sea. *Again.* Arthur was outraged. And he felt persecuted. He was being stifled. Bonney was taking up all the space there was. He had stood there, *exactly there,* for days, indulging in his agonies. Now when he, Arthur, had most need of a place to wail and pray alone—Bonney was back.

He took a few more paces toward him. Wild thoughts of seizing the fellow and flinging him down from the rail. But at that moment— surely sensing something rather than hearing it, for Arthur had been advancing on him with the extreme stealth of the hunter—John Bonney turned. Stared full at him. Arthur came to a stop. Gazed back.

"Mr. Crichton," Bonney murmured at last. "You have come up here to tell me she is dead?"

"No, sir," snapped Arthur at last. "Certainly not."

He was so angry at this piece of presumption from Bonney—how dare he imagine that Arthur would stoop to playing messenger for him in such a tragedy—that, for a moment, he contemplated seriously effecting what had hitherto, he saw, been mostly composed of pretense. He *would* hurl himself upon this young fool, they *would* roll around on the deck, punching and tearing at each other. And he would be satisfied at last. But before he could start himself into motion once more, the young man was upon him, had wrapped his arms around him, and, too late, Arthur remembered what his life, and certainly his marriage, was always teaching him: that there is a world of difference between twenty-one and fifty. Specifically in the present case in the matters of speed, agility, and striking power. He had not even begun to make his first move, and already he was imprisoned, and certainly about to be thrown to the deck.

At that moment he felt rather than heard a deep sob rack the body that was pressed against him. And it dawned on him that the arms that held him did so with no belligerent intent. Rather, Bonney was using his hold on him to hang on as if for dear life. Arthur stood there, in this embrace, for several more moments, nonplussed. Then, not knowing what else to do, he reached around the young man's back, patted him awkwardly.

"Now, now," he said. And "It's all right."

He helped Bonney toward a nearby bench, sat him down, lowered himself beside him. Arthur looked around him. This was, he remembered, the same bench that they had used when he had given Bonney advice about how to deal with his desertion. In better times. He glanced back at the youth. He appeared to be struggling now with something, had his hand in his coat pocket, was tugging away. Whatever it was came loose at last. A large something, wrapped in one of the napkins from the dining tables. Bonney unfolded the cloth. A circular pasty of some sort lay upon it.

"A steward gave it to me," the young man sighed. "Said I *must* eat. I can't think why I should . . . Would you care to share it, Mr. Crichton?" he added, and Arthur, whose mouth had unexpectedly begun to salivate at the sight of the crisp, golden crust, nodded.

He watched as Bonney tore the mass in half. Some of the brown interior squirted out over his coat. Bonney didn't seem to notice. He handed Arthur his half.

"She will die," Bonney mumbled at last, his mouth full. "I know she will."

Arthur cleared his throat of pasty. "Nonsense."

It was strange to hear his own fears coming from another's lips. Arthur felt some resentment at having to share them in this way. But the circumstance had the advantage, he recognized, that hearing them uttered out loud they seemed much less likely than when they were locked up in his own mind. They appeared hysterical, in fact, anticipatory in a callow, ghoulish fashion. And simply wrong. Suddenly he felt confident that Olivia would survive. That there had never really been a danger that she would not.

"She will die," Bonney groaned again.

"It isn't at all likely, you know." Arthur brushed crumbs from his lap. "Dr. Davies says that pneumonia is a scourge only to the old and infirm. Very few young persons die from it."

" 'Very few'? Then some do?"

In spite of his recent rush of confidence, Arthur felt his stomach endure a sudden lurch.

"Well, yes, I suppose *some* do. But—"

"She will die," the young man said yet again. "And it is I who am to blame for it."

"Now that is absurd. For heaven's sake, Bonney—"

"Yes, I am guilty. I have killed her... Don't you remember"— Bonney sighed—"the night that Negro fellow sang? I left the saloon— abruptly. Like a fool, I know that. She came after me to calm me. She came to my cabin. An angel!—she agreed to do that. And we talked. For hours we talked. In that cold cabin."

"If," Arthur started, trying to inject a note of brisk derision into his voice, "you are saying that talking to you in your cabin"—she had been in this man's *cabin*? alone with him? at *night*?—"could have caused her sickness, then I must tell you that the doctor is reasonably confident that my wife picked up the disease before we even boarded the *Laurentia*."

But Bonney wasn't listening. He was looking away from Arthur, along the poop. And now his right hand came over and he clutched Arthur's arm. Arthur turned in his seat. Looked. A steward was making his way toward them, picking his way between the benches, hurrying on. The two men got to their feet. The napkin fell to the deck unheeded from Bonney's lap.

"It is the messenger of death," he stated in the least melodramatic of tones.

"It's nothing of the kind." Arthur felt such joy, as if his heart had been suddenly released from a thousand imprisoning strings. "For don't you see, Bonney? He is smiling!"

=

Three minutes later, having parted from Bonney without noticing the event, he was in Olivia's stateroom. The patient was tired, weak, complaining—but better.

"How long until she is fully cured?" he asked a smiling Dr. Davies.

"As to that—I can't give you an exact date. She'll be quite weak for a while yet. But she's young and her constitution is strong. She'll be out of bed, I daresay, inside three days."

"On the day we reach harbor?"

"That's it. Oh, she'll leave this old tub under her own steam, never fear."

50°52' N, 12°22' W

But Olivia confounded them all by being ready to leave her room in the early afternoon of the following day. She felt so much better, looked so much better—and the weather outside was so delightful, the sea calm, the air quite balmy. For the first time the poop was almost crowded with passengers strolling to and fro and lounging on the benches. The sun was bright enough that the ladies, almost all, went to their trunks and each retrieved from the bottommost layer a gay parasol to protect her complexion. The stewards moved animatedly among the crowd, bringing drinks and cakes and pastries. (Their uncommon energy and attentiveness reminding passengers for whom this was not their first voyage that the end of this one, and the season for tipping the servants, was getting close.) The ship's officers, in dress uniform, were out in force and striking manly poses seemingly everywhere one looked. It wanted only a military band for the scene to be a replica in miniature of a holiday afternoon in an English civic park. A cheerfully noisy game of deck quoits broke out on the main deck. The sun shone and shone. Everywhere the European passengers were chaffing the North Americans on how much more salubrious conditions were on *their* side of the ocean. In short, the *Laurentia* had suddenly taken on the aspect of quite a normal ship, almost a pleasure boat.

Olivia was driven nearly frantic by the reports Arthur was bringing to her of the wonders going on up above. At last, having eaten an excellent lunch, she demanded to be taken aloft. Dr. Davies was sent for. Shook his head gravely at the request. Did not advise it. Could not be responsible for . . . *However*—this after a hasty glance at his patient, who was evidently gathering herself for an onslaught—if Mrs. Crichton *insisted,* then it might be possible. For one hour only. And she must be thoroughly wrapped up.

So, in nightdress, cardigan, topcoat, and bundled up still further in shawls and blankets, wearing a wide straw hat to protect her head from the sun, Olivia was taken up in the arms of two strong young stewards. Arthur joked, as they were maneuvering her out of the cabin, that she looked like a caterpillar emerging from a gigantic cocoon. Olivia stuck her tongue out at him. One of the stewards laughed so hard he almost dropped her. When they were gone Arthur stared at the doctor. Who shrugged, and looked a little ashamed.

"She is strong. It may do her some good. It won't do her any harm."

"Your word on that, Doctor?"

Pause, then the doctor said, "She must not remain on deck above an hour."

Arthur could hear Olivia's laughter in the corridor. It sounded wispy and strained to him. He hurried after it.

But his anxieties were all swept away by the reception that Olivia received when she arrived on the poop. People rushed to assist her into her chair—generally indeed getting in the way of the two stewards, who were perfectly capable of doing the job on their own. But at last, and without after all her being spilled out onto the deck, she was settled upon a canvas-backed chair. Arthur stooped to tuck in the blankets around her. From their midst her little face smiled up at the people thronging around her, nodded and laughed at the hubbub of congratulation. As the sun shone down on the cheerful spectacle, she received a steady stream of well-wishers. It seemed to make her so happy to greet them all, even those passengers she used to laugh at and find absurd. Even the dreadful Harris, for instance, was received with that smile. He showed her a daguerreotype of his two daughters back home in Pictou, N.S. Very ugly children, both of them. She told him he was a fortunate man.

"I know it, ma'am," he said.

"Then why do you look so sad, sir?"

(Arthur was still standing over her, ready to interpret any of these foreigners to her, or to refill the glass of lemonade that she'd taken, or to take her up and hurry her back to her cabin—whatever she wanted. It made him happy to watch Olivia in this mood. She so often fell to the temptation of being sharp and mocking about other people; he felt the habit too frequently served to disguise a nature that, as it was showing itself now, was really kind and sympathetic.)

"It's you, ma'am," Harris blurted out.

"Me?"

"Just so sorry to see you this way. So thin and wasted and all."

"Naturally you have lost a little weight, my dear," Arthur said hastily as a dismayed expression appeared on Olivia's face. "You've hardly eaten a thing for days." He got hold of the numskull Harris by the shoulders, moved him firmly on.

A new wave of well-wishers arrived. It included Mrs. Charvet and a completely unexpected Mrs. Farrow, apparently wife to the diplomat. These ladies formed a tight ring around the patient and, edged away from the center by their jostling crinolines, Arthur soon found himself no more than an outrider to the herd. For a moment he stood there somewhat at a loss. He looked to one side. Mrs. Stewart, enjoying the mild breeze on a nearby bench, bowed to him from under her parasol. He swallowed, bowed in return, then looked quickly to his other side. Saw the captain bearing down on him. Relieved, he went to meet him. At the last moment he suddenly remembered that he'd hardly communicated with McDonough since that moment, just before the Negro had been introduced to the saloon, when he'd instructed the first officer to take an abusive message to his captain.

Had Hartley delivered the message?

"Came to wish our fair patient a welcome return to our midst," the captain boomed gallantly, and put out his hand to shake Arthur's. Arthur took it gladly, he could see no animosity for himself at all in the old man's eyes.

"I'm afraid you will have to wait your turn. The ladies make a formidable phalanx."

"They do. So they do. God bless 'em."

The captain put his hand on Arthur's arm, steered him along the deck. Their way led them then past Mrs. Stewart. The captain cleared his throat quite noisily ... And had he just seen then, Arthur wondered in the next moment, a flash of something, something intimate, between the lady and the captain? He couldn't be certain, but—no, surely not. But then again—this particular female? Why not indeed?

"You must be very relieved, Crichton."

"Beg pardon? ... Oh. Yes. Indeed I am."

"Yes. Our doctor has pulled her through, eh?"

"He has certainly worked assiduously on the case."

"Glad to hear it. He tells me, by the way, that this ... this infection was almost certainly picked up before the poor lady came onboard."

"I hold the Inman company," Arthur said gravely, "not in the least responsible for what has happened to my wife."

"Excellent." The old man came to a stop, pressed himself against the deck rail. "Excellent," he repeated to himself, snuffling contentedly at the mild air. "It's a weight off all our minds, you know. Sickness onboard has a depressing effect on the whole ship."

"I'm very sorry we have been such a burden."

"Not your fault, I suppose," McDonough conceded. "But it did get so damnably gloomy in the saloon, I can tell you. I couldn't bear to go there after a while. Nobody dared utter a word for fear it would disturb your wife. Ridiculous, of course, how could she hear it so far below? But people wanted to do what they could."

"I'm grateful for their concern," Arthur said sincerely. "We are both grateful. But you're right, they took it all much too far. Why, I noticed that even the cardplayers had stopped their game. They need not have done that."

"Mark of respect, I suppose. Superstition, perhaps. People do these things. I remember a crossing in 'twenty-three. By sail, of course. We were becalmed off Bermuda. Fever appeared in the crew's quarters. Five dead within twenty-four hours. The passengers terrified it will get to them. This fellow—American, very wealthy chap, not noticeably a religious maniac—announces at lunch that a sacrifice must be made to ward off the peril. He volunteers to be that sacrifice. The captain, who's trying to eat his lunch in peace, is just looking around him to choose which of the stewards will fall on this lunatic and carry him below when the fellow marches out on deck, followed by the rest of the passengers, and jumps overboard. The other damn fools cheered him down. Sharks got him almost immediately—not a pretty sight. But do you know, Mr. Crichton? Seven more of the crew died before we reached New York Harbor, but not a single passenger so much as caught a cold."

"I am glad," Arthur said, "that no one felt impelled to such desperate actions in aiding my wife. Though canceling the card game is going pretty far, I suppose. The saloon won't be the same at all. And it's quite unnecessary for them to do without. I shall speak to Burgess about it."

At that moment he felt a hand touch his elbow. He looked around to find Mrs. Stewart standing there. He stared into her violet eyes. She is about to denounce me, he thought. He felt very calm about it. He wondered, with quite a stir of interest, what would happen after she did.

"Sir, excuse me for interrupting . . ." Beneath the brim of her bonnet, her eyes were now downcast. "But I believe your wife is asking for you."

He gazed at the woman a second or two more. Then, comprehending at last what she had said, he turned and hurried along the deck. On his way the Reverend Stibbards appeared in front of him, hands outstretched to seize his own and, no doubt, a piously joyous sentiment for the occasion already on his lips. Like a rugby football-player at full pelt, Arthur turned his hips and swerved around the encircling grasp. He pushed through to the center of the circle around Olivia's chair. She looked up at him. Her cheeks were flushed, her forehead gleamed. When he felt it, it was warm and damp to the touch.

"You're ready to leave, my dear?"

"Yes, Arthur," she murmured. "Quite ready."

Cursing himself for having let her take such a risk, he looked around for the young stewards. They were nowhere to be seen. No servants at all. Everywhere he looked there were only the sweep and swing of colorful spring and summer dresses, set off by the gentlemen's more sober garb.

"Steward!" he shouted. "Where in damnation is the steward?"

Running feet. The men appeared. Olivia was plucked out of her chair, carried toward the stairs. Arthur thrust his way through the crowd after her, not bothering to look into the faces of the people he pushed aside.

Their path to the lower deck led them past the saloon door. Arthur, without thinking, glanced in. Saw that among the other signs of Olivia's recovery—which he may now have so idiotically jeopardized—was the fact that the card game was back in progress. Only the adherents had changed. Major Cutler and the Negro were still playing, but Burgess had gone now, and the Nova Scotians were still keeping away. Their places were taken by Farrow and Mr. Barlow of Rhode Island.

=

"I shall stay with her," Arthur said at the cabin door as the doctor was leaving. "Please tell Mrs. Logan her attendance isn't required for now."

Davies nodded. "I doubt she'll wake though. Probably sleep through till late tomorrow. Best thing for her too."

"I know—but if she should wake, I'd like to be here."

The doctor left. Arthur went back to the bed. Sat beside it. Olivia lay under the covers, her face turned away from him. Even so, he could see that the flush he had noticed on deck was gone from her cheek, and that her skin appeared cool and dry. Examining her, the doctor had admitted that it had been a little unwise to set her free so soon.

"But it'll have done no real harm. Tough as an ox, your good lady."

The day passed. Arthur listened to Olivia's breathing, watched the light change at the porthole. As always it was shut. Even on such a balmy day as this, Dr. Davies still deprecated a constant flow of fresh air. It seemed a curious prohibition after Olivia had been allowed onto the poop, where all the dangerous fresh air in the world was available to breathe. But then it had been admitted that that expedition had probably been a mistake.

At some time during his vigil that afternoon, Arthur dropped off to sleep himself. He remembered afterward waking at one point to find Olivia too awake. They had had a strange, disjointed conversation. By now the light in the room was yellow, golden, thousands of dust motes drifted and spun in the shaft that fell from the porthole. It lay between them so that he could not exactly see her face as they talked. Then he must have dozed again. The next time he woke it was because of a knock on the door. He looked up to find Mrs. Logan watching him from the doorway. She asked him if he was ready to be relieved yet, adding by way of encouragement that they'd just started the dinner service in the saloon. He was about to shake his head, to say no, when he discovered that he was indeed very hungry. He tried to remember when he'd last eaten. Not at lunch, he was sure. He'd been down here then, arguing with Olivia over whether or not she should go on deck. He looked down at her now. She was breathing deep and easy. There was a slight smile on her lips, as if she dreamed well.

"Yes, I think I will go up. If you would take over here, Mrs. Logan."

＝

He pushed eagerly through the saloon door. Saw that—for the *Laurentia*—the room was crowded. Could see at first glance no absentees at all. Then as he crossed the floor he searched for, and could not find, first Bonney, then Burgess. The soup course was just being cleared away. He dropped into his usual seat. The place at his right hand—Olivia's—was vacant, the cutlery laid out on the cloth before it. He supposed it had been so all through her illness—the empty place, the unused knife and fork—as if loyally in waiting for her. The only time he had dined in here while she was sick, he had been too distracted to notice if there had been this vacant place next to him. It put him in mind of a mournful ballad that he'd heard sung in a tavern in New York, where he'd been waiting to talk to a fellow. How had it gone? "We shall meet but we shall miss him/There will be one vacant chair/We shall linger to caress him/While we breathe our evening prayer." Sad stuff. About the war, of course. The dead. Pathetic. He was glad he hadn't thought of it while he still believed Olivia lay close to—

Arthur turned hastily, nodded to his neighbor on his left hand, then, as a bowl of soup arrived before him, he picked up his spoon. Between mouthfuls he glanced around the room. Noticed with satisfaction that Charles Stuart had taken his place among the diners. Of course he had probably appeared at the dinner service before now, perhaps as far back as the day following his introduction to the saloon. It was the first time Arthur had noticed him, however.

He took his gaze away from the Negro then, let it drift over the other diners—and then, as he was raising yet another spoonful of soup to his lips, he came to a stop. Spoon frozen in midair, mouth half-opened to receive it. For he had suddenly seen that all the people in the room—the Negro only excepted—were staring at *him*.

It came to him then that the last these people had seen of him he had been rushing white faced from the poop, following his sick wife, who lay limp in the arms of two stewards. They had seen him enter the saloon just now—and had not the least idea what Olivia's circumstances were. Some of these people he had roughly pushed aside in his frantic rush along the poop. He owed them all ... well, a bulletin at least. He set his spoon down on his plate, got to his feet. Even, he saw, Charles Stuart stopped eating to watch him.

"Very happy to say"—he was smiling awkwardly to right and left— "that Mrs. Crichton received no ill effects from her outing this afternoon. The doctor says her improvement will continue, and she should be almost entirely recovered by the time we reach harbor."

The applause came from all the tables, and First Officer Hartley led the gentlemen in pounding away with his fork upon his water glass. As the noise died down, a score of animated conversations sprang up. The stewards set out a fish course amidst the cheerful din. The wine bottles appeared. Arthur was called upon and responded to several toasts from well-wishers at other tables. Soon he was feeling extremely jolly. He fell into conversation with his next-door neighbor, a man of about his own age. Once Arthur had had an idea that this fellow might be the ship's elusive purser, but it turned out not to be the case. His name was Cameron, and he was an American—which had been almost the full extent of the information Arthur had managed to extract from him hitherto. He had seemed, in fact, an extremely reticent type. When Arthur had tried to talk to him at a couple of dinners earlier in the voyage, he could make no headway at all, and had always turned back with relief to Olivia.

Perhaps because of the congenial atmosphere in the saloon this evening, matters were quite different now. His neighbor seemed to have a great deal to say for himself. Arthur could hardly get a word in. And it occurred to him as he listened to Cameron's near-unstoppable flow that another reason for this sudden garrulity—Arthur had noticed the same phenomenon on the *Persia*—was that the end of the voyage was in sight, and everybody knew that whatever acquaintance-ships were struck up now did not have to be maintained for very long should they prove disagreeable.

Cameron spoke mostly about himself, and fortunately he had an interesting tale to tell. He was, it appeared, on a mission to Great Britain to recruit teachers, male and female, on behalf of several localities back home, which in his case was a new territory of the Union called Colorado. Colorado apparently had a near-infinite requirement for teachers—"as many as Old England can send us. Old Scotland and Wales too, come to that"—but on being pressed a little Cameron reckoned that if he could persuade just a round dozen of the article to go back across the ocean with him he would consider his mission to have been a success. And he had no doubt he could do that.

"Why, if I could just *show* the people over there what Colorado is, there'd be such a rush to the boats the whole of your little country would be just about *de-populated*. In no time at all!"

For Arthur he ran through what he was going to tell the teachers to persuade them to come. As he talked, Colorado grew and spread and flowered across the tablecloth. And, even bearing in mind the national propensity to exaggerate for patriotic motives, it did sound a splendid place, confirming for Arthur certain rumors of its wonders he'd heard before. Alpine meadows more beautiful even than the European originals. Snowcapped mountains, fertile valleys, air the purest in the world, fast-running rivers, sparkling in the sun. Forests full of game and fruit where no one need ever go hungry. Room enough for the entire populations of two major European countries to move in, and plenty of acreage left over after they'd been satisfied.

"A Garden of Eden without a snake?"

"Rattlers," conceded Cameron, "and coral snakes, some. Moccasins too. But they're no problem at all, if you just take care. Hell, I never knew a man who got bit who wasn't asking for it. Not in Colorado!"

Arthur was smiling at the man's enthusiasm. The dessert plates were being cleared away by now. The wineglasses refilled. Rarely for him, he had accepted a cigar from the box the head steward held before him. He puffed on it now. About a quarter of the passengers who had dined tonight still lingered at the tables; the rest had gone or were now walking away, heading for the easy chairs, or for their cabins, or to walk off their full stomachs on the decks outside, where—the information had been relayed back into the saloon—the night air was just as balmy and invigorating as the day's had been. Out of the corner of his eye, as he smoked and listened to Cameron, Arthur saw that the cardplayers were settling down at their table. Tate, he noticed, had now joined their number, which surprised him a little, though he wasn't sure why.

He was reminded suddenly that he had not yet given his decision about the plan of business that had been brought to him. Of course Tate had not tried to press him on it while Olivia was ill. But now she was better. He would have to grapple with that matter right away. Give the fellow an answer. At the moment he was pretty sure it would have to be a negative one. However ingenious Tate's scheme was, it was certainly premature. To start a whole new manufacturing industry in the prostrate, beaten South—no, too bold. Let other men lose their fortunes trying it. And yet . . . he could not bring himself entirely to dismiss the idea. There was something in it, he knew. Something of value. If he could only sift what it was out from the dross.

—

At last even Cameron ran out of things to say about Colorado. He professed himself also to have become a little befuddled from the wine, and said he thought he'd like to walk it off on deck. He added that he'd be glad of company, but Arthur declined the invitation, for he wanted to go below soon to check on Olivia. They shook hands as they parted, Arthur standing up to do this.

"I must say"—Arthur grinned—"I'm confident that you will succeed in your mission. You'll get all the poor, pale English ushers you could want. Why, Mr. Cameron, the way you talk of the place, if I was twenty again I'd be off to Colorado myself!"

Cameron eyed him up and down in a friendly though deliberate fashion.

"No offense, sir," he drawled, "but I believe back when you were twenty I'd have recommended you to go on no such expedition. That far back there was nothin' but Mexes and Indians in Colorado, and trash like that."

Arthur watched as his new acquaintance crossed the saloon floor toward the door. He thought he might take just another half glass of wine before he went below. Though, for him, he'd drunk quite an unusual amount tonight, he seemed to be feeling no particular effects from it, except for the rather pleasant glow that was presently spreading through his veins.

And, he noticed, a moment or two later, except for the fact that he was having some difficulty exactly repositioning himself in his chair. It was curious. Each time he tried to sit, the seat of his trousers came into hard contact with one of the chair's arms. He turned the upper half of his body, so as to attempt to look behind him and see what the problem was. He was still occupied in this ungainly contortion when he heard a voice speak up from his right, from exactly where Cameron had been sitting.

"You are happy tonight," it said. "I am glad that you are happy."

"Miss Faversham!" he cried, turning around, seeing her sitting beside him. He sank into his own chair—with no difficulty now whatsoever—and gripped her hand in his. "I'm so pleased to see you. I have to thank you for—"

"Nonsense."

"—for being such a kind friend to me while my poor Olivia lay sick."

The spinster beamed back at him, pressed his hand. "I'm glad to hear that. I was afraid that you might be avoiding me—"

"Avoiding you?"

"Because we *have* talked frankly—and I know sometimes that things that are said in moments of great distress are not recalled with pleasure when the distress has passed."

"Not the case with me," Arthur promised—though suddenly he did then remember one or two intimate details about his marriage that he had confided to Miss Faversham, and he felt all at once naked and exposed. "Not at all," he insisted, trying to inject into his voice his previous certainty.

"But yet we won't speak of those things," Miss Faversham said, watching him shrewdly. "Not ever again ... Unless you wish it."

Arthur nodded. They understood each other. He let go of her hand. "Perhaps you will take a glass of wine with me?" he suggested. "A toast to friendship?"

"I won't. It disagrees with me, if I take it at night. I can't sleep. But I'll toast you in water gladly."

"Good enough." Arthur looked around. Seized the water jug from its container. "You can use Livvy's glass."

"To you, Mr. Crichton. And to your happiness."

"To yours as well, dear Miss Faversham."

"May it warm you. And bless you. For it is a fine thing if you can be happy. Even when not everybody tonight is as fortunate as you."

Something. The smallest, slightest something—no more than a wisp of cloud in the very corner of the sky. Arthur drank his wine thoughtfully, then set down his glass.

"I wonder why you said that, Miss Faversham?"

She placed her own glass—Olivia's glass—back on the table, used a lace handkerchief to dry her lips.

"It's nothing, sir," she said. "Nothing that should intrude upon your happiness tonight."

Arthur nodded. Prepared to pick up his glass again.

"Except that it concerns a friend of yours."

"Which friend of mine?"

"It is Mr. Burgess, in fact."

"Burgess? Is he ill?"

"Not in body, no."

"What on earth do you mean, Miss Faversham?"

"I mean, that he has been robbed."

"Robbed?"

"Of a great deal of money."

All at once, without at all knowing how he had got there, he felt as if he were trembling on the very brink of a precipitous slope. A slide of ice. Or mud, more likely. Whose descent dropped beneath him toward a bottom so far away he could not make out what it was made of. Sharp rocks, he guessed, or a sinkhole of black, icy water, fathoms deep. He thought longingly of the chance he had missed ten minutes ago to quit the saloon in the company of Cameron. He might now be promenading the deck, comfortably talking of such fairylands as Colorado. Instead of which—

He eyed Miss Faversham uneasily.

"If Burgess has been robbed, he must report it to the captain. Has he done that?" And when she shook her head: "But if there is a thief aboard—"

"Oh, there is nothing so honorable on this ship as a decent, straightforward thief. Mr. Burgess has been tricked out of his money. Cozened. Duped. *Cheated* out of it. By those two card-playing villains."

Arthur's gaze went directly to the card table. Drifted over the mild features of Mr. Barlow. Tate was inspecting his cards with a frown of concentration on his brow. The woman's words made no sense at all to him. Farrow was looking up now from his hand with an anticipatory smile...

Miss Faversham gave a snort of displeasure, seeing his lack of comprehension. "Oh, I mean the villain who calls himself a major, of course. And the black man. Two scoundrels working in collusion!"

Arthur's first thought was to laugh out loud. His next to hope earnestly that she had gone mad. He gazed at her, a smile hovering on his lips, not wanting to be caught out looking drably sober if she was trying—as she *must* be trying—to play an absurd joke upon him. She glared back at him, she looked outraged.

"For shame, Mr. Crichton! There is nothing to smile at. I repeat: poor Mr. Burgess has been robbed by those two miscreants."

Her voice was not low, and at that moment Arthur saw Charles Stuart look up from sorting his hand and cast a questioning glance at them. He bent toward his companion, who was staring defiantly back at the Negro.

"Miss Faversham," he urged, "pray, be very careful what you say. Certainly how loudly you say it."

For a moment, it looked as if her indignation would boil over and she would jump to her feet and start hurling accusations at the players. But after a short internal struggle, she nodded, subsided a little. At the same time, he felt his own inner temperature rising fast. He stared balefully at the source of his disorder.

"What are you saying? It's—preposterous! Those two men hate each other."

"Rubbish."

"They are mortal enemies. Have you forgotten," he ground on, crushing in his course the objections she was trying to make, "the effort we spent to get the Negro to the place where he is now sitting? And that we did this against the most strenuous, most *violent* protests of Major—"

"More fool us, if we did. If *some* of us did. It was a charade. The whole thing. A professional masquerade. To make us unwary. And to lure their victims into their trap. And Mr. Burgess—" There was something sounding very like a sob in her voice now. She couldn't go on.

Arthur's mind was reeling. He couldn't help himself turning back to the table. Major Cutler was throwing two cards into the center; Stuart, who had the deal, flipped him two replacements, facedown; neither of them looked at the other during the transaction.

Except for these mechanical exchanges, there was nothing at all in their manner that showed even a recognition of each other's existence, let alone friendship. Or what had the spinster's word for it been? Collusion. Nothing. Yet even as he noted the clear facts that gave the lie to her denunciations, Arthur felt a creeping certainty steal over him that she had not been wrong.

"What is Burgess accusing them of exactly?"

"Of cheating, of course. Of being cardsharps. Swindlers."

"Quieter, *please*. Has he seen them cheating?"

She was silent.

"If he saw anything underhand, he should have instantly challenged them—"

"And risk being—?"

"Or reported it to the ship's officers as soon as he was able. Did he do that?"

Again she fell silent. She shook her head angrily. Then, as if reluctantly: "It was not like that. He had no chance to report it."

"What do you mean?"

"I mean, that it didn't really occur to him that he was being cheated while it happened. It was afterwards—looking back."

There came suddenly a burst of laughter from the card table. Both Miss Faversham and Arthur looked up. Farrow was smiling, had laid out his hand on the table. Arthur could see it from where he sat. Two cards facedown, and three tens turned up: hearts, spades, and diamonds. As they watched, Farrow reached into the center for the little pile of wooden counters that lay there. Stuart was shuffling the cards, waiting for him to finish so that he could deal again.

Arthur turned back to his companion. She was now watching him with the greatest urgency in her eyes. "Oh, Mr. Crichton—something must be done. I believe the sum of money that Mr. Burgess has lost is very large. I fear if it isn't recovered, he may be *ruined*. Won't you help?"

"What on earth can I do?"

"You can come with me and talk to Mr. Burgess. Perhaps between us, we can rally him to take a stand—"

"He has to be *rallied*?"

Miss Faversham shook her head and gave a faint, indulgent, forgiving smile. There was something about her expression in that moment that reminded him of another's. Another woman's. "He is loth to," she sighed. "He talks—childishly—of debts of honor. How can there be honor in the face of knavery? But if you were to speak to him, I know that he would take what you had to say very seriously. He admires you, Mr. Crichton, I know he does... And then between the three of us we could come up with a plan of campaign."

"Plans? Campaigns? Miss Faversham—why *should* I? This is none of my business... And we will be in Liverpool in under two days."

"What has that got to do with it?"

Arthur didn't know. He could only shake his head once more and repeat, "It's none of my business—"

"Oh, but I think it *is*, sir."

Arthur heard Stuart's calm, easy voice drifting from the table, as he called the other players in turn to make their bets. The spinster had gripped his arm, was staring directly into his eyes.

"You spoke of the effort that was spent to translate the Negro from his place of confinement. But was it not *your* effort, Mr. Crichton, that was largely, almost entirely responsible? Was it not *you*," she insisted, "who raised up that savage man to the society of the saloon, where, with his odious confederate, he could prey with impunity upon hapless, unwitting victims? Such as Mr. Burgess."

=

Mrs. Logan looked up gratefully as he opened the door. He apologized to her for returning at least a half hour later than he'd told her he would. He hoped he had not caused her to miss her dinner.

"Not to worry, sir, they'll have kept something hot for me in the galley."

Olivia was sleeping, though not very deeply it appeared. At one point she even opened her eyes for a moment and seemed to stare up at him, but then they closed again and he was pretty sure that she had been unconscious all through.

"She's been dropping off like this, every now and then." Mrs. Logan was putting on her shawl. "She sleeps for a quarter of an hour, never longer than that."

"Is she troubled?"

"Not at all."

"Has she eaten?"

"A piece of cod, and some boiled potatoes. She ate with a fine appetite too."

Arthur nodded, sat down in the chair the Scotchwoman had just vacated. She paused for a moment, looking down at him, studying his countenance.

"Are *you* all right, sir? . . . Would you like me to ask the steward to bring you something? A dish of tea?"

"No thank you, Mrs. Logan," Arthur said. "I want nothing."

Mercifully, a moment or two later, she was gone. Immediately, Arthur covered his face with his hands. For the second time on this voyage he found himself with his faculties impaired by having taken strong drink. He, who on land could let a year go by without indulging in a single episode that departed in the slightest from the abstemious standard he had set himself after a series of too-public carouses in London long ago had threatened to end his days as a student of law. And now on this confounded ship—twice in less than a week. He got up from the chair, groped his way across to the porthole, and, damning Davies and his theories, unbolted it. Air that was cool only by the standards of this grossly overheated room flowed in to soothe his forehead. He stood and breathed it freely. But only for a minute or so. After that, and after a guilty glance toward the bed, he pushed the window shut again, bolted it.

In truth, he thought, as he made his way back to the chair, of the two episodes, this was the worse; there was nothing in his present state suggestive of pleasure. In this mood, he would be incapable of taking even the first step toward sowing his wild oats with Mrs. Stewart. At that memory, another pang smote his consciousness, though of shame this time rather than intoxication. Again he put up his hand to his face. The world was too much with him. Christ, it was, he groaned inwardly. In the shape of Miss Faversham, it had come close to smothering him.

It was as if she had been wrestling for his soul. Her hand had seized his arm in such a grip it would have needed actual violence to break free from it. Her eyes had burned into his; whichever way he had twisted and turned away from her, he could not seem to escape them.

"My dear Miss Faversham," he had implored her, "I simply cannot involve myself in another set of charitable adventures. I have righted all the wrongs I am capable of for one voyage. Indeed, considering the apparent failure of the single endeavor I did manage to complete"— he nodded surreptitiously toward Charles Stuart—"I can't think why you should wish to encourage me into another fiasco."

Olivia stirred now under her cover, and he half-raised himself to peer across at her. It was not so easy to see her. The night was almost on them. The single candle in its glass case strove to dispel the shadows, but ineffectually. Arthur sank back in the chair. Olivia muttered something, but nothing that made any sense.

Again and again he had tried to convince Miss Faversham that he would not—*under any circumstances*—engage again in experiments to alleviate the lot of whichever stray sufferer happened to catch his attention.

"But Mr. Burgess is not a stray. He is a friend of yours."

"I don't know why you keep saying that. I hardly know the man. Before this voyage, I did not know that he existed. After this voyage—" Arthur stopped, he shook his head. "I don't know him," he repeated.

"He may not be your *friend*. Yet you were happy enough to accept his help when you had need of it. When you were busying yourself on that black man's behalf. And you believed—he has told me you believed—there might be considerable danger in the affair. You did not turn poor Mr. Burgess away then."

"Oh, *rubbish*. Rubbish!"

Major Cutler looked up. Stared across the room at Arthur—who, after a moment, could not return the gaze—and then chuckled and threw in his hand. "That's 'xactly what I got," he told the others in a voice just loud enough to carry to Arthur. "Nothin' here but rubbish." Tate and Farrow smiled at the quip. Stuart turned to Barlow. "Your call, sir," he murmured.

Miss Faversham was rising to her feet. Arthur made some sort of gesture of politely following her up, but the expression on her face froze him before he could leave the chair. She looked down on him. He was bracing and arming himself to receive her last, and no doubt most devastating attack. But when she spoke her tone was quite mild: "I asked Mr. Burgess once why you should have taken such an interest in the Negro's plight. He told me he thought you had once been a lawyer. And he said he believed you still had a passion for justice—"

"Yes, yes," Arthur broke in impatiently. "And now you know not only that I am not the one any longer but that the other is quite extinguished in my breast. Is that it?"

"No, sir. I don't believe a passion such as that can ever be entirely extinguished. But I remind you: this voyage is nearly done. You risk living with a shameful memory for the rest of your days if you do not act in time."

After which preposterous threat, she turned right around, crisply as a guardsman, and marched away toward the door—an exit so impressive that even the cardplayers forfeited a few seconds of poring over their hands to watch her go. She left Arthur in tatters. In the five minutes he stayed on in his place, he drank two more full glasses of wine. Furtively he watched the activity at the card table. He could see no contact whatsoever between Cutler and Stuart, except what was required by the ordinary maneuvers of play. No nods, winks, secret smiles, gestures, nothing at all.

And yet it hardly mattered that he didn't see them, he acknowledged in the end: true professionals would never make such elementary mistakes.

=

"Arthur? Is that you?"

He got up, went to sit on the edge of her bed. He took her hand in his, bent over and kissed her cheek. It was warm but dry. "How are you feeling, dear?"

"Very well. But I keep falling asleep."

He helped her sit up against her pillows. She seemed very light under his arm.

"I'm sure it's entirely natural. How weary you must be."

"Mm. But I want to get up too. I'm so tired of this room."

"You were up," he reminded her. "You went up on deck. This very afternoon. It did not agree with you altogether."

"Was it only this afternoon?" she said vaguely. "It seems ages ago."

A silence fell between them. Not strained exactly, but not comfortable either.

"Are you thirsty, my dear? There doesn't seem to be any fresh water. I'll ring for a steward."

She shook her head. "No...what I would like—" She stopped. Seemed to be inventing her desire. "I would like an orange. I think there's one in the bowl."

As the table had been removed from this cabin to allow more room for those who waited on the sickbed, the fruit bowl—which the cooks' galley had sent down yesterday at the news of Olivia's recovery—led a wandering existence, being shifted around from washstand to armchair to floor and back again, wherever a space opened up for it. Arthur located it finally in the corner, on top of his trunk. He selected an orange and, returning to the bed, began to peel it with his fingers.

"The people at dinner were very anxious to hear how you were. I had to make a little speech."

"You must have hated that." She smiled.

There was a squirt of juice from the pierced fruit. It hit him rather painfully in the right eye. As best he could, he joined in Olivia's laughter at the mishap. When she had finished, the previous silence imposed itself once more. He completed stripping the peel and divided up the segments. Most he gave to her, the rest he ate himself. She smiled her thanks as she accepted each piece of fruit. Her eyes did not rise to meet his, however, and after she swallowed, her mouth always returned to the same tense, anxious line. Arthur couldn't watch her after a while. He looked away toward the porthole. The sky was deep gray now, tending swiftly to black.

He would have to speak soon. One of them would have to. In real life, healthy life, the last he had seen of Olivia she had been flying from the saloon, in pursuit of John Bonney. Now he knew she had gone so far as to enter his cabin. Alone. At night. This had to be spoken of. To wait any longer would be so cowardly.

He glanced at her again. She had lifted her chin bravely. She was ready, she was saying. Or—at least she would not resist, if he insisted on speaking. Yet he sensed that she was silently pleading with him at the same time to put it off...

He couldn't do it. Not now. Not while she still lay on her sickbed. It was probably cowardice—but better that, he decided, than cruelty. He would wait until they were on land again. This ship would remain a sanctuary for them. Though but a temporary one, of course. Cowardice would win them only two more days of grace.

"Yes," he said, "enormous sympathy in the saloon. Farrow offered a toast on your behalf. Most ridiculous thing I ever heard. Well, you know what a pompous, diplomatic ass he can be."

He saw the tension on her countenance break up, and a look of perfect gratitude flooded her eyes. She sat up much taller against the pillow, wrapped her arms around her knees.

"Tell me," she laughed. "What did he say? Tell me everything. What did everybody say about me?"

＝

For the next thirty minutes or so they talked of neutral, cheerful, unimportant things, until Olivia professed herself suddenly very tired again. Would Arthur mind? Of course he wouldn't. He got up from the chair, and they bade each other an affectionate good night. He promised to send in Mrs. Logan to help her with her toilet. She vowed she would be well enough tomorrow to leave her room again, "perhaps for breakfast." He urged her not to exert herself in the least. She said she would wait to see what the weather brought before absolutely deciding. "Perhaps I'll wait until lunch."

At last Arthur turned away and went to the door. When he glanced back, Olivia was looking down at her bedspread. He hesitated for a moment, but could think of nothing more to say than to repeat, "Good night, my dear."

He didn't hear if she answered. He closed the door after him, walked to the end of the corridor where Mrs. Logan's cubbyhole was situated, and knocked on the door. When she appeared, he asked her to look in on Olivia soon. The stewardess nodded, without speaking. She seemed to have something in her mouth, and he feared he had interrupted her meal. He retraced his steps and opened the door to his own room. He stretched out on the bed, gazed up at the empty bunk above him. He felt as little like sleep as if he'd just woken after eight good hours of it. He thought to drag his watch from his waistcoat. He held it up to the light from the glass lantern. It was barely quarter past nine. In the saloon they would be offering supper soon. But he didn't feel hungry just now. Anyway, the thought of revisiting the saloon after this afternoon's debauch appealed to him not at all.

But nor did brooding on the day's vexations, which seemed to be his only alternative. It proved to be inescapable, though, and as between thinking of Olivia and thinking of Miss Faversham the latter appeared less painful, he concentrated on her. He tried to turn her into a figure of fun in his mind. How ridiculous to seek to push him into action on behalf of Burgess. A man he hardly knew. But who was surely old enough to take responsibility for his own follies. And not go hiding behind a woman's skirts.

It didn't work. Miss Faversham refused to be turned into a joke. Was it really true then? That all the effort and resolution and high-minded agitation spent on the case of Charles Stuart had done nothing more than set loose a cheating rogue upon the saloon? He thought of First Officer Hartley visibly summoning up his courage— and of McDonough shaming himself, poor old man—and the others,

Burgess, Bonney, himself after all, all had played a part. And to what end? A waste of time, all of it.

For the first time he felt a stirring of private anger at the way he had—perhaps—been tricked. He tested himself as he lay there to see if it was enough to make any inroads in his profound desire to have nothing at all to do with this business. He found, to his relief, that it was not. But then another line of reflection began to grow in his mind, equally—no, much more—troubling. For he remembered the look on Miss Faversham's thin face at the point when she was talking of Burgess. Of Burgess's honorable inability to protect himself against the wiles of those who had—allegedly—fleeced him. She had smiled. An indulgent, forgiving, *doting* sort of smile. Watching it, he had known at the time he had seen it before. On another woman's face. Now at last it came to him: his wife's expression, long ago, when she had used to talk of John Bonney's military predicaments. It had made him so angry to see it then. And he had felt something, a shadow of the same emotion, seeing Miss Faversham smile so as she talked of another man. Miss Faversham who had become his dear friend; to whom—as Olivia lay, possibly, near death—he had confided his innermost secrets.

Good God.

"Good God!" he said out loud. He was jealous. Of *Burgess*. Of Miss Faversham's regard for him. He had failed to volunteer his help to Burgess because he was jealous of the fellow.

The moment he thought this—and even though he knew it to be only a possible fraction of the truth—Arthur was off his bunk and heading for the door. He hurried along the corridor to the staircase. There he paused. At this hour Burgess could be expected to be in the saloon sitting down at supper. But something held Arthur back from immediately heading for the upper decks. Some notion of a wounded dog crawling back to his lair. Burgess's cabin, he knew, was among the cheaper first-class accommodations, situated along the corridor that went forward from where Arthur was standing, and passed closest to the noise and rumble of the paddle wheels. In that direction Arthur now headed.

He had never been in this part of the ship before, and, as he groped his way along, he found himself comparing it with his own corridor.

Surely the dimensions were narrower and lower along here? And the light from the overhead lanterns seemed even dimmer. With difficulty he read the cards affixed beside each door. Harris. Mr. and Mrs. F. T. Barlow. Crossley—Arthur had no idea who Crossley was or were. Surely there could not still be people lurking in their cabins, people who had never yet found their way up to the saloon? Though he had heard of the phenomenon—close cousins to moles who passed the whole, broad Atlantic coffined up in their staterooms.

It occurred to him that he had not the least idea what he was going to say to Burgess when he found him. He realized he was still playing with the idea that he could discover what the situation was without having to commit himself to any kind of action. He saw now he had been deceiving himself. He couldn't raise this matter as if out of idle curiosity. Starting on it with Burgess meant that he was volunteering himself to become involved. Which was a thought to slow down his walk along the corridor to a snail's pace over the last few yards. He stood at last irresolutely outside the door that bore Burgess's name. The racket from the paddle wheels was almost intolerable this far along, and every grind and turn seemed to be speaking to him, telling him to have nothing to do with this unsavory affair.

He was on the point of turning away and returning to his own part of the ship—but then a renewed apprehension flooded him that his reluctance to proceed here was really due to so base a cause as jealousy. Over Miss Faversham! And somehow that got tangled up in his mind with thoughts of Olivia. And of how she had hurt him. What the one had to do with the other, he could not say. But it all reeled around in his mind in a confusion of alarm and unhappiness, harshly orchestrated by the paddle wheels' din, until at last, more to drive away the demons that were plaguing him than because of any rational motive, he leaned forward and knocked on Burgess's door.

No answer.

He stood for a minute, looking down at the floor, waiting. There was a line of light under Burgess's door, but that meant nothing. The glass-cased candles in all the rooms were lit from outside by the steward each evening, whether or not there was anyone at home. He couldn't hear anything. Again, that probably had no significance. If

Burgess was in, Arthur guessed, he'd be most likely engaged in what *he* had just been doing: lying on his back, contemplating his misfortunes on the underside of the upper bunk. A silent activity if there ever was one. Trumped only—Arthur's thoughts turned down a very dark passage now—by the silence of one who had decided to resist the tide of adversity no more, and whose inert form now perhaps lay inside this cabin, as still and silent as it would be for all the ages to come.

Ridiculous. A gambling debt. Only in stories in the magazines did men take their lives for such reasons. Yet when he knocked again on the door, it was with much more force than before. No answer.

Reasonably he concluded that Burgess had found some other refuge on the ship. Or else he needed no refuge after all, it had all been a figment of Miss Faversham's overheated imagination. He would withdraw to his own stateroom. Sleep, perhaps, would drive away the various goblins that gnawed at him. Sleep would certainly remove the last traces of his dinner-time debauch. He would awake refreshed, ready to deal with all challenges and problems—the latter category having been satisfactorily reduced by one. For this, he vowed, was the very furthest he would venture in *l'affaire Burgess,* and insofar as this futile visit to the least salubrious part of the first-class accommodation had marked the final limit of his involvement, he was not sorry to have made it.

He was in the act of turning away from the door when, from behind it: "Yes?"

"Ah…" Reluctantly, he turned back, faced the solid oak. "Burgess—good evening. It's me."

"Who," came the courteous query at last, "is 'me'?"

"Oh—Crichton. You know. Arthur Crichton." A pause. "Burgess? Hello?"

"Yes. Hello, Crichton."

"May I—may I see you? I know it's rather late—but just a quick chat, you know."

"Yes, it is. Rather late."

Pause. Arthur had never stared so long at a shut door.

"Would you rather *not* see me, Burgess?"

"Will that be all right? Only I've just gone to bed, you know."

"Of course." Arthur stepped back from the door, as nimbly as if it had suddenly grown spikes. "Very sorry to have disturbed you."

"Quite all right. Good night, Crichton."

Arthur's lips framed the proper response, but nothing came out. He waited still by the door, listening, expecting to hear perhaps the shuffle of bedroom slippers as Burgess made his way back to bed. He heard nothing, and after a while he had a strong impression that the drummer was waiting too, just on the other side of the door. At length, Arthur started back up the corridor. In a contrary fashion, he found that the episode outside the door, which might have been expected to ratify his decision to have nothing more to do with Burgess's case, seemed to have had the opposite effect. At least he found himself with no more inclination to doubt Miss Faversham's perception. The drummer was in trouble. Otherwise—Arthur thought he knew him well enough to conclude—he could not have done anything so discourteous as to refuse to open his door to an acquaintance.

Of course, knowing the man to be in some difficulty still did not mean that he was required to do anything about it. He was quite clear about this.

=

He was approaching the stairs, beyond which lay his own corridor, when he heard a solid clatter of feet, and in a moment a man burst into view, bareheaded, wrapped in a rubber garment like a Mexican poncho. Arthur stopped as the man reached the foot of the stairs, looked him over with interest. It was Babcock. Babcock from Nova Scotia. Arthur had never really studied the fellow before. Feeling a general antipathy toward him—some of which was the result no doubt of a quite marked dislike he entertained for his fat compatriot Harris—Arthur had consigned him to that large category of fellow passengers who might be summed up in the single word *blur*. A verdict compounded in Babcock's case in that for most of the voyage he had appeared just as one of the figures around the card table, performing their monotonous, automatic rituals.

Now looking at him closely, Arthur saw a much more striking figure than he remembered. A big, vigorous-looking fellow of about thirty-five. He looked in exceptionally fine fettle, an appearance of rude good health evident even under the dim light of the corridor. His dark cheeks were flushed, his eyes bright and alert, his black hair blown back away from his broad forehead. Face, hair, eyelashes, all were thoroughly damp.

As if his appearance needed some sort of explanation, Babcock grinned and said, "We've been out on deck for the past hour, trying to get our first glimpse of Europe."

"At night?" Arthur wondered.

"Oh, the lighthouse on Fastnet Rock, you know. The third officer says the lamp can be seen twenty miles out to sea…But not tonight. Probably fog along the coast. Hope it's gone by tomorrow. Should be. Wind's coming up strong now. Had a wave come over the rail, smack me right in the face. My God!"

Arthur smiled at the other's excitement.

"Is this your first visit to Britain, Mr. Babcock?"

"No, sir. I was over here in 'fifty-six. But still I'm just as keen to see the old place as I was back then. Wonder if it's changed any?"

It was not a question that demanded an answer. It was not really a question at all. Babcock was moving even as he said it, starting toward the corridor down which Burgess's cabin also lay. Eager to get out of his wet clothes, Arthur guessed. Towel his hair dry. Arthur called a good night that was cheerfully returned, and resumed walking toward his own corridor.

He had taken just a few steps when he stopped and turned suddenly around. "Mr. Babcock," he called.

Though far on his way to the sanctuary of his own cabin and dry clothes, Babcock turned good-temperedly back toward him.

"Sir?"

"May I ask you a question?"

"Why—surely."

The two men drew together again.

"A day or so ago—I don't know when exactly—you quitted the card game in the saloon. Your friend Harris did the same…May I ask why?"

The smiling generosity of Babcock's countenance—a temporary condition only, Arthur deduced, caused by his recent exhilarating encounter with the night sea—disappeared in a second. To be replaced by what Arthur remembered as more typical of the man's everyday demeanor: a reserved, somewhat unfriendly watchfulness. He waited for the answer, trying to keep a genial expression on his own face, as if the air between them had not become suddenly colder and laced with suspicion.

"Just got tired of it."

"Tired of it?"

"Sure. I'd been playing since we sailed."

"I see. Harris felt the same way?"

"You'd have to ask him that."

Babcock was edging away from him. He had to bring him quickly to the point.

"It was a coincidence then that your departure coincided with the arrival of the Negro at the table?"

Babcock's sideways glide came to a stop. He shook his head.

"I played a couple of days there with Stuart sitting in."

"And then you stopped. Was there anything about Stuart's style of play that displeased you?"

Babcock frowned.

"Did you think, perhaps, he was playing in collusion with another?"

"Look, Mr. Crichton," Babcock came in strongly, "you have to be real careful when you start—"

"Did you lose much, Babcock?"

"No more than I can afford to." Babcock stopped, looked away for a moment. He sighed heavily then, looked back at Arthur. "I don't know if you're familiar with poker, Mr. Crichton, but there's no problem if you find yourself in a game which ain't exactly ... *square*. You just throw in your hand, get up on your feet, say 'Thanks, gents' for the lesson, and walk away from it. Only a fool"—Babcock nodded—"keeps trying to win back his money in a game like that."

"Are you talking about Burgess?"

Babcock was silent.

"Apparently he has lost a great deal of money."

"He *is* a damn fool when it comes to cards, Mr. Crichton. I'd say he got what he deserved."

"Not if he was cheated out of it."

"Now there," warned the Nova Scotian, "you are saying what I never would. Unless I wanted to see myself in a whole lot of trouble." He regarded Arthur at first quite censoriously, and then—as if some remaining trace of his encounter with the sea had stirred up his better parts—he went on in a kinder voice: "Say, Mr. Crichton, I don't know how it is in England, but where I come from...well, it's all part of the game. If you run into a couple of fellows—"

"There were two of them then. Major Cutler was the other man?"

"If," Babcock bore on, "you happen to find yourself in a game with some slick fellows, why—like I said—you just get up, and walk away. No hard feelings. *It's part of the game.*"

"By 'slick fellows'—you mean cheats?"

Babcock shook his head, evidently finding Arthur incorrigible.

"You yourself have lost money because of these—"

"I didn't lose anything," the Nova Scotian snapped. He was silent for a moment. Then: "I paid out a certain amount of money to find out what I needed to know. And when I knew, I quit the game. That's all it was... *Good night,* sir," he almost shouted, as Arthur tried to open up another seam in his inquiry, and he turned firmly away and marched off toward his own corridor.

51°43' N, 7°20' W

The day was hardly begun—no more than a scraping of white in the east against the sable sky. A keen wind searched Arthur out as he stood in the doorway to the main deck. A wet mist gathered upon his unprotected face. It tasted salt upon his lips, and he guessed the dew was from sea spray rather than rain. But there was rain in the air, he was sure. He blinked his eyes, and peered along the gradually lightening deck. Even so early there were men about. The stewards and their helpers had surrounded the lifeboats and were taking from underneath the last of the fresh provisions, and ferrying them across the deck to the galley. Other men were scrubbing the planks.

He had lain restless in his bunk for forty minutes after waking, his brain seething with all the questions that had failed to trouble his sleep, which had been dreamless and deep. As if making up for lost time, they buzzed and stung him without mercy now. He tried to dodge them by shifting his attention to other, less painful debates. Such as the Tate business, still shamefully unresolved. He had been brought an interesting, serious business proposition: a scheme of really heroic proportions, whose undertaking would not only affect his own fortunes, or Tate's, but perhaps be the means of helping bring new hope to a devastated portion of the earth. And he'd done nothing much since hearing of it, except hide from its author. And now they were little more than twenty-four hours from Liverpool. He must make a decision. Was it to be no after all? He was almost sure it was. And yet... and yet—

It was no good. He couldn't keep his mind on the damn thing. No matter how big, heroic, momentous. He hauled himself out of bed, shrugged on some clothes. Olivia and Burgess. Burgess and Olivia. If he had to spend all his time on such tortuous themes, he would at least do it away from this airless hole.

The sea wind hit him with thumping force as he tried to move away from the shelter of the doorway toward where the stewards were working. A general idea of coffee was propelling him onward. He hoped a small tip might persuade one of the stewards away from his present task. He recalled that Miss Faversham seemed able to get a cup at any ungodly hour of the morning. With luck he would discover her supplier.

But he had been unprepared for the strength of the wind and had set off into it too weakly. With ideas of regrouping, so that his next assault could be more vigorously mounted, he turned back into the doorway—and nearly collided with John Bonney coming out onto the deck.

It was the first time he'd seen the young man, Arthur realized, since their peculiar encounter on the poop immediately before he'd received the good news of Olivia's recovery. If Bonney had not looked his best at that meeting, his appearance had actually deteriorated since then. He looked awful: bleary-eyed, features tired and drawn, hair, clothing awry. He looked, as Arthur couldn't refrain from pointing out, as if he'd been up all night.

"I have," Bonney said bleakly. "Most of it anyway. I couldn't sleep. Came up from my cabin, about midnight. Been in the saloon since then." His face twisted with disgust. "God, the stench in there."

"Yes, better off out here. Bit of fresh air. Though perhaps rather too fresh at present for my—"

"I'm glad to find you, Mr. Crichton," Bonney said. "For I wish to talk to you."

"Yes?" Arthur waited.

"Oh, not here..." The young man's glance traveled briefly toward where, not far off, the stewards were clustered. Some of them were larking about now, calling to each other, laughing. "Somewhere more private."

His eyes returned to consider Arthur. In the gray dawn they seemed very large, very dark. Unmistakably the eyes of a man with much on his mind. But then, Arthur told himself firmly, so have I. And am not going to find a better time of day than this to concentrate on what vexes me. Without a soul to trouble me. Except this gaunt, imploring specimen.

Well, he would just have to be put off. Arthur had opened his mouth to do exactly that—when he noticed that he had lost the other's attention. Bonney was looking past him now with such concentration that Arthur had the oddest feeling that he himself had just disappeared.

"Why, what is that?" Bonney said in a wondering tone.

Arthur turned to look. Saw nothing at first but a gray, heaving sea. And then it came to him. The horizon wasn't empty anymore. And it wasn't so far away as usual. There was a brownish line intruding on its grand receding sweep, cutting it off.

"It is land," he said at last.

Bonney was silent for a moment. Then: "That is *Europe?*"

"Yes, I suppose so. Its furthest reach. The west of Ireland, you know."

A steward was passing nearby. Arthur beckoned to him. Pointed to the line as he came up.

"Where exactly are we, steward?"

"Ten miles east of Kinsale, sir" came a prompt reply. "Did you not see the light from Old Head as we went by?"

Arthur and Bonney shook their heads.

"Good and clear it was. If you keep on looking, we should be off the Roche's Point light at Queenstown pretty soon. Shining red, that'll be."

Arthur nodded his thanks, and the steward left them. Too late, he remembered his need for coffee. He thought of calling after the man, but he had already disappeared. Arthur shrugged and turned back to deal with his companion. The young man was still staring at the distant land, an expression on his ravaged face of—well, what exactly was it?

It was *wonder,* Arthur saw at last. Bonney was staring at the land with a look of almost childlike awe. A child at his first circus, seeing his first elephant... And yet, coldly considered, the bit of land they were observing was as flat seeming and uninteresting as almost any would appear from so far out at sea.

It was the fact that it was *Europe,* Arthur understood suddenly. And for a moment, sympathetically, he shared in what must be passing through the other's mind. Raised in the vast interior of his own country, he would feel it something—something so *extraordinary*— to find himself here, for his eyes to be taking in their first glimpse of another world. A New World it was for Bonney. It must be as strange almost as to find oneself looking out across the surface of the moon. Arthur tried to remember if he had felt such great wonder on his first glimpse of America. He had been excited certainly, but not nearly as enthralled as Bonney seemed to be. But then he had not been twenty-one either, and America had not been his first foreign landfall.

"Mr. Bonney," he said at last gently.

The young man shifted his glance reluctantly from Europe to Arthur.

"This—*talk* that you wished to have with me? Perhaps after breakfast would be best."

All notions of other worlds, of wonder, of concern about anything beyond his own self fled from Bonney's eyes as Arthur watched. His mouth tightened into a grim, impatient line. "Now would be better," he said. Cracks of worry, almost of fear spread across his tortured countenance. "I must settle things soon, Mr. Crichton. Or else I shall go mad."

Arthur watched a little longer, then sighed, gave the merest bow to show his acceptance of the inevitable.

"We could go into the saloon?" Bonney suggested.

"I'd rather not. As you said, the air in the early morning is vile in there."

"Then..." Bonney looked up and down the deck, seeking inspiration. "Do you know the capstan galley? Forward of the kitchen. There are seats in there."

Arthur studied Bonney's features. Could see no mischief in them, no suggestion that his proposing such a site for this discussion—*her hand, in the fog, groping along his thigh*—was inspired by any malevolent motive.

"Very well," he said at last, and turned away and started off up the deck, not looking to see if he was being followed. The wind hadn't died down at all, but it no longer seemed to impede his progress. He rather welcomed striking against its force; battering it down, hurting it.

=

"Where would you like to sit, sir?"

"Thank you, Mr. Bonney. I prefer to stand."

They were in that place, that attenuated rectangle, where almost all the more memorable moments of Arthur's recent life appeared to have taken place. Here Olivia had sat reading her book, waiting for him, that first day the seasickness had yielded its grip. And then days—only days—later it was here that she had sat with Bonney, and at a distance he had strained to see through the sea mist whether the pictures that burned in his mind of his wife caressing another man were products of the weather and of his own drunken confusion, or were true. Another day, the actors had changed. He was bowed over in grief, telling Miss Faversham of all the murk and mess of his married life. All in this little space.

"I shall sit," Bonney said. "For I am so tired."

He slipped down onto the bench—same spot almost exactly as where Olivia had sat, reading; a little way off from where she had sat, fondling. Arthur looked down on him. Tried to remember how much he hated this man. How much at any rate he ought to hate him. Bonney looked utterly haggard. He had closed his eyes, was breathing shallowly. He had tried to shave himself recently, Arthur noted. But he had done it most ineptly. In places the skin was entirely bare, but mostly not. The whiskers stood at various elevations. There was a trace of blood upon his chin.

"Well, Mr. Bonney," Arthur said as coldly as he could. "What do you have to say to me?"

Bonney opened his eyes. "I want to see Mrs. Crichton," he said.

A pause as Arthur waited for more. Nothing came.

"You want to see my wife?"

"Yes, sir."

"But why shouldn't you? You certainly did not have to ask permission of me. Mrs. Crichton is well enough to receive visitors now. Even yesterday, a couple of the ladies dropped in to see her. And then, of course, she came up on deck for a while. Were you not able to speak to her then?"

Bonney was silent. Arthur nodded.

"Yes, I should think anytime after, say, eleven o'clock this morning will be convenient. Though I must warn you that she may easily become tired, so you should plan that your visit will be a short—"

"Oh, I don't mean like that." Bonney shook his head impatiently. "There is always somebody around her now. You—or the stewardess. I want to speak to her alone."

A scream in the sky. Human sounding. But how, from up there? Humans not having the gift of flight. A gull, of course. Must be a gull.

"You wish to speak to her alone?...About what, may I ask?"

At first it looked as if the youth would refuse to tell. But then his show of defiance crumpled, he looked down at his knees. "Want to apologize to her," he muttered.

"Apologize?"

"The last time I saw her...at the end I spoke to her...I was—angry—unfeeling...I want to say how sorry I am."

The screaming trailing away now, the beat of wings beyond the foremast.

"It's not the first time you have felt obliged to apologize to my wife," Arthur remembered. "Perhaps you two were not meant to be friends. You don't mix well. Like oil and water, you know? Chalk and cheese."

"Why are you talking about cheese?" demanded Bonney angrily.

"It's an expression. Is it unknown in your country? It makes sense in England. Which is where we will be in quite a short time."

"I must see her alone. I must—"

"No, you mustn't. Really."

Bonney stared at him.

"My wife has been ill. She needs rest and peace. She does not need excitements. And you, Mr. Bonney, are always too exciting."

"Are you *forbidding* me to speak to her?"

"Well, yes, I suppose I am. Unless either myself or Mrs. Logan is present."

"You have no right—"

"Of course I do."

The young man was glaring at him now in the most belligerent fashion. Once again Arthur had a vision of the pair of them coming to blows. Their fight would spill out from the galley onto the deck. In full view of everyone. A scandal. Olivia would hear of it. Would she appreciate his gallantry, his springing to her defense? More to the point: whose side would she be on?

"Come now, Mr. Bonney," he began again, as steadily and good-humoredly as he could.

But the other was not listening to him. He had lowered his head, and now he shook it slowly, miserably, from side to side.

"We had become so close," he murmured. "And then—we disagreed . . . and then she fell ill—and I have suffered so."

Amazingly Arthur found himself to be quite cool. Showing no signs of discomfort. Except that he was blushing. For what reason, he did not know. It was not *he* that had any need to blush. But for a moment then he had a bizarre vision of Mrs. Stewart standing, smiling and compliant at the door to her cabin. He shook his head firmly to sweep the image away. Not relevant to the present issue.

"Mr. Bonney, really—" he started, hoping it didn't sound too much like bluster.

"Has she spoken of me at all in the last few days?"

"Never once," said Arthur. "In my hearing."

"I love her," the youth suddenly cried out. He covered his face with his hands. From behind his clutching fingers, he repeated the declaration a moment later, but muffled this time, as if it was choking him, ". . . love her . . . and I believe she loves me."

There was nothing, Arthur supposed, that in propriety he could do after that except turn on his heel and walk out of the galley. Oddly though, he felt more sure of himself now than before, and less unnerved by the young man. The blurted confession, and its wistful postscript, had rendered Bonney suddenly naked and defenseless. He was revealed as an adolescent in a tantrum of calf-love. In such a circumstance, it was clearly the job of an adult to ease the child's passage back to reason, not throw petrol on the fire by taking the outburst in the least bit seriously.

"It's not fair," Bonney lamented. "Why should you have her? You are so old."

Arthur came to the bench where Bonney was hunched over and sighing behind his hands, and settled himself down beside him.

"Listen to me, Bonney," he said at last. "It's over, you know."

Bonney's hands dropped from his face, he looked up.

Arthur nodded. "These ocean trips are curious things. Unnatural. People are complete strangers at the start, and by the end of it... Well, there was a couple on the *Persia* going over—but never mind them. I understand that a sympathy has grown up between yourself and my wife. I'm sure it has been a fine, a precious thing. But we are not very far from harbor now. And invariably the end of a voyage brings an end to such connections. *Invariably*, Mr. Bonney. Apparently you do not yet understand this. I believe my wife does. As I say, she has betrayed no concern about you or your whereabouts in all the time she has been convalescing. No doubt the ordeal of her illness in some way has helped her towards wisdom. In your case, your own sense of what is right and fitting must suffice. But it *is* ended, Mr. Bonney. It's finished. Over."

⸻

Silence, as the young man continued to stare at him. Arthur met his gaze calmly. On the whole, he felt pleased with the way he was handling this extraordinary interview. He had let Bonney say what he wanted, and had offered no direct opposition to him, except on the crucial point of his not seeing Olivia alone. Another man might have let the thing slide into noisy confrontation, violence even. Arthur knew better. Years of business meetings had taught him that the directly aggressive tactic rarely succeeded.

Pleasure in his success even spread to his contemplation of the cause of all the bother. Bonney was a nice enough fellow, he supposed. Perhaps, like the second Pitt, his only real crime was that of being young.

I would have made far too indulgent a father, Arthur thought sentimentally, as he watched the youth. (His own son would have been about Bonney's age now if he'd lived, or a year or two younger.) Perhaps there was some good fortune in the fact the role was denied me. Unfair to Laura though. Very unfair.

"Don't tell me," the young man growled suddenly, "that I don't love her."

"Now, Mr. Bonney—"

"I do love her. But I'm unlucky. I love her. But I can't speak to her. I love her. And I almost killed her."

"Now you are being absurd."

Bonney said nothing. Only glared at Arthur. His expression had changed yet again. There was no more vulnerability there, nothing crushed about it at all. Nothing now but anger and spite.

"If"—Arthur sighed—"you are referring to that . . . visit she made to your cabin—"

"Yes," said Bonney, almost gleefully. "That is just what I am referring to."

Arthur was silent for a moment. He felt the veins in his face and head had become suddenly thick and engorged, as if he was literally bulging with rage. He looked down, found his hands were balled into tight fists. He should not go on, he knew it. He should get up and walk out of this galley. Go along to the saloon. Get himself some coffee. Then go down and see if Olivia was awake. If she was, he would order her to have nothing further to do with this young reprobate. That was certainly what he should do.

"One day, Mr. Bonney," he gritted out, "we will both no doubt realize how disgraceful is this competition as to which of us contributed most to a young woman's serious illness. But if you must know—if there was anything that brought on the disease to its last, dangerous stages, it was because my wife that night—wanting so to speak to me—sat in the dark, freezing corridor outside my door, waiting for me. A foolish, fond gesture, far more dangerous for her health, I think you must admit, than talking to you in your cabin, however cold."

"Oh, she didn't just talk."

"What?"

In the gray morning light, the young man's eyes glittered with evil. "Talking wasn't all she did. Not at all."

"What do you mean?"

"I mean what I said. She did more than just talk ..."

People—passengers, early risers, females—moved past the galley entrance. Arthur did not identify them. And they seemed not to notice the two men inside, as if he and Bonney were locked away invisible inside their grotesque interview. In the numbed clarity that had come upon him, he heard one woman say distinctly: "—quite beautiful, scarlet with black velvet bands; the dress is silver-gray poplin; belt, collar, cuffs, epaulettes, all scarlet too and trimmed with black velvet." And the other said: "It was at Henderson's? On Church Street?" Then they were gone.

"I ask you again, Mr. Bonney. Just what do you mean by that?"

The last of the sunlight flickered and went out. A small rain began to fall. His life, it occurred to Arthur, was now in the hands of this evil, destructive boy, whatever he chose to say next. It all seemed to be happening, though, very slowly, and as if at about a hundred miles' distance from where they sat.

=

Up and up, through the falling rain: he grumbling, objecting, falling back; she a step behind him all the way, cajoling, urging, and, when he became especially recalcitrant, practically ordering him to go on.

"For pity's sake, Miss Faversham—I don't want the poor fellow dragged into this!"

"Not a question of 'dragging.' He will be proud to do his duty."

"Doubt that most strongly," Burgess grumbled.

"Nonsense. Didn't you tell me he came to your cabin last night?"

"But I don't know what *for.*"

"It's plain as can be why he did it. His conscience was working upon him. He wishes to help you.... And please don't come to a stop while we are on a ladder, Mr. Burgess. It is a most precarious situation. Go on. Go on!"

At the top of the ladder, they huddled together under the umbrella Miss Faversham had thought to fetch from her cabin before they'd set out. Through the thick, weeping air, they surveyed the poop. "There he is," she murmured.

Burgess had already picked him out. On a bench on the starboard side. Crichton was sitting in an almost negligent manner, his legs crossed, his arms folded. For protection against the rain, he was wearing no more than he might have if he had confined himself to the saloon—no coat or mackintosh. No hat. His head was deeply bowed, he was staring down as if subjecting his folded arms to a most intense study.

"Doesn't look like a chap who wants to talk to anyone."

"He *looks*," Miss Faversham stated, "like a 'chap' who is getting very wet. He will be glad to shelter under my umbrella."

And with that she began her advance along the poop. For a moment, Burgess glanced back longingly down the ladder they had just mounted—but at last he sighed and, head down against the rain, followed her along the deck.

"Mr. Crichton!" she beamed as she came up. From the man on the bench there was no response, he did not even look up. Various explanations for her presence—such as the pleasure she always took in a walk in the rain, the advantage of rainwater to the complexion—died on Miss Faversham's lips. She looked down uncertainly at the silent figure on the bench. But Burgess came up then, and, emboldened by his arrival, she said again, louder, "Why, Mr. Crichton—here you are."

At that, he started and looked up. He seemed to have difficulty at first recognizing the intruders—or perhaps it was, she guessed, that he could not be bothered to identify them. His gaze drifted incuriously from her to Burgess, then back again. At last, he nodded, propelled himself very slightly upward to acknowledge her arrival.

"Miss Faversham," he said, in a voice that sounded not so much tired as empty. And: "Hello, Burgess."

"We have come," cried out Miss Faversham, in a determinedly sprightly voice, "to share your vigil. And to talk with you."

As she spoke, she settled herself on Arthur's left side. Burgess seemed to paw the deck with one foot.

"Not my idea, old man," he muttered.

"And you, Mr. Burgess, will sit on my other side. And thus my umbrella will shelter all three."

For a moment, as Burgess grudgingly sank down beside her, and even though she was still somewhat dismayed at her own effrontery in bursting upon poor Mr. Crichton like this, Miss Faversham experienced a moment of pure happiness. That such a little thing—to be perched between her two men, holding up her umbrella to protect them both—could give her such intense delight quite shocked her. Yet she thought she would not change her present occupation for the world. Pleasantly experiencing the warmth of a male body on either side of her, she listened to the patter of raindrops on the stretched material of her umbrella.

"Well, look here, we won't take up much of your time," she heard Burgess mumble at last, addressing Crichton, but really nudging her to begin.

Miss Faversham, somewhat reluctantly, woke again to her responsibilities. She shifted the umbrella's shaft from one hand to the other.

"Hardly any time at all, Mr. Crichton..." She took a breath, composed herself. "When we last spoke, I believe I became much too—heated. Incoherent even. I did not explain myself well. I was certain you would see things differently if you could hear the story from Mr. Burgess himself. Well, I know—I think—that you agree with me. And that is why you tried to get the truth from him last night in his cabin." Her voice became rather less confident then. "And so—I have brought him to you. As you see."

"Awfully sorry about this," Burgess mumbled from her other side. "Sorry about last night too. Nothing personal, old man. Just didn't feel up to talking to anybody."

Arthur did not appear to hear him. He gazed at Miss Faversham.

"Forgive me," he said at last. "What are you talking about?"

"Why—I'm talking of Mr. Burgess, of course. And how he was cheated by those card-playing villains. And how much money he has lost because of their knavery—" She stopped quite suddenly. She studied Arthur's face, shadowed as it was by the umbrella. "Are you well, Mr. Crichton?" she said then, in a very altered tone.

"Am I well?"

"Are you?" she persisted. "You don't look well—you look...you look rather *odd*."

"I'm perfectly all right. By the way, Miss Faversham," Arthur added, "I think you can put away your umbrella now. The rain has stopped, I believe."

"So it has," Burgess boomed out, evidently delighted they had moved on to a neutral sort of subject, like the weather. "Wretched clammy mist, though, ain't it? Don't need a map to know we're off the coast of Ireland, eh?"

Miss Faversham reluctantly lowered her umbrella. She kept her eyes all the time on Arthur's countenance. He was looking now toward Burgess, the faintest gleam of curiosity in his eyes.

"How much did you lose, Burgess?"

Before the drummer could answer—or even decide whether he would answer—they became aware of another presence. They looked up in unison. A steward stood before them. He held a note out to Arthur. Arthur took it, opened it. Miss Faversham had a glimpse of letters in bright blue ink, small letters, dashed off, evidently feminine. Having read the note, Arthur crumpled it, put it away in his pocket. He looked up at the steward and shook his head.

"Tell her I can't come now," he said.

The steward waited as if expecting more. But then, as there was nothing further added, he turned and left them.

They had lost Mr. Crichton again, she saw. He was staring at the deck before him as if he would bore through it to the chambers beneath, and then through them to the very hull and on through to the ocean beneath that. His expression began to frighten her. He looked so utterly lost, so inconsolable. As if to protect her against such a sight, he raised his hand then, and covered the upper part of his face, his haunted eyes. She noticed, without consciously absorbing the fact, that the skin of his knuckles was barked and bleeding slightly.

She thought there was nothing to be done now but for her and Burgess to get up and leave the poor man to whatever sorrows were tormenting him. That which had seemed so important a few minutes ago—and which had brought her bustling up here to intrude upon his solitude—shrank to nothing almost beside such overwhelming pain.

She looked across his body at her cointruder, meaning to signal to him that it was time to go.

Burgess wasn't looking at her.

"I lost fifteen hundred pounds," he said.

"*How* much?"

Only such a monumental sum, Miss Faversham knew, could have burst through the armor of Crichton's preoccupation. Though she had known the dreadful truth for a day and more, it shocked her anew to hear it said out loud. Fifteen hundred pounds. A small fortune! Burgess now nodded solemnly. With a stir of irritation, she guessed that he was starting to feel a perverse pride at the immensity of his folly.

"One thousand, four hundred and ninety-three pounds. To be exact."

"Such a sum has actually changed hands?"

"No. I gave three hundred in cash. The rest in a check."

"You were carrying three hundred pounds in currency?"

Burgess nodded. "My firm has an office in New York. I drew most of the commission I earned on this last trip from them."

Pierced once again by the enormity of what he had done, Burgess uttered a high, despairing yip of grief, and he jumped to his feet, and rushed over to the starboard side. For a moment Miss Faversham feared he would hurdle over it, and take his shame down to the bottom of the sea. But he only stood there, gripping the iron rail.

Miss Faversham turned back to her other companion.

"Mr. Crichton..." He turned his gaze to her. She saw again his unhappiness—worse than that: his desolation. "Forgive me," she said. "We have come to trouble you with our own affairs—and I think you have something else on your mind."

"I do," he said, without hesitating. "Something horribly on my mind. I wish to God I hadn't."

"Once you were able to talk to me about what distressed you. Couldn't you do so now?" Her glance shifted for a moment to the tormented little figure at the rail. "I can send *him* away..."

Arthur shook his head. "This, I can't talk about."

Miss Faversham nodded. Thought for a moment. "Then perhaps," she said, as brightly as she could, "it will ease your disquiet to think of another's plight. Mr. Burgess has lost so much—and he's not a rich man. I believe it will ruin him."

"Men must take responsibility for their actions. Women too, I suppose," he added in an undertone.

"But when that man is beset by *villains*—must he still pay the penalty, Mr. Crichton? In full? To swindlers?"

He shook his head again. "You are so sure they are swindlers?" he asked, though it seemed not so much a question directed at her as a rebuke for her easy use of such a term.

"Mr. Burgess is sure," she maintained firmly. "And Mr. Bonney seems to be too."

"Bonney?"

"Yes, old man" came Burgess's voice. "It was that young chap who tipped me off in the first place."

The drummer had come back to them, unnoticed. He sank down once more onto the bench.

"What do you mean: tipped you off?"

Burgess nodded. "Absolutely. It was—oh, I don't know—about a day after the colored chap joined us at the table. I'd started to lose rather regularly—"

"To Stuart?"

"Actually ... no. It was mostly to Cutler at the time. Anyway, I was sitting at lunch with Bonney. We were the only two left at our table. I started to tell him I was having a run of bad luck. And he said he'd been wondering if our precious pair might be 'sharps—"

"*Cardsharps,*" Miss Faversham explained.

"Well! Course I was pretty shocked to hear that. One doesn't go bandying around words like that—I mean, there *is* such a thing as slander ... But then I started to think about it—"

"How on earth would Bonney know that they were cardsharps?"

"Exactly what I asked him. Turns out he's spent a lot of time on those riverboats in the States. Went twice to New Orleans, before the war, on business with his father. Well, you know those boats are just gambling hells on water. And his father was a keen poker player. So young Johnny sat behind him and watched and learned. Few thousand miles of that, he reckons he can spot a cheat all right, he's a bally expert at—"

"And that's what he called Cutler and Stuart? Cheats?"

Burgess hesitated. "Not exactly," he admitted at last. "He just said...there was something about their style reminded him of the shady fellows he'd seen operating on the riverboats. Lot of trickery goes on there. Gangs that pretend they don't know each other, and then get together to pluck some—" He hesitated for a moment. Then nodded bleakly. "Some damn fool."

"But he's not sure?" Arthur persisted. "Not certain they are 'sharps?"

"He said he'd have to get into a game with them before he could be positive of that."

Arthur shrugged. "There is your course of action, then. Bonney must play against—"

"He won't do it," Burgess grunted. "We just asked him. Turned us down flat. He would hardly listen to us. Would he?" he appealed to Miss Faversham. She shook her head, she was still studying Arthur. "He's sitting down there in the saloon, pale as death. Except—" Even in his distress, Burgess couldn't help grinning. "His nose is red as a drunk's, and he's got the ripest of bruises coming up under his eye. Said he walked into a door. Well..." He smiled again. "That *may* be so."

"Then if Bonney declines to help, I can only suggest that you accept the loss of the three hundred pounds as best you may. It's an expensive lesson against playing cards with strangers. As for the rest, you can surely stop the check as soon as we land."

"Without proof those cheats *are* cheats? I'd be branded as a welsher all over England."

"Oh, surely not. People are not so attentive to every little scandal."

But Burgess seemed to ignore the comment, and after watching him a little longer, Arthur shrugged again and turned away.

＝

They had lost him now, almost entirely, she knew. His eyes were again without luster or light. He had managed to chase away for a time the harrowed look that had alarmed her a few minutes back, but to do so was costing him much effort, she saw. There were pinpoints of impatience at the corners of his mouth. They had taken up too much of his time. He longed so evidently to go back to what he had been doing before they had made their blundering appearance. He wanted to think of nothing but his own trouble.

She resolved again that he must, in pity, be left to think of his affairs without being subjected to *their* harassment. Again she looked across toward Burgess to warn him that it was time to go. She took a grip on her umbrella handle. She offered the distracted man beside her a polite and, she hoped, encouraging smile in parting.

"Thing is, Crichton," Burgess rumbled into speech once more. Miss Faversham closed her eyes. Mr. Burgess had noticed nothing. Nothing. "We thought of coming to you, to see if you wouldn't mind having a word with Bonney. We decided you were the only chap onboard who could change his mind."

"*I?*"

"Why, yes, old chap. He admires you very much, you know. Told me so himself."

"When did he tell you that?"

"Oh..." Burgess considered. "Few days ago, I think."

Arthur laughed shortly. "It would have to have been some days ago."

"Well, whenever it was, he was absolutely sincere. Said you were a very wise chap. That's it! Very *wise*...So we thought, he'd listen to you, if—"

"No." Miss Faversham could take it no more. She got to her feet. Burgess automatically rose after her. Mr. Crichton seemed to have forgotten his manners. He stayed seated, staring now directly ahead of him. "We will go now," she said, mainly for Burgess's benefit.

"Ah...will we? Well, all right. Suppose it was a pretty feeble idea, wasn't it? Definitely a long shot. Sorry about—"

"All right," said Arthur.

Miss Faversham and Burgess exchanged glances, returned to Arthur. He was buttoning his coat; he seemed surprised to find that the garment was rather wet.

"What did you say?" she asked.

"I said 'all right.' I'll talk to him, if you like." He got up. "Did you say he was in the saloon?"

"He was," Burgess nodded. "That was a while ago, mind."

"We'll look there first, then, shall we?"

With that, Arthur was away along the deck, heading for the stairs. The others stayed in place for several moments more before, with quickening steps, following him down.

They caught up with him outside the saloon door. He was turning away from the window, he looked satisfied.

"We're in luck," he said. "He's still in there."

He put up his hand to press the door open. At this point, Burgess—who had been dragging his feet rather for the last few yards—spoke up.

"I say …" They looked. He gave a smile, at once apologetic and stubborn. "D'you know … I think I'd just as soon not go through with this."

"Mr. Burgess!" Miss Faversham was shocked.

"Yes, I know, but … well, it's been your idea all along that I should brawl with these fellows. Hasn't it? I don't mean I'm not grateful, but …"

"Fifteen hundred pounds, Burgess," Arthur said quietly.

"I know. What did you call it? A damned expensive lesson. I shall have to pay for it. Though God knows how. But something like this"—he nodded at the saloon door—"it's the sort of thing—even if it turns out all right—it can show up when you least expect it, and give you a nasty poke in the eye. And I can't afford it, Crichton, that's the fact." Burgess drew himself to his full height then. "Dash it all, I'm a *drummer*. My word is my bond, you know."

He gave a last contrite smile, and picked his way past them, heading for the stairs down to the passenger berths. The other two looked after him, seeming too surprised at first to speak. Miss Faversham was struggling for breath.

"Well!" she said at last. And then: "The *coward*—"

"Now, then," Arthur objected gently. "I should guess a mixture of motives."

"When I think of the trouble I have taken over him."

"Which he forced you to take?"

Miss Faversham, in the midst of her indignation, caught Arthur's eye. After a moment, she subsided considerably, even fell victim to a reluctant smile.

"Yes, all right. I forced him." She sighed heavily as if contemplating the great waste of time it had been. "Well, at least you are relieved of your unwelcome commission."

Arthur glanced at the saloon door window.

"Perhaps I don't wish to be relieved of it."

Miss Faversham was smiling now, thinking Mr. Crichton was dealing with a situation that had become suddenly absurd by being humorous.

"You can hardly be expected to proceed on Mr. Burgess's behalf when he has himself just run for cover."

"Then I shall proceed on my own," Arthur said quietly, and then as she stared up at him: "Didn't you tell me I had a particular responsibility for this business? In that I raised the Negro up into the saloon?"

"It was an argument only—"

"You didn't mean it?"

Miss Faversham hesitated, not quite sure whether she had or not. She chose to avoid a decision.

"You can't involve Mr. Burgess in this when he has expressly asked us not to."

"I shan't involve him. He is not the only person to have played at cards with those gentlemen. He may not be the only one they have cheated...Anyway—his name need not be mentioned."

"But it is such a faint possibility"—Miss Faversham glanced at the saloon window—"that you can persuade Mr. Bonney to help us."

"Perhaps—perhaps not." He would not look at her. He stared past her, toward the dark interior where Burgess had gone. "It may be," he murmured at last, "that I am in a position to offer Mr. Bonney some inducement to join our cause."

"What inducement?"

But he had already pushed upon the saloon door. He held it open for her to go through, then stepped in after her. Bonney was sitting in a banquette at the far end.

"I'd like to speak to him alone, Miss Faversham," Arthur murmured. Then, without waiting for a reply, he advanced upon his objective.

＝

After all, she was not completely sorry to be excluded so. Two-thirds of the way to where Bonney sat, she dropped off to find her own place in another banquette situated at a diagonal from Bonney's. She watched as Mr. Crichton covered the rest of the distance. He was almost upon the young man when the latter looked up, and then got hastily to his feet. It looked to Miss Faversham—though she knew her imagination, which seemed so heavily overworked at present, could be playing her false—that Bonney had fallen immediately into a defensive crouch, as if expecting attack, as if preparing to fight back. From where she was now sitting, she could clearly see the ripening bruises on his face. Without conscious mental effort, a vision came to her immediately then of the fresh cuts and grazes she had seen on Crichton's hand.

But she didn't wish to dwell upon the conjunction just now, nor consider what it might mean, or whether it meant anything at all. A last look at the two men—they were seated now, at either end of their banquette, Crichton was talking—and she turned from them to survey the rest of the room.

The last of the breakfast things were being collected by the two stewards left in the saloon. Across from her, Mr. Harper was reading a book. Over at the card table, the men who were about to play were standing around it, talking, waiting as the cover was taken off. Though not all of them were here yet it seemed. She heard the villain called Major Cutler ask Mr. Farrow if Tate knew they were to start at nine. She couldn't hear Farrow's response, he was blocked from her sight and hearing by Mr. Barlow. She looked back across the room to the banquette where Bonney and Crichton sat. They were leaning close together now. The older man still seemed to be doing almost all the talking. They weren't looking at each other. They seemed like conspirators, but conspirators who wished each other no good at all.

Miss Faversham wished suddenly, heartily that she was not here. Whatever blaze of energy and indignation had brought her to this point had quite died away now. The sight of Bonney and Crichton muttering together over there—something was going to happen, she sensed, something real to replace the enjoyably muddled crusade she had been leading so far on Burgess's behalf. And perhaps what would now be done was worse, more evil by far, than the wickedness it was meant to fight. She did not know why she sensed this; but she saw these things, as if in a row: Crichton's despair on the deck above—it could only have been because of his imprudent young wife; then Bonney's battered face; last, Crichton saying he might be in a position to offer the young man an inducement. And she had said, "What inducement?" And he would not answer her.

One-two-three in a row. And they had not even the sanction of Mr. Burgess's support anymore. For he had run from the fight as soon as it risked turning serious. As she so much wanted to run now.

Miss Faversham had too much pride to accuse herself of being frightened. She was pretty sure though that she was out of her depth. She tried to remember how she had got so deeply into this affair. She had been feeling, she remembered, rather at a loss that day, rather sorry for herself. It was after Mr. Crichton had got the joyful news that his wife was on the mend. Of course he wanted nothing else than to be with the young woman; of course, *now* he had no need of the old one. Miss Faversham had served her purpose. She had been a devoted confidante when he had needed one most desperately—and now he didn't anymore. She had understood the situation perfectly. She had also felt suddenly lost, lonely, discarded. Almost desperate.

Unluckily, as it was rapidly seeming to her, it was while she was in that particular state of mind that she had become entangled with Mr. Burgess and his woes. As if she now had some sort of weather vane device installed within that directed her inevitably to whichever gentleman onboard was currently in most trouble. Toward the evening of that day, she had found Burgess pacing the main deck and—with some difficulty—had engaged him in conversation. Monosyllabic at first, within five minutes the whole story had come pouring out of him, all the shame and anger and the ugly details: the vile cheats, the stupendous losses, what Bonney had said.

At that last thought, she glanced again toward the far banquette. The young American was speaking now, and it was Mr. Crichton's turn to nod. She did not like to see the expression on Bonney's face; it was very close to gloating, she thought. She turned back to the card table. Mr. Tate was hurrying up to it, apologizing for his lateness. The other men—Mr. Barlow, Mr. Farrow, the two villains—were already seated. The black man was about to deal.

Was there in me, Miss Faversham thought, some small voice that told me as I listened to Burgess's complaints: here is something I can go back to Mr. Crichton with, and he will become engaged with me in this new drama, and we will be friends again? Really though, she knew it needed no speculation on her part. It was so. She had thought exactly that. Had she then, in that time when she had been his friend, his *confidante*, fallen—just a little—in love with Mr. Crichton?

Miss Faversham closed her eyes. It was all too much for her. She thought longingly of the little cottage in Teynham, and of the quiet, even temper of her life there. It was true that six months ago she had felt that both cottage and temper of life were driving her mad with boredom, and for that reason only she had hurled herself across the ocean, taking up an invitation from someone who was barely even a friend, an invitation that she knew full well had never been seriously meant. She had thought she would endure any embarrassment just for a change of scene and to view some new faces. But now, in this moment, she did not care if once again her entire acquaintance should consist of her maid, of the man who came to dig her garden, and of the postman who walked by her cottage three days each week to leave letters at some other address. At least once back home, she would not have to wrestle with such murky, probably unholy emotions. In love with Mr. Crichton? A married man? The idea!

"We have him" came the voice from above her. She looked up, gazed almost fearfully at Crichton's countenance as he loomed over her. He was smiling, but with little humor in his gray eyes.

"We have him?" she repeated numbly.

For answer, he nodded to where John Bonney, having risen from the banquette, was now passing the card table on his way to the saloon door. He did not glance at the gamblers as he went by, nor they at him. All were staring at their cards. Mr. Farrow pushed three counters into the pile in the center of the table.

"He will sit and play with those fellows." Crichton slipped into the seat beside Miss Faversham. "If they will let him in the game."

"Why shouldn't they?"

Crichton shrugged.

"Where has he gone now?" Miss Faversham persevered.

"Said he needed to pick up something. I don't know what. Maybe a rabbit's foot. Lucky charm, you know."

Miss Faversham studied him. His expression was calm, almost contented. She could not read his eyes, though.

"Oh, what have you *done?*" she said in a low, urgent voice. "What have you promised him?"

He gazed back at her. He didn't speak at first. Then: "I have persuaded him to help us. Perhaps he will clear up this wretched situation soon. Isn't that what you wanted?"

"What I want..." She stopped. Still she tried to search his eyes for the truth. "I don't know what you are doing, Mr. Crichton. I think—I fear—something is not right."

He only shrugged again. Looked away from her. In a moment she followed his gaze. The gamblers. Mr. Harper and his novel. In the corner nearest the kitchen door, a steward waiting for orders. Monsieur Charvet at a far table, writing in a notebook. It struck her that they were all men in here, except her. She felt engulfed in maleness—their games, their morals, their dangerous contests. She was suddenly warm, much too warm—this though the day was cool, and the damp air clung to the skin like clammy perspiration. She fumbled for a moment in her reticule for a handkerchief to wipe the moisture from her lip and brow. Seeing her need, Crichton produced his own handkerchief. It was large, clean, stiff. Male. She waved it away. Found her own at last.

She came to a decision. Got to her feet. He rose after her. She put out her hand to urge him back to his seat.

"I shall go to my cabin," she said, "for I don't wish to be part of this."

It appeared to her edgy perceptions that an ironical gleam appeared in his eye. But he only nodded and said, "Perhaps it would be for the best."

She thought of making excuses for her flight. But then she remembered Burgess humming and hawing with that uneasy smile on his face before he had broken away like a rabbit, and she resolved to stay silent. Except she could not help herself, after she had taken a couple of paces away from him, turning back and muttering, "Are you *sure?*"

"Perfectly sure," he replied. It occurred to her as she pushed her way out of the saloon that she had not needed to explain, or he to ask, just what she had meant by that.

===

Five minutes after Miss Faversham had left the saloon, John Bonney reentered it. Arthur had occupied the time in watching a steward top up the stove with coal. He didn't glance once at the card table, though the murmur of play was always in his ears.

"Are you ready, Mr. Crichton?"

Arthur looked up. Bonney appeared very stern, very handsome. Against the light that fell from the skylight above, the fresh cuts and bruises on his face only served to increase the glamour of his presence: a soldier newly delivered from the field of battle. Arthur found it hard to understand how he had caused such damage with a single blow. From a sitting position too.

"You go ahead, Mr. Bonney. I think you know what is expected of you, and I should be an unnecessary addition to the game."

"You don't care to play?"

"I don't know how to play this game. Nor any other game practically. I do," Arthur added, hardly addressing Bonney now, "occasionally play a game against my wife. It is called Beat Your Neighbor. I doubt it would find favor at that table—though I assure you the play can wax fast and furious."

He watched as Bonney approached the card table, made his request to join the game. There seemed some hesitancy, he thought, on the part of Major Cutler, but fairly quickly the young man was nodded into the company by Tate. Cards were dealt. They began again to play.

So far away, the game appeared mechanical, without variety. Sitting there, watching, listening, not really knowing what was happening, Arthur grew bored. And from that he turned sleepy. Farrow was saying: "I check," and Bonney: "Three cards here." Hearing their voices, Arthur looked up, stared at the players for a while, looked away again. Now he felt no longer drowsy. Everything inside was suddenly dark and empty. And he seemed to hear Olivia speaking out of the blackness. She had sent to him twice this morning, asking him to come to her cabin. He couldn't. He couldn't face her. He did not want to talk to her.

Bonney had said: "Talking wasn't all she did. Not at all." And he had said: "What do you mean?"

"I mean she did more than just talk … Though we did talk." The young man had sighed. "It seemed that we talked for hours. Perhaps it wasn't so. But we spoke of everything. In the end I could not help myself. I told her that I loved her. And she"—Bonney had smiled so joyfully—"she said it was so for her too." His smile had faded, the eyes become hooded, distant. "I said to her, if she loved me, she would give herself to me. Give herself now. Upon my bunk. I begged her. I demanded to know"—he had shaken his head, though whether in disapproval of his own behavior was not clear—"how, if she loved me, she could send me back to the war without granting my desire."

How could she indeed? Arthur found he was holding his breath. He had let it out in a long, silent sigh.

He felt a hand on his shoulder. Arthur looked up, dazed. Saw the drummer smiling down on him.

"Burgess," he muttered. "Why are you here?"

From the card table came a strangled cry. Both men looked immediately toward the source. But it was only Farrow moaning about his luck. "I was sure you wouldn't have had the pair," he was saying now, and Barlow was grinning across the table, saying, "Been sitting on it since the deal."

At the banquette, the two men looked back at each other. Arthur made room then for Burgess to sit down, but Burgess preferred to stand.

"I was—well—I was *skulking* down in my cabin just now," he explained. "Thinking what a bad showing I'd made when I called the thing off. Pure funk, of course." He grimaced unhappily. "And in front of Miss Faversham too … When I suddenly guessed—you hadn't taken a blind bit of notice of me. You'd gone to see Bonney. You were carrying on in spite of what I'd said."

"It's out of my hands now." Arthur gestured at the gamblers. "I'm afraid you're too late if you've come up here to stop me."

"Not a bit of it, old boy. I've come to say I'm sorry for being so bally spineless. And present myself ready for whatever comes along. Returned to duty, you know. Just like the old days." His gaze strayed back toward the table. "Has anything happened yet?"

"Nothing. It has been as you see it now, for forty minutes at least."

Together, they watched the game. The same low voices, the same small gestures and movements as the cards rose and fell from the players' hands. In a little while, as if he too was now wearied by the tedium of the spectacle, Burgess moved over to the banquette and settled upon it. His feet, Arthur noticed, did not quite touch the carpet.

"Why did you guess I would ignore your request?" he asked suddenly.

"Oh, I suppose—" The drummer thought about it for a moment. "Knowledge of the man, you see. Not," he added quickly, "that I really *know* you, old boy. Wouldn't presume to say that. But I think I can sum up people pretty quick. Not intimately perhaps—but the general outline, yes... It's my job to know people. I'm a drummer."

He said the last with such reverence that Arthur couldn't help remarking, "You rate your occupation pretty high, I see."

"I rate it at the highest. More than an occupation. A vocation."

"And yet—forgive me—the world in general does not seem to esteem the profession greatly."

"Because any number of scoundrels have unfortunately enlisted in our ranks. The nature of the work makes it easy to pervert it from its true ends, and so it has become a sort of home away from home for confidence men and tricksters. It doesn't change the worth of the work itself. Which—yes—I put at the very highest. Don't forget, Crichton, that Christ Himself was a sort of drummer. With supervisory responsibilities for twelve junior drummers under Him."

At that precise moment, a commotion broke out in the middle of the room. His head still spinning from Burgess's outrageous claim—Christ a *drummer?*—Arthur forced himself to look away from the little man. The rumpus centered on the card table. And though everything there was really happening with great speed, it seemed to Arthur afterward that there had been an infinite amount of time in which to watch the events unfolding.

He saw Bonney lurching to his feet. Heard him shout: "Stop him! Don't let him—" In the same moment, it seemed, with a sudden, subtle movement, Major Cutler transferred the cards in his hand to the middle of the table, where they joined a small heap of other cards already there. Bonney, baffled, was shouting now, "I saw you, you damn cheat!" Farrow was getting to his feet, crying, "What the devil—?" Barlow was pushing back his chair as if about to fly from the scene. Cutler was up now, snarling back across the table at Bonney: "You saw nothing, you goddamn—" Bonney wasn't listening. He was occupied with reaching under his coat, tugging at something. Stuart had his head down and was stroking open his hand of cards.

Arthur heard Burgess beside him say, "Oh, Lord." In the same instant he watched as Bonney took a long-barreled revolver from under his coat. But he seemed to—what? trip? stumble? lurch?—his hand knocked against the side of the table. He must not have had a good grip on the gun butt. The weapon fell to the floor, the carpet hardly deadening the sound it made on impact. Now all eyes—the Negro's still excepted—turned to Cutler. He was standing erect, the terrible alarm that had shown on his face moments before now rapidly leaving it, to be replaced by a gloating smile. Now he reached swiftly inside his jacket, and in a second there appeared in his fist the little pistol that Arthur had been shown long ago on the poop. When Bonney for a moment showed an inclination to drop to the floor to retrieve his own gun, Major Cutler waved the pistol at him and kept him upright.

"What is happening?" Farrow cried. "What's wrong?"

"*He* is wrong," Bonney gritted out, and he pointed across the table. His color was very high. Arthur guessed it was mainly due to mortification at his own clumsiness. "He is a damned cardsharp."

"Well, I do admire your guts, I guess," Cutler drawled comfortably. "To say that when you're holdin' a gun on an unarmed man is one thing. When *he's* holding the gun, and you don't have a damn thing in your hand—well, I declare that is pretty cool."

"Didn't you see?" Bonney demanded of the other players. "Didn't you see what he just did?"

There was a general shaking of heads. "I saw nothing," Tate said, and "Me neither," said Barlow. Cutler chuckled.

Bonney shook his head angrily. "If I could have counted his hand, I swear I would have found five cards."

"Five cards?" said Barlow, sounding confused.

"Three kings on the table," Bonney said impatiently, "means he should only have had four cards left in his hand." He pointed to the stack of cards in the center. "If we count them up, I know we'll find one more than there should be."

"What does that prove?" The major grinned. "I ain't the only man to throw in my hand."

"Mine's in there," Farrow nodded.

"And mine," lazily from Stuart.

"So maybe *some* gen'man had one more card than he ought to. But why pick on me? Anybody see me do anythin' underhand?" Major Cutler looked around the table confidently—as he was entitled to, Arthur thought. He was asking a question that had already been answered favorably for him.

"But that's why, don't you see?" Bonney persisted, though, it seemed to Arthur, with failing spirit. "Why do you think he threw in his cards like that?"

"Because the hand was finished," Cutler said easily. "Three kings beats two pair. That jackpot is mine."

The silence that followed bore testimony to the completeness of the major's victory. Bonney at last came to see it too. He shrugged and saying, "Well, I saw what I saw," he made to sit down in his seat.

"Stand up," the major commanded. "It's not over yet."

He waved his pistol again impatiently. Bonney slowly drew himself erect again. Arthur's eyes were entirely on the unfolding drama. He sensed rather than saw that Burgess, who had got up to stand beside him at the beginning, was now drifting toward the card table. He kept pace with him. In a moment they had joined the ring of spectators. Major Cutler glanced at them briefly. He did not seem distressed to find his audience had grown. Indeed, he appeared to swell a little internally as he turned back to Bonney. He was the man of the moment, the focus of all their attention.

"You called me a cheat, and you couldn't back it up," the major declared. "You pulled a gun on me, and you didn't use it. Now I am entitled to take your life. You sack of shit."

The profound silence that followed this was broken by the rustle of Stuart's chair legs against the carpet as he pushed back from the table and stood up.

"Looks like there won't be no more play for a while," he commented. "So if you gen'men will excuse me—"

"Why, Henry," Cutler blurted out, "you're not going to miss all the fun, are you?"

The Negro shot one brief and perfectly expressive glance across the table, and then sank back into his chair. He placed his hands before him, locked them together, studied them thoughtfully. He wore on his face an expression of complete forbearance, as of an adult caught up in some childish activity that he cannot for a time escape. Meanwhile, the cardplayers—those who had had no inkling of the truth until now—were staring at each other in disbelief.

"Henry?"

"I thought he was called—"

"How would Cutler know—?"

"I thought they were—"

"What is going on?"

"Jesus!"

Cutler himself seemed to realize that he had made a blunder. For the first time since Bonney dropped his gun, he appeared at a loss. "All right," he blared. And "That's enough!" And by waving his pistol about he was able to suppress the noise. The other cardplayers looked at one another, uneasily. Suddenly recent events, which had hitherto seemed to unroll themselves like some interesting but unbelievable play, appeared to them as unvarnished reality. There was a man with a gun, facing a man unarmed. An accusation of cheating had been made and—as Major Cutler had pointed out—made by the man who had now no means of protecting himself.

"Now then, gentlemen," Farrow spoke up, trying to inject a note of official command in his voice. "This won't do."

He was ignored. Barlow at this point pressed his hand to his chest, slumped back in his chair. "I must go down to my cabin," he moaned. "I must get my medicine."

"You stay there. And keep your mouth shut," the gunman advised.

"But I have a weak heart."

"Doesn't do to play poker with one of those, Mr. Barlow," Stuart observed in a mild voice, showing he had not completely abandoned the others to their folly.

Cutler, now reveling in his advantage, raised the pistol so that it was pointing at Bonney's head.

"I want to hear you apologize," he grinned. And when Bonney remained silent: "By all the laws known to me, written and unwritten, your life is forfeit. If you don't apologize, you will die."

At this last, Arthur, watching, listening, with the others, felt a throb of gladness. A picture flashed across his mind: Bonney, bleeding from the head, slumped across the table.

The next moment, as if to put a distance between himself and his pleasure in such a vision, he took a step forward. The pistol in Cutler's hand moved a little way toward him, until the major saw that he represented no threat. Then it returned to aim at Bonney.

Arthur said gruffly, "May I point out, Major Cutler, that we are sailing in a British ship and within British territorial waters. Your present course of conduct, if it should lead to injury or fatality upon the body of Mr. Bonney, will be judged in a British court on the basis of codes and statutes laid down by English common law. That law does not recognize the right of any man, in a private capacity, to take another man's life for any reason whatso—"

"Oh no, old boy," Cutler jeered. His hand was steady, the pistol now aimed directly at a point just above Bonney's mouth. "You bluffed me that way once already. Can't do it a second time. Besides," he added, "*he* ain't English. He ain't even a goddamn Easterner. He comes from where I come from, and *he* knows I got a right to kill him."

Bonney was silent. Again Arthur found himself tempted into a scoundrelly way of thinking. He couldn't help for a moment rather wishing that the boy would crack, and fall to his knees, and beg for forgiveness...

Forgiveness.

Bonney had asked her how, if she loved him, she could send him back to the war without granting his desire. In the capstan galley Arthur, then as now, admiring him, hating him, helpless to resist the glamour of youth and battle, had not known how she could.

He had found he was holding his breath. He had let it out in a long, silent sigh.

"She would not," the young man had grieved, clasping and unclasping his hands as he crouched upon the bench. "She said she loved me—but she could not do that. She would not be unfaithful"—he had looked up at Arthur with a kind of incredulity—"to *you*. And I could not move her. I begged, I think I wept—still she would not. But she said then"—he had carried on, just as Arthur was closing his eyes in shameful relief—"that as she loved me, she would do *something* for me. She would reveal herself, she would give her body to my eyes at least. And there and then—she did that. Took off her dress—and her shift—and everything... Until she was entirely naked. And she would turn this way and say to me, 'Do you like me like this, John?' And then she'd turn another way and say, 'And do you like me like this, John?' Oh, you cannot imagine it, Crichton—" Bonney's voice had rung out, angry with scorn. "It was something just for me. Only for me. And"—the voice was humble now—"it was the most beautiful sight I have ever seen..."

He had been silent for a moment, as he remembered. Then again his expression had turned baleful. "Goddamn brute that I was," he had rasped. "I could not stop looking at her. I made her stand naked before me for—I don't know how long. Long after she should have stopped. She was freezing, shivering, yet she would not clothe herself again until I had looked my fill. But I could never do that, and would not let her cover herself... Until she was truly suffering. But by then it was too late. She was ill. And it was my fault." He bowed his head. "But still I wanted to look. She started to dress herself. I begged her not to. I begged that she would let me touch her. I...I shouted at her, how could she think any man could endure to see her—and not take her?...And—she got frightened. And she ran away—"

At this point, having heard everything, Arthur had punched him in the face as hard as he could.

And shouldn't this boy, he thought now, be required to beg for forgiveness? Grovel for it? Humble himself upon the ground, forehead
rubbing into the carpet?

But Bonney did not. He only stared back at the jubilant major, his
one good eye showing the utmost contempt.

"Stop it now, Cutler," the Negro spoke then quietly. "You've had
your fun."

"Not by a long chalk." The major nodded. "He called me a cheat.
And now I'm going to shoot him down like a—"

"Oh, horseshit. You know you never shot a man in your life before."

Cutler frowned briefly. Then his face cleared. He giggled.

"Can't think of a better time to start," he said. He moved the pistol
upward a little, so that it again aimed at Bonney's forehead. "Say your
prayers now, you corn-holing little bastard."

Afterward, Arthur could have sworn that he actually saw the finger
tighten on the trigger. But whether Cutler would have shot Bonney, or
was just drawing out the moment in order to torture him, would never
be known. Arthur saw a blur of movement at his left-hand side.
Burgess had gone into action. And what was even more remarkable—
as if he was joined to the little drummer by a bond of steel—Arthur
found himself moving after him. They seemed to cover the ground
with wonderful speed. Cutler hardly had time to register the approaching danger before the two men were upon him. Burgess
wrapped his arms about his body, Arthur grappled for the hand that
held the gun. That hand had been knocked upward at the first impact.
A few moments of struggle, then there was a sudden *crack*, no more
than that, crisp, metallic, not loud. The gun fell from the major's newly
nerveless fingers. Burgess released his grip on him. Everybody looked
upward. In the glass of the skylight now, there was a small, neat hole.

"Now there, see what you done." Major Cutler's complaining voice
split the silence that followed. "Somebody's goin' to have to pay for
that—and I'll be damned if it's gonna be me."

He sank down upon his chair. Bonney was across to him in a second. He got hold of the major's left sleeve and pushed it back. Cutler

made no resistance at all; at this moment he seemed entirely detached from the proceedings.

His left arm was bare. Bonney reached over and rolled back the right sleeve. On the underside of the major's newly exposed forearm, secured to it by a leather strap, was a square of metal, a rectangle about three and a half inches by two and a half, a little larger than a playing card. It had a thin slit of an opening at the end closest to the wrist.

"Jeff Cutler, you are the biggest goddamn fool in the universe," Stuart said then. "With a new man at the table"—a nod at Bonney—"Why couldn't you be careful until you had seen what he was about?"

"It ain't my fault, Henry," Cutler whined. "I put it on when I got up this morning. How was I to know the sonbitch was goin' to show up?"

"But when he did show up—you didn't have to *use* it, did you?"

At a command from Bonney, Cutler undid the strap. With a sulky shrug, he handed over the little metal box. As the others watched, Bonney held the box above the table. Then rapped it against the surface once—a queen of spades sprang from the open slit at the top.

=

A powerful party—composed of Burgess, Tate, Farrow, and Barlow—volunteered to escort the major back to his cabin. There they planned to extract from him that portion of the drummer's cash he was holding and to tear up the check for the remainder of the sum. After that, they would make sure that Cutler stayed down there. On their way out, Burgess had called to Arthur, "Will you see the other rogue to his cabin, Crichton?" Now Arthur sat at the card table, facing Stuart, who had not yet moved from his seat.

At the insistence of the aggrieved victims of the pair, Stuart like Cutler was being required to pass the rest of the voyage confined in his cabin. (It was put to them that it was that or a report to the captain, probably followed by an interview with police detectives in Liverpool.) However, *he* was not being required to return the money he had won. He had resisted the notion with a passion, declaring that none of the money he had won from Burgess had been gained by underhanded means.

"I don't need to," he kept insisting. "I'm too good a player."

Burgess had had to admit finally that he had never seen a single trace of misbehavior on the Negro's part in all the time he had been playing with him, and Bonney, when appealed to, agreed that he had seen nothing exactly wrong either—though it was clear that Stuart was hardly ignorant of what had been going on, for they'd heard from his own mouth that he was aware of the need to be careful during this morning's play.

Now he was flicking casually through the pack of cards. He looked up then, pushed the cards over.

"Cut," he commanded.

Arthur cut. Stuart picked a card from the middle of the deck. "Ten of clubs," he said, without looking at it. It was. He drew another card, his eyes all the time on Arthur's face. "Jack of hearts."

"Yes." Arthur nodded. "You are a 'sharp, aren't you?"

"Only when I have to be." He flipped up another card. "Four of diamonds."

"Are you a singer, Stuart? An entertainer?"

"Professionally? No."

"Those playbills in your room—they're not genuine?"

Stuart shuffled the deck again. "Had a fellow in De-troit run them up for me." He thought for a moment, then started dealing out a hand of solitaire. "You know, I was an entertainer once. Kind of. Used to sing with my family when I was a kid. My father and uncles, my brother and me. Around Philadelphia that was. We'd sing spirituals, mostly. Mostly in private houses. Singing to de quality, you know . . . I had a pretty good voice back then."

"It's still pretty good. You showed that in the saloon the other night."

Stuart nodded, stared at the cards. "But it isn't strong enough. Not for regular work in a theater. And that's where the money is. No, I had to face it early on. No singer's life for me."

"So you became a cardsharp instead."

"I'm not a cardsharp. Cutler's a 'sharp—"

"And you are his partner. Why?"

"Because he's *white*, goddamnit. I can't make money playing against my own kind. They don't have enough of it. And I can't ask white men to sit down and play with me. Jeff Cutler—he gets into a game, after a while he says, 'You gen'men want some real action, I got a coon back in the hotel'll give you a helluva game.' And they rise to it, most usually—'No nigger can beat me at poker,' all that—and back they come to the hotel with Cutler, step into my parlor, and that's all I need. But I can't do it without Jeff—he's my *bait*."

"He's a reckless man. He will get you into deep trouble one day."

Stuart seemed to bridle for a moment at having to hear this unsolicited advice. But after a moment he shrugged, nodded. "I know. He's a fool. That's why he's having to go to Europe. He's made things too hot for himself in the States. At least the states where we operated." He flipped some cards in Arthur's direction. "See that? Third one came off the bottom."

Arthur shook his head. He hadn't seen. Stuart settled the pack back on the table. Sat for a moment thinking. Then he began, almost shyly: "Reason I agreed to come along when he axed me . . . well, see, I have heard—don't know if it's true—that things are different on this side the ocean. Concerning the coloreds—" He stopped. Then, uncertainly, as he probed forward into unfamiliar country: "I thought maybe I could come over with Jeff—but cut him loose pretty soon. I could sit in on any game I wanted. Nobody'd object to me."

He brought his gaze up to meet Arthur's now. So much hope in that darkness, such openness to hurt. And he was so *young*, Arthur saw. He had not really thought to give an age to the Negro until now. Moreover, the flavor or sheen of sophistication and old wisdom that Stuart habitually carried around with him appeared to add years to his age. Rather to make him seem ageless. But seeing him as he was now, unguarded, wistful, it was manifest that he was hardly any age at all, perhaps only twenty or twenty-one. Olivia's age. Or Bonney's.

It was as if the whole world had turned suddenly young, Arthur thought, and he the only ancient left staggering about on the face of the earth, still, by some freak of nature, not buried underneath it.

"Would you," the youth said hesitantly, "know if that was true in England? About the coloreds, you know?"

It was Arthur's turn to hesitate. And seeing him so uncertain, Stuart's expression hardened again. He nodded.

"I guess it was a lie after all. I should have known it."

"I'm not sure," Arthur said. He wanted very much to drive away the bleakness in Stuart's eyes. At the same time, he feared the worst thing he could do was be overoptimistic, and set the young man up for future humiliations. "Of course, we have had no such laws or civic ordinances against colored people as have disfigured America, not for very many years. But still…" Again he hesitated. "As to whether you could sit down to play at cards anytime you wanted, wherever you wanted, in clubs or private houses—" He stopped, shook his head.

Stuart sat for a while in silence. Then he nodded again. "Thank you, sir," he said, "for being honest."

"But I'll tell you what," Arthur spoke out again, his voice rising as the hopeful idea came to him, "you may find things quite different in *France*. Paris anyway. For I believe—and I believe it's true—that over there social standards are a great deal more—" He stopped. "Lax" was what he had first meant to say. "Much more liberal than ours," he finished at last.

The Negro thought it over. An interested smile began to spread upon his elegant countenance. "Paris, eh?" he said at length. "I like the sound of that. Is it far from England?"

"London to Paris? Less than a day with a smooth crossing. You may have to learn a whole new language," Arthur warned, but the Negro shrugged as if that was the least of the difficulties he anticipated.

=

They talked for a while longer. Stuart opened up a little on his mode of operation on the *Laurentia*. It had been, it seemed, a trial run for the campaign to be waged in Europe, to see if a bluff could be convincingly operated that presented himself and Cutler pitted against each other as deadly enemies. It had worked extremely well—as Mr. Crichton would have seen—though it had not been anticipated that Captain McDonough's cowardice would have kept Stuart in his cabin for *so* long.

The point of the exercise had been to make it easy for him and Cutler to secretly collaborate and exchange signals, once he had joined the game.

"Then you did cheat?"

"I told you"—Stuart sighed—"I told all the gen'men: none of the money I won from Burgess did I get by cheating."

"And from the others?"

"Not from them either." He was silent for a moment, then shrugged. "Though I helped Cutler pick up a couple of pots, just for the practice ... I'm a damn fine gambler, Mr. Crichton. Not the best there is, I'll admit that. And sometimes I need a little of the kind of help that ain't exactly in the rule book. But against those *amateurs*?" He shook his head scornfully.

At last, the Negro said, "I'd best be heading for my cabin. Before those fellows get back to *make* me." He got to his feet. As Arthur started to follow him, he put out a restraining hand. "No need to escort me, Mr. Crichton. I can find my own way."

"It seems a curious thing. We took you out of there—"

"And now you're sending me back." The Negro's right forefinger described a small, neat circle in the air. "Curious is one word for it. Oh, I don't argue with it," he said as Arthur tried to speak. "We've been lucky here. Hell, on the Mississippi boats, before the war, if they found something like what Cutler had on his arm, they'd throw him in the river. And use the nigger to weight him down."

Arthur held out his hand.

"Good luck in Paris. If you get over there."

"I believe I will try that." Letting go of Arthur's hand. "Good-bye, sir."

"Good-bye, Stuart ... But is that your real name?" he called after the retreating back. The young man paused, looked around.

"I guess it is."

"You *guess* it is. What does that mean?"

"I mean—certainly it's my name. Professionally speaking. Good luck, Crichton."

$$=$$

Stupidly, while he had given Bonney a definite period of time in which to try his fortune, he had not exactly defined when that period would begin or end. After one o'clock, he had told him.

"I've already arranged with Mrs. Logan that she will leave my wife's cabin at one. She has duties elsewhere on the ship then. I've told her not to worry if I haven't arrived yet. She must go ahead and leave, I will be along in a little while. But I shan't be along. Mrs. Crichton will be alone. As you desire."

He had explained this. But he had neglected to give a time when he would himself at last arrive at Olivia's cabin. So he had no notion when precisely Bonney would expect his own "time" to begin. One o'clock on the dot? One-oh-five? One-fifteen? He did not think the boy would wait much longer than that. He must be so impatient to put his case. Rushing to discover his destiny.

But then he *might* wait. He might need to pluck up his courage. He could not be so certain that his entreaties would be kindly received . . . One-twenty then? Later even?

Above all Arthur did not want to walk in and discover them still together. Shameful as so many aspects of this business were, he didn't think he could bear that final indecency. To see them together. Waiting for him so as to make the happy announcement? He shuddered at the thought.

He would wait until two then. By two o'clock, Bonney must be finished and gone.

He wandered about the ship. Tried the main deck, the capstan galley, climbed to the poop. There was nowhere he wished to settle. He thought of finding some companion to pass the time with, but then he realized that there was no one he wished to see. Except he had a faint desire to extend his conversation with Stuart—but not enough of one to make him want to go belowdecks, to walk along that corridor, to go past her room, to hear the sound of laughter from within—or, worst of all, no sound at all.

Colorado.

The single word that could speak for everything that pressed so hard upon his mind. *Colorado.* Though, he supposed, it might be interchangeable with a few other words. Such as *Nebraska, Nevada, Utah, Oregon,* and the great *California* itself, all those lovely, novel American names that he had heard so often dropped into conversations over there. Usually in conversations he was having with greedy, plundering businessmen—his colleagues, he acknowledged—who could hardly wait to get their hands on the spoils awaiting in those fabled lands, once the minor distractions of what was left of the war were cleared away. Nevertheless, out of whomsoever's mouth, the names resounded in the imagination like that—more than that—of El Dorado. They spoke of such immensity, such beauty, of a great unknown.

He had heard that the Mormons before the name of Utah had been adopted had wanted to call their territory Deseret. Deseret. In the interminable spaces of Deseret a man could easily lose himself. A man and a woman together could disappear in Deseret. Or Colorado.

He could not now precisely locate when the notion had first come to him, perhaps as far back—though he had no inkling then of how grave the crisis in his marriage was, how recklessly Olivia had struck at its roots—as his conversation with that rabid advocate of emigration to the great West, Mr. Cameron. Cameron had certainly given him the name of Colorado—but it was more likely that he had realized its utility for himself, and for his wife, during the terrible conversation with Bonney that had ended with him striking the boy. Or perhaps just afterward—though he had been so stunned then at the revelation of Olivia's misconduct, it had seemed that no other thought could occupy his brain except, over and over: she has bared herself to him, she has let him feast his eyes upon her nakedness. She has done before him what I had thought was mine alone to take pleasure in. My rights. All that was left of them. To see her.

Yes, most likely then: the tendrils of a new thought growing and spreading. A thought that said: this boy may not only be a destroyer, a butcher. He may be a savior too. Our savior, Livvy's and mine.

For he could see, dimly at first and distorted by his own rage, the image of something, a possibility, showing through the murk. He moved slowly to clear away all the dust and debris, and the image started to look like, very like...hope. Hope that there was a future possible for himself and Olivia, other than the bleak pair that had seemed their only options. Divorce, and social disgrace and isolation for her. Or to spend the rest of his life fearing, then enduring his own cuckoldry.

America. Arthur, like so many before him, had begun to consider whether the best chance for the future lay to the west. But not his own future. Olivia's. Before, when he had imagined her trying to make a life after a divorce, he had set that life against the settled codes of some European society, in London, or on the Continent. And he could not see how in those surroundings she could ever find a position that would make her existence bearable. Even with a protector by her side. Even if they were husband and wife.

But now—considering that protector to be Bonney: naturally he would want to take her home with him. To America. From what he had seen over there, Arthur did not think that the society of the eastern seaboard was less strict in its demands that the surface proprieties be observed than anywhere in Europe. Rather more so, perhaps. A second marriage, with the first husband still alive ... if it got out—and doubtless it would get out, he had enough connections over there now that rumors would find their way eventually across the ocean—her position would be untenable in such places as New York or Boston or Philadelphia, in almost any society that she might find herself, except the shabbiest. Bonney came from the interior of the country. Indiana, Arthur thought he remembered. Far from the East, yet all that region had been settled for several decades now, and there had been time enough for the codes of the older civilization to fasten upon the new in all their grim rigor. He had heard that the best society in St. Louis, for instance, was now quite stifling in its insistence on almost inhuman standards of propriety. It might be, Arthur saw, that whatever love he professed for Olivia, Bonney would be shy of producing her in his own place, before his family and friends, before his father.

But beyond that, beyond Indiana, beyond St. Louis—into those far lands that had hardly been touched yet by the civilizing, annihilating hands of Church and Society ... In Colorado. Or distant California. Or—just the day before they had left for England, he had heard casual mention of a brand-new territory, a just barely intruded upon colossus they were calling Arizona. Twice the size of England. *Arizona*. Where everything was still fluid. Where cities were springing up overnight, and the First Citizens had only gathered in the place the morning before. Where all manner and kinds of folk were still shifting themselves about, still not frozen into place. Where there could be no idea of an "irregular liaison" because there was no regularity yet, no regulations.

Arthur saw the immensity of the West as a vast ocean in which Livvy and Bonney could swim free, in ever-increasing circles, and never be sunk by a social iceberg or devoured by a sea monster of propriety. Where she might be the queen of Arizona. Or Colorado. Nevada. Utah. Queen Olivia of Deseret. And nobody dare point the finger at her. She was spotless, washed clean in an ocean of space.

═

The problem was: just as he was beginning dimly to see that the young American might be some sort of knight come out of the West to resolve the awful dilemma of his marriage, Arthur—in the role of outraged husband—had been pushing Bonney as far away from him and Olivia as he could. He had forbidden him to speak to his wife alone. He had then concluded the business by punching him hard in the face. He could hardly, in fact, have put a greater distance between themselves and their possible savior, and there seemed no way at all that it could be bridged.

But then, he remembered—he had by now found his way back to the capstan galley, was drumming his fingers nervously upon the bench on which he sat—then Miss Faversham had appeared on the poop, with Burgess in tow, and a story that had held no interest at all for him, until she had mentioned Bonney's name. As if in a flash, he had seen the way forward. He would go to Bonney and, in return for his assistance in uncovering the card cheats, he would offer him an interview with Olivia, alone, undisturbed. And in that interview, Arthur knew, Bonney would put his case, make his plea. The escape door would open for Livvy. The chance not to have to live a fractured life with an old man. The chance for spring to lie with spring, as was proper, as—he knew, he guessed—she longed for.

Colorado.

It had seemed such a brilliant idea that Arthur had even allowed himself to smile inwardly—and a little spitefully, he acknowledged—at the fact that the redemption Olivia would achieve should be located in the country she professed to detest.

His fingers beat away at the wooden bench. Time passed. He thought of looking at his watch again. Decided not to. Anyway, Bonney would be there by now. Bonney. Bonney.

He looked at his watch. One-thirty-one. He thought of going somewhere else to wait out the remaining time. Thought he wouldn't after all. Then got up and left the galley and went to the side rail. Nothing to be seen, though he was looking landward. They should be off the southeastern tip of Ireland by now, if not already turned into the St. George's Channel...

Not the least valuable part of this scheme to convert Olivia into an emigrant to the great republic—he mused—was that it might turn out to be the making of her. Out there, in the harsh wilderness, in the company of a fellow adventurer like Bonney, she would have to re-create herself into something more than what she was now: a rich man's darling, a captive bird in a gorgeous aviary. It was true that Olivia had never shown the least signs of deploring her imprison-ment—at least not her imprisonment to his wealth—in fact very much the opposite. Which was so unlike Laura's attitude, of course...

A gull called. He looked up. It was sitting in the rigging. There was a splat on the deck then. He looked down. A glistening white circle had appeared on one of the planks. He looked back at the gull. It flew off. Spirit of Laura?

He became aware of a feeling then, the strangest feeling, that was stealing through his body. It was such a coldness as made him shrink inside as it passed upward through him. It had got to his chest before he could quite locate what had begun it. He thought at first it must be an effect of thinking—however briefly—of his first wife. But as he traced back his thoughts, he found it wasn't so. It was the other Mrs. Crichton for whom he was now suffering this icy burning. For as he'd watched that gull fly away, and as he'd been mourning the disaster of his first marriage, he'd also been congratulating himself on how much better he was dealing with the fiasco of his second. Yes, he had been thinking of his *plan*, how smoothly it had worked out. How he had gone to Bonney and offered him his wife—no! Offered twenty min-utes of her time. Be clear about that. And in return... Yes. That was all clear. He had used the pretext of Burgess's troubles to—yes, that was clear too.

The problem was—and this was the source of the chill that his mind had released upon his body, it was at his face now—the problem was: *Why?*

Why had he done it?

Who was he deceiving in linking Burgess with this bargain he had struck with Bonney?

Only himself, all at once he saw. He had used Burgess as an acceptable way to bring himself to do what he had done.

In the guise of assisting a friend in trouble, he had done this: gifted an unstable, dangerous *adolescent* with a visit, alone, with his wife. Who had been very ill. Who was still recovering. He had set them up against each other, in an unequal contest, that could only end repulsively, like putting a spider and a fly in a bottle together.

To do . . . what? To solve his own confusion. His own. Arthur Crichton's. To take the weight from *his* shoulders. Because he could think of no way in which his and Olivia's stories could be played out satisfactorily together. So he would divide them. Remove her from his conscience. His presence. Shuffle her off. Bury her in America. Bury her anywhere.

His clever plan had been nothing more than a disguise for a crude trading in flesh. As, he had heard, in the English West Country in the old days, a man no longer willing to endure his wife would take her to market and sell her to the highest bidder.

He did not blame Bonney for acceding to this infamous bargain. Naturally he had jumped at it once offered. The queen of Deseret— a tasty dish to set before his dazzled eyes. But *himself*. Oh—he jumped to his feet. The chill in his frame had been replaced by its exact opposite. The shame was pouring out of him in great drops of sweat. *Livvy*. How could he have done it? Even if he had little hope that she could ultimately avoid a life of disloyalty and self-indulgence, he had no need to force the choice upon her. From him, at least, she had the right to expect that he would not actually dig the pit into which one day she would fall.

And now, rising like fire, there was something else. The young man was in his cabin. Now. *Toying* with his wife. Seducing her. It was intolerable. No matter how he had got there. (Good God—by invitation!) Nevertheless, he thought he would assassinate him if he caught him—doing anything at all to her.

He actually considered going to Burgess, who, after the excitement at the card table, had taken it upon himself to confiscate the major's pistol. Arthur fancied the thought of confronting Bonney with *that* in his hand. But there was no time. It was one-thirty-four. The die *must* be cast by now. He groaned. Turned. Ran along the deck. Several people smiled at him, called out to him. He didn't see them, hear them. Inside, he almost collided with the first officer.

"The very man!" Hartley cried. "Do you remember, Mr. Crichton, that I told you I had a book that explained Great Circle sailing admirably? I've found it, and here it is."

Smiling proudly, as one who confidently expects his proper measure of applause, Hartley held out a thick, brown-leathered volume.

"Oh, damn the Great Circle," Arthur muttered through his teeth. "And damn you too. Get out of my way."

He thrust the officer aside, took the stairs down to the passenger deck three at a time. Raced along the corridor. Came to her door. Thought of knocking. Then sneered at himself for a cowardly punctilio. He pushed open her door.

It was as he feared. She lay back upon the pillow, her nightgown unbuttoned, her breasts exposed, and a male head bowed before them as if in worship.

"Now, Olivia!" he cried out in a voice of Old Testament thunder.

She sat bolt upright at the noise. And the man reared back from his occupation. He turned then. Raised himself from his crouching position. Removed the brass stethoscope from his ears.

"Really, Mr. Crichton! You are much too loud. I would still prefer that my patient did not have to suffer such shocks as that."

Arthur found himself staring at the thick orange whiskers and indignant blue eyes of Dr. Davies. Olivia began to cry weakly.

=

It was all soon mended. The tears were a result only of a combination of surprise at Arthur's roar—for which he was still apologizing profusely—and what remained of the fatigue of sickness. As to the latter, the doctor's report was most encouraging.

"She is entirely out of the woods. In fact, a few moments ago I would have said it was past time for her to be out of that bed and up in the saloon where she belongs. Now, however"—a censorious glance at Arthur—"perhaps a few more hours of rest are indicated."

The doctor was finally got out of the cabin. Arthur closed the door behind him, came back to the bed. Olivia looked up, gave him a tremulous smile.

"You know, my dear," he said, "I think Davies is being a bit of an old woman. I'm sure it wouldn't hurt if you wanted to get up now."

She shook her head. "Not just yet, Arthur. But I do want to rise this evening. For the last night's dinner, you know. I expect there will be singing after, and—well, I want to be there for that."

He noticed that her room had become much cooler, was no longer unbearably stuffy. He looked around, saw that the porthole was a little open, and that the captain's stove had gone. Nothing, he thought, could better indicate Davies's faith that she was "out of the woods" now.

"Shall I leave you alone until then?"

"Oh, no," she cried. "Please don't, Arthur. Don't leave me."

"Very well," he said, taken aback a little by the urgency with which she'd said that. He smiled down at her. "Dinner is some way off. How shall we pass the time?"

"Cards?" she ventured. "It's been so long since we have played."

"So it has. Yes, let's do that."

He went over to his trunk, found inside a pack of cards. It was a pack he had picked up from the little table in their sitting room on their last day at home. It had traveled with them to America, and had been much used on the voyage over, and while they were there. The packet itself was rather battered looking now. It bore a tartan pattern, in blue and green and yellow, the same as was on the backs of the cards inside. Quite extensive research had failed to discover any Highland clan that claimed this particular design, so they had adopted it as their own: the Crichton tartan.

Arthur looked at the object in his hand, so redolent of home, of long, slumberous evenings by the fire, of looking up occasionally to see Livvy curled up in the armchair opposite. For him those evenings had represented a kind of perfection, marred only by a guilty supposition that they must be dreadfully boring for her, though she always said she loved those times above all.

"Are you all right, Arthur?" she called from behind him. "Can't you find the cards?"

He straightened up and turned and showed her the pack. He saw her eyes widen a little as she looked at it, saw that she remembered too. "The Crichton tartan," she smiled. The smile seemed to hang then at the corners of her mouth, her eyes searched out his, watched him.

He dropped into the chair near her bed, then bumped the chair across so that he was next to her. He shuffled the cards.

"Livvy, I wonder if you would like to learn another game?"

"Another game?"

"Mm. It's called poker. I have watched it so much of late, I think I know most of the rules by now, and—"

"No, Arthur," she said firmly.

"I just thought it would be a change."

"But I don't want a change."

He divided the pack, gave her half. They began to play. He seemed to have no face cards at all. She kept winning. He could hardly concentrate though on the play. He looked up at her. She seemed thoroughly involved in the game, smiling at her successes.

"Now, Arthur, what are you thinking of? Only one card for the knave."

"I'm sorry, my dear."

"I win again." She scooped up the pool, fitted it under her other cards, and gave the whole, thick stack a complacent tap with her hand.

They had played through the deck once, and it had been shuffled and divided again. He had found himself with more face cards this time, and was actually beginning to get a little interested in the game, when she remarked very casually: "Mr. Bonney visited me this afternoon."

He laid down an ace. Watched as she followed with four cards, none of them face cards. He picked up the pool from her counterpane.

"Did you hear me, Arthur?"

"Yes, dear. You said Mr. Bonney has visited you."

"It was rather inconvenient, as I was quite alone. Curious that he should have chosen just that time to call."

He happened to glance up at her then. Saw staring at him a pair of the shrewdest blue eyes . . . then her lids drooped to cover them. She played a card onto the one he had just laid down.

"I *told* him it was inconvenient. But he would not listen."

He wanted to keep on with the game, to give no show of apprehension, to keep his dignity—but he found that his hands and wrists would not move. He sat still, head bowed. They have made their pact, he thought, and she has been left to break the news to me. At least that showed a certain delicacy of feeling on their part: he would not have to receive his dismissal in the presence of his successful rival.

From somewhere Arthur found at last the strength to move his hands. He placed a queen on the upturned cards.

"I hope that Mr. Bonney did not become difficult."

"Difficult? Oh, no. But he did get rather noisy at one point. I quite feared he would give me a headache. He was as loud as you were when you came in just now."

"I've said I'm sorry for that, my dear."

His queen won him another pool. He picked it up. Laid down an ace.

"What was the young man so noisy about?"

"Oh, nothing of consequence. Really, he spoke so wildly I could hardly make head nor tail of it . . . Except near the end: he said that he has found a Cunard steamer bound for America that leaves Liverpool shortly after we shall dock. He intends to take a passage on it."

Five—three—ten—her king—four—six—his queen—

"How did he find out about this steamer?"

"I believe he said the ship's purser told him."

"Then such a gentleman does exist?"

Three—her knave—another ace—

"Must do . . . It is the *Persia* Mr. Bonney will be traveling on. Our old *Persia*! With Captain Shannon. Remember, Arthur?"

"Indeed I do."

Eight—two—four—

Seven.

"I win," Arthur said. And she growled in comical anger.

I have won, he thought vaguely then. And mine is the prize. He felt oddly flaccid. And discontented. Colorado, in its splendor, was sinking and expiring before him. He could not tell himself it didn't make him a little wistful to see it die.

"So Bonney was never actually offensive?"

"Oh, not that. Though after he'd said about going home, he became so very loud and wild again and waved his arms so much that I thought I was going to have to order him from my room. But luckily Dr. Davies arrived just then. And Mr. Bonney left."

THE
GREAT
CIRCLE

53°27′ N, 4°42′ W

A gust of laughter from the saloon windows behind him. Another song started up. A shout from high on one of the masts—a lookout was it? A hand settled on his arm. He looked around, implicitly expecting to find Olivia there. In the moonlight Miss Faversham was smiling up at him.

"Heartbreaker," she said. "Cruel man!"

Without needing to consult each other's wishes, both turned in the same moment and began to walk along the deck, Miss Faversham's hand still resting upon his arm.

"I thought you had gone below long ago," he said.

"I had. My cabin is just underneath the saloon. Those singing idiots kept me awake. So I climbed up to the deck. To find you baying the moon. Heartbreaker!"

"I know you must have some cause for what you say, ma'am. But I really cannot think what it can be."

"I'm referring, sir, to the very evident partiality shown you by the lovely Mrs. Stewart. And—what was equally evident—your sad failure to respond to it."

He was silent for a moment. Then: "And when was this evident partiality shown?"

"Why, during her recitation, of course."

The recitation. Late during the after-dinner entertainment, Harris, swaying and grown bold with drink, had brayed forth that of all the ladies present only Mrs. Stewart and Mrs. Crichton had failed to contribute to the singing. Mrs. Crichton, of course, was excused by reason of her indisposition. But Mrs. Stewart…? Excited, the diners had shouted out for the widow to perform. "She must be better than the rest of the gals," Babcock had remarked ungallantly, so incensing the husband of Mrs. Barlow that thereafter he made frequent uncomplimentary references to the Nova Scotian's own ill-received rendition of "Rocked in the Cradle of the Deep." Thankfully, Mrs. Stewart had stopped all this before it got out of hand by raising a graceful, yielding hand. Smiling, she had professed herself completely incompetent to sing, but said that she would be happy to declaim a short verse, if that would be acceptable. Another full-throated roar of encouragement had told her that it would. She rose then, making a most striking figure, with her head thrown back, and one hand resting upon her breast.

"I did not," said Arthur, his words rather falling over each other, "exactly notice that she showed marked attention to me."

"Well, she did," Miss Faversham promised. "But you are excused for not having noticed it—for I think she showed just the same amount to every other gentleman present. I suppose it was the nature of the particular piece. It seemed to tap a certain vein in her."

Mrs. Stewart had waited for silence—which took longer than might have been expected because in a corner banquette Burgess and Miss Faversham appeared to be rowing with each other at half volume, and it took the shushes of most of the saloon to get them to be quiet—and then she had waited still longer until not a pin could have been heard had it dared to drop. Then had said very simply: "Untold Love." Somebody had cleared his throat huskily. When it was all still again, she began:

> *In the depth of the ocean a flowret may bloom—*
> *Though its beauties for ever lie hid from the eye;*
> *Unadmired it may scatter its gentle perfume;*
> *Unheeded may live and unmourned may die.*
> *So oft in the breast the fair blossom of love,*
> *Concealed from the world all on secret may sigh;*
> *Uncherished, save only by angels above,*
> *And the hearts in whose deepest retreat it doth lie.*

"Very fine words, Miss Faversham."

"Indeed they were. But *can* flowers bloom in the ocean deep?"

"Seaweed, perhaps?"

"Possibly. Anyway, she scored a great success. I noted that several of the gentlemen turned quite red in the face trying to suppress their emotions."

They had reached the end of the port-side deck. The options were to continue around to the starboard side or to turn and retrace their footsteps. As they hesitated, there was a sudden bang toward the starboard, then a whooshing sound, followed by a second report and another *whoosh*. Their eyes turned to the sky. A few seconds, then the rockets broke one after the other in showers of blue and white. From the saloon, where the spectacle must have been visible through the skylight, came a cheer.

"So was it to the fair declaimer that you were offering your silent devotions just now?"

"Hardly."

"I am glad. Otherwise you would certainly quarrel with her intended, and it would be nice for the final stage of this crossing at least to be completed in peace and quiet."

"Her intended?" Arthur asked after a moment.

"Why, surely you have noticed?" They had started to walk back along the port-side deck. "Or have heard something? It is the great event of the whole voyage... Mrs. Stewart has landed her catch."

"I *thought* so," Arthur cried.

He felt suddenly quite elated, and he didn't know why. Then he thought he did know, and he grew less merry. For if Mrs. Stewart had truly found her match, then it seemed to him that the highest possible barrier had been erected against any revelation of that appalling scene between himself and the widow in her cabin. Even if she was at all inclined to reveal it—blackmail?—she would hardly now jeopardize her future happiness by doing so. Which was a mean thought to entertain, but there it was.

"Yes"—he nodded—"I had guessed something... So—the widow has captured her old salt?"

Miss Faversham peered up at him. "Well," she said uncertainly, "I have never heard those gentlemen called *that* before."

Which puzzled him. "Surely if anyone is entitled to the designation of 'old salt' Captain McDonough is?"

"Captain…?" A long moment, then she sighed. "It isn't McDonough."

"It isn't?"

"I should hope not. Otherwise his wife would have something to say about it, I should think."

"He is married?" asked Arthur, groping.

"He is. And his wife is always near him… Onboard, she calls herself Mrs. Logan. The stewardess. Did you not know?" She sighed again, much more pointedly than before. "Really, Mr. Crichton, you are the most unobservant of men."

"It isn't true. I can't believe—"

"Of course it's true. Inman does not allow officers' wives to follow their men to sea, so Mrs. Logan has had to take up the occupation of stewardess, for her husband is fond and does not like to be away from her. But it's an open secret. Everybody knows it." A pause, then: "*Almost* everybody, it seems."

═

The Reverend Stibbards it turned out was the actual object of Mrs. Stewart's affections. Arthur, still baffled by the revelation of who exactly had been toiling on Olivia's behalf for the past several days—dressing her and washing her and carrying her chamber pot—reacted almost with apathy to this news, which at another time he would have found fairly sensational. Miss Faversham though was still fascinated by the case.

"It's all signed, sealed, and delivered, barring only the parson's words. Immediately after landing, they are to make a tour with the Charvets through Lancashire and Yorkshire. They will stop in York at some point, and there will plight their troth at the minster itself. At least that is the reverend's plan. He is talking very grandly about it. Perhaps they will be allowed to. I hope they are." The spinster nodded firmly. "Though I found out that *I* could not stand him, he is a decent enough man, I suppose. And now is a very proud and happy one. And so he should be. She is certainly a fine-looking woman. By the way, the children turn out not to be her own."

"Not her own?"

"No. She says she was asked by a friend in Canada to bring them over to deliver to their grandparents. In Burnley, I believe. She cannot imagine, she says, how the impression got about that she was the mother... I think the reverend was mightily relieved to find that he would not have to play the fond papa *just* yet. Indeed, I do not think the business would have gone ahead had she not made it absolutely clear to him he would not be obliged to."

They had reached again the position on the deck where she had first found him. In silent consent, they stopped, leaned over the rail. Moonlight glittered on the water. The noise of the paddles had been stilled for several minutes now. The *Laurentia* sat in the water almost without motion, like a plump partridge waiting for the beaters.

He felt her shiver beside him, and he turned to her.

"Are you cold, Miss Faversham?"

"I will be soon. But not for a few minutes."

They returned to their silent contemplation of the silver stretched out below. Somewhere out there, Arthur knew, was a pile of rocks called the Skerries. They had passed them in daylight coming out. Behind them lay Holyhead, from whence the pilot boats would be approaching out, if their rockets had been seen.

And at that moment two more shot into the air. The cheer from the saloon this time seemed much more ragged and faint.

"Are you happy, Mr. Crichton?"

"Happy?" he said, startled.

"Yes," she said briskly. "It is a condition quite easy to recognize. Are you happy, sir?"

"I don't know, ma'am. I don't know what I am," he said at last. "I think I am in course of becoming something. But can't tell exactly what it is."

She was peering now up into his face. He returned her gaze, tried to smile for her. Under the moon they could see each other quite clearly.

"You have worried me greatly on this crossing."

"Very sorry for that. Thankfully, you won't have to worry for much longer."

"Don't sound so full of self-pity, sir."

"Don't be impertinent, Miss Faversham."

Injured silence—but then her face broke into smiles.

"I *am* impertinent, aren't I? Busybody. Nosy old woman."

"Since you have already told me you are younger than myself, I take that as an insult. Besides," Arthur added carefully, "I know that you are trying to deceive me. *My* concerns have hardly been the most important feature of this voyage for you. Nor even, I think, has Mrs. Stewart's romance completely occupied your attention. Or, to put it another way: it's my belief that the widow is not the only lady who has made a conquest on this crossing."

=

Miss Faversham looked away. She seemed to be torn now between smiling and frowning.

"It must be very obvious," she muttered at length, "if even an unobservant man like you can see it."

"Thank you, ma'am. I think it is the deal of arguing that goes on between the two of you that opened my eyes first."

"We do argue, don't we? Mr. Burgess irritates me so much, you see."

"Excellent basis for your future happiness... There is to be a future?"

"Perhaps."

"He has asked you to marry him?"

"Of course not. We have only been aware of each other's existence for—well, you know just how long."

"But... Isn't there a but?"

"But we have concluded that our friendship is at a point when it would be wrong to end it absolutely tomorrow. So I have invited him to visit me at my cottage in the near future. It will be a very proper visit, Mr. Crichton. I shall ask my sister to come over from Hythe and stay with me at the same time. So I will be rigorously chaperoned."

He laughed, and wanted to say something, to congratulate her on this enterprise. But he saw that she was thinking, and so held his peace.

"I know so little about him," she said quietly at last. "And it is not easy for me to know how to go about finding out. I have tried to discover where he stands in matters of religion, for instance. He appeared at first inquiry to have a strong though primitive faith—but then unhappily we fell into an argument upon a point of doctrine. And I could not proceed further on my quest."

Arthur wondered if this "point of doctrine" was connected at all with the Christ the Drummer notion. He trusted Burgess had had the sense to hold this back, in reserve as it were, otherwise he could see considerable difficulty ahead in advancing his suit. One thing he was sure about concerning Miss Faversham, even on their short acquaintance, was that her orthodoxy was profound.

On the other hand, it struck him then, that quality might make her a perfect match for an eccentric like Burgess. Perhaps.

"What do you think, Mr. Crichton?" She was staring up at him, her expression serious, yearning, as if she would drag the truth out of him, come what may.

"I think he is a fine chap. And he would be a very lucky chap if you were to accept him one day. In the meantime, this visit sounds like a good idea."

She was silent for a moment, then, in a voice quite unlike her usual firm and confident tones, said: "Mr. Burgess is a very short person, is he not? For a gentleman, I mean."

"He is, I suppose."

"And I am rather a tall one. For a woman... Together, do we not risk looking ridiculous?"

"What on earth do you care about that?"

She watched him for a little more, then nodded and looked away, smiling to herself. Arthur waited for a moment or two. Then: "The reason I mentioned your ... *friendship* with Burgess was not just to embarrass you—"

"Which you have succeeded in doing greatly."

"The thing is, you see, it's been in my mind to make a certain proposition to him. But I think you should hear of it first."

"A proposition?"

Very briefly he outlined the plan that Tate had brought him. Explained why he didn't believe it would work in its present form, at the present time. She was frowning, concentrating as she listened; he did not think she missed a word he said.

"Then if the plan is a poor one—?"

"Oh, I don't mean that. Indeed, it's a most interesting plan. My guess is that only time, a decade or two, is wanting to make it an excellent one. But in the here and now I believe we must proceed in other ways. Though it's also my belief that one day our path will take us exactly where Tate wants us to go."

Briefly again, he summarized what he saw as the immediate steps. A foothold at first, then something more than that, in one of the traditional American centers of cotton manufacture: Massachusetts, for instance, or Rhode Island. That would give the new firm an entrance into the hugely growing domestic market of the States. And then, if the firm could establish a strong base over there, when in the fullness of time the opportunities arose—south, east, west, wherever—they would be perfectly positioned to strike.

"I haven't said a word of this yet to Burgess. Nor even to Tate. My guess is that in tandem they will make a rare team. Tate understands very well the practical side of the business, but he is not perhaps the most easy of men in the personal line. I do not think he would be capable of generating much goodwill on his own, and that will be vital for a new firm, setting up in a foreign country. But on the other hand, your Mr. Burgess—"

"My Mr. Burgess," she said slowly, "is a good-natured, companionable, easygoing fellow—"

"Exactly. He makes friends wherever he goes. Also—at the stage we go into manufacture, I should certainly like to have his commercial skills on our side."

Her eyes kindled with pleasure. "You think Mr. Burgess is good at what he does?"

It was on the tip of Arthur's tongue to say that any man who thought his occupation could most appropriately be filled by the Son of God was worth employing. But in the end he said only "I think he puts a very high value on what he does, ma'am. Which means he most probably won't let us down."

She nodded, was quiet for a while. At last she looked up at him again.

"Why do you tell me this?" she asked.

"Because it occurs to me that I might not be playing the part of a friend if I was to make this offer to him."

"A friend to who, Mr. Crichton?"

"Why to you, Miss Faversham."

"He will be in America all the time?"

"Most of the time."

"When will he leave if he takes your offer?"

"Not for a few months."

"And would you not offer the position if I said I was opposed to it?"

He shook his head at last. "I suppose," he murmured, "I am giving you advance information, and no more."

"It's good of you." She touched the rail beside her, ran her gloved hand along it. "By the by," she said, "have you decided what this new firm will be called?"

"I thought Tate and Burgess would be quite adequate."

"No Crichton?"

He shook his head again. "After all, they will be doing nearly all the work. I shall merely be supplying the capital."

"And receiving the lion's share of the profits?"

"If there are any profits—indeed I shall, Miss Faversham."

They grinned at each other. Then she nodded. "Make your offer, Mr. Crichton. I suppose a few months will give us long enough to settle our minds. And if Mr. Burgess does make *me* an offer, and I should look favorably upon it, then . . . Well, yes"—she heaved in a great gulp of air—"yes, even Massachusetts."

=

As she left him, she asked if he intended to stay out here all night. On the whole, he couldn't think of a good reason why he shouldn't—or at least stay out until the pilot boat arrived. If it arrived. The clear night air was cold, but he was well protected against it. Earlier, after he'd seen Olivia to her cabin, he had gone along to his own. His trunk was in the middle of the floor, already packed for the morrow, and on the top of it lay a cloak that he planned to wear for the first time to celebrate reaching land.

He had bought it during his trip to New York, at A. T. Stewart's great store on Broadway. The famous marble palace outshone most of the merchandise it contained—but not this cloak. It was lined in silk of deepest crimson hue, and woven of the very finest wool. Woven in

American mills too, and cut and sewn by American manufacturers. Seeing it in Stewart's, he had coveted it as he rarely did any item of clothing—but not least because he wanted to bring it back to Lancashire and show it to a certain few people as an example of what the Americans were now capable of. For fear of exposing it to dirt or damage, he had kept it folded in his trunk all during the crossing. Olivia had never seen him wearing it. In fact, he hoped to surprise her pleasantly when she did for the first time next day.

He'd decided then that it was already next day, or very nearly. And the night was cold. He'd put it on.

Now, enjoying its deep warmth, he strolled along the deck. Late as it was, he felt quite alert and even cheerful. Buoyant. He knew he did not have to look far for the source of this—talk of business always left him exhilarated. At least, of a certain kind of business. Anything above the humdrum. And this new idea was certainly that. To burst into a market new to him—with deep-laid plans to open up a whole new territory to the manufacture one day . . . He tried to quiet himself then by telling himself that neither of the other two partners of the firm of Tate & Burgess had agreed to join him yet, indeed neither was even aware of its still-phantom existence. He would have to do a great deal of talking tomorrow.

All at once, as if to relieve the excitement building up in him, there came again the bang and then the harsh, trailing gasp through in the air. He watched the blue and silver lights falling then. From the saloon this time came no responding cheer. He sensed—without knowing why—that this was probably the *Laurentia*'s last effort to attract attention this night. The lights were dying now all around him. If the pilot did not arrive tonight, it would be better for him, he supposed. It would give him more time tomorrow to persuade the other two men to join him.

Little by little then, as if following the stars as they drifted down toward the sea, his spirits settled and quietened. Now, his earlier exhilaration seemed rather strange to him, almost artificial. He felt himself at last in a state that was—not gloomy exactly. Melancholy, though. Something like that.

So I am saved, he thought. I am Arthur Bartram Crichton, Esq., man of business, resident at Stormont House, Chorlton-cum-Hardy,

Lancs, and Olivia is my wife. My faithful spouse—as far as anyone can tell. The building still stands, just; the circle is still intact. And so they would go on. For she had not actually yielded to Bonney, not the very last redoubt anyway, not according to the boy, and he with every reason to boast and lie about their transaction. She had shown herself naked to him, that was all. (All!) And he had seen Mrs. Stewart similarly unclad. They were quits therefore. He could look at things that way, if he wanted. He supposed a detached observer might look at them like that.

She must have got scared that cold night after what she had done—whatever she had done—in Bonney's cabin. She had run from it straight back to him. She was running from it still. Poor Bonney, poor fool. This afternoon he must have felt very confident as he started out to see her. Why shouldn't he be confident? She had already permitted him nearly every favor within her power to grant. A thing like persuading her to bolt from her husband must have seemed the merest of obstacles.

Arthur saw him next, a bit later: urgent, desperate, beginning to gabble his words. How had she said it? He had been loud, had talked wildly, waved his arms. No doubt he had—for he was already breaking up on the rock of her irresolution. No more than her husband could she do the decisive thing, it seemed. They were alike. Blessing and curse. A knight had come out of the West to rescue a damsel from the clutches of the ogre—and the damsel had sent him away again, all shiny, undented shield and drooping lance.

=

Another rocket mounted in the air, startling him much more than it would have had it not been completely unexpected. He felt disgruntled—the previous one was meant to be the last—then, as he watched the falling stars, he smiled wryly, thinking that an exhibition of the limits of his own judgment was probably not a bad thing to have to face. Not that reminders of *that* were scarce on the ground just now. For instance, he had probably let Olivia stay too long in the saloon this evening. He'd wanted her to leave when the covers were cleared, but she had insisted on staying for the toasts and the singing. And he hadn't the heart to argue with her. She had been so happy there, since that moment when he had taken her in, just as dinner was about to begin. How proud he had been to have her on his arm. A great roar of welcome had gone up from the assembled passengers, the reception even heartier than that shown her on the poop the day before. He had felt her hand squeezing and then releasing his arm in her pleasure. "Thank you," she'd murmured, bowing her head this way and that, quite like a queen. And again: "Oh, thank you."

So they had stayed, through Babcock's dirge, and Mrs. Barlow's "Coming thro' the Rye," and Harris's riddles (sample: What is the difference between a stubborn donkey and a postage stamp? You lick the one with a stick and stick the other with a lick). And "Come Where My Love Lies Dreaming" sung as a duet between Mrs. Farrow and Mr. Harper. Then had come Mrs. Stewart's recitation, and after that Olivia had admitted she was tired and wished to go below.

In her cabin she had sunk upon her bed, and then had held up her arms and asked him to undress her. He had done it carefully, gravely. Her eyes had been closed throughout. She might have been fast asleep except that she responded whenever he asked her to move a limb or a finger to make his task easier. When she was naked she had put her arms around him, held him to her.

"If you would like to … to love me now, Arthur," she had whispered, "I am ready."

He had found within himself no desire at all for that. He'd kissed her cheek, told her that he thought now was not the time, what was of the first importance was that she should get better, and nothing should be done that might impede that.

"But I am out of the woods now," she had protested.

He had thought she would be glad to be excused, but she didn't seem so. He held her in his arms. Her naked body seemed different from how he remembered it from the distant era when he had still been allowed to caress it freely. Of course she had grown thinner while she had been on Dr. Davies's regime of slops and wheys and lemon water. The skin felt rather slack under his hand. He had no doubt that as she got better this condition of looseness would disappear. But of a sudden he was struck by the thought that the quality she had once had, that bloom of youth, that perfect perfection, might not ever return entire and unblemished. He considered that—and then the next moment felt an absolute stab of shame at the sly pleasure the thought had given him. Pleasure that Livvy, even she, was now on course downhill. The looseness would never go away. The first lines would appear on the perfect skin. The wrinkles would not be far behind. The queen must come down from her throne one day and join the common herd, where such as he were to be found.

=

He stared out at the night. He could see no stars at all now, whether made by man or by God, none of them. Only moon and sea...

And as he waited, as if drifting in vapor from the silver surface, a memory rose before him, at first quite indistinct, but sharpening as it came closer. It was from the time when Olivia lay sick. Or rather—it was still closing on him—from that day when she had seemed better, had come up on deck, but then had suffered a relapse and had had to return to her bunk.

He had been sitting near her, himself dozing on and off, as the afternoon wore on. At one point though he had woken up to hear her say, quite distinctly: "Little fool!"

"Olivia?" he'd asked, when she did not add to this pronouncement. And then when that failed to get a response: "Who is the little fool?"

"I am."

He had thought to humor her. "How true, my dear. I wonder it has taken you so long—"

"Don't laugh at me, Arthur. I am a fool." He had heard her take a long, trailing breath. "And I have been such a disappointment to you."

"Olivia—you are nothing of the sort."

He had leaned over, taken her hand from where it lay on the cover. Held it tight, felt how warm it was.

"But I'm not a clever woman, am I, Arthur?"

"Dearest, don't talk any more. Davies says—"

"Laura was clever. Wasn't she?"

"*Laura?*"

"She was so clever and she...she did things. And I am so stupid. And useless."

"Livvy, dear—"

"Say the truth, Arthur."

He had shaken his head. "What a thing to be talking about now."

"The truth."

"Livvy, if ever I was—a little—vexed with you, it certainly wasn't on account of your intelligence."

"You won't answer me."

"All right." He had sat, holding her hand, thinking upon her question. The answer when it came quite surprised him.

"No, Livvy. I believe it's you that has the greater intelligence." She had opened her eyes, searched for his. He'd nodded, shown her he was serious. "It's just that you've not had to use it much, have you? But Laura's way was hard from the start, she had to struggle, and use her wits."

Until I took the struggle away from her. Made her into a scrounger upon a money-grubber… Olivia had turned her head then upon the pillow. He'd reached out, touched her cheek. Hot.

"And I… I am distinctly stupider than both my wives. There, is that what you wished to hear?"

She had laughed as she'd looked back at him. Then a little while later they had both fallen asleep again. And afterward, so taken up had he been both with her recovery and with the excitement over the card game that he had forgotten what they'd said that night, until this very moment.

Now why had she thought to speak so of Laura? He had always believed her to be quite incurious about his first wife. She was invariably respectful if ever Laura's name was mentioned, but her attitude had seemed entirely impersonal. He imagined she had no more feeling for her predecessor than, say, for his father, who had also died before he met her. Yet on her sickbed she had spoken of Laura with an envy that was almost fierce.

Not envy, he thought then. Something else. A yearning. As for something she wanted and had misplaced. Or had never had. And he realized now he did not know what it was.

He did not know her. It was the truth. They had lived together three years almost and he did not really know her. And he suddenly hated the fact.

Yet on the heels of his regret, it came to him too, like a benediction, that it was not yet out of his reach to try to know her. She had not died at sea, nor left him for another, and so he had only to wait, and choose his time and ask her whatever he wanted. She lay sleeping only a few yards below where he stood. In the morning he would see her—and the morning after that, and after that, and after that... For this right—for her living presence beside him—he had wrestled with Bonney across the ocean. Had hurled his single punch for this right. And much else that had happened on the crossing had the same root, he thought. In some obscure fashion, it was to keep her beside him that, say, he had brought the Negro up from captivity. And even that he had once found himself stumbling around in Mrs. Stewart's cabin, with his trousers down and his cock waving in the air.

All for Livvy.

53°24' N, 2°59' W

All around were buildings in the mist. The *Laurentia* drew to its mooring in the Queen's Dock. Almost all the passengers were gathered on the deck, watching a curious scene unfolding on the wharf. Forming themselves into two ranks were about twenty or thirty policemen. The moment the *Laurentia* settled at the wharf, before it was even completely tied up, there occurred a sudden eruption of humanity at the fo'c'sle end of the ship. Man after man came welling up from belowdecks and began dropping over the side. The lines of police lay across the only exit from the dock. As the passengers watched, the *Laurentia*'s late unlawful human cargo tried to break through or elude these lines. Some chose to do it independently. For the most part they were not successful, yet it was quite a spectacle to see them running and dodging and diving, with the constables on their tails. Others looked for safety in numbers, advancing against the police lines in a determined mob. Here was where the most serious battles broke out, the police using their sticks, the would-be immigrants replying with fists and boots.

Up on the decks, the passengers began by enjoying the contest as if they were spectators at a horse race or a prizefight. They were calling out, clapping, cheering, jeering. At first the support for each side was pretty evenhanded. But then a distinct bias toward the ex-crew became apparent. For they had been as much a part of the ship as the

passengers. They were Laurentians too. And, though they had presented a rather unruly, and even threatening presence at times,
nothing very serious had ever occurred. They had helped—or at least
had not hindered much—the steering of the ship all the way along
the Great Circle. Between them, passengers and crew had crossed a
mighty ocean together. They had been shipmates. So the passengers
cheered at the occasional success, as a man wriggled and fought his
way past the lines and then hared through the gates into the streets of
Liverpool beyond.

Perhaps two dozen stowaways eluded the police cordon, the rest
were dragged off to waiting coaches, en route to the jailhouse, and then
presumably—certainly the most flagrant criminals among them—to
be returned to the North American shore. The passengers went their
separate ways after a while, quite a few looking rather guilty, as if they
had taken part in something shameful.

Arthur had seen nothing of this. In fact, he had seen very little of
the entire course of the *Laurentia*'s approach to harbor, since the moment the pilot boat had reached her at last in the early morning. He
had been too busy below on other business. His first port of call had
been Tate's cabin. He'd spent nearly two hours there in close discussion. Then he had gone in search of Burgess, found him in the saloon.
As befitting an old ocean hand, the drummer was ostentatiously paying no attention whatsoever to the scenes of approaching arrival beyond the saloon's windows. Arthur had spent a further hour talking
with Burgess, then had gone below again with the intention of sitting
with Olivia until the ship docked.

He found down there a scene of fury and confusion into which he
was drawn the moment he passed into her cabin. Mrs. Logan was on
her knees before the open trunk, tight-lipped and angry-eyed. Olivia
had collapsed upon the bed, and was alternately weeping and complaining. It was certainly because she was tired and still not fully well.
She had stayed too long at supper last night, and she was paying for it
today. And not only she was paying. There appeared to be real danger
of an explosion from Mrs. Logan. Arthur wanted to dismiss her from
the room, but with his new knowledge that she was the captain's lady,
he found himself reluctant to order her about. But at last he con-

cluded that if she had decided to accept the role of servant then she must expect to be treated so, and he told her to go.

When they were alone, he turned back to survey first Olivia, then the jumble of clothing in her trunk.

"What I don't understand, my dear, is why it took you under an hour to pack this trunk in Massachusetts and it is taking so very long to repack it now."

"That is because I could not get that silly woman to do what I wished."

"But what does it matter in what order things are packed this time? The train for Manchester leaves Lime Street at three o'clock. We will be at the Adelphi for only a couple of hours. How many changes of costume do you intend to make in that time?"

At which point, she collapsed entirely, crying, and complaining that he was not taking her seriously. He never took her seriously. He was a beast.

After twenty minutes of this, Arthur went in search of the stewardess and, without bothering himself in the slightest over the question of her status, offered her a huge tip to go back into the cabin and deal with Olivia. Lavish as it was, Mrs. Logan did not leap at his first offer, and they stood in the corridor for some long time, bargaining keenly. From above their heads came all the tantalizing noises of arrival: ship's whistles, shouted orders, the ever-slower turning and the final cessation of the paddles. Then came a grinding noise that went on and on. He felt the ship's timbers shaking under the strain, and he knew they must be right up against the wharf. Still the Scotchwoman haggled away. From above now came a confused murmuring, punctuated by loud cries and shrieks.

At last she consented to accept a sum so large that it was greater than the amount he had on his person, and—as she insisted on cash on the nail—he had to go to his own cabin to fetch it for her. Which involved reopening his trunk and unpacking half of it. When he had paid off the woman, he hurried up to the main deck. By the time he got there, some of the passengers had already left the boat. Of the struggle on the wharf between policemen and stowaways, all that remained was a dismal file of the latter being crammed into waiting police coaches. Arthur found Burgess among a few other watching passengers, and had the story from him.

"How did the police know they were onboard?"

"Captain must have sent word ashore somehow. Perhaps on the pilot boat when it went back to Holyhead. They must have telegraphed it to Liverpool. Sly feller, eh?"

As the other passengers went below, Arthur and Burgess maintained their watch, and took up their earlier conversation from where they'd left off. Arthur had begun his approach this morning by ascertaining that, as he'd suspected, the drummer's immediate career prospects were not promising—on account, as he said, of a contraction in the trade.

"No call for telescopic sights?"

"Well, not over there." Burgess had nodded in the general direction of America. "I'm afraid that market has pretty much closed down. In fact, there's not much call for the item anywhere just at present, though I've heard there may be opportunities in Central Europe soon. But not just yet."

In spite of this, Burgess had not been at all keen when Arthur had finally broached the idea of them working together.

"No offense, Crichton, but your line of business—shuffling bits of paper around—not really my dish of tea. When I sell something, I like it to be—well—something solid. Something I can point to, pick up, use—you know. Solid."

"Yes. Solid. But that's just what I've been thinking... You know, Burgess, I began in business by making things—not just shuffling paper. I owned a mill. It was a good mill, I think, though I was really out of my depth. Got rid of it fairly soon. But I believe I should like to explore that world again. As far as I am able to anyway. And you can help me. You and Tate."

After that uncertain start, the drummer had been warming to the idea all morning. The sticking point at the time Arthur had left him to call on Olivia had been the need for him to live indefinitely in America. This now seemed not to be so much of a problem, and Arthur guessed that in the time they had been apart, Burgess had been able to have a reassuring talk with Miss Faversham. He knew they had met, for the drummer had told him he'd just missed her. She had seized an opportunity that had suddenly arisen to share a coach with several other parties, all heading for the depot and a train leaving in twenty-five minutes that would deposit them in a very few hours at Euston Square in London. Arthur was untroubled by not seeing her leave the boat. They had already met this morning—on his passage between Tate's cabin and the saloon—and had said their farewells. Addresses had been exchanged, promises to write, he had kissed her upon the cheek, she had actually blushed.

He wondered now if Miss Faversham had also mentioned the name of the new firm when she'd last spoken to the drummer. Tate & Burgess. Hard to turn that down, Arthur guessed. In fact, he counted on it.

=

As they watched, other passengers started to leave the ship. The Barlows went down the gangway looking very small and huddled from above, then the Canadian fellow Harper, peering around him in an eager fashion, and holding on to his stovepipe hat to stop the breeze picking it off his head and bowling it along the cobbles. Both parties found coaches waiting for them at the foot of the gangway, their luggage was already strapped on top or wedged inside.

Then Burgess murmured: "There go the villains."

They watched as Charles Stuart and Major Cutler, each carrying a bag made of carpet material, slipped down the gangway and made off in a hansom cab.

"Common-looking beggars really, weren't they?" Burgess said. "Good riddance to bad rubbish, say I."

"I suppose so."

Arthur had no kind thoughts for the major, but he did find himself briefly hoping that Stuart would find some congenial place over here, where he might freely and profitably exercise his several talents. Perhaps in Paris.

"Though the darkie had a fine voice, there's no denying that." Burgess nodded. "But did you see how they didn't give so much as a backward glance at the ship? Too ashamed, I suppose."

Mr. and Mrs. Farrow went down the gangway next. At the bottom, Farrow turned, looked up at the ship, and seeing the two men at the rail, waved.

"And Tate," Burgess asked as he waved back, "how does he feel about the plan? About me?"

"Tate is very sorry that he and I don't see eye to eye on a timetable. Still, he is wise enough to know that a chance for the future is better than no chance at all. As for you, he would be honored to work with you."

"Honored? Did he say that?"

Arthur replied with a movement of his head that could well be interpreted as an affirmative nod, and Burgess smiled happily. In fact, Tate had by no means been so positive in regard to the news, his reserve deepening when Arthur was forced to confess that it was largely instinct that had decided him on the drummer. He had promised that a proper inquiry would be made of Burgess's current employer before a contract would be offered, and that in any case the contract would give them means of escape if the drummer's performance did not prove satisfactory. In the end, Tate had said only that if Arthur thought it a good idea, then he wouldn't object. Arthur saw no reason, while they were still trying to recruit him, to put this rather grudging response before Burgess.

The drummer sighed gustily now. "Honored," he murmured again contentedly. He had convinced himself, Arthur saw. He would certainly enlist in the cause. It was only a matter of detail now, and that could be taken care of at a later date. Having no further business to do up here, he really ought to go below and deal again with Olivia. At least see that she and Mrs. Logan had not yet actually come to blows.

"There goes Stewart," Burgess announced.

Startled for a moment, for he thought his companion was referring to the Negro, and he was sure he had already seen *his* departure, Arthur looked over the side. To find a party of four descending the gangway. It was led by Mrs. Stewart. Behind her, the Reverend Stibbards was giving her rather ineffectual assistance. At the bottom of the gangway, the coachman was holding out his hand for her to grasp. At the end of the procession came M. and Mme. Charvet.

The party gathered at the coach as the last of their cases was being slung aloft. On the reverend's face was a look of fatuous joy.

"Shouldn't somebody warn the poor fellow?" Arthur murmured.

"Of what? Of winning a most handsome woman? D'you think a better opportunity will ever arise for the 'poor fellow'?"

At that moment, as if aware she was the subject of their conversation, Mrs. Stewart looked directly up at the rail. From under a demure gray bonnet, her violet eyes seemed to sparkle. They were looking directly at him, Arthur knew. From this distance, he could not quite read their expression. At first he thought it must be anger. Then he was not so sure. At any rate she appeared to be waiting for some reaction from him, and after a moment he doffed his hat and bowed to her. She nodded then, as if satisfied, and turned to follow Mme. Charvet into the coach.

Burgess gave a faint whistle of admiration.

"What was she?" Arthur wondered, as they watched the coach pull away.

"Oh, a harlot. Definitely."

"Just that?"

Burgess hesitated. "D'you know, I rather believed her story about the dead husband. Dead something anyway, some sort of a reg'lar partner. My theory is that she was once in the gay life, but was able to quit it. I don't think she came onboard with the idea of earning her passage on her back. But the opportunities came up and—well, she didn't see why she should turn 'em down. But guess what," the drummer went on, "it's a curious thing, but apparently she called time long before she need have."

"Called time?"

"Mm. Couple of chaps I spoke to, who'd had her earlier on the crossing, went back later for second helpings and found she'd shut up shop. Seemed to happen after that night Stuart sang—"

The day of his own disastrous showing in her cabin, Arthur thought. Had it so appalled her?

"—which must have been about the time that she started to properly get her hooks into the reverend."

"Yes," Arthur said. "Must have been."

"*I* think he's a lucky chap. And if anybody needed a warning against the match, it was her. By the way," the drummer went on, quite as if he was continuing the same line of conversation, "that's a damn fine cloak you're wearing, Crichton. Is it your tailor's work? If so, I wouldn't mind getting his name off you, if that's all right."

≡

It was the first of what Arthur was rather hoping would be a ripe cluster of compliments to be garnered by his new cloak, and he intended to enjoy it. He looked down smugly at the gorgeous folds, took a moment to show Burgess the intense red of the silk lining.

"In fact it's ready-made," he revealed. Burgess murmured his surprise. He told him where he had bought it. "American manufacture, you know. Puts most of our stuff to shame rather, don't it?"

"I must see if they have any left next time I'm in New York City."

"Which may not be so very far distant." Arthur nodded. He grasped a fold of the material, turned it over again for Burgess's benefit. "You can see what a fine weave it is. Obviously they have made great strides over there in the last—"

He stopped for, looking up, he found that Burgess was paying no attention to him, or his cloak. Rather he was looking past Arthur's shoulder, his eyes widening all the while in amazement. "Lord," he breathed then. And then again: "Good *Lord*..."

Arthur swung around. Looked where Burgess was looking. Found standing at the top of the gangway the tall form of John Bonney. The young man looked pale in the damp, misty light, tending to green, as if, to be contrary, the *mal de mer* was about to visit him just as he was leaving the element. But none of this had excited Burgess's amazement, nor now was causing Arthur's mouth to drop open.

A short jacket of heavy wool, dyed dark blue, with silver buttons, a black belt, light blue trousers with a dark stripe down the sides, a pair of well-worn black brogans. On the arms of his jacket were golden chevrons, with three downward-pointing stripes on either arm. On his head a crumpled blue cap with a black leather peak.

"What the devil is that getup for?"

"It's the uniform of—"

"I know what it *is*," Burgess said. "I've seen enough of 'em walking about the streets of Boston and New York and Washington these past few months. Why's *he* wearing it?"

The thought of having to explain Bonney's tangled military record defeated Arthur. Luckily Burgess was too agitated to concentrate on the question for long.

"He can't leave the boat like that. He'll be——"

"I think it's all right," Arthur said. He nodded over the rail toward the wharf. There was now only a single vehicle, a hansom cab, waiting there. Its driver had just got down from his seat. He came to the foot of the gangway. Bonney went down it. He was carrying a large carpet-bag, very like that borne by the two gamblers. Arthur supposed his regular, his civilian clothes were inside.

They watched as Bonney handed the bag to the driver, who put it in the back of his cab. Burgess shrugged.

"I suppose he'll be safe inside that." He nodded at the cab. Bonney was still on the wharf talking with the driver. "D'you know, Crichton," the drummer went on, "I heard an extraordinary thing about that young man. Apparently, he is turning right around and going back to the States by the very next boat. D'you credit it?"

"I've heard something of the same myself." Arthur nodded. "I suppose he will be taking that cab direct to the *Persia*'s wharf."

"But isn't it most extraordinary? Can you make any sense of young people today, Crichton?"

"My wife affords me some means of penetrating their mysteries."

"Ah yes, of course." Burgess grunted, not quite sure whether he had just made a blunder. "Of course she would. Fine young woman, Mrs. Crichton. Very fine . . ."

Arthur turned away from the rail. After the first shock of seeing him in uniform had faded, he had felt very little at the sight of his defeated rival's exit. He thought again he ought to go belowdecks. See to getting Livvy out of her cabin. And after that they would have to leave the ship. Normal life—their life with each other—would be resumed. Arthur found himself feeling subdued as he contemplated that resumption. The optimism that he had taken to his bed last night had not really survived his waking; his notion that the irregular and sometimes disgraceful events of this voyage had in some way contributed toward the saving of his marriage now seemed awfully like wishful thinking. And he rather suspected he had communicated these despondent feelings to Olivia during their brief, hectic meeting this morning. It might be that they had contributed to her distress.

It might be too, he thought now, that she shared his reservations about what had happened. The end of Colorado, all of that. Yesterday she had made a decision about Bonney, about himself. Perhaps it was the right decision, the only one she could have made. But still—there might be lingering regrets.

Thankfully, at least the spark that could have ignited any remaining dangerous fuses would no longer be around. Very soon, Bonney would be bobbing away on the tide, and every hour would take him farther and farther away from them.

"Ah, my God—that tears it!"

Arthur, who had almost forgotten the drummer's presence, glanced at him, then down again at the wharf. The cab was now moving away across the cobblestones, zigagging among the piles of baggage and cords of rope. But Bonney was not aboard. He had just started to walk briskly after the cab. His hands were free and swinging, his legs striding forth in steady rhythm. In his uniform, the impression—no, rather the reality—was of a soldier on the march.

Burgess and Arthur stared at this, then at each other.

"Now there"—Burgess nodded—"is a problem."

"What will happen to him?"

"Well, at the least he'll be brought back to the ship, to have the matter sorted out. Anyway, he'll find himself in quite a pickle with the peelers. No sailing to America today for young Mr. Bonney, I'd wager."

"No," Arthur cried out violently. "That mustn't be." He stopped then, aware that the drummer was eyeing him curiously. Striving to reach a moderate tone, he added, "I shall go after him. I shall—" He scarcely knew what he would do. He stared after the tall, receding figure. "We've said enough, have we?"

"Think so." Burgess nodded. "For the time being. You have my address?"

Arthur had. He thought he knew the place. Small hotel off Bold Street. He took the drummer's hand.

"I'll be in touch to tell you when we are to meet."

"Three musketeers, eh? Hope it's before the month is out. In April I plan to be away from Liverpool."

Arthur thought of Miss Faversham, of the little cottage in Kent, of the sister coming over from Hythe as chaperone.

"Yes, I must go to Germany. Settle my accounts over there."

"And then . . . are you not to visit Miss Faversham?"

"Ah, she told you that, did she?" Burgess nodded. He was silent for a few moments. His features now were showing a curious mixture of embarrassment and bravado. "It's the damndest thing, Crichton," he sighed at length. "Always happens on these crossings. I don't know what it is. I have sometimes thought it might be that the ceaseless rocking of the vessel has the effect of exciting one's sensibilities. Anyway, it's always the same: I get pally with a lady, rather too much is said between us. A situation is created, y'know. And then at the end I have to wriggle out of it."

A pause. "I see," Arthur said. "And have you wriggled out of this situation?"

"Not yet. Should have spoken up just now, but I funked it. I shall have to write her a letter."

"Poor Miss Faversham," said Arthur, after a moment.

"What? Oh, yes, absolutely. Wretched business." The drummer chuckled ruefully. "But what can one do, Crichton? I am the most confirmed of bachelors—and yet I do love the company of the ladies."

=

There was no time to mourn Miss Faversham's awful luck. Bonney was covering the ground at a great rate. It was clear that he would be at the dock exit long before Arthur could catch him up. He himself was making very heavy going. For all that the *Laurentia* had been almost stationary at its mooring for the past hour or so, when he reached the bottom of the gangway Arthur still found the complete immobility of the wharf disconcerting. Also there was the fact that the cobblestones underfoot had been made greasy by a recent light rain, which, as he started after Bonney, was turning into damp snow. He found himself swerving and staggering in his pursuit of the tall figure ahead. Bonney, for some reason, appeared quite unaffected by the conditions.

Arthur stopped at last, panting, and threw back his head.

"Mr. Bonney," he called. And: "Oh, Bonney!"

The figure kept marching on.

"Bonney!...For God's sake, man—*Bonney!*"

From a nearby knot of porters came sarcastic echoes of "Bonney, Bonney!" And it seemed it was to these calls rather than to his own that, after Arthur had given up hope, the young American at last responded. He stopped, turned, looked—and waited then as Arthur, who had sprained his ankle slightly skidding on a patch of unidentifiable slime, limped toward him.

As he came close, Bonney looked away. He seemed to be in the grip of some strong emotion, so that he could not meet Arthur's gaze. For his own part, occasional sharp pangs in his ankle were effective in taking Arthur's mind off the uncomfortable aspects of this—please God—final meeting. He came to a stop, inhaled deeply a few times to get his breath under control. Took the opportunity to look the young man over. This was their first encounter since yesterday afternoon in the saloon for, like the two gamblers, Bonney had absented himself from the last-night dinner—though in his case voluntarily. Seeing him now, Arthur felt suddenly very grateful he had never worn this uniform in front of Olivia. Such martial glamour might have tipped the balance in his favor. The thought silenced him for the moment, just as he was about to speak.

"I'm glad to see you, sir," the young man said. "I wanted to find you, to say good-bye. I guess I didn't have the nerve." He nodded. Looked down. The peak of his cap was casting a shadow upon his eyes. "I wished I could have spoken once more to Mrs. Crichton too. Is she...is she well?"

"Perfectly well. You would hardly believe that she had ever been ill."

"That's good." Bonney nodded. "Very good...I fear that the last time Mrs. Crichton and I saw each other we parted on a disagreeable note."

"Again?"

"Yes..." The young man looked up, as if to check that he wasn't being mocked. "Yes, again. Perhaps you were right, sir. Chalk and cheese, was that it? . . . Well, then: good-bye, Mr. Crichton. I'm afraid I can't stay to talk with you, though I should like to have—"

"I hear you are to sail on the *Persia?*"

"Yes, sir. I must be aboard in under an hour. But I'm told it's only thirty minutes to walk there, and a straight road. I thought I should like to see something of England before I left it."

"And so you dismissed your cab?"

"It's gone ahead with my bag."

"And"—Arthur nodded toward the ship—"there appear to be no other free cabs available for the moment."

Bonney stared at him, in perplexity.

"The thing is, you see, you can't go out in the street dressed like that."

Bonney looked down at himself.

"Why shouldn't I?"

"Because it's a uniform."

"Yes, sir. Last night I resolved to live no longer in daydreams. I am a soldier. Nothing else. And a soldier wears a—"

"But it is a *foreign* uniform."

"How—foreign?"

Arthur sighed. "Mr. Bonney, wide as the borders of your splendid republic now stand, they do not yet include this side of the Atlantic. That"—pointing—"is a foreign uniform. And it's not really the done thing in England to be wearing such outfits in public—unless, I suppose, you're on some sort of official mission from your government, which manifestly you are not. You may therefore excite a great deal of interest."

Bonney shrugged. "Can't help that. Yesterday, after she—" He stopped. His voice had begun to tremble. He took hold of himself. "Last night, I resolved that I would wear nothing else from now on, all the way home."

"It's against the law. If you go out in the street like that you may be arrested. And put in prison."

A pause. Then on Bonney's lips a faint, disbelieving smile.

"I think you should take this seriously. It's unfortunate you are wearing that particular uniform. You know there are plenty of rumors afloat over here that the treasonous Irish revolutionaries are expecting help soon from discharged members of the American armies. Incidentally, there are many Irish in Liverpool... I don't suppose you'll want to get yourself mixed up in that particular brew?"

"Lord, no."

"Or they may think you are one of the number who have crossed the Atlantic to secretly recruit our English poor to feed the needs of your Federal army. There is a law against that sort of thing. It's called the Foreign Enlistment Act, and the penalties for contravening it are heavy, I believe. Probably you'd be able to talk yourself out of it in the end, but—"

Bonney stood there, irresolute.

"But is it really serious, sir?"

"It's very serious. Look—" Arthur nodded toward the dock gates, about fifty yards away. There were three or four policemen standing there, veterans of the battle against the stowaways. At present, gathered in a tight, businesslike group, they were looking toward himself and Bonney, showing a definite interest. It seemed to Arthur that at any moment they would make a move toward them. He looked around for someplace that might give them a temporary concealment, found a watchman's hut nearby, glowing brazier outside. He nodded Bonney toward it. Looking in at the door, they found a watchman inside, who was happy enough to let them enter and share his fire but disinclined to leave the shelter himself, until Arthur gave him a shilling to go away.

They stood just inside the hut, warming their hands at the fire.

"This takes me back," Bonney remarked.

"Beg pardon?"

"To camp. I have stood like this, with some other fellow, a hundred times, just warming my hands... Well, I'll have to change my clothes, I guess. But I've nothing, my bag is on that cab. Can you help me, sir?"

"I could lend you some things. But my trunk is already on deck. It will take some time to find it, then to open it—"

Above all Bonney must be kept away from the ship. Away from a chance of his meeting again with Olivia. Particularly with him looking like this.

"But I've no time. I've cut it fine enough as it is... There's nothing to be done." Bonney groaned. "I'll have to miss the *Persia*. I won't be able to go—not until tomorrow."

He sighed, and shook his head, then looked down at Arthur. Already, Arthur noted with concern, the resilience was showing in the youth's dark eyes. He was seeking—and finding—the silver lining.

"At least"—Bonney nodded—"it will give me a chance to properly say good-bye to you. And to Mrs. Crichton. With your permission, of course," he hurried to add. "And in your presence, if you like." He was silent for a little while. Then, rather shyly: "And do you know, sir, I have been wondering... perhaps this attempt to return straightaway is folly. And I should stay over here, as I first intended."

In the darkness of the hut, Bonney's eyes gleamed interrogatively. Arthur maintained a stubborn silence. If he did open his mouth, he was unsure if anything more coherent than a roar of frustration would come out.

"I wonder if you could advise me about that," Bonney pressed him at last.

"No, sir. I think this time I must decline the office." He was rather proud of the even tone he'd found to say this. It did not seem to satisfy the young man, however. He continued to watch Arthur—almost hungrily it felt like. "All I can suggest you do, Mr. Bonney, is to weigh up what you would lose by staying, with what you might gain."

"What would I lose?"

"I believe you said your father's love. And so your home... and your country... And perhaps, I don't know, your self-respect."

"Then you think I should go back."

"That isn't my advice."

"You think I should stay?"

"That isn't my advice either. I give you no advice."

They stood side by side looking out. The short day was beginning to fail. A few flakes of damp snow came whirling past. They hit the brazier, hissed, died.

"I must go back. There's nothing else for it..."

His decision, Arthur told himself. His alone. *He* had given no advice.

The young man held up his hands helplessly. "Yet I have no civilian clothes to wear. So I must stay."

To attain a great object, a great sacrifice is sometimes required—in war and peace it is the same, Arthur supposed. He held out his hands for a last time at the comforting embers.

"I believe I have the solution," he said sadly, "to your difficulty. First you must remove that cap, and put it away somewhere."

His hand was already at his throat, he was unbuttoning the cloak.

"And then you must take this"—he held it out—"and put it on. You may walk out from here then without fear. It will conceal what you are wearing underneath."

The young man took the cloak. Felt it with his free hand.

"But it's a very fine cloak," he said.

"I'm aware of that, Bonney."

"I'll send it back, of course."

"No matter. But look after it. As you say, it's a fine piece of work. I never thought the Americans could do so well."

The young man drew the cloak around him. In it, he looked almost impossibly dashing.

"Thank you, sir," he said suddenly. "Thank you for your kindness. Since we first met, you've been kind to me. And what have I done for you?"

"Well... not much, I should say."

"It's no more than the truth." Bonney nodded solemnly. He hesitated, then, not looking at Arthur: "Mr. Crichton, there's something I told you once, and I regret having done so. About what Livvy—Mrs. Crichton—well, what she got up to in my cabin that night... It wasn't true, you know. Nothing like that ever happened."

"I never imagined it had."

"Oh?" Bonney sounded taken aback.

"Of course not. You made it up out of disappointment. She refused your advances. So you invented all those disgusting fictions, caring not who you injured."

Silence. For a moment, Arthur thought the boy would give him an argument. But at last Bonney only nodded heavily, and said: "Well, all right. If you like... Yes, I guess that's how it was."

They stepped out of the hut. Arthur looked toward the dock gate. The policemen had lost interest in them. The way out was clear.

"I'm sorry too," he said then, surprising himself. "Your eye seems to be getting better, and I'm glad of it—but I regret that it should have ever come to that. Not a habit of mine, by the way, hitting people."

"Oh, that's all right. It was a pretty good punch, I guess."

"For an old man?"

"For anybody who's sitting down."

Bonney put out his hand then. Arthur took it. He felt oddly unwilling then to let the young man go.

"You know, Bonney," he said at last, "it may be that your time of danger over there will be of short duration. When I was in New York, I heard that Lee's army is very close to the breaking point."

"Yes." The other nodded. "They are always telling us that we have them licked. It always turns out to be a lie."

"But I heard this from a gentleman who is a member of General Grant's staff. Southern desertions over the winter have been enormous. There is scarcely an army left to face you. My informant said the end of the war can be only a matter of weeks away," Arthur urged. "By May certainly it will be all over. June at the very latest. You have only to keep yourself safe until then."

"May," intoned the young man. "June." He named the months as if referring to epochs deep in the hazy future.

"It's not that far off surely? We are nearly in March."

Bonney smiled.

"Grant is able to waste men in less time than you could believe, Mr. Crichton. At Cold Harbor, seven thousand were shot down within ten minutes. Seven thousand men. And we gained not a yard of ground."

Arthur watched as Bonney swung off toward the gate. He wished suddenly that the police would stop him there. Instead, they saluted as he went by.

After which, he turned, waved once at Arthur, and then was gone.

———

A couple of minutes after Bonney had left the scene, the coach that was to take the Crichtons to the Adelphi Hotel arrived on the wharf. It could have been lent to the young American, so that inside it he could have gone to his new ship without exposing his uniform to the streets. In which case Arthur would still be the proud possessor of the cloak. It served him right, he supposed. The idea of getting rid of Bonney had been so pressing, it had precluded thought of more sober, practical solutions.

Perhaps it was a good thing after all, he thought, as he stood at the top of the gangway, watching his trunk being hauled onto the coach. A good lesson. He had loved that cloak too much. He was not ordinarily vain, he knew, and the infection had become all the more virulent because of that. It was best that the source should have been removed.

But he would never cut a dash in it now on Market Street, and he had looked forward so to that.

Shaking his head, he made his way across the deck. Met First Officer Hartley coming through the doorway that led from the saloon. They shook hands, exchanged cordial farewells. There was no reserve or coolness between them—the unfortunate incident of the day before, when Arthur had cursed the officer en route to Olivia's cabin, had been fully apologized for at dinner last night, if not entirely explained. The first officer had been very decent about it ("Strain of Mrs. Crichton's illness—quite understand").

Hartley now was in as much of a rush as Bonney had been and, curiously, for the same reason. He was going back to America this very day, and on the *Persia*. He had long wished to transfer from Inman to Cunard, and now at last a vacancy had opened up.

"Better for me, I think," Hartley said. "Now the American war is played out, I know Inman plans to concentrate again on the emigrant trade. But I've got a taste now for the society of the saloon. And—I believe—have an aptitude for it."

Arthur assured him he was not mistaken in this, but commiserated with Hartley on not having the least break between ships.

"Yes. Shan't even have a chance to see my wife this time. Worse luck."

Arthur thought of Mrs. Stewart. Of the first officer and Mrs. Stewart. Stopped himself. Rumor only. And no business of his in any case.

"But who will fill your place on the *Laurentia*?"

"No one. Indeed no one is required. It has been confirmed. She is to be towed across to Birkenhead and broken up."

"Ah...and what of Captain McDonough? Will he get another ship?"

"I think not," Hartley said after a moment. "I'm sure he doesn't really expect to be given one. He has bought a house on the Cheshire coast, you know. He can sit and watch the Liverpool steamers come and go."

"In the company of Mrs. Logan?"

Hartley cast a quick upward glance. He hesitated, then nodded. "You are observant, sir. Yes, with Mrs. Logan."

"And shall you be sorry to change captains?"

"D'you know, in spite of everything, I think I shall. Captain McDonough"—here Hartley lowered his voice—"has somewhat declined of late, it's true. He is no longer the man he was even five years ago. But all in all: a first-rate seaman. One of the finest Great Circle sailors I ever knew."

Below, Arthur went warily along his corridor. He listened but could hear no advance warning of squalls or squabbles. He came to Olivia's door. It was a little ajar. He looked in. She was sitting at the table, dressed in her outdoor costume. She was very still, her back straight, her head bowed. She did not see him looking at her. He wondered how long she had been like this, alone, in the dim light.

=

He pushed open the door. Miraculously, the wild confusion of an hour ago had melted entirely away. Her trunks had been removed. The cabin was in a state of perfect order. They could leave the ship whenever they wanted, they could start for home.

She looked up and smiled at him. He came to the table, and sat down opposite her. He could hardly believe that last night he had thought that her malady might have taken the bloom from her forever. As he looked at her now, she seemed flawless. She looked as if she had never had a day's illness in her life. Nor even a moment's worry or concern. She looked perfect.

"The oddest thing has just happened to me, Arthur. Mrs. Logan and I had finished the packing. And I'd started to thank her—and to apologize a bit too, because I knew I had been rather trying...And she told me to shut up. 'Shut up!' That's what she said. And then she called me 'a spoiled little bitch.' And walked out of the room. And would not come back no matter how loud I called."

It daunted him a little to look at her, and yet he felt such admiration too, and interest. What a fraud he had been, he thought, with his shows of reluctance and indifference this morning. When the truth was he must have her. That was all. Whether it was "good" for him, or "good" for her—what did he care? He must keep her.

"Did you hear me, Arthur?"

"Yes, my dear. Mrs. Logan told you to shut up."

"And called me a bitch! *Well,* I was very angry, of course. But then I thought—I had been *so* dreadful to her all morning. That's true, isn't it, Arthur? I was dreadful."

"Well, Livvy..."

"Just like a spoiled little bitch, in fact. So she was right...But still. To be called that. By a stewardess. Isn't that extraordinary?"

"It would be, I suppose. By a stewardess."

He saw her hand slip across the table and into his, and he looked up. Her face under the high brim of her bonnet was calm, her blue eyes steady and affectionate.

"I'm going to try to change, Arthur. And not be such a vain, selfish little...well, you know. I'm sure I wasn't always so. I got very gloomy and out of sorts in America. And then I think I fell into bad habits on the way back."

"Livvy, you were quite ill. And then—"

"Yes, yes. I know all of that, but still—I think Mrs. Logan's words are a warning that I ought to heed. Even though I was absolutely *furious* at the time."

She got up, came around the table to him, put her cheek against his. "Oh, Arthur—I want to be home. In our own dear room, in front of the fire. Do we really have to stay at the hotel for hours and hours?"

"Where else should we wait for the train?"

"Do we have to wait?"

"Unless we want to walk all the way to Manchester, I think it would be best."

She giggled, held him close. Amazingly, he found himself on the brink of actual tears.

"Livvy," he said. "I should like you to invite Miss Faversham to stay with us."

"Miss Faversham? What an odd idea. When should you want her to come?"

"Soon...You see, I think she will have need of friends quite soon, and—I'm not sure she has many where she lives."

"Then she shall come to us, and stay as long as she likes," Olivia promised. "Poor old thing."

"I'm so very glad, Livvy," he murmured, turning his face against her bosom. "Truly I am..."

"But I'm happy to invite Miss Faversham."

"Not her. Us—" He could hardly go on.

"I know," she said. "I know, my dear old boy."

She put her face down again to his, nuzzled his ear, his beard.

"Now I *want* to go to the hotel," she whispered. "And shall I undress for you there? Shall I say: 'Pray, do you like me like this, Arthur?'... And shall I say: 'Or pray, do you prefer me like *this*?'"

═

The circle is completed. We have come so far—yet nothing has happened. Nothing really has happened. Except that we pull back safely from another precipice. Is it the next that will prove fatal? The one after that?

"Arthur?"

This one was not quite fatal. Not to *us* at any rate. As for Bonney— he was going to join his ship in any case, marching along in his uniform through the falling snow, like a damn doomed fool. At worst I only gave him a little shove. Gave him a cloak. A shroud.

"Arthur, I'm speaking to you."

Last night, in this cabin, he had fetched her nightdress and lowered it over her naked body.

"You won't ever leave me, will you, Arthur?" she had murmured as her head emerged from the hole.

"What a thought, my dear."

"Sometimes I am so afraid that you might."

How should I leave you, Livvy? For we are married. We are locked in the deepest, snuggest contract there is. And there really is no way out of it, except Laura's way.

"Arthur!"

He collected himself.

"I'm sorry, my dear. I was wool-gathering. Yes, that would be very nice."

"You didn't hear at all what I just said, did you?"

"What did you say, dear?"

"I asked: have we any further business upon this ship?"

"None at all, as far as I know."

"Then, my dearest old boy—let us go ashore."

RETURN

47°50' N, 41°3' W

FROM *THE PERSIAN TIMES*, MARCH 5, 1865

INKY-GRAPHS (FROM THE SALOON)
"A chiel's amang ye takin notes."

Last evening, after supper, the Saloon was entertained and instructed by a lecture from our popular first officer, Mr. Hartley. His subject was the maritime technique called "Great Circle sailing." He began by posing the question: "Was there ever a circumstance when the shortest line between two points might not be the straightest?" A hearty chorus of "No!" resounded throughout the Saloon. Whereupon, Mr. Hartley, by means of a globe, and a large map of the Atlantic which he had set upon an easel, proceeded to show how this apparent contradiction in Nature might after all be true.

It appears that when Herr Gerhard Mercator published his famous map in 1569, the particular projection he chose in order to represent a curved surface upon a flat chart necessarily distorted the true position of the latitudinal lines. This did not invalidate his work—a straight line drawn between any two points on his map will give a correct compass bearing, which, if maintained throughout the course, will lead a ship from one point to the other. This is known as the rhumb line, and is in universal use because of its simplicity.

However, it is not the shortest course—which course, because the planet itself is curved, must of necessity be curved itself, and thus fall under the denomination of a Great Circle.

Here the first officer proceeded to show, by means of the globe, how, for instance, while the rhumb line between The Lizard at Cornwall and St. John's in Newfoundland is about 1,980 miles in length; by approaching the same destination on a curved course, on the Great Circle, the distance between the two points may be reduced by above 30 miles. And while the difference may appear insignificant in an ocean passage of near 2,000 miles, yet the fact that the Great Circle line may at its furthest distance from the rhumb be as much as 330 miles apart, gives the navigator—if we have perfectly understood Mr. Hartley's meaning—great scope in being able to pick a favoured course across the sea, and yet hardly increase or even reduce the number of miles to be sailed.

Having successfully demonstrated that at sea all land-based certainties should be put aside, and that certainly the surest course may not be the straightest, Mr. Hartley gracefully concluded his lecture, which was received by all present with loud applause and many expressions of gratification.

The Saloon then proceeded to a rather noisy exchange of comical toasts, having been munificently gifted by our distinguished fellow passenger Mr. Barkworth of Rochester, New York, with two cases of champagne—under whose stimulating influence, it must be admitted, your poor scribe Winkle was only able to note down two or three of the better sallies. Viz.: "To Mrs. Russell, who makes such eyes at a certain Official Personage—whether her course be set by a 'rum' line, or a Great Circle, may it bring her at last to the *tête-à-tête* she longs for with her 'True Heart-ley.' "

And "To Mr. O'Brien, whose nightly carousals remind his 'fellow Persians' that not every Son of Erin is blessed with the Gift of Music."

And finally "To Miss Kate Bartlett—who has become so very smitten in so short a time—rejoicing with her that *her* 'Bonney' lies, not over the ocean, but upon it just now."

The last we think perhaps wanted more polish, but it seemed to strike home, judging by the blushes of one of the parties mentioned, and the abrupt scowling departure from the Saloon of the other!

Vale
NATHANIEL WINKLE

PETER PRINCE is the author of the novels *Play Things*, which won the Somerset Maugham Award, and *The Good Father*, which was made into a film starring Anthony Hopkins. He has also written for the screen (*The Hit, Waterland*) and television (the PBS-BBC series *Oppenheimer* and the BBC adaptation of Muriel Spark's *Memento Mori*). He lives in London.

ABOUT THE TYPE

The text of this book was set in Janson, a misnamed typeface designed in about 1600 by Nicholas Kis, a Hungarian in Amsterdam. In 1919 the matrices became the property of the Stempel Foundry in Frankfurt. It is an old-style book face of excellent clarity and sharpness. Janson serifs are concave and splayed; the contrast between thick and thin strokes is marked.